P9-DWY-857

Certificate in Lieu of Discharge

Familienname: ...ackenberger
Surname:

Vornamen: Claus
Christian Names:

Geburtstag u. -ort: 26.3.27 Schweidnitz Schlesien
Date and place of birth:

Familienstand: ledig
Marital status:

Beruf: Schüler
Civil occupation:

jetzige Wohnung (genaue Anschrift): Simbach am Inn, Moos 8
Present address:

wurde entlassen am 8.1.1948 von der*) französischen Kriegsgefangenschaft.
was discharged on from the*)

Beglaubigt durch:
Certified by

Unterschrift und Dienstsiegel des Mil. Reg. Offizier
Signature and Official Seal of Mil. Govt. Officer

Name, Rang und Stellung des beglaubigenden Offiziers.
Name, rank and organization of the certifying officer

(Abdruck des rechten Zeigefingers)
(Print of the right forefinger)

*) Hier ist anzuführen: Heer, Marine, Luftwaffe, Volkssturm, ähnliche Organisation wie RAD usw.
*) Insert Army, Navy, Air Force, Volkssturm, or para military Organisation, e. g. RAD, etc.

(A. Seidl)

Personenbeschreibung:
Description of person:

Größe: 181 cm
Height

Gestalt: mittel
Figure:

Farbe der Augen: blau
Color of eyes:

Farbe des Haares: dunkelblond
Color of hair:

Unveränderliche Kennzeichen: Narbe an der li. Hand
Invariable distinguishing marks:

Veränderliche Kennzeichen: keine
Variable distinguishing marks:

1000 7.10. 47 Kambli'sche Buchdruckerei, Pfarrkirchen

March 2003

A LONG WALK

Claus Hackenberger

Have always peace in Your Heart

HARA
PUBLISHING GROUP

Published by
Hara Publishing
P.O. Box 19732
Seattle, WA 98109

This is not a work of fiction.
It is an autobiography presented in novel form.
All events happened at places and locales cited in the story.
The names and details of people involved have been changed; any resemblance to actual persons, living or dead, is entirely coincidental.

ISBN: 1-883697-69-7

Library of Congress Catalog Card Number:
2001089618

Manufactured in the United States
10 9 8 7 6 5 4 3 2

Editor: Vicki McCown
Cover Design: Scott Fisher
Book Design & Production: Scott and Shirley Fisher

To all of those who walked with me
and are home by now.
Koenig
Ivanovich
Leo
Bauer
Max
The dead man whose boots I wore
Kate
Victor Schäufel, our teacher
and Tommy, my son

Many people helped me write this book. During dark hours, they showed me that there was light. In moments of highest elation, they pulled me back to earth. They read my chapters, critiqued my story, and never tiring, corrected my lines. I want to extend my sincere gratitude to all of them.

My daughter Christine unwaveringly set straight my grammatical blunders, and never stopped asking where, when, why? My sister Ingrid helped me with the timeline of events that happened when we were young. Dennis Sather, a well-read friend of mine, urged me to share with others what life has taught me. Larry Barr, took time out and cleaned up my spelling, encouraged me to keep going. He let me know whenever I had come too close to the edge or even had faltered beyond. Gail Beck, my dear friend and mentor exuberantly told me on any possible occasion that I say the right things, that I must allow others to read my script. Candy Cullen's critique and consistent encouragement let me find my way through the pastime of a cruel and senseless war. Dr. Edith Mroz read and scruitinized my manuscript. She softened the hard spots in my text. Charlene Casem, my neighbor, like a mother she always voiced concern when my lights kept on past midnight. In her shy way she told me so often that my book will be 'a good one.' Deborah Dvorak helped me find a publisher. Vicki McCown, my editor-in-chief, arranged my lines, bridged the gaps, and made a book out of the manuscript. Scott Fisher, the architect and artist, designed the cover and arranged this book. And last but not least my publisher, Sheryn Hara. She took me on and brought these chapters to the marketplace.

I do thank you.

memories from a long time ago reach into this day.
at dawn the fog ushers them back,
drifting from meadows and ponds.
memories rise in the warped flickers the sunset leaves
at the end of a hot summer day.
memories whisper while the moon stretches silver shadows
over the floor in my dark room. some though
forever stay enshrined deep in my soul.
I only touch them in my dreams.

Stettin

Stettin

The tall, lean, well-dressed man, a slender woman on his arm and a small child in tow, made his way cautiously down the icy streets of Stettin. A bright yellow streetcar clanged by, capturing the boy's attention.

"Vati, look, look! They have choo-choo cars running on the street!" cried the boy in wonderment.

On this cold and dreary Sunday afternoon in January of 1932, Georg Berck, with his wife, Margarete, and their little son, Paul, strolled along the sidewalks of the city that was to be their new home. They would be moving from Striegau, a small village in Selesia where Georg had worked as a head teller at the Reichs Bank. A month ago he had been promoted to loan officer, specializing in industrial loans, and transferred to Stettin, a fair-sized city in the province of Pomerania, near the Baltic Sea.

Paul tugged on Georg's sleeve insistently.

"The choo-choos," he repeated, "I don't see the locomote making white clouds. Look, Vati. Do you?"

Georg bent down to pick Paul up and tightened the woolen shawl around that sweet, tiny face. This coming March, Paul would be five. Georg loved him very much, though he wondered why the child sometimes seemed so hesitant in returning the affection.

"Why don't we take a ride on one, and perhaps the conductor will tell us the secret? And then we can see the harbor too."

The harbor near the mouth of the Oder River gave Stettin a cosmopolitan air, with its majestic palace buildings of the Haaken Terrace towering over the western shoreline. Georg, anxious that this first look at Stettin make a favorable impression, knew the harbor would delight and amaze his wife and son.

But Margarete had other ideas. Shivering under the cold winter wind that blew through the empty streets rimmed by snow berms, she shook her head.

"No, Jorg, it is too cold for Paul." This nickname was the only way in which she ever addressed her husband. "Let's see the harbor tomorrow. Maybe by then the wind will have died down a little."

"Grete...we will be warm in the streetcar." Seeing her look of dismay, he admonished her, "Come on, woman, don't worry, Paul is all right. Hey, little one," he said to Paul, "you are not too cold, are you?"

Of course, he knew the answer. Even if it had been too chilly, Paul would never admit it, warmed as he was by his excitement. Cold? No, Paul would not be cold. This was all so new to him, his head turning back and forth so fast that his father feared his neck might snap.

Little Paul hammered Georg's chest with his gloved fists.

"No, no, not cold! Warm, hot!" he bragged, throwing his arms into the air to emphasize his point. "Come, Vati, tell the train to stop." Then, as he so often did, he broke into a sing-song voice. "We ride a train, ride a train, choo-choo ha, choo-choo ha, tsh, da, tshata, tsh, da." Paul could make anything into a song.

Even as she stood shivering in the cold, Margarete thought about the piano lessons she must soon have him start.

Georg, too, was eager to take a ride in those yellow-painted cars whose sides carried banners with slogans like:

Margarine tastes better than butter...He who works is not hungry...We are making a new world...

Georg Berck had been in Stettin twice before, first for his interview and then to search for an apartment. When his new supervisor, Mr. Hanske, had given him a tour of the city, Georg had felt like a king. Coming from a small town where he walked or rode his bicycle to work and cars were rare, Georg's first ride in an automobile had been exhilarating.

Of course, Georg had not mentioned to Mr. Hanske that these experiences were new to him. He almost gave away his ignorance the very first time he had seen a real streetcar. When sparks flew at the point where the rods met the black wire, it reminded him of lightning, scaring him a bit.

As they made their way to the streetcar stop, little Paul let the shawl come undone once again, trailing it down the sidewalk as he ice skated on his shoes, like a kite drags its tail.

Ever the worrier, Margarete cried out, "Jorg, he will get pneumonia. Stop him. He will fall and hurt his head. Jorg!"

Georg fetched the laughing boy just as the streetcar stopped. The three climbed into the empty car and moved to a bench at the far end.

Georg leaned toward his son.

"Now listen, Paul, your mother is right, you could catch a cold. Come here on my lap. Sit still or I..."

But Paul wiggled out from under his father's arms and ran to the front of the car where the motorman stood behind a handrail. As Paul watched, the motorman sounded the bell three times and shifted into gear. The streetcar began to roll smoothly down the street. As it curved around the corners, the wheels, chafing against the rails, squealed in protest.

Paul, too overcome by wonder to be shy, pointed to a wheel and asked the motorman, "Is this your steering wheel?"

The man smiled. "No, little one. I have no steering wheel. The rails in the street make the cars go around the corners. This is my brake wheel. Here, watch me. But hold on tightly to the railing. I don't want you to get hurt."

"Good afternoon, mein Herr. I hope this disobedient child does not disturb you."

At Grete's urging, Georg had come forward to collect his son. He, too, was embarrassed that his boy had disobeyed him and behaved so childishly in public.

"No, no, he's fine. He has never been in a streetcar, has he?"

Georg shook his head, grateful for the motorman's kindness, thinking that it must be obvious that they were from the countryside and knew little about city life. He watched the motorman, busy running the car all the while with a faint smile on his face. Every so often he spun the brake wheel to slow down when a traffic light changed to red, then slowly accelerated again when it turned green.

The motorman motioned to Paul.

"Hey, little guy, you want to ring the bell? Come over here. Ja, duck under the handrail. See that big button down there by my right foot? When I tell you, step on it. Make sure to do it hard."

"Why do you have a bell?"

"It lets people know I am coming. Everybody on the street must watch out for my car. I can't move out of the way, because it is stuck to the rails."

In the warmth of the heated streetcar, little Paul, still wearing his heavy winter coat, began to perspire, but he didn't notice, so swept away was he by this ride. Emboldened by the motorman's friendly manner, Paul hopped up and down as he held the handrail, for the windowsill was just a shade to high for him to look out into the street.

Georg, who had forgotten that he was going to spank little Paul for running away, looked at his child with a mixture of pride and dismay, and asked himself, "I wonder from whom he got this wild streak? We'll have problems with that. Yes, I must do something about this wildness."

"Now!" The motorman's command cut short Georg's thoughts. Paul, on cue, stomped on the bell button with all his might, but no sound rang out. Georg started to move to help the boy, but stopped himself. What would this motorman think of him? A grown man, a loan officer, wanting to make a streetcar bell ring? He knew his father, a federal judge in Schweidnitz, would not approve of such a peasant urge. Yet somehow Georg's foot found its way to that shiny button on the floor. His heavy step brought a loud peal, so loud that it scared little Paul, and the motorman laughed.

Georg and Paul sat down on the bench off to the side. The boy was still puzzled. How did the man steer the car? He had not understood the motorman's explanation. The toy truck under his bed had a steering wheel. Without it there was no way to have it turn right or left.

"Vati, how does the car go around the corner?"

"It is difficult to explain. I will tell you when you are older."

Georg always gave this answer when he himself was in the dark. He had no feel for mechanical things. Even with a job as simple as hanging a picture, Georg would manage to hurt himself and leave deep hammer marks in the papered walls. These jobs were left to Grete.

Soon little Paul would no longer be too young to understand. A year from this coming March he would celebrate his sixth birthday, and school would soon follow. In time, the "little" in front of his name would fall away, and he would be forced to join the Jungvolk and then the Hitler Jugend, where he would learn the real messages of those banners on the outside of the cars.

After a short while, the tram stopped at the railroad station down by the river, where the family stepped from the car onto the sanded sidewalk. They turned north, heading towards the harbor along Dock Street. At one point they passed under a long railroad bridge that spanned the river. Trains steamed overhead, traveling east through Pomeranian farmland to cities like Danzig, Königsberg, and Schneidemühl at the Polish border. Just a few years later locomotives would pull trains crammed with soldiers over this same bridge on their way to war in Poland and Russia.

This same Dock Street twelve years later would become Paul's only escape route after bombs had flattened the city.

January 1944. On the sixth day of the new year, the Feast of the Epiphany, Paul returned from his Christmas leave in Schneidemühl, where his family had been living since 1939. The navy had drafted him a few months before at the age of sixteen and stationed him at an air defense base in Swinemünde that covered U-boat repair bunkers.

He arrived in Stettin at night to find thousands of soldiers in town waiting to be transported to the Russian front or into France. Paul planned to pass the time at a twenty-four-hour movie theater near the railroad station, where soldiers between trains could relax and watch movies any time of the day or night. Then the air raid sirens let go, and he raced to a shelter in a cellar not far from Dock Street already packed with men, women, and children, old and young. Within minutes the floor rolled with swells, accompanied by the unnerving howl of oncoming projectiles.

The first bomb carpet went directly over them. Explosions pressured the air in the cellar and Paul felt the compression hitting his chest. The devastating shells missed the building, but the lights had gone out, leaving the shelter in pitch dark. Lightning from bursting bombs showed through the cracks in the door, and the oxygen-poor air turned thick with pulverized mortar dust blasting off walls and ceiling.

Somebody yelled, "Cover your mouth with a piece of cloth, a shawl, whatever you can find!" Paul took off his navy overcoat and breathed through its sleeve.

Women screamed. Children whimpered. People began to cough and vomit. Some sounded like they were suffocating. It became very hot. Suddenly someone started to push people aside, wanting out. Panic set in. Many, mostly children and the old, were trampled to death.

Here in this cellar...it could be the end...all of us buried alive...

Paul could not stop trembling. He bit into his coat to keep his teeth from chattering. Some older soldiers finally calmed down the delirious crowd.

The B-17s laid four more bomb carpets. The cellar shook violently as explosions upon explosions crumbled buildings, tore up streets, flattened the railroad station. The raid lasted for more than an hour. A distant siren's steady sound said it was over. Yet it never would be.

It took five men to push the door open, and only wide enough for one person at a time to get through. Caustic smoke drifted in and made it nearly impossible to breathe. Paul pressed his coat against his mouth and got out. The concrete stairwell, barely passable, was littered with broken bricks and burning debris. Buildings above were bathed in flames. Torn bodies covered the street. Their clothes were on fire too. Nobody would need to bury them. Not even their ashes would find a place to rest.

He raced down Dock Street to escape the roaring firestorms that raged through the streets. A horrible wind sucked up debris that tumbled about until it disintegrated in the intense heat. Whole city blocks were collapsing as their burning roofs fell, and ignited the floors beneath. The snow and ice that had blanketed the city just an hour before had since evaporated. Magnesium sticks were burning everywhere. The bombers had dropped them by the thousands to assure total destruction. It was an inferno, and far worse than Dante imagined.

The screams echoing in Paul's ears seemed as though they could not come from humans. He would hear those screams for as long as he lived.

He could hardly breathe. It was so hot! When his heavy overcoat caught on fire, he let go of it. Running for his life he ripped open his jacket and held it over his head and face with one hand while the other shielded his eyes. Then he saw the harbor. The warehouses on Dock Street were burning, but an icy wind blew from the east, fanning smoke and flames away from the piers and docks.

There were people, soldiers, farther down by the jetties where the harbor tugs were moored. Paul kept running. And in the midst of this disaster his mind gave way to the day when his father had brought him to this harbor for first time. It must have been the cold chilling wind that reminded him of the ride in the streetcar, of his trying to push the tug...

The Bercks kept on walking, heads bent down against a stiff northerly wind blowing with full force off the frozen Baltic Sea. Inland icebreakers kept a narrow river channel open between Swinemünde, Penemünde, and Stettin. Harbor tugs and fishing vessels moored along the quay slept in the ice of the harbor, their deck and pilothouses hiding under drifts so tall, one could think that the snow was the cargo they had brought back from the sea. A little farther down, by the old Hanse Stadt warehouses, men wearing heavy coveralls, rough gloves, and snug-fitting earmuffs unloaded a cargo ship. Long derricks roped to masts hoisted netted loads from the vessel's hold onto the dock. The hefty wind made the whining of the cargo winches fade in and out, the calls of the men sounding like barks. When the freighter had arrived the night before, it had been greeted by an ice-locked mooring, from which tugs had pushed large sheets of ice into the channel.

Although Grete knew it was not wise to be out in this freezing weather, she had given up arguing with her husband. She watched as Georg rubbed his ears which were red with cold. He wore a felt hat with no headband, flimsy gloves, and no shawl. The snow melting around his ankles soaked his Sunday shoes. She could not understand why he did not wear his boots. During winter back in Striegau, he had often wrapped his legs with cotton straps like mountain climbers do to keep warm.

When she pointed out his inadequate attire, he had refused to listen.

"We are living in the big city now," he'd told her with some exasperation. "Things are different here. I'm no longer a simple bank teller. I am higher up, Grete. We need to lose that small-town appearance, and you—"

Grete had cut him off in mid-sentence, something she rarely did.

"What are you talking about? Do you mean that in the city we have to dress so flimsy that the icy wind can chill us right to the bone?" she had asked scornfully.

It was not surprising that Grete should choose being practical over being stylish. Margarete Kinzel had been raised to be practical. As the elder of two daughters of a prosperous grocer in the town of Schweidnitz, she had taken it hard when her mother had died of cancer when Margarete was only six. Her father married again not long after, and his second wife was expressly strict with Margarete and her younger sister, Käthe. One could not help but get the impression that those two girls were being prepared to enter the convent.

It may have been the impersonal relationship between the stepmother and Margarete that had trimmed away much, if not all, of her womanly softness. She kept her emotions to herself, never showing joy or sadness. Disappointment—or was it bitterness?—seemed to live inside her.

Paul never heard her laugh. He could think of no friends that she had. And never had she given him a hug that he could remember. Paul knew more about the mothers of his friends than he did of his own. Still, she did love him, Paul knew that.

As they walked along the harborfront, Paul took off running ahead of his parents, shoe-skating on the ice-covered planks of the pier. The bows of the moored tugs pointed toward the wharf, their stems showing just a little above the bolder rail. Paul tried to push one of the boats away from the pier, thinking of his little ship at home that he easily maneuvered around the bathtub while his mother gave him the weekly bristle-brush scrub down. When nothing happened, he beckoned to his father.

"Vati, I push, but it doesn't move. Come help me, please."

Georg held onto him and answered against the wind.

"Paul, it is far too big, and the ice is holding it tight. Nobody can push it away, even if the harbor were not frozen over."

Grete stood away from the boats, watching from behind a nearby shed that sheltered her a little from the chill. She pulled the luxurious mink coat her father had given to her as a wedding present more tightly around her. As Georg glanced back at Grete, he couldn't help noticing that the worn hat and rubber overshoes certainly did not match the well-tailored pelt. Again he wondered how he could wean her of that small-town habit, for he knew that the more he encouraged her to change, the more she would cling to her provincial upbringing.

The Berck family lived in a gray apartment complex as long as a whole city block on Burscher Street, Number 10. Broad streets bordered it on all four sides onto which portal-like entrances faced, giving access to six floors of units. Living room windows looked toward the street, while the kitchen doors opened onto small balconies, fenced with black wrought-iron latticework, overlooking the backyard. During the summer Paul's mother fastened flower boxes to the railing, bringing a splash of color to the drab surroundings. Each year, as Christmastime approached, a dead goose would hang there in the cold, freezing her feathers off.

At street level, small shops and daylight-basements alternated with cellars where the renters kept their coals, potatoes, carrots, crocks with sauerkraut, and pickles. A few manufacturing buildings between vegetable gardens occupied the soccer-field-sized backyard. There, too, were paved areas for children to whip their tops, play ball, or ride their roller scooters.

In a nearby workshop in the large backyard, a carpenter worked, mainly building furniture for taverns. Paul could see the small, makeshift building from his balcony up on the fourth floor. The humming of woodworking machinery made him wonder what was going on behind those windows blinded with sawdust.

One day he could stand the wondering no more.

"Mutti," he called, using his baby name for his mother, "I want to go play with my new top. Okay?"

Grete did not look up from the dishes she was washing in the sink. "Don't get dirty, and come up right away when I call you. Do you understand?"

His hasty "yes" drifted back to her as he slammed the front door.

Taking her hands from the water and drying them on the dish towel, Grete moved to the window that overlooked the backyard. She was not at all sure about Paul. He was always so wild and so embarrassingly inquisitive. Just the other day she had noticed him lying under his bed. Doing what, she had wondered. Then he had come running into her and pulled down his pants to show her his tiny erect penis.

"Mutti, Mutti, look. Why does it do that?" he asked, oblivious to her embarrassment.

What in heaven could she have said? Her face flushed.

"Well...when you are older...yes...don't worry about it...after a while..." she had stammered, unable to find the words.

But he had not waited, slipping up his pants and hurrying back to the safety he found under the bed. As little as he was, he sensed already that neither his father nor his mother would ever answer his questions in a way he would understand. It was always "Later, when you are older" or "Well, that is just the way things are." In those days children were often told "One does not talk about that." Paul sometimes had questions that his parents did not dare to ask themselves or anyone else.

Paul worked his top for a while on the concrete pad, skillfully whipping it closer and closer to the cabinet shop. When a planer's high-pitched whine screamed inside, Paul clapped his hands over his ears, keeping them covered even after the machine had stopped running.

The cabinetmaker turned just then and noticed him outside the door.

"It's loud," he said with a grin, then asked, "Where do you live?"

The boy looked up to see a not-too-tall man covered head to toe with the fine, downy sawdust of his workshop, except for his bushy black mustache from under which a short, brown pipe could be seen.

Paul pointed up to his balcony. "There!"

"And what does your mother call you?"

"My name is Paul and I am almost six. I'll be going to school soon."

"Okay, Paul. They call me Tischler, Mr. Tischler. Do you want to come in?"

Paul could hear his mother's warning ringing in his ears: "Don't, don't you go into that shop, ever! You hear me?" But he looked at this man who spoke slowly and with a smile, and he nodded his yes.

"I've wanted to find out what you are doing in there for a long time."

"All right. Come in then. Just don't touch anything. Here, I'll put you up on this workbench. You watch. Tell me when you need to go home." Then he added, laughing, "No need to get into trouble."

Paul smiled back, thinking this man must have a mother like his.

Mr. Tischler and his helper were gluing a front panel to a curved wooden frame, part of a bar table they were building for a tavern on the next street over from Burscher. A can containing sticky brown stuff that looked like syrup to Paul sat on the workbench inside a pot with boiling water. The men spread this thick, hot adhesive over the wood with a wide brush, then fastened clamps to hold the pieces in place until the glue would set up.

Paul was fascinated. Tischler took him around the shop, showing him the large band saw, the long sanding belt, a couple of drill machines, and the tall glue press, all covered with sawdust.

"Here, this is the machine that makes all that noise. It's called a planer. I use it to smooth out those rough boards over there in the corner."

Then the cabinetmaker pointed at the ceiling. Hanging from the rafters was an array of shafts, wheels, and wide, flapping leather belts that drove the machines on the floor. Paul's cheeks had turned rosy-red with excitement, his hair, jacket, and pants white with dust. There were so many questions to ask...

Mr. Tischler saw her first. Grete stood in the door, her face a mask of anger. The cabinetmaker beckoned her to come in, but she ignored him, shouting at Paul through the hum of running machinery.

"You rascal! Did I not forbid you to go inside this shop? And you did not hear me call you! I will ground you!"

"Are you his mother? Madam, you have quite the young man there. Why do you not allow him to watch a little? I can tell he likes machines. I'll see to it that he does not get hurt. Come, please, sit over there in that chair." He took a rag and slapped the dust off the wicker chair. "I would like to teach him to straighten my bent nails."

Again Grete pretended not see Mr. Tischler. She came over to Paul and grabbed him by the arm as though she were going to pull it out of its shirtsleeve, and dragged him crying back up to their tiny apartment. Back in her domain, she handed down her sentence.

"Here, boy, you stand in the corner of this kitchen with your face to the wall until your father comes home!"

Little Paul stopped his tears after a while, but he held little hope for his fate. His father was not interested in glue, lumber, clamps, or nails. Upon hearing the story, Georg grounded his son for three more days and sent him straight to bed after dinner.

May 1933 brought Paul's first day in school.

His mother had bought for him the customary long, cone-shaped tube filled with chocolate, cookies, and candies, brightly decorated with colorful ribbons and streamers. The frilly red paper lid wore a light-blue bow. Georg had arranged to take off from work for a few hours and he and Grete brought their son to the Catholic school the pastor uptown had recommended.

About thirty young boys dressed in Sunday outfits had congregated at the school, all holding similar cones, one or two taller than the boy holding it. Many of the new students shed tears, and here and there a mother cried as well.

Grete did not cry, but barely managed a smile as the teacher introduced himself. He was a man of medium build, strong but on the fleshy side, with large cigarette-stained hands.

"I am Mr. Macke, your boy's teacher," he said, an insincere smile revealing his yellowed teeth. "This will be my class until the fourth grade." His smile melted into a more serious expression, and his narrow eyes seemed to hold a hint of menace. "This is a very strict school. We do not tolerate boisterous behavior and we expect you to help us with good oversight at home."

Georg nodded his concurrence. It was exactly as he had expected.

"Would you like to stay and observe today? No? In that case, classes will be out at three. Does he have a card for the tram? Good. Sister will put him on the streetcar heading for Burscher Street. But we will only do this for the first few days. After that he has to do it himself."

With a quick goodbye to Paul, Georg and Margarete left the classroom, relieved to be on their way.

There had been no kindergarten to prepare Paul for entering school, nothing to cushion the shock he felt at that moment. He did not cry, but he held onto his tube like he would his beloved teddy bear at home. He had tucked the stuffed animal under the blanket on his bed, reassuring him. "You wait here. When I come back this afternoon, we'll go down to Mr. Tischler's. Okay? Come, I hug you. Yes, don't worry. I'll be back soon." As his mother called impatiently for him to come, he hugged the bear and gave him a long kiss on that brown nose.

Paul's words were meant to console himself as well, for he somehow knew that an era had come to an end, that things would never be the same again. It would have been a little easier for Paul had his parents helped him to understand this, had they given him a hug, a pat on the head, some reassuring words. Maybe they did not know how. Maybe they did not know that love needed to be shown, a priceless gift— not to be hoarded, but shared.

At school, Mr. Macke directed the children to small desks that had been arranged in two double columns, each eight deep. He motioned to Paul, but he did not move, his legs simply did not want to go.

"Hey, boy, come! You sit in the second row over there by the window." Just 'boy'? No name? thought Paul.

He began to shiver. Suddenly, he let go of his tube, turned, and ran out of the room. Irritated, Mr. Macke sent Sister Lillie to find Paul, who was hiding under the sink in one of the restrooms.

"Hey, little one, come, der liebe Gott, the Lord wants you to sit with the others. They are waiting for you. Come."

Paul did not look at her, did not seem to hear.

"If this were not your first day, Mr. Macke would have you stand in the corner for at least an hour," the Sister admonished.

She grabbed his arm and led him back to the classroom. Paul did not resist, but his eyes betrayed his fear. Mr. Macke pointed to the proper desk and the sister had him sit down next to another boy, one who was still crying. His name was Petrus, and Paul found out later that he also lived on Burscher Street, in one of the daylight basements across from Number 10.

The teacher explained about school, schedules, and homework. He would teach them to write and to read, and every day a priest would come by to teach them about good, bad, and God. Then Mr. Macke talked about confession, communion, sin, grace, penance, Jesus, and the Holy Ghost.

"And, remember, the sign of the cross will always protect you from the devil!"

Though this first hour of school represented a very special moment for these children, Mr. Macke seemed insensitive to it. These kids were leaving something they never again could recapture. Could he not see how lost they felt at this moment? He was the steward of their pure, innocent souls. They were new plants, entrusted to him to be bedded in good soil. But he had endured those "first hours" so many times, for so many years, that he had become dull. He no longer cared about those precious little hearts.

Perhaps it didn't matter, this ambivalence by the schoolmaster, for soon Hitler's men would take over. They would scatter infected spores into the minds of these young people and destroy decency for generations to come. They would alter the meaning of right and wrong, distort their values. They would teach these children to kill and make them abandon their God.

The bell rang. Their first morning of a new life had passed.

"Okay, children, we'll go outside. Sister will play ball with you. Then you eat your lunch and afterwards we will start with the letter 'A' of the alphabet."

Paul did not get up. He held onto his wood-framed slate so hard that his tiny knuckles turned white.

"Come on, you too. Go with the others, go play."

Paul looked at Mr. Macke, paralyzed with fear.

"Come, let go of your slate!" Mr. Macke glared down at Paul, thinking that although he'd forgotten the little bastard's name, he'd learn it soon enough. No doubt he'd have problems with that one.

Paul looked down at the slate, unable to let go of it. Somehow it seemed welded to his fingers. Then, whack! The teacher smacked him across the back of his hands with a wooden ruler, and the slate dropped with a crash onto the desk. With his knuckles turning an angry red, Paul jumped up and ran to catch up with the other children. He played, but without enthusiasm. Something had broken inside him. A new unknown feeling had been born. He had no name for it, but it was not pleasant.

His mother noticed the change in Paul the moment he stepped off the tram that afternoon. She had never seen that shadow in her son's eyes. She immediately noticed the marks the ruler had left on his small hands, but said nothing. They walked home in silence. Once inside the apartment, Paul took his teddy bear and slipped under the bed. He began to feel safe again.

"Hey, Paul," called his father from the dinner table, "if you don't come and eat with us, you will go hungry tonight."

Paul did not answer. After Grete and Georg had finished eating they pulled him with some difficulty from under the bed.

"Jorg, do you see how swollen his hands are?"

"Well, he must have done something bad. You remember the teacher telling us..."

Paul held his teddy so tight the bear seemed to be gasping for air. But he said nothing.

"Wash your face and then go to sleep. School starts early tomorrow."

Paul settled into the routine of school, doing his work and receiving adequate grades, although they were never good enough to satisfy Georg. His memories of those four years in that Catholic elementary school consisted mainly of the abuse Mr.

Macke meted out. His punishments rivaled the barbaric methods of old English orphanages. Often he would pull a boy forward over the desktop and slug his fist into the back just below the rib cage, or even lower, directly into the kidneys. Once, when Paul broke out laughing, remembering his teddy falling in the bathtub the night before, Macke stormed from his cathedra and beat Paul so hard in the back that his nose started to bleed. For a few panicky seconds he could not breathe.

"One more time you disobey and your parents will need to look for another school!"

Georg blindly believed every negative report from the teacher and frequently added some red streaks to Paul's bottom with the thin willow stick that was always waiting to be used on him. The anxiety and stress began to wear him down.

During the first year in school, Paul became very ill with diarrhea. All known home remedies, even dried blueberries, failed to stop it. The family doctor could not help. Paul lost weight, and he was often too sick to go to school, missing over a hundred days of first and second grade.

In desperation, his mother considered taking him to a homeopath, an idea her husband forbade.

"But, Jorg, this can not go on much longer. I feel so sorry for our son. He has become so frail."

"You want to take him to a quack? No, never!"

She silently overruled her husband and secretly took Paul to see the homeopath. After examining Paul, the new doctor gave her three bottles of tiny, colored pellets.

"I know they don't look much like medicine, but you have him take those green pills in the morning, the blue ones at noon, and these yellow little balls just before he goes to bed. Trust me, it will make him well."

"What is it he has? He's been sick for over a year. Nothing has helped."

"To be honest, I cannot tell for sure, but I think it is one of those new types of bacteria. They call it a 'virus,' an organism too small for us to see. Our microscopes are not strong enough. All I know is that my medicine has been tested. I don't know why, but it stops a virus from growing."

She knew she should discuss this with Georg, but, of course, she couldn't. She would just have to wait and see. In the meantime, she followed the diet the doctor recommended for Paul, which included dove, calf meat, and liver. As predicted, in three weeks' time, Paul recovered.

During Paul's illness Grete relaxed her boycott of Mr. Tischler, allowing Paul to go into the cabinet shop whenever he wanted.

Paul had been ecstatic, proclaiming, "Oh, Mutti, thank you, thank you! I will help you every night to carry the coal bucket up from the cellar. I will!"

Each room of the apartment had a kachelofen, a stove, built into a corner, reaching from floor to ceiling. Its sides, about four feet wide, were tiled, usually in light green, beige, or brown, with a narrow bench on one side. Grete made a new fire in each stove every morning, using wood first and then covering the flames with a sizable pile of coke mixed with coal. When the fire was going strong she would close the oven door and adjust the draft. The tiles absorbed the heat and warmed the room all day, providing a steady and comfortable temperature. But it was hard work to carry a bucket of coal and a pail filled with coke up those five flights of stairs.

One day after school, Grete sent Paul downstairs to Mr. Harold, the shoemaker, to pick up a pair of shoes she had left to be resoled. As Paul walked timidly into the shop, he found a heavyset man with short, gray hair that wanted combing. He worked intently at a his bench using a small hammer, holding in his mouth what appeared to be several small, white sticks. As Paul entered, the man turned to look at him, revealing a friendly face with kind eyes.

"Hello," Paul started, shyly. "My family...we live above you on the fourth floor. My mother asked me to pick up my father's shoes." Paul looked around, suddenly aware of the dozens of pairs of shoes in the shop. "Are they ready?" he asked uncertainly.

The man spit out the sticks. "Your father's shoes? Berck? Ja, they are, but I still have to polish them." His voice was gentle for such a large man. "You want to stay a little and watch?"

Of course! The shoemaker turned on the polisher, which hummed like Mr. Tischler's band saw. All sorts of wheels and discs turned swiftly on a long shaft; some of the rollers had sandpaper on them. Mr. Harold held Georg's shoes against a brown brush-wheel, and in no time had polished them to a shiny luster, making them look brand new.

As he handed the shoes to Paul, the shoemaker said, "Mr. Tischler tells me that you are helping him. He says you know how to hammer his bent nails and make them straight again. He is very proud of you."

"Ja. He showed me how to do that," Paul beamed, then an idea hit him. "Maybe I can help you too? Do you have crooked nails too?"

"No, little fellow, I don't. My nails are made out of wood. See those short little pegs over there, the ones sharpened on the end like a pencil? I use those to hold the soles in place. I'll show you sometime how that is done."

But Paul was not ready to give up. "Well, maybe you will let me sweep your floor? But I need to talk to my mother first. I'll run upstairs and ask." He was almost out the door when Mr. Harold reminded him to take the loafers with him.

When Grete came downstairs the next morning to pay the shoemaker, she brought a hopeful Paul with her.

"Paul says you have said he could visit you here in the shop. Is that true? Are you sure he will not disturb you? He can ask a lot of questions."

Mr. Harold got up from his stool—and it immediately fell over. Paul leapt to pick it up, but could not make it stand. Then he noticed the stool had only one leg.

"Mr. Harold, did the other legs break off?"

"No, Paul, my stool has only one leg, right in the middle under the seat. See? We shoemakers move and turn around a lot when we work. One leg is all we need. I'll teach you to sit on that stool over there, okay?"

Satisfied with the situation, Grete said, "Paul, you can stay. But be polite and don't disturb Mr. Harold. Keep away from those sharp knives, and..."

"Mrs. Berck, don't you worry, he will be all right. He'll keep me good company."

As the months went by, Paul spent many hours with Mr. Harold, especially on those days when he stayed home from school. By the time Paul was well again he had learned to prepare shoes for the work that had to be done to them. He learned to read the instructions Mr. Harold wrote on the repair slip. For those that needed cleaning, the laces had to be taken out and hung onto a rack. The numbers on the pegs had to match the ones on the tags stuck in the shoes. When shoes needed new heels, Paul would pull off the old ones, and Mr. Harold would fit them with a new pair. He was not strong enough to rip off worn soles, as the wooden nails did not let go easily. But he polished almost all the repaired shoes, strung the laces back, and displayed them on the return shelves.

On most days, school let out around one in the afternoon. The ride home on the tram took half an hour, after which Paul had to walk a few blocks home, making it by two. A glass of milk was waiting and the kitchen table cleared, ready for him to spread out his books. It took him about two hours to do his homework, which his mother would check. If his handwriting did not suit her, she would have him do it over again. On those afternoons Tischler and Harold waited in vain for Paul.

Saturdays were good workshop days. School got out at eleven, and weekends were homework-free time. Paul kept both shops clean. Mr. Tischler paid him ten pennies a week, but the shoemaker and Paul worked out a different deal: Paul could polish the family's shoes every day for free. The arrangement had been Paul's idea. He had watched his mother every night, after she had brought up the coal from the cellar, buffing his father's and his own shoes. She always looked so tired, he wanted to spare her this one task.

"Mutti," he told his mother one night, "Mr. Harold said I can polish all of our shoes down there in his shop. I will do this job from now on. You can rest." He hoped this consideration would please her, that she would yield a hug or some other sign of affection. But he was disappointed.

Those ten pennies he earned from Mr. Tischler bought all kinds of goodies in those days. Paul could get ten candies or a glass of raspberry water for one penny; a large sweet roll cost only two cents. Grete bought a piggy bank for him, a hollow ugly-looking thing made of porcelain with a narrow coin slot in its back. She made him drop two pennies into that bank every week.

"When it is full, we'll break it and bring those pennies to your father's bank. He has already opened a savings account there for you."

Paul watched that piggy. Whenever he felt the porcelain belly was getting too tight he would relieve its stress, using a kitchen knife thin enough to assist a penny to escape. He did not blow his stolen treasure on candy. Instead, under his bed, way in the corner, stashed behind one of the bed legs lay a matchbox that held the loot—Paul's own secret savings account. Never mind the one at the bank.

One morning as Paul left for the tram, his mother straightened the collar on his coat, an uncharacteristic familiar gesture.

"Paul," she said, "I won't be home today when you get back from school. I need to see the doctor."

"Are you sick?" he asked anxiously.

"No. I just have to get a check-up."

"But how will I get in? Oh, ja, you put the key under the mat. Mutti, can I go and help Mr. Tischler?"

"Homework first, you know that. Now run along or you'll miss your tram."

Paul had grown into a strong young boy of eight. Despite the cruelty of his teacher and a lack of outward affection from his mother and father, he looked at life with a positive attitude. He was a well-mannered boy, friendly and outgoing. Sister Lillie had taken a liking to him and always smiled warmly at him when they passed each other in the dim hallways.

In early May, Georg told Paul that his Aunt Käthe, Grete's younger sister, would come to stay with them for a while. She would sleep in the same room with Paul. A new bed had been bought just for her.

"Your mother and I will move into the room adjacent to the kitchen," his father had explained.

This puzzled Paul even more, for that room, known as the "master's room," was kept closed and strictly off limits for Paul. Its wooden floor was partially covered with a red and green rug, the walls flat with faded violet-colored wallpaper. A sofa with washable armrest covers, a heavy, black oak desk with drawers, and some ungodly looking chairs underlined the "emptiness" of this lonely chamber.

Only at Christmastime would Paul be allowed to glimpse inside this room. Each year a tall tree, stretching right up to the ceiling, would find its way into this room. Georg would spend hours behind the locked door hanging foil strips one by one onto its branches, so that it glittered with twinkling stars and tinsel strands. The whole tree would be studded with white beeswax candles, to be lit just five times: on the eve of Christmas, the two days of Christmas celebration, New Year's Day, and on the sixth of January, the day the three kings brought their gifts to the manger. And under the tree the colorful wrappings of the presents, brought by the Christkind, brightened the room, seeming to make it breathe easier.

The gramophone, a good-sized dark, wooden cube, stood in one corner of this room, strong and silent except during this one season of the year, when his mother would turn its crank, the needle scratching the grooves to fill the apartment with songs of that holy night.

But now the usual year-long silence of this room was about to be shattered, its space taken possession of by a new life.

Aunt Käthe arrived and took over the household duties. Taller and thinner than his mother, she had sad-looking looking eyes rimmed with dark shadows, making her seem not well. She cooked, cleaned, and hauled coals and coke for the fires in the stoves. She saw to it that Paul got to school on time. Paul did not understand why she had come; the only explanation given was that his mother wasn't feeling well and needed rest.

"Quiet! Go play in your room," Aunt Käthe would often admonish him. "You must not disturb your mother."

Paul wondered but could not guess what was happening in his house. In later years, as he thought back on this time, he could not recall noticing that his mother had been pregnant.

His parents kept this secret from him and deprived him of taking part in the miraculous wonder of creation. They hid the new child in his mother's womb from him, never allowing him to participate in the anticipation of the new life growing in the same womb that had carried him into this world. Incapable of reaching beyond their own upbringing, his parents shrouded the event as though they were ashamed of it.

Paul would often wonder throughout his life why his parents seemed unable to show love, intimacy, warmth. Perhaps the First World War and the hard times that followed destroyed their ability to be open and loving. They were not willing to risk living with any kind of hope of happiness, fearing the pain that would follow should they lose everything once again. Both seemed intent on teaching Paul that life was hard— his mother by being efficient rather than affectionate, his father through a strict adherence to rules and his harsh and frequent punishment of his son.

The right time would never come to talk about these failings within their family. It would not be until much later, long after the Second World War had ended, that Georg, old by then, would let Paul come close, but by that time it would be too late. Ill feelings would not dissolve, and love suppressed over so many years could not be suddenly kindled. Questions would always remain unanswered. And the hugs that had been so desperately wanted those many years ago would seem stiff and unnatural when at last given. The day Paul finally stood at his father's grave, he shed no tears. He knew the time had come to accept and to forgive, that no one can step into a new day without having forgiven what happened yesterday. But although Paul understood this, it took years for him to do it.

On the twenty-sixth day in May of 1935, Paul's mother came to his bed in the middle of the night.

"Paul, Paul, wake up. I must go to the hospital."

Half asleep, Paul rubbed his eyes. "What for?" he asked, confused.

"I need to go there to pick up our new baby."

Jarred awake by this, he jumped out of bed.

"A baby! You mean a brother? Where did you get..."

But he was interrupted by Aunt Käthe. Fully dressed and with a suitcase in one hand, she handed out orders.

"Come, Grete, we must go. Paul, you go back to sleep. But you can stay home from school today. You wait here until I am back."

Paul's father went to work as usual that day, and Paul entertained himself in the apartment until lunchtime, when his aunt came back with the news.

"Paul, you have a little sister."

Disappointment mixed with worry on his face. "But, where is Mutti?" he asked.

"She had to stay in the hospital. You know the stork that brought the baby, he bit her on the leg. So it will be a few days until she will be home again."

Alarmed, Paul asked, "Did the stork bite her bad? Does she hurt? I want to go there and help her."

"Let's eat something and then we'll go, okay?"

After lunch, they took the same tram Paul usually rode to school. The hospital, a tall, red-brick building, sat on a tree-lined boulevard just about halfway between home and school. As they entered the large glass doors to the vestibule, Paul stared at the nuns dressed in white tunics.

"Are those sisters Catholic too?" he asked Aunt Käthe, who shushed him without answering. "Where is Mutti?"

They hurried up the stairs to the second floor. The door of Room 15 was ajar, a strange smell floating from the room. They knocked and when he heard her voice telling them to enter, he started to cry. She lay on a strange bed that stood on tall legs, and she looked pale and weak. When he threw himself onto her blanket, she took him into her arms. It was this moment, though very short, that had been set aside for both of them. For the first and only time, she let him feel her soul. He would never be this close to her again.

A few days later, his mother returned home and life settled back into a routine, one dominated by the needs of the baby, Ingrid.

Each afternoon, Paul would watch as his mother diapered the baby on his bed.

Staring at Ingrid's naked bottom, he asked his mom, "Mutti, why is there no little thing down there. Is she okay?"

"She is just a baby, Paul. It will come later."

Paul graduated from elementary school in 1936 and was enrolled in the gymnasium in Stettin, which was located just a few blocks from the bank where his father loaned money to important businesspeople. This school had nine grades and offered a variety of academic subjects in the curriculum, including three foreign languages. Latin instruction began in the first grade and continued through the ninth. In third grade, students were required to begin studying Greek. Those boys slated to become professionals—lawyers, doctors, teachers and the like—would take French in the fourth grade. Young men leaning toward the more technical side in life would skip this third language and focus on mathematics, chemistry, and physics. And, of course, religion was taught to all.

Paul did not do well at his new school. Although these teachers were not masochists like Mr. Macke, but civilized, well-educated men, Paul could not make contact with any of them. And he had no friends among his classmates. His visits to the shops of the cabinetmaker and shoemaker became less frequent, for his homework took up most of his free time.

In late 1937, Georg left Reichs Bank to join the army again. He had served during the First World War, achieving the rank of lieutenant, and had been taken as a prisoner by the French. Paul did not understand why his father left a good job for a new career in the military. Georg, anticipating another war, hoped that by joining the army early on he would have a better chance to advance to higher positions, which proved to be true.

The whole affair seemed timely. The years after World War I had been filled with disenchantment for the people of Germany, fueled by the failure of an array of governments. The heavy burden of Versailles had made it all but impossible for the country to once again become a contributing member on the European continent. The fertile soil of the Germans' nationalism seemed ready and waiting for the empty, golden promises. Men and women alike believed the propaganda, which preached that they alone belonged to the Herrenrasse, the race selected to conquer and rule the whole world. Children were lured into radical ideologies, given sharp-looking uniforms, and led to regard Hitler as their real father. Songwriters composed music with stirring harmonies and simple but patriotic words that urged people to be strong and victorious. Hitler was grooming Germany and her people to fulfill his fanatical ambitions.

That Paul's father wanted to be a soldier again seemed somehow to fit into the framework of this euphoric era that concealed the hideous slaughter of millions of innocent human beings, that distorted the souls of children, encouraged them to break their bonds with their parents, and eventually destroyed their homes.

After Paul had completed just one year at the gymnasium in Stettin, the family moved to Stargard, about forty kilometers to the southeast. The military had a training facility there to which Paul's father had been transferred. This city, much smaller and older than Stettin, boasted ancient ruins of stone walls and fallen towers, high berms and low gates that still told of the times when the city had defended itself against the Huns. The Bercks rented the second floor of a townhouse on Klappholz Gasse, a suburban street garnished with the fragile pink blossoms of almond trees.

Paul entered the second grade of the local gymnasium in the middle of the school year. He found the transition difficult, and it took him time to catch on. Although this school offered the same curriculum as the one Paul had left in Stettin, the overall level of knowledge of the student body was slightly lower. That, of course, could have helped Paul, who had struggled in his studies in Stettin, but he failed to take advantage of the situation. Dealing with new teachers, strangers as classmates, a new home in an unfamiliar neighborhood—all this made him feel isolated. Unlike Stettin, where at least he had Mr. Harold and Mr. Tischler as adults to whom he could talk, here he had no one to whom he could look for help in making the transition from a boy to a young adult.

Nowhere was there joy in Paul's life. He incurred his parents' disappointment when the quarterly report cards placed him in a "C" bracket, closer to minus than plus. His sister Ingrid did not exist for him, and it seemed as though he had lost his mother as well, as she gave all her attention to the baby. He withdrew into himself, shutting down his feelings, his hopes, his dreams, so as not to be hurt. Little did he know that in no time a brown shirt, white socks, and black pants would get him going again.

Several events spiked Paul's time in Stargard during the years of '37 and '38.

Paul was "invited" to join the Jungvolk, a group of boys aged ten to fourteen who were encouraged to march together and to do great things for the Third Reich. At age fifteen, these boys would progress into the Hitler Youth, and the armed forces would take over at age seventeen. Prior to being transferred to the military, every young man had to serve at least one year in the Reichs Arbeits Dienst. This was an organization that taught the future soldiers basic work skills. By the time Paul was transferred into this organization, the men spent most of their time building earth fortifications in Poland. German soldier-children would die in those ditches trying to stem the flood of oncoming Russians columns. The RAD also repaired railroad systems and assisted in the clean-up of bombed cities. Paul signed up, as did his entire class, with the encouragement of their teachers.

"It is good to belong to the Hitler Youth," their professors assured them. "You will learn to become a soldier, a fighter for our Führer, for Hitler. You'll see, it's going to be a lot of fun. We are very proud of you!"

Like hundreds of thousands of German children, Paul found excitement in the prospect. Wearing his uniform made him feel good, with his brown shirt that fitted perfectly, and the black-leather shoulder strap holding his belt and buckle firmly in place. The group leaders, barely older than he, were outgoing, friendly, determined, clean-cut young men.

"Heil, Hitler! Whenever we meet, your shirt must be clean and ironed. You ask your mother to teach you how to do that. And your knee socks must be clean. We want them to be as white as snow."

Grete had bought him the mandatory two pairs of short black corduroy pants. He took pride in wearing them, thinking that he really looked sharp. He kept his shoes polished to a sheen like Mr. Harold, the shoemaker, had taught him.

Wednesdays and Saturdays they would gather to march around town and sing "new world" songs. Paul enjoyed singing, especially those songs that told about heroes and victory.

People walking the streets would halt and cheer the singing youths passing by, often joining in song with them. Afterwards the boys would gather in a large meeting hall and listen to hero stories about Hitler and the Third Reich he was in the process of building.

"We, the German people, our nation, our race will 'rule the world as far as we can see,'" they were told. That phrase actually belonged to Alexander the Great, who had used the same slogan to drive his armies into the battlefields some two thousand years earlier. It proved just as effective in the 1930s in rousing mere children to dress in soldier clothes which would later be riddled with bullet holes.

"Heil, Hitler, heil! When you meet with your friends, when you greet people on the street, in stores, everywhere, you want to shout out his name: Heil, Hitler! And remember we are all the same, the 'Pimpf' next to you, in front of you, and in back of you. We all are comrades. Heil, Hitler!"

And with their right arms stretched forward straight, hands flat as discs, those little boys repeated again and again and again. "Heil, Hitler!" Their eyes shined with the misguided idea that they were strong, even invincible. They were never given a hint of the deadly opposition they would face.

Hitler was their role model, their icon, their mentor, a figurehead replacing the bonds these boys should have shared with their families. Parents were shoved into the background, and Hitler became the head of the German family.

How could fathers and mothers let that happen? Where were the teachers? Why did not the priests use their pulpits, the bishops their influence, the cardinals their power? What did this Hitler have that they could not have beaten? These questions still beg to be answered.

At the meetings, the propagandizing went on for hours, always ending with their voices raised in song, loud and proud: "Deutschland, Deutschland über alles, über alles in der Welt...(Germany, Germany all over the whole world...)" And then the SS song: "Die Fahne hoch...(Raise high the flag and march together...)"

One day they were given a picture of the Führer to hang on their bedroom wall. Their leaders instructed them to express their thanks to this portrait each night before they went to bed. None dared defy this edict.

The day Paul brought that picture of Hitler home, his mother turned pale, though he did not notice.

"Mutti, we have to hang it up right by my bed. You help me, please?" She gave him a look of dismay, but went along, protesting only at its placement.

"No, Paul, not next to your crucifix!" Snatching the hammer from him, she drove the nail in by the door, just above the light switch.

It wasn't until many years later, after Paul had escaped from the prison camp, home from hell, that Grete told him that she had prayed all night long after hanging that picture. So distraught at what she saw as a sacrilegious act, she had thrown the hammer into the river the next day.

"Why did you not say anything if you knew that all this was so wrong?" he had accused her.

"Would you have believed me? I lived in fear that you knew what I thought, that you would inadvertently give it away. The Gestapo would have been at our door within the hour. They would have taken me away and shot your father. I know I did not help you, but it would have been in vain had I tried. It was risky enough to go to church, risky enough for you to be an altar boy. Your father knew I did not believe in Hitler. He wanted me to keep my mouth shut. He did not tell me what he thought. He probably never will."

As the months went by, the indoctrination became more serious. The children were made to assemble at eight in the morning on both Saturday and Sunday mornings and then march to the nearby forest where they played "cops and robbers" the Hitler way.

"Make your faces dirty, dark with mud. Find tree branches and grass. Let's find out who camouflages himself so we cannot see him, just like our brave and cunning soldiers..."

These Sunday morning practices served not only to heighten their skills, but to keep the boys from church. Only after the leaders were sure that the last Sunday Mass had started would they discharge their soldiers-in-training, too late for them to attend the services.

Summer went by quickly, filled with marching, swimming, school, growing up. The "cops and robbers" games became "cops and Russians" or "cops and Frenchmen," their true enemies. New words infiltrated their vocabulary: "commando," "plan of attack," "rifle," "storming," "holding the line," and many more. The children became increasingly excited, even Paul, hardly able to wait until Wednesday and the weekend, the times they would assemble to wear their uniforms and practice being "Hitler's Kinder." As if the schools sought to ease their responsibilities, they no longer had any homework on those days.

Fall passed and winter descended, December blowing bitterly cold days into town. The River Ina, which flowed through the middle of Stargard, froze under a cap of ice. The north wind shaved the snow off its surface, polishing the icy river so that one could see right through to the bottom. But this bottom harbored warm springs, which thinned the ice and made it treacherous, as Paul would find out.

It happened one day as he and another boy, both new to Stargard, were skating south of the bridge. They didn't notice that they were the only ones skating there, that the rubberlike surface of the ice might not be reliable. Suddenly, the ice beneath Paul's skates cracked and he slipped into the icy water clear up to his shoulders. Although he was close to shore and could touch the bottom, the mud of the riverbed sucked him deeper with every step he took. Within a few minutes numbness swept over his entire body, his hands beyond hurting as he tried to pull himself up onto the ice, which only broke away under his desperate grasp.

Terrified, the other boy yelled over and over for help, but the wind stole his voice away. Afternoon was turning to evening, the light growing dim. And then a woman crossing the bridge caught sight of Paul; realizing his plight she hurried to a nearby corner store for help. The owner, who had been decorating a tall Christmas tree out front of his shop, grabbed his ladder and quickly ran to the shore near where Paul was trapped. He laid the ladder across the ice.

"Grab that rung boy!" he called to Paul. "Come, on, grab it! Last year a kid like you drowned right on this spot. We don't want that to happen again. Wake up! Grab that rung, grab it!"

Paul looked helplessly at the ladder, no longer able to move his arms.

Skaters from the other side of the bridge saw the commotion and came running. Some had lanterns they took with them for night skating, which they used to light the disastrous scene. Everyone kept shouting, "Hey, you! Grab that ladder!" But Paul, though he tried will all his strength, could not do it. Finally, a boy who Paul knew lived up the street from him slid on top of the ladder and crawled toward Paul. Grabbing him by the collar of his parka, the boy held onto it while the others dragged both of them to shore. They had to pull hard to break the hold of the glutinous mud of the river bottom on Paul's feet.

Once out of the mud and ice, Paul was rushed to the store, where his rescuers stripped off his clothes and began rubbing him all over. After a few minutes, feeling started to come back into his limbs. The woman who had first seen his plight had fetched Paul's mother and some dry clothes.

A passing policeman, looking in on the scene, scowled at what he saw.

"Can't you read, boy? There are signs all over telling you not to go near there. Your old man ought to ream a second hole."

Next morning, when Paul showed up in class, they welcomed him as a hero. He had broken the ice, both literally and figuratively. His father, however, felt quite differently. When Georg returned home from training the weekend after the incident and heard the story, he took the thin willow stick from the cupboard and frizzled it on Paul's rear in a furious rage.

Whenever he had been punished before, Paul had shed repenting tears. Not so this time. He bit his right index finger till he drew blood, determined not to let his father know the pain he felt. This defiance made Georg all the angrier, and he increased the tempo of the beating. And then a sharp voice halted his assault.

"Jorg, stop! That's enough."

It was one of the few occasions on which Grete intervened, and Georg did as she asked. As he withdrew from the room, he added a parting shot.

"You are through skating this year and, for all I know, the next one too!" As it turned out, it didn't matter what his father said, for he would not be around to enforce his punishment. He would be too busy marching into Poland and France and later into Russia, helping to bloody the ice of the Weichel River, the Volga, and the snow in Stalingrad.

Georg finished his training to be an officer in the German army in late October 1938. One autumn evening, as Grete and Paul had just begun to eat their evening meal, the doorbell rang.

"Who could that be?" Grete wondered aloud. As Paul jumped up to answer the door, she stopped him. "No, Paul, stay and eat. We do not need to speak to someone so rude as to call during suppertime." Those were the rules, rigid and unbendable.

Whoever was at the door would not go away, and the bell continued to ring. Paul wondered if it were the police, perhaps searching for a thief, or the fire department come to evacuate them from a burning building. Little Ingrid, startled out of her sleep as she lay in her crib by the table, began to scream. Finally Paul's mother had no choice but to answer the door.

Surprise!!! In marched Georg wearing his full uniform complete with gloves, cap, and something Paul had never seen before: a monocle pinched between the right eyelid and his cheek. A thin, black, leather lace fastened to the glass ran down to the breast pocket. Paul wondered if this funny-looking piece of glass belonged to the uniform, or if his father wore it to look more important.

He turned to Grete, her face pinched in an anxious frown.

"Sit down, woman. Make the baby quit crying. All of you, listen!"

He clicked his heels and saluted.

"I am a captain now. My battalion is stationed in Schneidemühl. We'll move there next month!"

There was a long pause. He had expected his family to congratulate him, to applaud this good news. But they did not like what they had just heard.

"Again?" protested Grete. "But we just moved here. And, Jorg, I was going to take Ingrid to Munich to see my sister next month. The timing is not good."

"You can still visit her. Give her a call and ask her if you could go there next week."

Reluctantly, Grete agreed, but she had to wait till Monday morning to contact her sister. Since the Bercks had no telephone, she would have to go to the post office where the clerk would put through the call.

Aunt Käthe had married right after Ingrid was born to a traveling salesman, who represented a large wine distribution company. Because of their wealth and stature, they had their own telephone and could receive Grete's call.

The trip was arranged as Georg suggested and the next day Paul's mother left with Ingrid for Munich, where they would stay for the next two weeks. On the recommendation of the local pastor, Georg hired a young woman to care for Paul while Grete was gone.

Paul guessed that Eza was about twenty-five. He, eleven by then, did not have an eye yet for womanly shapes and beauty. He had observed that she was better looking than his mother, and she smelled as though she bathed in perfume every morning. But that was as far as his interest went.

When Grete and Ingrid left on their trip, Paul felt profoundly alone. He brooded over the upcoming move. Neither Georg nor Grete seemed to be concerned with what moving so soon again would do to him. Starting over was difficult for him, both socially and academically. The news made him sad and angry, and feeling a bit rebellious.

The evening of the day Grete left, Paul paid a visit to the store owner who had saved his life.

"I'd like to buy a pack of cigarettes," Paul said, hoping his voice didn't shake.

The man gave him a long look, then pushed a mini-pack containing three thin smokes across the counter.

"Now, son, don't let that old man of yours catch you with those. He'd take the skin off your ass. You'd never be able to sit again."

In this small town, the "river-folks" had learned how Paul's father had beaten him severely after the skating mishap.

"I won't. I just want to see how it tastes. Do you have some matches, please?"

Outside the store he lit a cigarette and took a few deep drafts, just as he had seen his physical education teacher do. Instantly, he became sick. His head began to spin and he shook violently. He felt as though his stomach wanted to leave his body.

He tossed the pack and the matches into the river and stumbled home, throwing up several times along the way. When he reached his door, he had no strength to push it open, so he rang the bell. When Eza opened the door, she gasped.

"My God, what happened to you?" she cried in alarm. Then she smelled the stench of cigarette smoke and vomit and instantly knew the answer. "Oh, boy. Do you stink!" Her face puckered in distaste. "What are we going to tell your mother? Well, come on in. I'll fix you some seltzer water. It'll make you burp. You will feel better in no time."

Fear fought through Paul's nauseous haze.

"Tell my mother? You're not going to do that?" he asked, his lip quivering.

Eza laughed. "Just kidding, my lips are sealed. Not a word, I promise."

"Promise?"

"Promise, yes." She handed him a glass of fizzy water, and once he got it down, it did help to rid him of his nausea. "Now take off those filthy clothes and get into the bathtub."

After his bath, Paul felt better. He lay on his bed, thinking about what he had done.

I don't think I ever will smoke again in my whole life. How can anybody enjoy that? What if Mutti finds out? Maybe I'll tell her myself. I feel so guilty, but at least it's not a sin. I don't have to tell the priest. What would Vati do to me if he knew? Come to think of it, I'd better not tell anybody. But what about Eza?

He went into the kitchen and ate the dry piece of bread she put in front of him.

"Eza, could you make some more of that bubble water, please?"

She did, and he drank all of it. He was sitting at the table across from her, squirming in his anxiety as to whether he could trust her. He needed to make sure.

Eza, slurping her coffee with all the manners of a pig, noticed his jumpiness.

"Hey, you! Why are you so fidgety? Can't you sit still?"

"I...well...you're sure? You will not say anything to my mother?"

"No, I'm not a tattletale, so don't worry about that. Right now, I think the best thing for you to do is go to bed."

Paul agreed, so exhausted was he from repeatedly throwing up. Eza tucked him in, touching and patting him in places where his mother never had. But to Paul this did not seem to be much out of the ordinary.

"I still have some ironing to do," she said. "Why don't I bring the board in here? We can talk, yes?"

"Sure," replied Paul, although he wondered what they would talk about.

He felt cozy in his bed, warm and safe. He watched as she started on one of his brown Hitler shirts.

"Now, I don't want you to feel so guilty," she said, turning the shirt expertly as she ironed. "Jesus, all the boys I know do things like that. And I myself wasn't any different. How can you learn, understand anything unless you try it yourself? Now you know that smoking makes you sick. They could have told you that, but you still would not know how bad it really feels, how awful it tastes. Right?"

"I guess so," agreed Paul drowsily.

"Having others just tell you about things doesn't work. You need to find out yourself. That is what learning is all about. Am I talking too much?"

"No," replied Paul, turning on his side to watch her. "But when you are a kid, they tell you what to do and what not. All I hear is 'No, you can't' or 'Yes, you have to.'"

"I know what you're talking about. Just remember we grown-ups don't always have the right answer for every question you ask."

"Ja, a few years ago I wanted to know what made my truck go. My father said it was a spring. But I still didn't understand, so I took the thing apart to find out. Guess what? He spanked me for that."

"Yes, but in time you might find it is better sometimes not to know the answer." Without looking up, Eza changed the subject. "How old are you Paul?"

"Eleven and a half."

"Do you have a girlfriend? You are good-looking. The girls should be standing in line just to catch a glance of you, no?"

"I don't like girls."

Eza set down the iron and looked at him. "Why not?"

"They're dumb."

A look of mock consternation crossed her face.

"Excuse me? You say I am dumb? I'll teach you!" She put the iron aside and spurted toward him. Hands around his neck, she pretended to throttle him. "You little bastard you! I might be stupid but I'm not dumb. You hear me?!"

He knew she was joking and tried to push her away. He had absolutely no inkling that those round mounds were breasts. He could feel her nipples, but the sensation meant nothing to him.

Then, seemingly by accident, her blouse came open a little, and she did not try to button it back up. Paul couldn't help but see her nakedness. He froze. A strange excitement took hold of his whole body.

"What is the matter with your face?" she laughed, moving a little closer. "Tell me, how does it feel to look at my breasts? Bad? Tell me."

Paul had a hard time speaking. He shook his head.

"But isn't that a sin? The priest told us not ever to look at a woman who is not properly dressed." Even in his state of shock he had to admit that these feelings bouncing around inside him, hammering his chest, making his heart flutter and his thing go hard...no, these feelings were not bad. All this was so strangely exciting. No, not really bad at all.

Eza stretched out next to him on top of the feather-bed blanket.

"Move over a little," she commanded, pushing his leg. "I want to hug you. Your mother forgot to do that this morning when she left." Her arm found its way under his shoulder. She pulled him close and touched his face. "You're such a nice boy. You really have never seen a naked woman? No? You are not pulling my leg?"

"No, honest, I haven't." His voice sounded to him like it echoed from another room far away.

Eza kissed his cheek. Paul squirmed.

"What if my mother finds out about all this? My father would kill me. I don't know what he would do to you. I know it would hurt."

Eza laughed. "How could she find out? Are you going to tell her? She won't hear it from me. I promise you that. Here give me your hand. Doesn't that feel good to you? It does to me. Leave it there."

Paul shivered. "Eza, I don't want to...I don't know..."

"Oh, come on. Don't you want to kiss me? Just a little? You'll have to learn how to do this some day. I'm a good teacher. Here, come, I close my eyes, okay?"

He hesitated.

That was going to be a hell of a confession. The priest sure wouldn't ask "How many times?" Or would he? What would I tell him? What will he ask me? How can I say it? I don't even know what to call all that. I think I'll go next Saturday, but not to our church. That priest knows me. I will walk to the north end and go to confession. I'll be a stranger there. But, I don't know. My penance, God, I'll pray all year on it! And all Mutti will have to do is look at me. She will know right away that I did something that just wasn't right.

He did not kiss Eza, but she kissed him.

"Oh, I like that," she sighed. "One more time." And this time Paul kissed back.

Paul had never experienced being struck by lightning, but he thought it must feel exactly like that. He was waiting for the thunder to roll in. She had slipped under the blanket, close to his feverish body, and placed his hand where she most wanted it.

Paul was reminded of Ingrid, how she seemed incomplete. Well, maybe all girls are missing that, thought Paul. But he was afraid to ask.

Nothing more happened that night except she had her throws. Paul, concerned, asked her if something was hurting her.

She only laughed. "Come, it is time to sleep."

During the night Paul got up and went into his mother's bed. For the rest of the time, until his mother came back from Munich, he either brought home a friend or stayed at the boy's house up the street. Eza went about her business like nothing had happened. Paul decided he would tell his mother about the cigarette.

Georg had left Stargard in August 1938 to take command of his battalion in Schneidemühl. The family would follow in early January 1939. Paul dreaded the move, which came again in the middle of the school year. He barely had made friends in school here. So far the Bercks had moved four times since he was born, and in none of those places had they grown roots. It would finally happen, though, in that new city close by the Polish border. When asked later where his home was, he would come to answer "Schneidemühl."

The early morning air felt frosty cold. Dawn had just begun to creep over the sky. Taking the scenic route to school, Paul walked along the river. He entered the old part of town through the medieval gate in the Mill Tower. The water here was channeled through a wide trough with gray concrete walls that protected the nearby houses from spring flooding. Low fog hung on trees and shrubs.

Paul wondered about the smell of burning lumber and tar that drifted toward him as he passed through the old portal. Then he saw where it was coming from. The synagogue across the river was smoldering. All the windows were broken. Golden icons scattered around the yard had been defaced. Some had been smeared with mud.

Something was very wrong. There were no people on the street, none. There was no fire engine, no firemen fighting the blaze. Frightened, he hurried by and started to jog away from the scene. Not far from the Jewish church, two stores had been ransacked. Merchandise torn from the shelves and racks littered the pavement. Someone had poured red paint over expensive gowns. A lot of broken glass covered the sidewalk. Again, there were no people around. He gathered that something terrible had happened. Why was nobody here to help? What was going on?

None of his teachers mentioned anything about all this. Paul finally asked one of his classmates.

"Oskar, do you know who smashed the windows of that jewelry store on Hermann Street? And on my way here I saw the synagogue burning. But in neither place was anybody there to help. Do you know what happened?"

"I'm not sure. Last night I overheard my father with his voice raised, saying to my mother something about showing those non-Aryans just who makes the rules in this town. He was very angry. I heard him say something like 'These bastards murdered one of our diplomats in Paris. I might be out all night.' When I left for school, he hadn't come back yet."

Paul decided to ask his mother about it when he got home.

That was on the morning after what came to be known as "The Night of Broken Glass," Thursday, the 10th of November, 1938. One day Goebbels would have to answer for that. Little did Paul understand what had happened, nor what was going to be. Yet, as a citizen of the German nation, he would have to share in the colossal shame his country and his people had begun to accrue. He would carry this guilt until the end of his life. It was so repulsive, hideous, unspeakably vile, and it would only get worse.

Schneidemühl

Grete's two weeks in Munich passed quickly. On a cold, rainy Saturday, Eza and Paul walked to the railroad station to meet his mother and Ingrid.

As they entered the station, Eza put a hand on Paul's shoulder."We are friends, aren't we? Yes?" she asked, her voice sounding unsure, concerned.

"I don't know. I guess so. Anyway, I'm going to tell my mother about the smoking. So whatever you want to tell her is fine with me."

The clerk in the check booth punched their tickets, and they pushed onto the tarmac, which was alive with sights, sounds, and smells. The station overflowed with travelers, some dragging suitcases so big Paul could have easily slept in them. People shouted and frantically waved to get the attention of arriving relatives or friends.

Engines blew off steam. The stationmaster whistled. Vendors hawked their wares: coffee, ice cream, cigars, cigarettes, and hot dogs. Passengers leaning out from their compartment windows hollered for a newspaper.

Pushing through the crowd, Paul could barely hear Eza as she spoke to him. Finally, she grabbed his arm and spun him around.

"Who got to you, boy? What do you mean you're going to tell your mother? I told you, I'm not going to say anything. You promised you wouldn't either."

"Eza, I went to confession. You want to hear what the priest said to me?"

As he waited for her to answer he looked around the station, drinking in the frenetic atmosphere. When he turned back to Eza, she was no longer behind him, having somehow disappeared in this anthill of hustling commuters.

Paul spent a few minutes searching the crowd for her, then headed for Track E, where his mother's train would pull in.

Maybe she had to go to the bathroom, or perhaps we just got separated. I think she'll show up here any minute.

Grete had written a postcard to Eza and Paul, advising her arrival details and giving specific instructions.

"Meet me at the engine, as I have to pass by it on my way out. And don't stand too close to the track! I'll see you soon." Paul saw a baggage handler leaning on his electric cart waiting next to the track.

"Sir, is this where the engine stops?" he asked the man.

"Ja, just about. Go that way a little. And don't stand too close!"

Paul took up his position, feeling that eight feet away should be enough. He did not have long to wait. The train came in fast, the engine's hot, moist steam suddenly engulfing him completely. The white stuff tasted oily, making him feel dizzy. Blindly, he grabbed the sleeve of another person caught in the same white cloud.

"Help me, please! I don't know which way to go!" But as quickly as the steam blew in, so did it dissipate. Finally, Paul let go of the sleeve, thanking the bemused stranger.

He spotted his mother, and was surprised to see her pushing a new kinderwagen, a large and expensive stroller with a big canopy to shield the baby. Paul looked inside to see his sister, but she was completely covered with a feather pillow behind a plastic see-through flap.

"Hello, Mutti! I'm glad you are back! I missed you."

"Where is Eza?" asked his mother, looking with concern over his shoulder.

Paul hesitated just long enough for her to sense that something was awry. "I don't know. We were here together, and then I lost her."

"I do not like that. She is to take care of you. I need to talk to her."

The joy of having his mother back became tainted with fear.

If she asks me, I don't want to lie to her. What am I going to do? I feel so guilty.

"Paul, tell me, how are you? Let me look at you." Grete shook her head. "You need a haircut. Never mind, let's find Eza." But Eza had already run back to the Berck apartment to hurriedly pack her things. She felt both angry and afraid.

"That little bastard with his priest!" she fumed to herself. "Sounds like trouble to me. Stupid little kid! We could have had so much fun."

After looking for Eza in vain, Grete and Paul walked home. He pushed the teeter-tottering stroller over the cobblestone sidewalk as if his life depended on it. Watching him, Grete sensed his nervousness. Whenever Paul did not have a clean conscience, he would bite his lower lip and sniffle—just as he was doing right this moment. Paul, who knew his mother was watching him, wondered what would be her first question. And how would he answer?

They found Eza's note on the kitchen table, which explained that she had taken the wages owed to her from the leftover food money. "You don't need me anymore," the note continued. "I left so abruptly because your son was not nice to me at the station. I don't know whether you are aware of this, but he lies a lot. He's kind of a strange kid."

Grete stared at that piece of paper for quite a while, piecing things together. Ingrid whined in her crib, but Grete did not seem to hear it. Instead, her attention fixed on Paul, who was turning a glass of milk round and round, stepping nervously on his feet. She gazed at him not knowing what to do. No one had prepared her for something like this. In the back of her mind she played with the possibility that nothing "serious" had happened. Maybe she just was imagining things... But then she saw that Paul's hands were shaking and tears had begun to spill down his cheeks. She looked again at the note. After a while she heard herself saying, "You don't have to cry. Everything is all right." She crumpled up the note and threw it into the garbage can under the sink. Then she started fixing supper. "Paul, here, take the bottle and see if Ingrid wants it." His mother never asked Paul what really did happen. And he never told her about his first cigarette.

Captain Georg came home one day early in December to take the family to Schneidemühl for a short visit. He wanted Grete to see the new home they would move into before Christmas.

Paul did not enjoy the train ride. There was nothing to see but fields rushing by, the fences and roads completely covered with snow. The sky was gray, heavy clouds nearly sitting on the chimneys of the farmhouses that hastened by the window.
He did not want to move away from Stargard. It was so hard to make new friends, to feel at home again in a new apartment. Why could they not stay where they were?

The last time Paul had traveled on a train had been when his mother had taken both children on their summer vacation to Henkenhagen at the Baltic Sea. At the beach Paul had made mountains and castles out of white sand. He remembered how the salty waters had come and rippled over the seashore, each little wave licking away at what he just had built. After an hour or so he could no longer tell where he had played. It was as if the sea pretended that his little buildings never had existed.

This happened over and over again, and seemed to be a metaphor for life. Would he ever be able to make something the sea would not wash away, that time would not destroy?

At the beach he had sat many times by the breakwater and let the dry sand run through his fingers onto his legs. The prickling of the warm crystals felt soothing. Other times he would press his fingers tightly together, trying to hold the sand from running to the ground. Yet the grains kept leaking. And soon his hands would be empty no matter how many times he tried to keep them full.

The train kept speeding east. Dark had settled on the landscape. The twinkling lights from houses and of distant street lanterns may as well have been stars that had fallen onto the snow. A lonely night slept out there, waiting for morning. Paul felt uneasy. He closed his eyes and leaned back into the soft cushions of their first-class seats. He kept feeling the sand running through his hands. Was that the way life was? Yes. Before long it would happen. Soon one morning he would wake up, and that life would stare into his face—hard, without compassion, without mercy.

A few days before the captain had come home, Paul was given his second-quarter report card. In religion and sports he received two C's; the rest—Latin, Greek, Geography, and all the other activities—were marked with a D. Mr. Gübel's comments stated that Paul was absentminded and listless, an intelligent fellow who needed to apply himself. Some tutoring would be advisable. Still, the teacher did note that Paul was well liked by his classmates, displayed honesty, and portrayed a sincere team spirit. Nobody asked Paul about the report card. His mother was too busy with the preparation for the impending move, and his father's mind focused on his battalion. Just as well.

After a year had gone by in Schneidemühl, the D's would turn into F's. The reason? Paul discovered girls. They no longer seemed to be so dumb. As a consequence, he would have to do the grade over again. That upset the freshly promoted lieutenant general, Georg. He learned of Paul's academic failing when he stopped at home on his way back to Schneidemühl after a meeting with field marshal Keitel in Berlin. He stayed just long enough to let Paul have a piece of his mind. This time Paul could not sit down for a couple of days.

The train finally slowed as they approached Schneidemühl. When they disembarked, an army automobile picked them up and took them to a fairly large apartment on Wasser Strasse #4, which Georg had reserved. Georg hoped that Grete would like it. Because his being a soldier again, he would be away much of the time. He wanted to be sure that the family would have a good place to call home. And he had the feeling that something big was in the making, something that would not let him be with his family for years on end.

The second-floor apartment had three bedrooms, a nice bathroom that included a tub, and a spacious kitchen with a balcony enclosed by a wrought-iron railing, similar to the one in Stettin. An electric stove with two burners sat on the counter next to the sink. A large, walk-in pantry boasted several shelves. A wood-burning cooking stove on fancily curved legs stood in the corner, its white-enameled oven lid fashioned with a shiny, black handgrip. A coke-fired furnace, situated in the hallway between the spacious dining room and the master's chamber, provided central heating.

Paul's sister was given a small room next to the master bedroom; another room, just off the dining room with a separate entry, became Paul's very own until after the war had begun, when he would move in with Ingrid. Grete would use his room to house a family from Stuttgart who lost their home to the bombs the Allied terminators had rained on that city.

In the snowy darkness, the backyard looked long and narrow. A bike repair shop bordered it on the left side, and an eight-foot-high fence ran down the right. A gate at the end of the yard opened into a garden. Georg had negotiated with the owner of the house, Mr. Jasinsky, for the use of a small portion of his garden so Grete could sow some flowers and grow carrots, cabbage, spinach, and cucumbers.

They could not see it that evening, but the garden stretched for some one hundred feet down to the bank of the Küdow, a narrow, shallow river winding through town. Two bridges crossed it, one old, one new. A larger-than-life statue of Frederick the Great guarded the west entrance of the old bridge. High on a marbled pedestal, the king leaned on his famous cane. His coat seemed to wave in the wind, as though it had been blowing when they poured the bronze statue.

A little over to the south was the Johannes Catholic Church. The prelate, Dr. Hart, lived next to the church in a grand mansion with an apple orchard in the back. One day he would catch Paul and his friend stealing apples there.

"Well, Grete," asked Georg, "do you like it?"

Typical of Paul's mother, she worried about the cost. "You think we can afford it? Isn't it too expensive? It is almost three times bigger than the one we had on Burscher Strasse in Stettin."

Georg calmed her fears. "Don't worry, I'll get promoted again soon. Yes, we can swing it."

Slowly, almost reluctantly, Grete nodded, looking around approvingly. "Okay, then, thank you, we can be home here."

Paul, of course, had no say in this matter. Georg signed the lease, paid Mrs. Jasinsky the first month's rent, and took the family to a fancy restaurant at the end of Posener Street to celebrate. The restaurant, considered the social hub of the city, catered only to a well-to-do clientele. During the ride to the restaurant, Georg gave stern instructions to Paul.

"You sit still and don't play with the silverware. When we grown-ups talk, you keep quiet. If you need to go to the bathroom, raise your hand. Grete, why don't you comb his hair a little..."

At eleven years of age, Paul had developed what could be thought of as his blank mode, deflecting his father's dont's and have-to's. Faking total acceptance and obedience, he could be polite, even managing to smile when spoken to. Over time he had nearly perfected this mechanism that deafened his father's intrusions.

As Paul had developed from an innocent boy into a thinking adolescent, he had grown further and further away from his father. Georg had raised his son with a stern rigidity, often driving home his rules with corporal punishment or emotional cruelty. Although he had wanted Georg's love and approval when younger, Paul now found himself traveling down the bitter road to hating his father.

At the restaurant, the Bercks were met by an obsequious headwaiter named Manfred. "Please, this way," he indicated with a sweep of his arm. "I have reserved a table by the window for Herrn Major." Paul was unimpressed.

What good does a window at dark do, one that even during the day had no view other than the dirty-gray building of the movie theater across the street?

Although Georg held the rank of captain at that time, Manfred understood the political benefit of upping the status of officers bringing their families here for dinner. Georg did not object, for his whole demeanor suggested that he thought himself important. Paul found his father to be more comical than commanding, sporting that silly monocle on his face. Such an eye-piece certainly could not have been comfortable.

Ingrid did not join her family; instead, she spent the evening in her new kinderwagen, keeping company with the woman in the coatroom. Children under six were not allowed in the dining room, and bringing in a baby would have been considered very poor taste.

The restaurant reminded Paul of the master's chamber, the parlor in Stettin: sterile and impersonal. Fairly good-sized dining tables, about twenty of them, were arranged like a chessboard, with only white squares, however, to play on. The silverware—made of real silver—was laid just so: The knife and fork, handles exactly two inches from the edge of the table, were stationed on the right side of a double set of dinner plates. To the left, a soupspoon, a tablespoon, a teaspoon, and a small sugar spoon glittered in the light of monstrous chandeliers hanging from an arching ceiling. The comfortable chairs were upholstered a deep maroon velvet, soft and luxurious to the touch.

"Put your hands on the table. No, not so far! And keep your arms in close. Yes, like that." Georg was proud of how he had taught Paul to behave like a gentleman at the dinner table. It had not been easy. But after having to sit at the table with a book under each of his arms for a week, Paul had learned to sit and eat properly.

A waiter arrived, bowing respectfully. He was nameless, for servants were considered third-class people who did not need a name. The patrons simply called them "garçon." Women were not allowed to waited on tables.

"Good evening, sir." He offered Georg a menu. "May I bring you some wine?"

"Of course," replied Georg, and selected a good Rhine wine. Then he studied the binder, which showed no prices. "We will eat beef tonight, yes, and mashed potatoes with asparagus and mushrooms, please. Oh, and bring a small portion of veal for my son here. Thank you." Another bow and the man in his white jacket disappeared.

Shortly, a different steward appeared with the wine. Georg held his eyeglass close to read the label, taking his time and making the waiter nervous.

"Is something wrong? Did we make a mistake? Is it not the right one?"Georg nodded gravely. This was a serious matter.

"It is okay."

The waiter opened the bottle and passed the cork to the "major," who sniffed it. Another nod. This one was tinged with a smile.

"Very good!"

The first waiter had come back. He took the bottle from his associate's silver tablet and wetted Georg's wine glass. First he inhaled the aroma, then he took the professional sip. A third and final nod eased the tension.

Georg pursed his lips and said, "Grete, this is a good wine. You will like the taste." She smiled her acceptance, then pushed Paul's elbows from the table. His chin almost hit the double set of the china in front of him.

"One doesn't do that. You do not lean all over the tablecloth," she admonished.

Grete tried the wine, which turned out to be dry and tangy, bordering on outright sour. Her face distorted and Paul could not help it, he laughed out loud—too loud. People at the next table raised their eyebrows. Georg turned and apologized for his son's behavior. After a few minutes the tension eased, although the "major's" face remained stern, like a warden's before pushing the button.

Grete was not a wine person. Beer and brandy, those were her beverages of choice. Paul would discover that one day quite by accident. Paul had always felt drawn to the master's room, probably because it remained off-limits to him. He couldn't help thinking that something was in there that they didn't want him to know about. If the room had been not carefully locked each time his mother and father went in and out, Paul never would have had the urge to go in there. Their secrecy made him determined to find out the chamber's secret. One day after the family had moved into the new place, Paul waited until his mother left for the grocery store. Then, using a screwdriver, he picked the simple lock. Cautiously, he entered. It was as sterile as all the other rooms, with a chair, sofa, and carpet of dark, uninviting colors. Its one fascinating feature was the telephone sitting on top of the oaken desk. He found nothing else that would warrant his notice.

On the way out, however, he discovered, by sheer accident, a bottle hidden behind the gramophone. "Kirsch brandy," the label read. Curious, he pulled out the cork and took a whiff.

Wow, that smells good! I think I'll just take a little taste. Nobody will notice...

After that, whenever he found himself alone in the apartment, he broke into the room and took the bottle from its hiding place. He found it puzzling that the bottle would always be half full. He would take a swig, enjoying the taste and the deliciously warm sensation that radiated throughout his body, then hide the treasure once again.

The main course arrived. The no-name man dished out the food from covered pans warmed by a candle burning beneath them. He then stood back, ready to jump when more mashed potatoes or gravy were needed.

Paul thought his food tasted good. The veal was fried just right. When he tried to cut it, the meat nearly slipped off his plate. What would have happen if it had? As he saved the plate from certain disaster, he caught Grete's look of relief.

Georg toasted his wife several times. "To our new home, Grete!" Paul kept expecting her face to turn funny again, but she had gotten things under control.

While they conversed with each other, neither his mother nor his father addressed Paul unless he was not sitting up straight, held his fork incorrectly, or had his mouth fuller than etiquette allowed. With nothing else to do with his mind, he began to play a little with the night Eza had fondled his virginity. Somehow it made him feel good that he knew something they did not. Grete had not mentioned anything to her husband about what she suspected, and Paul felt safe enough to fantasize.

After a dessert that was not shared with Paul— "It would give you a stomach ache!"—Georg put Grete, Paul, and Ingrid back on a train to Stargard. He had to be with his soldiers, who were training in a maneuver that simulated an all-out war.

On the ride home, the steady clackety-clack of the train on the rails lulled Paul to sleep.

On moving day, a van arrived with three men. They took care of everything: packing, loading, even cleaning, although they couldn't find a speck of dirt. Grete had shined the place up before they had gotten there. Cleanliness was one of her "eleventh" commandments. She impressed on Paul that, no matter how poor a person was, there was no need to walk around dirty or live in a filthy place.

"Soap is cheap and water doesn't cost anything!" she would insist. Another one of her commandments, "Do not pick up a pin if it does not belong to you," would come to haunt Paul during the years after the war, when he would be forced to steal to stay alive. Still, many of her rules, though not among the famous ten Moses brought back from the mountain, stuck with Paul and guided him well through life.

A week before Christmas of 1938 the Bercks found themselves comfortably settled into their new home in Schneidemühl. The town lived under a heavy blanket of snow, five feet thick in places. High berms rimmed the streets. Horse-drawn sleighs ferried milk, bread, and brown beer down the narrow streets, their drivers' sharp yells alerting the neighborhood. When the milkman passed, he would clang his bell, and Grete would run downstairs to have her glass carafe filled with three liters of heavy cream milk. With the beer vendor, she exchanged empty beer bottles for full ones. This way of doing business brought a new experience to the family.

Because Georg was on maneuvers with his battalion, they celebrated Christmas without him, the first time in Grete's married life that she had done so. As always, she hid her emotions well, never wanting her family to know how she truly felt. The Christmas tree she had bought stood in the master's room, just as always. No one would call it a beautiful tree; some of its few branches looked naked, and much of the tinsel hung crookedly. But it did not matter. Like every other year, Grete had managed to convince her children that there would be no Christmas tree.

"You see, your father is not here, and I don't know where to buy one and worse, how to decorate it. So we'll have to do without." That sounded very plausible, and Paul believed his mother. He would have been glad to help her, but, of course, that was out of the question. Still, he wondered why the keyhole in the door of the master's room had been masked by a band-aid on the inside, so that any peeking would be impossible.

"Mutti, do you think the Christ Child will bring us any presents at all?" asked Paul. "If He does not see a tree through the window, He might just fly by."

At this suggestion, Ingrid started to cry. "Why don't the both of you say a few *Hail Marys*?" suggested Grete. "The Child has fine ears and hears everything we say."

Obediently, Paul went to his room and knelt by his bed. But his praying gave way to letting Ingrid ride on his back in a game of "horsey." This kind of play was risky for Paul, for should Ingrid fall off, she might scream as though she were mortally wounded. And Paul one more time would have to spoon up all the blame. At one point he felt so wronged by Ingrid and his mother that he decided to run away and stay with Ortwin, his best friend in school. Unfortunately, Ortwin's mother did not go for it, so Paul was forced to endure the injustices at home.

This Christmas Eve all went fine. In the afternoon Grete put them both in the bathtub. Paul played with his toy boat while Ingrid splashed about as she sucked on the washcloth. When his mother took Ingrid out of the tub, Paul looked up and asked, "Mutti, why doesn't she have hair down there?"

Grete felt like someone had hit her, and hit her hard. Even if she had an answer for him, she could not speak it. The room began to spin around. She had to hold onto the top of the counter. Eza? What had happened while she was gone? Paul, for once, did not seem disappointed that she didn't answer another one of his questions. He forgot the question quickly, moving on to more important matters.

"Mutti, you count how long I can keep my head under water, okay?" Paul, it turned out, could stay under until the count of twelve. Grete relaxed. The Lord had taken that chalice away from her. While she rubbed Ingrid down, she said a prayer for Paul. She really believed that prayers could move mountains.

"Pray until your mouth gets dry, and then some more. The Lord will hear you, Paul," she often told him, another of her own "commandments."

Grete helped the children get dressed in their Sunday outfits. Paul hated the long, home-knit stockings she made him wear. They felt to him like they were made of sandpaper, for he was highly sensitive to scratchy clothing. But as with so many other things, he had no choice.

Grete wore a champagne-colored blouse, a blue cotton skirt, and shoes that did not match the outfit, giving her an awkward appearance.

"What's that smell on you, Mutti?" asked Paul.

"Don't you like it? It's Eau de Cologne 4711. Your father gave it to me and I am wearing it in his honor. Now you wait out here and I will open the windows in the master's room to let the Christ Child in. When you hear the bell you can come in."

Paul bit his lip in impatience, while Ingrid danced around in the hallway. The tension became unbearable. Finally the bell rang, very soft and yet so clear and bright. Paul opened the door, with Ingrid right on his heels. He was stunned. In the corner stood a tall tree with real wax candles burning in the holders on the branches. Wow! How could that be?

Grete closed the window. "The Christ Child just left and He asked me to pass onto you this sign of the cross." She knelt in front of them, dipped her finger into the holy water bowl she took from the oaken desk, and drew a little cross on their foreheads. Ingrid wiped it off right away with the back of her fat little hand, but Paul bowed his head. As he did so, he could see out of the corner of his eye a shiny new bike. Ingrid had already gotten busy with the bell on her brand-new red tricycle.

"No, children, not yet. We'll play later. I want to read you the Christmas story first." Paul bit his lip harder yet, and his sister threw a fit when Grete pried her loose from the tricycle's handlebars. After a bit, they settled down to listen: "...and they wrapped the baby in diapers and put Him down onto the straw of the manger. There were angels and shepherds from the fields. They all praised the Lord.... Now, let's sing the *Holy Night* song." She went over to the new piano Georg had given to her for Christmas and played for them.

The Bercks usually had fish for supper on Christmas Eve; this evening it was carp. Carp had so many fine bones, Grete always feared they would get stuck in Paul's throat, so she would always give Paul the fish's head. He liked to eat those soft cheeks and whatever else was inside this head with its so-sad-looking eyes.

Georg's absence became much more noticeable at dinnertime, for it used to be he who always cut the roast, deboned the chicken, or parted the fish. Grete now felt uneasy doing his chores. His chair at the head of the table was empty, but his authority still oozed from it, penetrating the festivities. The gramophone played Christkind songs and dinner ended with a sweet, raisin-studded bread pudding. Paul thought it very good and out of the ordinary, and Grete allowed him two helpings. As they ate, Grete told Paul he was to be enrolled at the Freiherr von Stein Gymnasium right after the new year.

"Your grades have got to get better," she added sternly. "They almost did not take you. Luckily, your father being an officer swayed their opinion."

Paul was thankful that his father was in the army, not because of his influence, but because it meant he would be away from home more and this would make life just a little easier.

Grete tucked Ingrid in her crib, and then told Paul to dress for church. "We'll go to midnight Mass while she sleeps. She will be okay. Your father needs our prayers and we must give thanks for all the nice things we got tonight."

Although the apartment was barely five minutes from the Johannes Kirche, the walk chilled Grete and Paul. The temperature had dipped below zero, and the iced snow on the sidewalk crunched under their boots. Grete wore her mink coat, while Paul looked like a mummy, all shawled up.

A woman who walked up from behind greeted them warmly.

"Good evening! You must be our new neighbor. We saw you coming out of Number 4."

Introductions were made. The woman's name was Frieda Mortz, and her husband, Max, was the organist for the church.

"And these are three of our children, Geela, Inge, and Mieschel. Our oldest son, Gerhard, is in the army." As Mieschel opened the door to the church, Frieda asked, "Would you like to sit with us up on the balcony where the organ is? It's less crowded." Grete agreed, and she and Paul followed the Mortz family through the slender door into the vestibule. The church was not much warmer than the street outside, for it could not be heated. The body heat generated by the many worshippers kept the temperature hovering slightly above freezing. The church, though not large, could seat some three hundred people. Tonight, however, not only were the pews filled, but people stood wherever they would find a spot. Young and old were dressed for the holiday. The women had taken off their heavy shawls and donned hats and fancy cotton scarves. They sat on the left side of the aisle; the men sat on the right. Small children had been left at home, and not a whisper could be heard in the sacred silence.

Only the wooden benches were allowed to squeak as the congregation shuffled for space.

Paul found the scene breathtakingly beautiful. Bright chandeliers cast their light through the colored glass of the Gothic windows onto the white snow outside. Inside the church, hundreds of candles flickered everywhere—on side altars, in every nook and niche, and before the various saints whose likeness had been cast in plaster. Two altar boys swung golden kettles with glowing myrrh that perfumed the air, giving a festive flair to the proceedings.

Mieschel grabbed Paul's hand and stormed up the narrow, spiral staircase that led to the balcony and, further up, to the bell tower. They squeezed by the organ's air bags to a spot where they could lean over the balcony railing. The members of the choir, busily sorting their songsheets, let their papers slip here and there, pages sailing down between the benches. Giggling, the boys retrieved the sheets and returned them to their owners. Frieda, thinking the boys too loud, hissed "Pssst!" and came over, her index finger pressed against her lips and a dark look on her face. The boys retreated to a spot behind the organ where it was safe to talk.

"I am an altar boy," said Mieschel proudly. "Would you like to be one too? It's fun to wear those frocks and ring the bells during Mass." Paul looked doubtful.

"I don't know. Isn't it hard to learn all those Latin prayers, the ones you answer the priest with?" Suddenly he had a thought. "If you're an altar boy, why aren't you down by the altar with the others?"

"We are about thirty boys," explained Mieschel, "but there are only twenty-five frocks. So we drew straws. Mine was a short one. But that is okay, as I like to be up here too." He jumped up, pulling Paul with him. "Come, I'll show you how to tread the air bags. Inge and I have to do this tonight when my father is playing."

Mieschel, who was the youngest Mortz child, was a couple of years younger than Paul. His sister Inge was just about Paul's age, Geela was sixteen, and Gerhard, the boy who had already been drafted into the army, was the eldest. In time the Bercks and the Mortzes would get acquainted in a deep and permanent way, but their friendship began that night with Paul having found his first new friend in an otherwise strange town.

Max played the *Bethlehem* song, and the congregation fell in: "...a child was born in the manger, and angels and shepherds came to see..." Paul stood by his mother. She was kneeling, her hands folded in prayer, covering her face. What Paul could not see was that her eyes were wet. He never in all of his life ever saw his mother cry.

The procession came down the aisle—altar boys, the smaller ones first, three priests, one carrying the cross, two deacons holding candles, the pastor, and then the prelate himself. The altar boys carried bright-sounding bells, ringing them gently. They all marched to the song Max played, as Paul watched Mieschel and Inge treading the air bags. The Mass had begun.

"Kyrie eleison, Christe eleison, Kyrie eleison. Lord have mercy..."

It turned out to be a tremendous celebration. Paul sang the "Te Deum laudamus...(Mighty God we praise you...)" as loud as he could. No Hitler Jugend song could ever be that moving, that powerful, that beautiful!

Paul settled into a surprisingly enjoyable life in Schneidemühl. He liked his teachers at the new school. They seemed friendlier, did not sit on such a high horse as the ones in Stargard. Maybe it was because Schneidemühl was a smaller place. People knew each other. Many went to church on Sunday and prayed there every night during the rosary month of May.

Hundreds of thousands of acres of farmland stretched to the north, the south, and the west. A large sawmill made lumber from timbers cut in nearby tall and deep forests, giving the city its name, which meant "cutting mill." The Polish border to the east was not farther away than seven or eight miles. Halfway between the city and the border rose the garrison where Georg's army regiment was stationed, its dark-red brick buildings spreading over eighty city blocks.

Paul had been accepted into the Untertertia, the third grade at the Freiherr von Stein Gymnasium. The younger Mieschel was in the Sexta, the first grade. The two boys became good friends and spent a great deal of time together in each other's home. The Mortzes lived on the ground floor of their building, with the windows of their one bedroom—in which slept the entire family—and the kitchen facing the backyard. Since Paul lived on the second floor of the adjacent building, he had a good view of the Mortzes' backyard, the garden, and the river beyond.

Frieda Mortz was a bubbly, outgoing woman. She wore her straight, gray hair pulled back from her round face, her short, corpulent figure maintained by her daily treat of a mocha and a slice of hazelnut tart at a downtown cafe. Her manners could be somewhat affected; when she sipped from a cup, she held it as though it were a raw egg sitting in a thin shell. She liked to think her piety rivaled that of the Pope, and perhaps this accounts for why Paul felt she never trusted him. Still, she managed to make her cramped apartment friendly and cozily warm, and Paul liked going there. Not shy about asking for a favor, Frieda used the Bercks' telephone, a habit that would sometimes irritate Grete, although she never mentioned it to Frieda.

Max Mortz was a heavyset man, with white hair that only partially covered his round, Slovenian head and noticeably large ears. Although his voice came out scratchy, his words were always warm and friendly, and the eyes behind his large, gold-rimmed spectacles were gentle. Unlike his wife, he was quiet, almost shy. Max worked for the city, where he oversaw utility billings. Every morning he walked the two blocks to his job in the administration building at the Markt Platz; at noon on the dot he came home for lunch, then took a short nap on the couch, his hands folded neatly over his chest.

Both Frieda and Max played the organ, although when Max played, Paul thought the music to be beautiful. On Sundays, he accompanied the Mass at the Frauen Kirche across town while Frieda answered Father's "Dominus vobiscum" and manned the organ at the Johannes church. Paul and Mieschel would take turns working the air bags. While Mieschel was a member of the Jungvolk, Paul joined the Hitler Jugend. He had "enlisted" in the music platoon, where he learned to play a long-stemmed bugle known as the fanfare. He became good at that and soon was promoted to group leader. The red-and-white braided chord swinging between the third button on his brown shirt and his left breast pocket attested to that.

Every Wednesday afternoon, the "Fanfaren Zug" gathered at the Post Platz. Paul stood in front of the group, holding the glinting brass fanfare in his right hand, the funnel resting on the upper leg so that the striking black-and-white flag attached to its long shaft hung straight down. The platoon leader would announce the program for the afternoon.

"We will march through town towards the Baggen hills north of the city..." he would order, and the troops would quickly assemble. The musicians marched first, then the "regulars" would follow in columns three deep, divided into platoons, up to three hundred kids altogether. Drummers hammered the skin of their long black-and-white barrels, and Paul blew his heart out on his extended trumpet. He always kinked his left arm with the hand welded to his hip, like the handle of a coffee mug. The fringed flag with the SS insignia swayed, as though keeping time with his steps. He was so proud. All young people were proud at that time: their faces glowing with excitement, hearts on their way to beat to the rhythm of the Third Reich.

When they got to the Markt Platz, they halted and sang songs of tomorrow, when the whole world would be theirs. They sang songs of heroes, songs that held no tears, only glory, songs of a future promised to them again and again: "Heute Deutschland und morgen die ganze Welt!...(Tomorrow the whole wide world)!"

Often on Sundays they would stand at the Danziger Platz with thousands of other boys and girls from different parts of the city: the boys sporting brown shirts ironed to a crisp and shined shoes, the girls clad in starched, white blouses and demure black skirts. They would stand in formation for hours, listening to propaganda speeches. In between they would sing "...strength and victory..." and pay homage to the swastika, the wheel of fire that would wreak havoc around the globe. Of course they would win this war! Goebbels, Göring, Alfred Krupp, Hitler—they all kept saying so, over and over again.

After the marching, the singing, the playing soldiers and war, they were let go to be boys again. They went cruising on foot down Posener Street after showing off for the Bund Deutscher Mädchen–BDM for short–the young girls of Hitler's Jugend. Together they ate ice cream at the parlor across from the movie theater. They all felt confident that there was no way Germany could lose.

In the fall of 1939 German soldiers invaded Poland. During the weeks preceding this event, the Berck family had seen nothing of Georg. Then, he appeared on the evening of August 30th unexpectedly. As he came into the apartment, Paul noticed that his driver did not bother to shut off the car as it waited across the street.

Grete ushered Paul and Ingrid into the master's room. Paul noticed the liqueur bottle was gone.

"Grete, Paul, Ingrid—I am going to war very soon. I don't know yet when. I came to say goodbye. Paul, you help your mother, bring home good grades, and grow up to be a good soldier. We will be fighting for our country, and you children will help us at home by doing the right things. Understand?"

Of course Paul understood. They had at least told him that much during their meetings at the Hitler Jugend's halls.

Grete looked somewhat derailed as Georg kissed Ingrid on the forehead. Then he sent the children out and closed the door.

The next time they saw their father he was marching with his regiment through the city, a farewell gesture. The march had been orchestrated so that the troops passed through the streets where the officers had their homes. Although police stood on hand to regulate the traffic, there was none. The streets were empty. Grete, Paul, and Ingrid leaned out the living room window. When they caught sight of Georg, he was riding a horse in front of the regiment. He wore a helmet, and a saber dangled from his left side. The monocle fixed in his right eye reflected the autumn sun, giving Paul the impression that a flashlight shone from his father's eye.

Georg looked up as he passed their apartment and gave a ceremonial wave. Then, resuming his military posture, he raised his hand to his helmet and saluted them, after which he rode on without looking back.

Little did the family know they would see him only three times during the coming seven years, and then only for a few hours each time.

Paul watched his father with confusion. The man on that horse was a different person, not fitting the frame of the past. Paul thought back to their days in Stettin and one particular dinner when Georg cut himself slicing the Sunday roast. His father had turned white and nearly fainted. And it was true that Georg had not really known how to use a hammer to perform the simplest function such as putting a nail into the wall. Now he wore a saber, knew how to ride a horse, and was going to war. Georg would ride among craters filled with shredded bodies, see men with their limbs torn off, hear the awful screams of burning people who did not escape the fire of the flame-throwers. He would use his pistol to shoot down boys who were as young as his own son. He would direct the regiment's guns to blow up houses, villages, even whole cities, and he would call it victory. Who was that man on the horse, the one who did not hug Paul before he left? There would never be a time for Paul to ask his father. Never would there be an answer.

One evening, not long after that day, Grete had the children put on their Sunday clothes, and they walked to church. Paul remembers her face as lifeless, a chiseled granite gray. She prayed but her lips did not move. Her folded hands showed white knuckles in the twilight of the cold cathedral. Many other families joined them in silent prayer. Hundreds of candles flickered at the feet of the Virgin Mary statue, each representing a hope, a prayer.

On the way home, the sky to the east in the distance sparked with what looked like lightning. They heard the rolling thunder of the first exploding shells.

A horrible war had started.

Grete held Ingrid's and Paul's hands so hard it hurt, but her grip made them feel safe. They returned her strong grasp, as though they never wanted to let go again. They understood little of what was happening, and even less of what was going to come. But an eerie foreboding saturated the night, and they felt that.

Death's sickle would go wild. With grizzly howls, the animal in man would waken, slurp blood, and feed on soil soaked with bodies. Mothers-to-be would be slit open and the soldiers from Siberia would rip out the unborn life, mangle it, stomp it into death. A civilized nation would build ovens and burn people who were gassed to suffocation on the way to the smokestacks in Poland. Millions of heroes would be killed. Nothing would be left of them on which to pin a medal, no grave or cross a wreath could decorate on Christmas Day. Whole countries—simple women, men, children only wanting to love, to live, and to be together—would be torn apart forever. Yes, people's lives would change. The war would wound them all, and many of the wounded would never heal. The ones who survived would carry their broken souls and hurting hearts through the years until they would join with those they had lost. Only death would finally erase the awful gruesome memories of their torched hours.

The next morning the radio kept broadcasting victory. "Sondermeldungen" (special updates) accompanied by orchestral blasts announced the fall of cities in Poland.

Paul worked hard to attain his C-average status in school. Mieschel kept urging Paul to join the group of altar boys. One Saturday morning, Mieschel and Paul went to early morning Mass. The priest looked at Paul.

"Come, I help you to get dressed up. You can kneel at the side step of the altar and watch, yes?"

"Yes, Father, if you think so."

For the next week Mieschel took Paul under his wing, teaching Paul how to recite the Latin answers. *"Confiteor Deo Omnipotenti...*I confess to Almighty God..." The prayer was long, and it took Paul quite a while just to memorize part of it.

"You know, sometimes I forget some of the lines too," confessed Mieschel, "so I just kind of mumble."

"Father doesn't notice?"

"No, because when we say the *Confiteor*, we bend our heads down." Mieschel demonstrated, kneeling and leaning forward, pulling his head down to his chest. "You see? My head always touches the next step up, so the priest can't really hear too well what I am saying." He straightened up, taking on the air of someone sharing a secret. "That works best when I am serving by myself. If I'm serving with others, then timing is important. I've got to know how long a mumble can be. It must be the same length as the real prayers, not shorter or longer—you see what I mean. When there are four altar boys, two on each side of the pastor, you have to make sure your mumble ends when they end, and then raise up at the same time."

To be truthful, Paul never said the *Confiteor* without mumbling some of the lines. But what he lacked in memorization skills, he made up for in his ability to get the timing just right.

One Wednesday afternoon, as Paul stood in front of his Fanfaren platoon, his section leader motioned to him.

"Follow me," the leader said, and took Paul over to one side. When they were out of earshot of the others, Hans look Paul square in the eye. "I hear you are an altar boy now at the Johannes Church."

Nervously, Paul replied cautiously, "Yes, I recently became one."

"Paul, you know that our Führer, Hitler, will do away with the religious stuff—this Catholic church business, the Lutherans, and all the other sects. Remember what he did to the synagogues? Yes, after we have won this war, we will understand that there really is no other God but him."

"Hans, I know. You've told us that so many times." Paul's thoughts were beginning to undergo a change, and he dared Hans with his reply. "You also asked us to pray for him. To whom do I pray, to the God who lives in my church and will be done away with?"

"I can see you need some more training. Obviously I have failed to get through to you." The young and earnest youth looked at Paul with anger and fear. "Look at me!" he commanded. "And listen well: Altar boys don't blow fanfares in my unit. Think about it." With a last dark look at Paul, the leader stomped away.

Paul, however, did not give up being an altar boy, nor did he have to quit blowing his trumpet. But this had more to do with his father's influence than Paul's.

One night, when Paul, Mieschel, and two other boys were performing their altar boy duties for an evening rosary, they did not finish until after the eight o'clock youth curfew. Knowing there would be repercussions if caught, they legged it home as fast as they could. Ironically, their running attracted the attention of the local police, who rounded them up and took them to jail. One policeman recognized Mieschel as the son of Max Mortz, the utility supervisor at the municipality, and he released the boy. When Mieschel returned home with his story, Frieda stormed upstairs to the Bercks to report the incident. Georg decided to show the police just who was who. After all, he was an officer on leave from the victorious front of the war. By God, they'd better show some respect!

Major General Berck donned his full uniform and went down to the police station. Within minutes, the rest of the altar boys were released. Paul never knew what his father had said or done, but a couple of weeks later, Hans again took Paul aside.

"So, your old man thinks he's someone," he sneered. "Okay, you can keep blowing your trumpet. But, just between you and me, the 'Major' is on our list."

Paul would learn later that Hans was referring to the blacklist of Hitler's storm troopers, the Waffen SS, feared for their scare tactics and ruthless punishments. No doubt they would take care of Georg some day.

Schneidermühl had become a major transportation hub between east and west, and trains now came and went with increasing frequency. Paul liked trains. The white steam blasts of locomotives as they set the long snake of cars in motion fascinated him. He could feel the power of the engines' spinning wheels when they slipped on the tracks. Often, after he had finished his homework, he would hop on his bike and wheel down to his favorite spot—a bridge near the railroad station that straddled the train tracks. He would stop right at the middle of the overpass, lay the bike on the sidewalk, and lean over the railing with his feet on the lower bar. The tarmac was not far from where he stood, and he could hear the whistle of the stationmaster followed by the conductor's shout: "Aaalll aboaaard!"

Sometimes the train would travel east, away from the bridge, and Paul's eyes would follow its puffing clouds until they became one with the sky at the horizon. He would forget where he was, falling into daydreaming about traveling to far away countries—Greece, Spain, Italy. Sometimes his mind wandered further yet, to far east islands, to India and China.

"One day," he would tell himself, "I want to go away, way, way far from here. Yes one day..." More than once, as he stood fantasizing about his future, a train would pass under the bridge, the dense steam from its engine engulfing him and making his hands and face moist with the white mist.

On the day following the first thunderous sounds of war, train after train arrived from the eastern front. The cars had red crosses painted on their white roofs and military ambulances waited on the platforms. Soldiers with Red Cross arm bands carried bodies on stretchers from the Pullmans to the vehicles. Even on the bridge, Paul could hear the moaning, could see the blood-soaked bandages covering heads, bodies, arms, and legs of wounded soldiers.

This...this, Hans, this you did not tell me when you had me aiming the rifle at my friends, the "enemy" in your games of war. Did you forget? Or did your leaders not tell you either?

Hans had spoken only of victory—yes, and about death, the glory of dying for Hitler. Not a single word had he said about soldiers losing their legs, becoming blind, leaving their arms and feet out there in the craters of the shelled land.

Vati, my father, you are out there too. How will you come home? What made you go there in the first place? You had been a soldier in the First World War. You have seen all this before when you fought at the Vosges Mountains against the French. You lost then, you and the German nation, you and the hundreds of thousands of other young men. Why are you doing it again? Have you forgotten those bandages, the gas masks, the pain?

Of course, in the end, Georg would have had no choice. If he had not gone willingly into the military, he would have been drafted. And if he had refused to serve, a concentration camp would have been his fate.

Trains continued to arrive, bringing mangled, half-dead men into the station.

They say this war will not last long. It soon will be over, over before they ask me to go where you are. Will it? I am afraid. I don't want to be a soldier. I don't want to kill another person who, like me, wants to live. I don't want to come back blind or maimed. Yet I know I have no choice. Because of you and all the other fathers, we children have no other way to go. We will suffocate with you in this inferno. Why? For what?

News came that Poland had fallen. It had only taken a few weeks to destroy this nation, her cities, her land.

You, my Father, you helped death to become alive. How can you ever look into my eyes again and talk about God?

In the winter of 1943, in the midst of their country's unrest, Paul and Mieschel found themselves trying to navigate the difficult waters of adolescence. Understanding the opposite sex became one of their biggest challenges, not without its pitfalls. One January afternoon, as the boys were ice skating on the Küdow River, they saw that three girls were chasing them.

"Paul! Paul slow down!" one of the girls yelled at the top of her lungs.

But Paul felt like having a little fun. "Come on, Mieschel, let's see if they can catch us." The boys bent forward, folding their arms behind their backs and weaving from side to side as they raced down-river. The girls, however, were good skaters, and kept pace with them. One of the trio was Beth, a girl about two years older than Paul, who had been trying to get close to him ever since she had seen him perform at the gymnastic competition. Paul's athletic body had caught her attention as he executed his giant swings on the high-bar. She had screamed with excitement with the rest of the crowd when he let go of the steel rod and, completing a double somersault, landed upright on the mat. The whole auditorium had broken into wild applause, and he had become an instant celebrity, with the local paper running his picture on the front page next day.

As Paul skated under the new bridge downstream, he felt the grip on his right skate coming loose. He shouted to Mieschel to stop. The girls came up behind them, Beth shaving the ice with her skates as she stopped, just to show off.

"I knew I'd catch up with you!" she gloated. Turning to the other two girls she said, "Our boy here got tired. He had to get his breath back. Ha, ha!" The icy wind burned Paul's face so deeply red that his blushing did not show. He was angry and embarrassed. Mieschel, who had sat down next to him, could barely keep a straight face. Not only was he enjoying Paul's predicament, he knew something Paul didn't. Beth's brother, Heinz, had told him that Beth planned to kiss Paul.

"But it's not that she has a crush on him," Heinz had explained. "She just gets a kick out of doing nasty things. I warn you, my sis is a little bitch. So tell Paul to be careful, not to make an ass out of himself, okay?" For some reason Mieschel had not passed this juicy tidbit on to Paul. Now it was too late.

Beth linked arms with the other two girls, Uschi and Maria, and skated toward Paul, who had gotten up, his skates dangling from his shoulder. The three girls formed a tight ring around him. Beth faced him and issued a dare.

"Now I've got you, my man. Come and kiss me or I will tell your friends what kind of a sissy you really are. Come on. Here, come, kiss me!" She removed her shawl a little exposing more of her waiting face.

Caught in their circle, Paul could not move. His arms were pinned down, pressed against his body. Mieschel watched in awe, knowing that if his or Paul's mother found out about this, the boys would be in deep!

"Well, my lover, will you kiss me? Please, pretty please?" taunted Beth.

Paul had to admit to himself that he found her attractive and had been thinking for some time of asking her to go with him for an ice cream cone at the parlor on Posener. He found himself remembering how pleasant it felt when Eza had kissed him. He wanted to see if it would feel like that with Beth. In excited expectation the girls squeezed in on him, making it hard for him to breathe. His skates dug into his ribs. One of the other girls, Maria, wished that she were the one whom Paul would kiss. She sometimes pretended that her pillow at night was Paul, caressing it in teenage fantasy as she fell asleep. In her dreams she and Paul would be together, perhaps swimming in the Küdow, playing tag under water, touching each other. Her heart ached with desire for Paul. She did not like what was going on, but neither did she want to leave.

"Well?" demanded Beth. "Come on, don't keep me waiting."

Paul leaned toward Beth, trying to reach her lips, but she turned suddenly coy and moved away a little.

"Try a little harder, big man. Here, I'll open them for you," she teased, licking her lips. "Come and get them."

With a burst of strength Paul broke out of the girls' circle of arms and grabbed Beth's head. And then, just before his lips met hers, she bit him. Blood spurted out of his mouth, running down his chin and staining his white turtleneck sweater.

"That'll teach you how to treat a lady! Come on, girls, let's leave before this kid does something else to me."

Beth turned to go, but Maria blocked her path and slapped with her iced glove so hard that Beth went sprawling on the ice.

"You...are...a...bitch!" she screamed at the startled Beth. Then slowly she skated away, tears stinging her cheeks. Recovering her composure, Beth grabbed Uschi and skated in the other direction, leaving Paul and Mieschel alone.

Paul pressed his glove to his lip to stem the bleeding. "Mieschel, listen, here is what happened: As I was skating, I fell and bit my lip. Can you remember that?"

"She bit you pretty deep. You're bleeding like a pig. Here put some snow on it." The lip started to swell, making it hard for Paul to talk. But, as it happened, he didn't have to say a word at home about how his face got that way. His mother jumped to the conclusion he hoped for all by herself.

"I told you not to go so fast," she admonished him. "Why can't you ever listen?"

Fortunately, because the next day was a Sunday, he had no school. The lip would heal some before he had to return to class. But if Paul thought that there would be no gossip, he was dead wrong. On Monday when he entered his classroom he saw all of his friends wearing red lipstick on their lower lip or smeared over the cheeks. Some had tied red-spotted handkerchiefs around their necks.

"How's the kissing boy today?" "Ready for some more passionate skating parties?" "Oh, Paul, will you teach us how to kiss a girl? Please, we want to know, we..." The interrogation was interrupted by the Latin teacher, "Globe," as the boys called him, because his head was as round as a soccer ball and completely without hair. A surly man who often had alcohol on his breath, he was always a bit unsteady after the weekend. Today his voice trembled about an octave lower than usual.

"You been in a fight, all of you?" he asked hoarsely. A coughing spell further reddened his puffy face, which was crisscrossed by a net of very thin, dark-blue veins. "Who won? Brutus? You look like you have been helping Cassius with the knives. Paul Berck, when did they murder Caesar?"

Why does he ask me? He couldn't possibly know about Beth and me. Gosh, when did they do away with Caesar? "Sir, some time in March, 44 BC."

"Berck what is the matter with you? I'm perplexed, a correct answer out of you? Go get a bloody lip more often."

Paul's lip healed soon; his battered ego took longer, and it happened in a way he could not have imagined. One day in late fall, the gymnasium's principal took Paul and his twenty classmates into the teacher's conference room.

"You are called upon to defend our country against the barbaric air-raiding enemy, the English and the American bombers," he announced without preamble. "On Sunday, four days from today, you will take the train and go to Swinemünde at the southern shores of the Baltic sea, where our Navy has several air-defense batteries. Secret weapons that will turn the tide of this war are being developed nearby. "The Hitler Jugend discharges you to become soldiers. You all are sixteen years and older, time for you to really contribute to our victory. Your education will not be interrupted; you will continue your studies while you are there. If you have any questions, ask them this afternoon during your Wednesday Hitler briefing.

"Go and help win the war! Help build the Third Reich." He thrust his arm in the air. "Heil Hitler!"

The boys filed from the room not quite understanding what just had happened. They would leave this town, their mothers, their families and be thrust into danger. Newspapers and films had acquainted them with the infernos the Allied bombers left after unloading their canisters and fire-sticks. They had seen in graphic black-and-white documentaries the gunners, the explosions, the tumbling planes. What they had not been shown were the live torches— burning people racing to escape the awesome firestorms in the cities that howled to heaven for hours on end. What they had not been shown were the mangled twisted bodies of soldiers that lined the battered landscape of Russia. And, of course, what they had not been shown were the ovens in Birkenau.

Paul would eventually see all that. Thankfully, though, the future kept its secrets from being spilled just yet.

When he got home his mother let him read the letter the school had sent to the parents of the "Marine Helfer." Helpers, that's what they were, not quite soldiers, though good enough to die.

"We'd better get some things together for you" was all she said. It seemed she had become harder still. He never saw her smile anymore, and she went to early morning Mass more and more. That afternoon Beth's brother Heinz came to visit Paul at home.

"We all know you guys are leaving soon. My sister asked me to tell you she would like to go to the movies with you."

"Oh, she would? And bite me again? No thanks."

"No, listen, Paul, she feels very bad about that. She does not want you to go away hurting. She wants to be your friend. Okay?"

Paul gave Heinz a wry look. "I am sorry she couldn't come herself and say that to me." He shook his head. "Tell Beth that I have forgiven her, but I have no desire to become her friend. People have feelings; maybe one day she will understand that." About to be uprooted, torn away from his home, tossed into an uncertain and dangerous new environment, Paul felt lonely already. And yes, he was afraid of what was coming at him.

As he left school on that last Friday, he saw Maria standing across the street. She seemed to be waiting for someone. He waved at her and she smiled back, motioning for him to come over to her. As he crossed the street, Paul thought back to how she had stood up for him on that day on the ice. Ever since he had felt a strange emotion whenever he saw her.

"Hello, Maria," he said.

She blushed, then asked softly, "Can you walk with me for a while?"

"Ja...I...a...Oh, may I carry your satchel for you? I left mine at home since this was my last day in school." She handed him her schoolbag, and they walked toward the town's central park. This sunny autumn afternoon would be one of Paul's last days as a boy.

They found a bench by the pond. Paul took off his windbreaker and spread it over the damp slats for Maria to sit on. As she helped him, the light breeze waved her hair by his face, and Paul felt a jolt. He closed his eyes and something vibrated in him, an emotion so beautiful, so pure, so new and unknown. He stood there frozen in time wishing this moment would last forever.

He opened his eyes again to find Maria gazing at him. "Paul, I like the way you just looked at me. I felt like...well, I don't know how to describe it, don't know how to tell you." He shyly reached for her hand. She opened it and softly locked it around his shaking fingers.

"Maria..." He looked away from her over to the pond where a few ducks wrinkled the still surface. "Maria, I never thanked you for what you did for me last winter. I want to do this now. I want to..." Her free hand pulled him close. "I also want to."

Two young, innocent people forgot time and what would come with the next day and the day thereafter. She kissed him and he responded, softly and yet with bursting passion. If there had been thunder and lightning, they would have been oblivious. The two lovers rose and, hand in hand, walked toward the low rolling hills of the Baggen, a forest not far from the outskirts of the city.

"I have had these feelings, this love for you, for some time," Maria confessed. "I wish this afternoon had come earlier so we could have had more time to be with each other."

"Maria, would you think less of me, maybe even see me as timid if I told you that I am afraid?"

"Of course not. Why should I..."

"No, please let me talk about it. You know being a soldier means that you have to be ready to kill another person—to kill someone like me or one of my friends in class. That is what I do not want to do, what I can't do. Maria, I am very afraid. They've told us, and you've heard it too, that if I do not shoot I will be shot by my enemy."

"Yes, Paul, I wondered often why girls in Poland, in France, in Russia should be my enemies. No, how can I think less of you when you share your heart with me? There is peace between us. Where else can we find that?" She held him tightly. "Oh, Paul, you make me love you. I never felt so giving before in my life. Come, hold me. I want you to take some of me with you when you leave on Sunday." Tears flowed down her cheeks, and he kissed them away.

On that cold and windy Sunday morning, Maria stood next to his mother at the train station. She begged him to be careful.

"I will pray for you to come home safely," she promised. Paul's mother had brought a small vial of holy water. She drew a wet cross on his forehead, which he did not dare to wipe off. He kept waving long after the train had passed under the bridge where he used to dream about faraway places.

The military lifestyle at the air defense battery did not allow for mourning. The kids had no time to feel lonely, no time to think of home and how things used to be. Some days the new recruits seemed to go twenty-four hours straight, with no opportunity to rest.

In the beginning Maria wrote often. Paul heard her voice in between her lines, felt the softness of her hair. Her picture hung inside his locker. Sometimes he would put it under his pillow and fall asleep with precious memories until the sirens brought him suddenly back to reality. And then there were no more letters.

Mieschel would send a few words here and there. "When are you coming home on leave? It's no fun without you. No, I don't know where Maria is. The family moved south, I think to Switzerland. I don't know for sure." He did not want Paul to know that Maria's mother had forced her into a marriage with a well-to-do man in Zürich.

In another letter, Mieschel reported, "The women in town are digging defense ditches—you know, where we used to play, north of the lake. Sometimes we hear the cannons east of us. I wish we could sit in the cherry tree just one more time. Do you remember?"

Yes, Paul remembered. The two would sit in the forks the tree had grown, often until deep into the night. Sometimes they would hardly talk. Often they took pieces of wood on which they had etched names, stars, and other symbols, and climb up the tree as high as they could, nailing their artwork to the branches. They had started to do these "sacred things" right after they had become friends a few years earlier. Around that time Paul had built a makeshift shed in his backyard from old rotting wood he had fished from the river. One day after school he asked Mieschel to come over. "Come see my little house. It's big enough for both of us." After Mieschel helped Paul finish the short bench inside, they sat there in silence. Then Paul looked at his friend.

"Mieschel, I want to be your blood brother." Paul had read about "blood brothers" in one of his Karl May books.

"Yeah, that'd be good. How do we do it?"

"We'll rub our blood together. Here..." Paul got out a pair of scissors from under his coat. "Roll up your sleeve. No, the one on your right arm." Mieschel grimaced, but did as he was told. Paul bared his left arm. He took the scissors and cut a small piece of skin between his hand and elbow. He did this three times, an inch or so apart. Three red pearls of blood oozed from the little wounds.

"Here, you do the same." Mieschel hesitated at first but then he cut himself as well.

"Now, you dip your finger into my blood and rub it into your cuts, and I'll rub yours in mine. See, now your blood is in me and mine is in you."

"Does that mean we really are brothers—and will be until we die?"

"Yes, until we die." Paul had also brought two odd-sized pieces of clean pinewood. They smeared their drying blood onto both boards.

"Now, let's go over to the meadow and climb that tall maple tree near the river."

"And?"

"We'll nail these pieces up in that tree. When we come back to this tree from wherever we may have been, we always will find one another. You or I will be right there."

Weimar

Weimar

The army truck jarred its way downhill, following a winding road spiked with chuckholes. Empty oil drums slid around on the muddy truck bed, pinging musically with the falling raindrops. The driver, an American soldier, figured he had another half-hour's drive to the hastily built camp where he was to drop off the prisoner.

The colonel's men had thrown the German soldier unceremoniously among the drums in the rear bed of the truck. A young guy, no more than eighteen, he looked like death itself, bloody and broken, his limbs askew. The driver had said nothing, but figured that his compatriots must have beaten the shit out of him. Taking him to a camp would probably be a waste of time; no doubt he wouldn't last much longer.

The six-wheeler swerved hard to the right and sent a barrel skidding into Paul's shoulder, jamming him up against the tailgate. His head slammed on the sideboard, leaving his ears ringing, shooting pain through his body so intense that he couldn't focus. Gingerly, he picked up his right arm; at least that didn't seem broken, just bruised. He cautiously worked his jaw and found he could lick the falling rain from his swollen lips. He reached for the back of his head, his hand fluttering weakly like the wing of a dying bird, where he found a nasty gash oozing blood. The truck came to an abrupt halt, and after a few moments, the tailgate was lowered and Paul was pulled roughly out. His captors carried him through the makeshift barbed-wire gate into a camp, somewhere in the isolated countryside. Strange, he could not make out what they were saying. Darkness fell, but the rain did not abate. The miserable cold of the night kept sleep from him but could not make him move. His mind drifted back to the events that had brought him to this hell.

September 1943. Paul found himself stationed with an air-defense battalion in Swinemünde at the Baltic Sea. Their well-camouflaged site sat under large green nets and boasted an arsenal of weaponry: four 10-centimeter cannons, two large-diameter listening discs, one 15-meter scope, and two 20-millimeter Oerlikon anti-aircraft guns. A Russian prisoner detail had been assigned to the battery. During the day, these prisoners worked at the U-boat readiness docks, helping to unload and distribute ammunition; at night they performed additional duties around the installation. One of these Russians, Ivanovich, had been assigned to Paul's bunker.

Ivan was a shy man, about forty, somewhat unpleasant at first sight. An ugly scar ran below his jawbone where, as a young boy, a bad case of the mumps had exploded on his face. He had the habit of jerking his shoulder when he spoke, while pulling on his ear when listening. He carried the smell of mold and decay in his tattered clothes. But Paul came to like Ivan, even to enjoy his company. His eyes were gentle, speaking of a wide, beautiful country left behind, of the love of his family whom he might never see again. Ivan knew a few German words he had picked up during his years in German prison camps, and he would try to converse with Paul.

When asked where he was from, Ivan gestured toward the East. "Siberia," he responded. "Far, far, Volga, farther Ural Mountains, Stanovoi, two son like you, dead, wife, don't know."

Sometimes Paul would ask him to speak in his native Siberian language. Though not understanding the words, Paul responded to the emotion in Ivan's voice, knowing that he was talking about his land, his people, his God. During moments like these, the two men touched each other's souls. Yet this closeness made the killings between their two countries hurt even more.

Ivan, like the other Russians, missed his vodka, but they had found a deadly substitute known as "torpedo juice," so named because it came from alcohol that leaked through the hoses as the torpedo propellor systems were cleaned prior to installation. The Russian prisoners would put hash cans under the leaky spots, and then later drink the drippings. The alcohol was poisoned—full of chemicals and not fit for human consumption. Several warning signs said so, but the Russian prisoners could not read them. Two of Ivan's friends had died from drinking the potion, but the Russians seemed unable to keep from imbibing the potentially lethal liquor.

One day, when Ivan cut his finger badly as he prepared another hash can for the take, he went off to see Fritz, the battery's medic, who bandaged it up. Having heard about the torpedo juice, Fritz asked Ivan to bring him three full cans. Shortly thereafter, Paul heard that Fritz had found a way to purify the torpedo-bay alcohol.

On Paul's seventeenth birthday, his fellow gunners threw him a small party in their bunker. They were also celebrating his promotion to platoon leader and chief gunner of the 20-millimeter group. Paul had asked Ivan to come to the party and, like any good guest, Ivan brought something to drink. Carefully, he slipped a can out from under his torn coat and passed around the cleaned-up torpedo juice among the other party-goers. Though Ivan had gestured that they should be careful, cautioning in his broken German, "Eeesssy, langsam, o, not fast!"

Paul choked on the vile concoction that tasted like turpentine mixed with gasoline. And then, just when the burning in his throat became bearable, the alarm sirens scared them back into the real world.

Paul jumped into the gunner's seat with the ease of a baseball player sliding into second base. Koenig, his best friend from school in Schneidemühl, swung him around. He expected to see three or four bombers, limping low and trailing smoke as they tried to make it to the Baltic Sea to save their skin. Paul took aim, but found he needed to be repositioned to get off a good shot.

"Hey, Koenig, more to the left, can't you see?" he yelled. "Come on! Move! Swing that gun! What's the matter with you?" Paul hurled his words against the bullets spraying from the machine gun bubble on the port side of the gyrating Fortress II. Then, suddenly, Ernst, the soldier who fed the ammo into the cannon, grabbed him by the shoulder and turned him toward Koenig. Paul gasped. Koenig's legs were gone, shot right off him. The dying aircraft had burped one more time, taking his friend with it.

Another life gone. Another city destroyed. And yet this loss was just one small blip on the bloody big screen of the war. Of what importance was one life of a friend, when during these bombing raids thousands of people burned in firestorms ignited by bushels of magnesium sticks the bombers dropped on city after city?

After that day, Paul would never be the same. Values he had accepted, had believed in, had lived for were desecrated by the blood steaming off the battlefield. In that instant a change took place in him. From deep within him a new direction, a different belief began to form. The shiny cage the German leaders had built to incarcerate his soul had cracked.

March 1945. No real German army existed anymore, just splinter groups like Paul's, roaming lost and hungry and with no direction, no orders. Just a week before, their sergeant had stepped on a mine and disintegrated before their eyes. Sergeant Mueller had been with them since Marine Corps boot camp in Weimar, to which Paul had been transferred in 1944, and his troops had come to love him as much as they had hated him. Two of the men, Walter and Utrecht, buried what was left of the sergeant. There had been no time to stick even a crude cross in the ground.

Paul's platoon had drifted aimlessly about the countryside until they were discovered by a lone lieutenant as they rested in an apple orchard. Drawing his pistol, the officer had shouted at them, "I am your new commander! You will follow me or I will blow your head off right here and now!" Paul and his fellow soldiers had gaped at the manic lieutenant, who wasn't much older than they, not quite believing what they were seeing. SS insignias studded his uniform and Nazi propaganda continued to spew from his mouth.

"We will win!" he cried with passion. "I know Hitler will soon fire very special new weapons that will bring victory to our country."

What an idiot. How can anybody be so stupid? He will get us all killed.

The nine of them, the remaining survivors from the original Mueller platoon of thirty-five men, looked at each other, silently deciding that it would be better to follow than to get shot. And they had no doubt that this fanatical officer would make good on his threat. They knew Heinrich Himmler, the infamous chief of all German police forces and the mastermind behind the ovens of Auschwitz and Birkenau, had created a special group of soldiers, the Waffen SS. These soldiers, trained to be the equivalent of political Rottweilers, were given the mission of infiltrating the German Armed Forces, local governments, and industrial complexes to assure compliance with Hitler's ideologies. Having been emotionally dismantled and then reprogrammed with the values of the Third Reich, the SS men had become illogical and dangerous extremists championing the Hitler/Goebbel ideal. Their new commanding officer belonged to this breed.

Paul knew a bit about this elite corps, for after he had been transferred from the air defense batteries in Swinemünde, the Waffen SS had targeted him as a draftee. But Georg Berck, by then a high-ranking army officer, and one of the "old guard" who did not like the anti-God propaganda of the SS corps, had been able to prevent that. Much later, Georg would discover that, by pulling these strings, his name had been added to an SS blacklist of men and women considered to be political "outsiders." No doubt, sometime after the war, when Germany reigned victorious over Russia, England, France, Poland, and the rest of Europe, the SS men would have paid General Berck a visit. "Hitler allows you to die with honor," they would have graciously advised him, placing a revolver on his desk. "It is suggested that you pull the trigger with the gun pointed at your head." Later, the men would return to retrieve his body and bury it at an undisclosed piece of ground. Hitler's gofers had done exactly that to the famed Desert Fox himself, Field Marshal Erwin Rommel, and no doubt to countless others.

Under the lieutenant's command, Paul's platoon had marched for three days toward the front line near Bechstead Vagt, a small village near Weimar, where German scouts had discovered an American fuel dump hidden by dense forest. The lieutenant then gathered his troops at midnight to lay out his plan for the attack.

"We must destroy the American depot, no matter what the cost," he had ordered. "We leave here before dawn, advance to the forest, and dig in. You know the drill: We succeed or we do not come back. The Führer is counting on us. Heil Hitler! Wearily, mechanically, Paul returned the salute with the others. What did it matter? The war was all but over. American and Russian war machinery rolled by in the distance to the right and to the left. The Allied Forces had formed a huge cul-de-sac and were netting prisoners by the hundreds of thousands.

Long before dawn, the lieutenant led the nine men into the woods. There he forced them to dig shallow holes just long and wide enough to shelter their bodies from hissing shrapnel. Heavy American artillery plowed the ground around them—hit after hit, closer and closer, until a near miss caved in Paul's chest, knocking the wind out of him and rendering him unconscious. Any closer and he would have been another statistic.

The Navy had taught him at the air defense base in Swinemünde to shoot at American incoming bombers which air-raided the country day and night. Penemünde, which had been only a few miles to the south, was the building site for the V-1 and V-2 rockets, under the supervision of the famed Wernher von Braun. Von Braun had shown up one day at Paul's training camp, shaking hands with the them, building up their morale. They felt proud, knowing they were defending their country, fighting for the starving women and children, the old and infirm, those hiding in cellars of flattened towns like Hamburg, Dresden, Leipzig, Stettin, Darmstadt. Wernher von Braun promised to fix all that with his new weapon.

"You young people are winning the war! You are winning the whole world!" he praised them. "I am working on a new bomb that will evaporate England and will make us kings of Russia! But you must keep on fighting!"

At daybreak, heavy machine-gun fire coming from the American fuel depot skinned the bark from the few standing trees the night's hauling artillery had missed. Paul came to abruptly and sneaked a peak out of his manhole. He could make out some American soldiers milling around in the distance near stacked oil drums. He yelled over to the next hole. There was no answer. All of a sudden the shooting stopped.

"Stoek!" he called again, so loud the Ammies must have heard him. "What's going on?"

Why did nobody shout back?

New bursts puffed the ground close to his dugout and he froze with sudden comprehension. *Quiet, Paul! Don't move!* He waited for what seemed like hours. Finally, he dared to raise his head above the rim of his hole. His eyes did not want to see the bodies—mangled, strewn about, blood and guts mixed with earth. Bile rose in his throat and he vomited violently.

He was the only one left. Death had spared him alone. Utrecht, Walter, Stoek, Borsutzki, Schilf, all his friends from back home were gone. He knew their brothers and sisters, their mothers and fathers. What would he say to them? Perhaps nothing, for his turn could be next. Frightened and in shock, Paul sank into survival mode, his instincts overriding all learned doctrines, the message the adrenaline carried throughout his body distinct and unambiguous. *I want to live!*

"Get that, guys! A German soldier never panics, is never afraid, would rather die than lose his honor and become a prisoner!" Sergeant Mueller's morning song back at the boot camp rang in his ears, taunting him now that he knew it to be a lie, a farce.

Welding his revolver to his shaking right hand, Paul burst out of his hole and ran with all that his lungs could give. Behind him, an American Sherman Panzer sprayed bullets randomly to the right and to the left of him. He did not try to dodge the bullets, instead putting his faith in prayer.

Dear God, help me run. Please help me run!

He did not stop until he reached a creek. A dam for the railroad tracks had been built there, a culvert carved in it for the water to flow through. He threw himself into the icy water. The searing cold shocked him back to sensibility, cooling his glowing body yet bringing home the reality of his desperate situation. Finally, he broke down, shivering uncontrollably, crying without tears. The intense fear loosened his bowels, and he fouled his pants. With his hand frozen around his pistol, he undid his pants, took off his underwear and washed the awful smelling dung out of his clothes. After filling his canteen, Paul rose and walked into the night, hungry and shaking, his wet pants clinging to him like a second skin, the cold numbing his body. He heard the rumble of rolling trucks to his left. The American troops were making their last trawling sweep. To the east, he guessed the Russians were closing in.

"Never, ever let the Russians catch you" he could hear Sergeant Mueller warning them. "They do not take prisoners. You get roped together with a bunch of guys, and then they hang a grenade onto to your belt. You all march away, and at a safe distance a Russian soldier aims and blows you up. That is why you carry those two bullets in your watch pocket. Use them, and you will die with honor. Your mother will be proud of you."

For two days and two nights Paul walked, stumbling along, often falling flat on his face. The hard, frozen ground felt like a brick wall as he slammed into its unforgiving surface. Sometimes it seemed as though his body could not go on, yet he never gave in to that thought. His determined "I want to live" got him up again and again and again.

He stayed away from the small villages that peppered the countryside, sticking to the main roads. These were littered with broken-down war machines—burned out tanks and rolled over cannons—but no soldiers. In fact, there were no people anywhere.

The only food he ate came from the cab of a smashed-up truck: a half-eaten loaf of bread just as hard and dry as the clumps of soil lying around shelled-out craters.

The third morning Paul woke up face down in an irrigation ditch far from the road, covered with stinking muck. The desperation and desolation overcame him. "I can't do this anymore! I don't want to go any further! I can't!" he screamed to the heavens. Then, a sudden thought sobered his hysteria.

The Luger! Where in all hell is my pistol? How, when, where had he lost it? How could he shoot himself without his gun?

A noise brought him out of his thoughts. Slowly he raised his head to find three American soldiers standing around him, their gun barrels almost touching at his head.

"Halt!" Paul's head dropped again.

"Alles man komm snell...Get up you bastard!"

A fourth soldier came by in a jeep. Paul had to raise his hands. They searched him and found the two bullets that he had hidden in the watch pocket of his army pants, just like Mueller had told him to do. They also saw the picture of his father in uniform. Paul had taped it to the last page of his "soldbuch," his water-resistant army passport.

"Major General, what do you know. This is your old man, isn't it?" Something else got their attention: a picture of a silver skeleton head attached to the outside of his wallet, the emblem of a club of students trained in emergency assistance and life-saving techniques to which Paul had belonged. Unfortunately, it resembled the "Totenkopf" insignia of the Waffen SS. On seeing this, the soldiers ripped off Paul's coat and his shirt, yanking up his arms to find the tattoo of his blood group, which Waffen SS soldiers had engraved on the underside of their upper arms. Of course, they could find none on Paul.

They tied his hands with a chain and fastened it to the frame of the jeep's windshield. The four soldiers jumped in, laughing and joking as they dragged him stumbling along across the crusted field, all of them smoking big cigars as though simply indulging in some harmless sport. After a mile or so, a seemingly endless stretch for Paul, they got to a patch of stripped forest.

They untied him from the jeep, but left the chain tightly wound around his wrists. One of the soldiers, whose two silvery bars on his shirt collar indicated he was a lieutenant, stood in front of Paul, legs spread, hands behind his back. He began to interrogate Paul in fluent though accented German:. "Wo ist deine Einheit? (Where is your regiment?)" He opened Paul's passport, which they had taken from him back at the ditch, and shook his head. Slowly, calculatingly, he pulled out the picture of Paul's father. He played with the two bullets, rolling them back and forth in his other hand.

"You must have killed a lot of Americans. You German Marines were very good at that. Tell me how many of our soldiers did you kill?"

Paul stood there, disconnected from what was going on, hearing the repetitive "I want to live" within, slipping away from reality. He looked at the other three soldiers crouched in a semicircle around him, using their guns as the third leg, yet he did not really see them.

Is it over? Mr. von Braun, you said, you promised... Why am I alone, where are the others? Oh ja, they still are at that forest with the naked trees near the village with those red-painted barns. But that was a long time ago. They should have been here by now. I hope they will find me soon...

"Answer me, you pig!"

Paul could not remember what the question was.

"I don't know," he managed to say.

"You want me to believe that? Look here, killers wear this." He held up the skeleton head emblem like a priest holds the Eucharist at Sunday Mass. The lieutenant took a step closer, forever imprinting onto Paul's memory his rage-twisted face, the whiskey-red eyes that held no life in them, the fetid smell of his breath. "We know who your father is. He is in Berlin. Too bad you'll never see him again."

What was happening to him still did not register. Paul watched the three in front of him, getting up, hipping their rifles.

"Hey, buster, you don't seem to care much about your old man." He backhanded Paul's face. "We need your attention, boy, listen up. How many did you kill?"

Blood spurted from Paul's nose; when he tried to speak, his jaw did not work. The spit had evaporated from his mouth entirely, and the chain had cut into his wrists, leaving them skinned and bleeding.

"What is with this guy?" sneered the lieutenant. "Must be one of those Hitler Jugend kids. We need to give him a lesson to remember." The officer was talking over his shoulder to the other three who laughed and fiddled around with their pistols as though they were Wild West cowboys. "Tell you what, we'll be nice to you; after all you're just a kid. We'll let you pray before we shoot you. How is that?"

That did sink in. *Shoot me? What have I done? No, the Americans don't do that, only the Russians.* Paul tried to fold his hands reverently, but he couldn't feel his cold-numbed fingers.

"You know, Paul—may I call you by your first name? Paul, your outfit was based in Weimar. Do you know how many people died in that concentration camp there? Dachau, does that ring a bell?"

This was a new concept for Paul. *Concentration camp? What was that? Dachau? What is this guy talking about?*

"Do you pray? Well, then, why don't you go ahead and start." The officer pushed up a sleeve and took off one of the ten or more wristwatches he wore strung up his forearm. Paul later saw many American soldiers with all kinds of wristwatches up their sleeves, all taken from prisoners. "You will not tell me how many men you killed? That's too bad. Listen carefully: I'll count from sixty down to one, and then it will be all over for you. I mean it. Are you ready? ...59...58...57..."

The other three soldiers had disappeared, but Paul hadn't noticed. *Is this it? No, it's a dream, it has to be. Would his mother ever know?* In the distance, Koenig waved at him. He wore his ice skates. *Paul, come on. The Kuedow River is frozen over. Let's go skating.*

"...54...53...52...51..."

I can't, Koenig, I need to get some flowers for Mother's Day first. She will cry if I don't.

"You're talking about your mother? You don't have to worry, she will never know that we shot you. Your father will not either...48...47...46..."

Why is this American counting? I've got to get the flowers before the store closes...

Paul had been about eight. After school one day, he went straight to his room and pulled out the matchbox from under his bed, carefully counting out the few pennies he had saved. At the corner of Burscher Strasse and Holzweg in Stettin, across the street from the bakery, sat a flower shop. He planned to surprise his Mutti with a bouquet, although he sure would catch hell if she found out that he crossed the big-city street all by himself. The lady at the flower store had been sweet and helpful.

"For your mother? Well, how about those blue forget-me-nots?" She wrapped them up in some fancy paper and picked fifteen pennies from the money he held in his hand. "Be careful on your way home."

Returning home, he saw his mother hurrying towards him on the street, her face grim, her eyes dark. How had she known? Who had told her? He had been gone for such a short while. Before he knew it, she had struck him across his face. Through his tears he had gulped,

"Happy Mother's Day, Mutti! I bought you some flowers from the store back there..."

"Thank you, but I told you never to cross the street!"

"...38...37...36... Are you ready? You want me to give your father a message? Hey, I'm talking to you. How many people did you kill, you son of a bitch?" Paul came around when the count hit "...9...8...7..." The two-silver-barred soldier had opened up Paul's shirt. "...6..." was the last number Paul remembered hearing, for he was struck from behind in the head with what he would learn later was a baseball bat.

The events that followed were hazy, unreal. The Americans must have left, for in the morning two German medics searched the camp for the ones the night had kept.

"Look, this boy is still with us," one medic said, then he asked Paul, "What did they do to you?" But Paul could not talk.

They let him have some water, wrapped his head, and propped him up against a fence post. "We'll come back tomorrow morning," they promised. They didn't. Or maybe they did. Maybe a day passed, or it could have been a week or two. Paul would never remember exactly what happened. He only knew that he reentered semiconsciousness after being dumped at the camp by the truck with the oil drums. The bloody turban the medics had applied around his head was no longer there. The gash in his head still hurt but it was dry. He found himself walking around with other prisoners. Where was he? There must have been some three thousand men milling around the camp, the guards herding them back and forth.

Once a day they were given cold meat from a metal can, but there was no shelter given from the chilly rainy weather. Paul felt at times that he was standing somewhere in the distance watching himself and the soldiers, who all seemed to chomp on big cigars. Once he saw a prisoner down in the mud. An American guard stood over him, yelling, "He tried to steal my knife! You bastards watch me. This is going to happen to you if you ever steal!" He struck the distorted body with his baseball bat again and again. To this day Paul hears the sound of the crunching noise the bones made as they broke, like the snapping of dry twigs under a pillow. "Don't anybody help this son of a bitch. He had it coming." The young prisoner didn't need any help, would never need help again.

Paul's memory of those days in that first prison camp resembled watching a television program during an electrical storm. Power on, then a flash and nothing, then on again, off again, over and over, no telling for how long. In one recollection that seeped through the sketchiness, Paul recalled being in a park with many American soldiers. The trees were starting to bud, and the ground was covered with grass. One soldier had tapped him on the shoulder.

"Hey, kid, do you want this? It's good stuff, but I'm not hungry anymore. Here you can have it. Just throw the can into the garbage over there when you're done." He smiled at Paul, making a fist with his right hand, the thumb straight up. "It's okay, go ahead."

Ham and eggs. God it was good! He had no clue what the thumb-up meant, but was thankful for the soldier's smile. One day the guards divided the prisoners into blocks of fifty. Long tractor-trailer rigs drove into the camp, and the groups were stampeded like cattle onto the trailers. Some of the German soldiers shouted exuberantly, "Man, we are going home! The war is over! You hear, the war is over!"

Paul watched the chaotic scene unfold. He heard the shouting. He wanted to climb that tailgate too. But the trailers were all pulling away without him. It looked like they had taken the fence with them, but they had left him standing there all by himself.

Kreuznach

Kreuznach

They must have come back for him, for some foggy memories emerged. A truck packed with prisoners; everyone standing, crowded into the bed like livestock; the crush of the others against him as the truck twisted and turned; the sudden jackknife of the truck to a hard stop; screams that rang out into the night.

Finally, the tailgate opened and Paul stepped into the slippery loam of a vineyard spreading over acres of sloped farmland. In the dark, even the branches of the lowly grapevines seemed sinister, silhouetted against the sky in this alien terrain. Soldiers, armed with the ever-present baseball bats, herded the load of scrambling prisoners into their new home.

Paul still wore the same uniform. The blood from his head wound had crusted onto the fabric of his jacket collar; his pants remained as wet as they had been when he'd climbed out of the icy creek.

The cold of the night bit through him. Somebody yelled, "Hey, get down you idiots! It's nighttime! Get down or you'll be shot!"

Suddenly Paul noticed clumps of live bodies, men hugging the ground like thousands of live molehills from which rose their steamy breath. The man next to him motioned Paul to sit down.

"They shoot," he said in a low voice. "I lost my friend last night. He could not take it any more. He went crazy. He got up and ran into the fence over there. See those jeeps with the machine guns? Every night they drive around this barbed-wire wall and shoot over our heads. If you stand up, you get shot." He moved over a bit. "Here. Come and sit down with your back to mine. We'll keep a little warmer that way."

The man eyed Paul's coat pockets hopefully.

"Do you have anything to eat? Something you could share? I am so hungry. Today I tried to get food, but I could not find my group. Finally, I couldn't walk any longer. You sure you have nothing to eat?"

"No," replied Paul with a shake of his head. "No food."

The dark of the night was made more dramatic by the bright lights that lit the twelve-foot-tall barbed-wire fence. Bad Kreuznach, a "Hunger Camp," as Paul would find out it was called, was home to some forty-five thousand prisoners, most of them no older than he. There were no tents, no cots, no blankets, nothing to give any warmth or shelter. Just cold, damp, gritty mud for the prisoners to wallow in like pigs.

"Look," Paul's new friend said, "pull up your knees against your chest as close as you can. Stick your hands between your legs. You will hold in your warmth. It gets cold here, cold enough that the puddles will wear thin ice in the morning."

Paul imitated the fetal position, and after a while he found that the mud warmed his ass much like the layer of water does in a wet suit.

"Where did they pick you up?" the man asked

"From somewhere around Weimar. I don't know for sure. You?"

"The Americans caught me in Göttingen. Did they feed you? We here get a little to eat once a day. A lot of people don't make it. Most of them die from the cold wind and hunger. Some eat sand. But, of course, that kills them." Paul could feel the man shivering at his back. "My name is Leo."

"I'm Paul. Ja, they gave us cold beef in a can every so often. It looked like dog food, made you shit thin and throw up."

"I've been here for over two weeks and I haven't had to go once. You'll find out what I'm saying. Put your head down on your knees and think of summer. Try to sleep."

The morning came early, bringing with it the cold sting of a light snow. Paul realized that men were moving about everywhere, walking aimlessly.

"Leo, let's get up. They are walking all around us. I don't want us to be trampled on. Come."

Paul had to roll on his right side and then onto his knees before he could stand up straight. As he did so, Leo fell back onto the ground. With his hands between his legs and his head welded to his knees, he had passed into the darkness.

"Jesus!" Death still came as a shock to Paul—but that shock would not last long.

Paul got up and stumbled on with the thousands of other men, who like him, had lost their beliefs, their youth, their innocence, their families, their hope, their reason to live. They had become hardened, so inured to atrocity that they no longer cringed when the kid in front of them fell. They simply stepped over his body and moved on. Death walked with them. And hell was yet to come...

Paul had been wandering around, his thoughts shutting out all else.

Leo, maybe I should have gone with you. Maybe I should fall down and let them trample on me. I am so cold. My head hurts so bad. Running into the fence—why not? It'd be fast.

He staggered, lost his footing on the mushy loam, and nearly fell. A man behind him grabbed his arm.

"Hey, kid, watch where you are going," he said gruffly, but not unkindly.

Paul managed a small "thank you" and fell into step with the man. He was older by a year or two, and taller by a few inches. Paul learned his name was Wallach—Wally for short. In the next few weeks, he would come not only to rely on Wally's leadership, but to trust him implicitly.

"Looks like you need to rest. Come on over to where me and my friends are."

Obediently, Paul followed the man over to a spot where two other bedraggled men sat.

"Hey, Emus, move over. This man here needs our attention. Do you have some water left for him?"

"Sure, Wally, coming right up. Want some lemon in it?" The man called Emus scowled at Wally. "Asshole! We can't get any water until noon, and you know it."

"I have a little left he can have." The second man, whom Wally introduced as Bauer, made this offer, although he did not look happy about it. He took an aluminum canteen from under his coat, uncorked it, and handed it to Paul. "One sip, just one, you hear? Or I kill you. No joke, I mean it."

Paul nodded and raised the canteen to his lips, barely moistening them with the water.

Wally eyed him. "How long have you been here?" he asked. "Do you have a name?"

Paul licked his lips and handed the canteen back to Bauer. "I am Paul. I...I think I got here last night."

"Shit, you must be one of those kids they brought in from Leipzig. I was sitting next to the camp gate when they unloaded you guys. I heard the drivers talking. One trailer rolled over. You were lucky."

Looking around, Paul wondered just how lucky he was.

For some reason, Wally had decided to take Paul under his wing.

"Tell you what. Emus, me and Bauer here need to go and find the rest of our group. If you are not in a group, you won't get any food. Why don't you come with us? Maybe not all ten will show up and you can get something to eat."

It took them an hour to get to the spot where the group met each day at "mealtime." They looked at each other—ten altogether, including Paul.

Wally gave Paul a smile, the first he had seen in a long while.

"Well, I guess you are lucky again. You're in, Paul. You stick with us. We've been here for a while. Bauer over there, Emus, and me, we went to school with each other in Stargard. We got drafted together and we stayed together through all that mess. Don't ask me how we did it."

Stargard! What a coincidence.

"My family lived in Stargard for a year. I must have gone to the same school you guys did."

Bauer narrowed his eyes, immediately distrusting this confession. "So? What street did you live on?"

"We rented a house on Klappholz Gasse, you know, the street lined with all the ash trees, with the red berries in the fall. Close to the River Ina," explained Paul.

Bauer wasn't satisfied. "What was the name of that bald Latin teacher, the one who was always so rude? God, he bugged the hell out of us."

"Globe? I know what you mean. He..."

But Bauer's scowl had brightened and he interrupted him.

"Hey, you really were there. I thought for a while, you were faking it. You are okay." He put out his hand and Paul took it. "We are four now. That's good, because we need to start digging our hole. It will keep us warmer during the night."

Wally got up from his yoga crouch.

"Emus and I will get our rations. You guys wait here."

"Hell, where would we go?" said one of the group.

Quite a while passed before they came back, and by that time Paul's stomach was grinding its own walls. He hurt in a way he had never known, from the inside out. Hunger became a big word, a way of living, changing the world around them, overshadowing all other thoughts and feelings. It transformed men into distrustful animals that would kill each other over a crumb of bread. Hunger challenged the survivors among them. Only the most fit, the most devious, the most deceitful creatures escaped its clutches. Paul would soon become a slave to his hunger, stooping to desperate measures, such as chewing wood and charcoal, to soothe the pain in his gut.

The nine of them knelt in a semicircle around Wally. He had put the food on the ground on a layer of toilet paper:

Two raw potatoes
Ten tablespoons of coffee in an empty Army juice can
Ten slivers of canned tomatoes
Ten C rations of hash
One loaf of Army bread, five inches square, five inches tall, with a round top
Ten teaspoons of sugar in an empty C ration can
Ten tablespoons of canned peas, also in some sort of a rusty container.

In two large hash cans with handles made of barbed wire, Emus carried their ration of water to help fill the stomach where the food could not.

Wally took his time. The gang, their eyes riveted on the food, chattered with their jaws, like cats before they jump for the mouse. Except for Paul, each had a small can or a plastic lid onto which Wally put their portions.

"Paul, you got to use your hands till you find something better."

Bauer produced a homemade scale, a shoestring tied to a short branch with a piece of cardboard stuck to each end. Wally weighed the bread and the chips of potatoes. It had to be right on the button. A hundredth of an ounce difference between portions could start a riot. The irony was that the same hunger that made them all so weak, also gave them the strength to kill each other.

Sometimes, a man might not eat right away, keeping the food on his plate until all the others had finished their meager meal. He would make sure everyone could see him, chewing on the thin slice of tomato for minutes on end, licking his fingers after every tiny bite. He might take an hour to eat what others had shoved in their mouths in fifteen seconds.

But this was a deadly tease, a way to get killed. In their hunger-distorted minds, the other men would be convinced that the slow eater had gotten more than they had, that he had somehow cheated. One night Paul saw this scene played out not far from where his group took their meager meal. One man still ate while the other nine had already finished. Eighteen hands reached out, not for the food but for the man's neck, choking him until he quit chewing. It happened in an instant, like thunder not waiting for the lightning. In less than a second the man's misery ended. When the litter-boys picked up the body later, it was naked. The nine had taken off his clothes and then traded the pieces among themselves. Calvary all over again, maybe worse.

During the afternoon they started to dig. Wally, Emus, and Bauer had dug a hole for shelter a few days after they first arrived. But the ground had been slightly sloped, and they had slid out of it during the night into the heavy rain. Now they had staked out a new spot, and with Paul to help them, construction began.

Bauer had the three of them lie down, close like sardines. He made a line in the mud and then asked to Paul scramble over Wally and Emus to the other side so he could measure for a hole that would fit all four of them. They used the water-hash cans to scoop out the dirt, an easy enough task the first few inches, for the ground was soaked. After that, the compacted loam had to be shaved in thin slices, much like cutting hard cheese without the benefit of a sharp knife. By nighttime they had excavated a hole six by eight feet, with a depth of about four inches. Paul had packed mud up around the rim of the hole, making the cavity deeper and slightly more protected.

Bauer tried it first. "It's okay. Paul, you and me will take the outside tonight. Tomorrow we will switch." His hunched shoulders and haggard face betrayed his weariness. "I am so tired, I don't know if will want to get up again." Wally, who had disappeared earlier, returned just before the jeeps fired their guns, the deadly signal for bedtime.

"These fucking shitheads have no manners!" he scowled, as they all dove into their bunker. "Here, I brought some grass and a few sticks from up the hill. Crawl out, Bauer, we need to spread the grass first. Tomorrow we'll make some sort of a roof over the upper half of the hole."

They worked flat on their bellies spreading the grass and twigs. Bauer had to be rolled back into his position; he had passed out. Concerned, Wally checked him.

"He'll make it," he pronounced.

Emus took off his long, German army coat, one of the few prisoners who hadn't lost it to the guards, and fanned it out over their chests and part of their legs. Lying on their backs they felt warm after a while. The grass, steamed by their body heat, released a smell like that which usually escapes a grave site during a funeral.

Wally remarked, "Emus, we need to get ahold of a knife. Cutting the potatoes would be much easier. Your thin wire wastes so much."

"You know what they would do if they found a knife on you, Wally? They'd make you eat it. Did you see the kid this noon? They had tied him to the fence post with barbed wire, right there where they passed out our food. I heard he had stolen from the bread truck. A guy told me the guards made him eat one whole loaf, and made him drink a lot of water on top of it. That kid..."

"Hey, jerk, that's enough! Not a good bedtime story. I'm dreaming already of too much shit."

Paul fell asleep thinking of a knife.

When he awoke the next morning, he noticed for the first time a city of holes, just like the one he and Bauer had built, spreading out from the center of the camp. Holes by the thousands pitted the landscape, making Paul feel as though they had landed in the excavated town of Pompeii that Mount Vesuvius had ashed so long ago.

As he wandered around by the fence that day, he found a nail. He didn't pick it up right away. The Jeep patrol was near, and the guards might get suspicious if they saw him do anything unusual through their high-powered binocs. After they had passed he retrieved the nail, which looked to be about four inches long and almost a quarter of an inch in diameter. He also picked up two rocks.

Paul thought of Joseph at his shoe repair shop in Stettin. He had continually hammered the edge of his leather knife to make it sharp. Maybe he could do that to the nail with these two rocks. It would take a while, but then he had nothing but time.

When Paul got back, Bauer was the only one there, busily making the hole longer. He seemed better than the night before, but worked with quiet desperation on that small piece of ground.

"Are you okay?" asked Paul. "Maybe you should rest. You scared us last night." He held up the nail. "Look what I found. I think I can make a knife out of it."

Bauer stopped his digging to stare at him.

"You can do that, Paul? Man, that would be great."

It took Paul three days to "forge" the nail into a small saber using the two rocks he had picked up. The larger rock acted as an anvil, the smaller one as a hammer. It was 1945, yet he might as well have been living in the Stone Age. On the second day of his forging, Wally had to find him another anvil, as the first one had crumbled from the constant pounding. The steel got harder the more Paul beat it, and tiny, brittle pieces of metal broke away from the cutting edge as he worked. The finished product resembled a serrated butter knife. The blade measured about half an inch wide and two inches long, with the rest of the nail and its head serving as a short handle. He drew the knife over the anvil a few times to sharpen the edge.

"Here, Wally, you cut Bauer's throat if he passes out again."

Impressed, Wally checked the edge with his thumb and cut himself.

"Son of a bitch, this thing is sharp! We hide it under the grass. Nobody knows anything. Got it?"

The days were getting longer now, and the weather became warmer and drier. Paul, who had worn all of his clothes constantly for warmth and protection, had not taken off his boots since the Americans had taken him prisoner, almost two months before. Constant wetting and drying had formed the leather around his feet, like an alabaster cast steadying a broken limb. One day he decided to let his feet out into the fresh air.

But Wally protested. "Paul, I wouldn't do that. Somebody might steal your boots. Even if they don't, chances are you won't be able to get them on again. You learned that from survival training, didn't you?"

"Wally, if I don't take my feet out of them, my toenails will grow right through the leather. I don't want to wear those suckers for the rest of my life."

But the job was not so easy. He could not undo the shoestrings, as they had melted into a Gordian knot. He used the Paul-knife, as the gang called it, to cut the shoestrings away. Even then, the shoes would not come off easily. Emus had to grab the heel and pull with all his might.

The first inkling of fear shot through Paul when he saw his toes. He flashed back to a now-distant memory of the carrots his mother had kept in a bed of sand in the cellar, trying to preserve them through the winter months. The remembered taste of the marmalade she made with those carrots flooded his mouth, so horrible on the dry bread that was half sawdust and half wheat. That had been when real jam was impossible to get—the soldiers on the front needed to eat, and so civilians had to go without. By February, the carrots had withered and darkened, like dead snakes unable to escape their den.

Looking at his shriveled toes turned brownish-black, Paul could think only of those disgusting carrots. The nails had grown over the toes, curving over the tops like misshapened claws. Paul spent hours on his pedicure, carefully wielding the makeshift knife. After the others saw this, they took off their boots too. The same mummy-like carrots greeted them.

At first, Paul reveled in feeling the warm sun on feet that had been cold for so long. But by nighttime, they had started to swell, the carrot-toes turning into overstuffed sausages. Their dark, brownish color had turned light blue then black, and with that change in color came excruciating pain.

Paul found he could not stand up, much less walk. He felt as though razor blades fought with his bones under the skin. He was not alone in his agony. The shoe removal had been contagious, and moaning could be heard in holes around them. The scene rivaled that of a battlefield littered with wounded.

Since they couldn't walk, the men crawled to the shit ditches on their hands and knees, feet held high above the ground. From above it must have looked like a train of tired fire ants coming home from a hard day of work. The outhouse ditches were some twelve feet long, six feet wide, and ten feet deep. The men sat on booms—logs spanning the length of the ditch—one per side.

Even though many outhouses littered the camp, there was always a waiting line. It took Paul almost an hour to get onto the log. In his condition, mounting the log posed a challenge, especially since he had nothing to hold onto to steady his balance. One wrong move and he would fall into the pit as others had, left to wallow in the urine and excrement, screaming for help that never came. Eventually they drowned. Nobody cared.

Paul had become like everyone else in the camp. He did not fall in, that's what was important. He had survived so far, that was all that mattered. Hunger had killed any compassion for others. Hunger had turned them all into self-centered, unemotional animals. *Survive, no matter what! Survive at any cost!* This basic instinct was what had kept him going.

Some prisoners at a nearby hole had discovered that wet loam packed around the bloated feet lessened the pain and swelling. But that took water, a precious commodity. Wally made the decision for them.

"Tomorrow we will use half of our water and make mud. No voting is required on this issue. Emus, you are in charge of the mud pie." No one argued, and after a few days of this treatment, their feet recovered.

Life, in its most primitive form, stripped bare, had become routine. Men around them died, were carried away, were forgotten. Nobody even noticed the litter carrier any longer in this live cemetery. Those who remained did what they had to do to keep going.

Bauer continued to deteriorate. He said little, moved slowly, each word he spoke braided with pain. His face had become fleshless, pale skin stretched over his sunken cheeks. He often sat in the hole staring into the distance with eyes that did not see anymore. He shivered like he had malaria, and spoke to his sister and mother in his waking and sleeping dreams. Worried that they were losing him, the others shared their rations, and Emus let him have most of his coat during the night.

In early August 1945, rumors spread through the camp that the Americans would let the men go home soon. A long tent was erected near the gate of the camp and within days German officers, all looking well-fed and healthy, gathered up men and brought them to the tent. New rumors spread like crystals in a saturated solution: SS men would be detained, as would prisoners without a home address. These unlucky souls would be shipped somewhere to repair airfields in France.

Paul listened to the rumors with mixed feelings.

No matter what my fate, nothing can be worse than this place. Getting away from here, I want that more than anything, dead or alive. I am so hungry, it makes no difference to me anymore.

He took a twig from the makeshift roof of their hole and began to chew it.

The rumor about the SS men proved to be true. Paul saw youngsters trying to bite out the blood group tattoo under their armpits, with only infected wounds for their efforts. The screeners were not fooled.

The shadows finally persuaded Bauer to come and drift with them. That night Wally, Emus and Paul shared the big army coat. They didn't talk about it. There was no tear left to cry.

The next morning two German officers came by their hole.

"You," they pointed to Paul, "come with us."

So weak was Paul that they had to help him make the walk to the big tent. Wally and Emus did not say good-bye, and Paul did not look back.

Why is it I don't feel anything? Wally saved my life when I came to this camp. I am leaving, and I feel nothing? Will I live, or are these two guys bringing me to where Bauer is?

The two men deposited Paul in the waiting line, which stretched all the way around the tent, and it wasn't until he had waited several hours that he finally stepped inside. American soldiers sat at several different tables, many of them smoking long, dark cigars. Some lounged idly with their feet up on the tables, as though they hadn't a care in the world. The smoke-filled air smarted Paul's eyes and nose, and the stifling heat nearly made him pass out. He leaned against the first table so he would not fall.

"What is your name?"

"Paul Berck."

"Outfit?"

"Marine Corps, Weimar."

"Your home?"

"Schneidemühl, Pomerania."

The soldier wrote something on a piece of paper and handed it to Paul.

"Go to the next table. Number 3," he instructed, his voice flat, disinterested.

At table number 3, Paul got a shock.

"Your town is Polish now. You can't go back there."

Paul stared at the man.

Shit, I'm not going home. I have no home. Maybe they will send me to a place where there is more to eat. If they don't, I'll die here.

The man had given him some instructions, but Paul hadn't been listening.

"Move it!" the man said sharply. "You're holding up the line. Table number 5."

At table number 5, Paul was handed a preprinted form:

I, ______, herewith certify that during the time I was a prisoner in this camp, I was treated properly, had sufficient food, and slept on a cot at least twelve inches above the ground.

Bad Kreuznach, August 1945

"Sign here," commanded the soldier, handing Paul a pen.

Paul stared at him in disbelief. "I won't sign this. It is not true. You know that."

"Boy, you better sign," said the soldier. Older than the others Paul had talked to, he seemed weary, resigned. He gestured to other German prisoners who had passed through the line. "See all those guys? They've signed already. It's your one-way ticket out of here. If you don't...well, son, you've been here long enough to know what can happen."

Paul looked down at the piece of paper filled with lies and knew the man was right.

I cannot fight this. For something to eat I'll do anything, anything!

He signed the paper and moved on. One table to go.

A doctor, or perhaps he was only a medic, felt Paul's glands at the neck under his jaw. He listened to Paul's heart and chest with a short, wooden stethoscope. When asked to breathe deeply, Paul fainted. The medicine man and his assistant spanked him back to daylight. The last lie came when they weighed him.

"Eighty-nine pounds," announced the assistant. The doctor, however, entered "125 pounds" on the chart, along with a note certifying that Paul Berck was in good health and fit to go to work.

They sent him to the end of the tent where he was to receive his sentence. Even though Paul wanted desperately to leave this place, he felt a knot in his stomach about what would happen to him.

When it was his turn, he asked, "What will happen to me? Where are you taking me? Home? The war is over, you know...."

"Yes, I know," replied the soldier who pushed him along. "I also know that you have no home. The town where you went to school is in Russian hands. You cannot go back there. We are shipping you to a city in France. You will work there for a while until the Red Cross finds your parents, which should take just few months. You'll be home before Christmas. Now go!"

It would take Paul longer than two years to get home, two very hard years.

A cattle trailer waited at the exit of the tent, already half full with prisoners. This time there was room to sit. They dragged Paul in, and the truck pulled out, taking the prisoners away from a vineyard that would not grow grapes for quite a while.

Bauer, Wally, Emus, I don't want to think of you now, I just can't.

The short ride ended at the railroad freight terminal. A hundred or so boxcars, some open, some with a roof, were being stuffed with prisoners. The truck stopped at the ramp and backed up to an empty, covered boxcar. Guards lowered the tailgate, and the fifty men crashed onto the straw that covered the floor of the gondola. Paul passed out as the heavy sliding door banged shut. It was dark and hot and stifling, just as one might imagine hell to be.

Rennes

The train pulled out of the terminal in Kreuznach, heading west to Paris. As a farewell gift, the prisoners were given C rations, one per person, accompanied by a handful of army can openers thrown into the straw. With that the Americans washed their hands of their captives, turning them over to the French government. Rumors flew as to their fate. One story reported that, just like after World War I, Germany would have to pay certain reparation fees to France. Those prisoners with a home address in the Eastern part of Germany would be transferred to the French government as part of those fees. For how long would the French keep them? How much repayment would be enough?

On the train, the sight of C rations incited chaos. Even in the weakest body, the animal instinct broke loose as the men fought for more food, some stealing two, even three additional cans. One American soldier had hidden an extra ration under the unconscious Paul's shirt, who did not notice. The man next to Paul did, however, and snatched it away the moment the soldier turned away. Soon, the men were wolfing ham and eggs from partially opened tins, their lips and fingers shredded on the razor-sharp rims. But these rail-thin bodies, deprived of any real food for so long, could not adapt to so much all at once. Violent stomach cramps squeezed awful moaning from the warping torsos of the prisoners. The boxcar began to reek of excrement and vomit. Paul's neighbor did not finish his meal, instead shaking fiercely and then suddenly falling still.

The fifty-five-gallon drums, filled with water for the journey, broke loose of their bonds and toppled over as the train jerked away from the tarmac. The water spread over the floor, adding humidity to the already unbearable heat.

It was almost midnight when Paul finally came around. He felt the wet straw that contoured his numbed body. The heat had dissipated some, aided by the draft of air hissing through the cracks in the walls, which also helped to vent the indescribably foul smell.

God! Again you push me away from your heaven. Why? Why don't you let me leave here, let me go to where Leo and Bauer are? Or maybe I am there already, and this is your hell? No fires and devils with horns and pitchforks like they told us in school? Just the slime of urine-soaked straw, the stench of putrid vomit, the nauseating decay of dung and dead bodies? I don't know, perhaps the flames might be preferable...

He tried to get up, but the rails jarred the car hard from side to side, pitching him onto his neighbor.

"Oh, man, did I hurt you?" Feeling dizzy, almost drunk with fatigue, Paul slurred his words toward where he thought the man's face would be, for the impenetrable darkness made it impossible to see. But no answer came. Pushing himself away from the body, Paul suddenly noticed that his own feet were bare. Someone had taken him for dead and relieved him of his boots. Staring into the dark he kept on mumbling to the corpse. "Do you still have your boots?" He felt his way down the man's wet pants till he found the feet. "Oh, you do, you do have your shoes. You think you still need them?" Paul pushed the other's feet to wake him, to get an answer. Swaying with the speeding train he fell forward and threw up a little bile. Still the man did not move. Paul continued his soliloquy. "You must be dead. Even if you're not, if you keep on just lying there, they'll carry you out before we get home. Remember how they did that back at the camp?" Even in the humidity of the train car, Paul's feet could not retain any warmth. "My feet are so cold. Maybe you can give me one shoe?" Paul slid his hand under the pant leg of the dead man and felt the cold, stiff leg. "I think you're through walking," he said. And then, as if to apologize, "Yes, I take your shoes, but I am not a thief. You don't need them any longer and I do. You understand? I am walking out of here." Paul slid close to the other's feet and tried to undo the shoestrings, but the tightly knotted laces and the blackness hampered his efforts. "Wally, I need the knife I made for us, I do..."

In his crazed condition, he could not stop talking. He felt the weight of the action he was about to take. He was going to steal; worse, he was going to rob someone just like himself. His feverish mind carried him back over the years to another time he had taken what was not his.

Young Paul had found a penny on the stairs leading up to the family apartment. He had put it into his pocket with his other treasures: the bent nail, the chipped marble, a couple of special pebbles, and his handkerchief.

When his mother went to wash the pants that night, she shook out the arsenal of "worthless things," as she called them. Out fell the penny.

"Paul, get out of bed and come here!"

Her raised voice alarmed him, but a quick review of the events of the day revealed nothing he considered punishable.

"Yes, Mutti?"

"Where do you get this money from? Speak!"

"I found it on the steps outside, I..."

"Was it your penny?"

"It might have been," started Paul, but he was cut short.

"Your money is in that jar up there," she said, pointing an angry finger at the top kitchen shelf. "Did you take a penny out of it, lose it, and find it again?"

Confronted with such logic, Paul had to concede, "Well, I guess this coin isn't mine."

"So you took it anyhow from someone who had lost it?"

"I guess so."

With her iron grip she grabbed him by the arms. "Don't you ever again pick up a penny that is not yours. Never, do you hear me! If you find something as small as a pin and it does not belong to you, don't touch it. Let it be. Now put on your clothes, take this money back to where you found it. And before you go back to bed, say an extra *'Our Father.'* Go!"

Mother, this time I steal not a penny, but my life. I am not a thief, but with no shoes I can't make it. Up there, "Our Father" doesn't want me yet. He's pushing me to keep on going. You see, Mutti, I need boots for that. Do you understand?

Paul lost consciousness again and remained in a deep sleep until the train stopped at a station at the outskirts of Paris. Outside, the sound of people shouting, screaming, and wailing began to pierce his fog. Rocks hurled at the sides of the boxcar scared him back to daylight, and he realized a riot was in the making. Men and women and children raced up and down the tracks, wanting to storm the train. Those Nazi prisoners must be killed! The open boxcars got it all: the shit wrapped in newspaper, the bottles with piss in them, the bone-breaking rocks, the pieces of scrap and debris and filth. Some threw small paper bags filled with salt that blistered the eyes and scorched the wet skin as the prisoners sat baking in the sun. They all had read it in the papers: A transport filled with German pigs would be coming through, and they had awaited the train's arrival with angry anticipation.

The train lay in the midday heat like a wounded snake, enduring, unable to escape the attacks of the vicious herd of brutal enemies. The moaning of the tortured was suffocated by the yelling and screaming of the hate-breathing crowd.

An eternity went by. Finally, police arrived and dispersed the lynch mob. The door of Paul's car was slammed open. Soldiers, none older than Paul, climbed in.

"Merde! Merde!" they said, over and over, although it meant nothing to Paul. The soldiers clasped what looked like towels around their mouths and donned rubber gloves. Then, shining their acetylene lights over the awful scene inside, they fell silent.

Paul had been trying to undo the strings that tied the boots to those dead feet, and even when four gloved hands grabbed the body and pulled it toward the door, he did not let go. The guards shouted at him, but he held on; they kicked him, but he persisted. Finally, one man stepped on his hand while the other one pried him loose from the leather. Then they hesitated, looked at each other, and nodded. Both bent down, slashed the shoestring knots with a pocketknife, tore off the boots, and threw them at Paul.

"Ici, cochon...Here, pig."

Ha, Wally you told 'em. I knew you would help me... Paul did not count how many dead people they took out, but the railcar now offered survivors more room to breathe. For a flash or less he wondered how and where they would bury the bodies, and if the people at home ever would know what happened to those for whom they would wait in vain to come back.

Guards righted the water drums and refilled them with a fire hose. Then the door banged shut and the train rolled on, heading further west. Around noon it reached its final stop, and the prisoners crawled onto the tarmac of a deserted freight terminal at the outskirts of Rennes. French soldiers herded them into covered army trucks that made the short ride to a camp near the River Vilaine.

The disembarking at the camp gate took some time. Many could barely walk. Resident inmates, hardly strong enough themselves, tried to help them get to their tents. Tents! Yes, a city of tents stood before them. Paul did not notice this right away. His mind drifted back to where he had left Wally and the others.

He was taken to Tent "A." Right inside by the flapping door was an empty space—three feet by six feet of bare, hard ground. The German chief of the tent motioned to Paul.

"This is your spot. From where did they bring you?"

"Kreuznach."

"Jesus! Was it really as bad as they say? Seventy-five thousand kids in a vineyard, no tents, no food, not even blankets, ja?"

Paul did not answer. He took off his filthy jacket, bunched it into a pillow, and lay down. He had not had any food for at least a day and a half, but since hunger had become his constant companion, he barely noticed.

After they shook him awake the next morning, the tent leader handed him a one-pound hash can. A few rusty spots tarnished an otherwise shiny interior.

"Come on," the man said, "we'll get you something to eat."

Paul got up, but then sank to his knees, weak and dizzy. The tent leader, a stocky man with long, muscled arms, looked down at Paul with what almost seemed like sympathy.

"What's your name?" he asked, extending a hand to help Paul up.

"Paul."

"All right, Paul. I'm Ernst. I think you may need a little help. Let's just take it slow. I'll stick with you."

Paul half walked, half crawled to the mess tent, with Ernst keeping close to him, urging him along. A long line winding around the canteen tent greeted them. Paul sat down to wait, creeping along as the line moved. Paul noticed Ernst's unusual dish, which had been fashioned from a hash can but had handles on either side bent outwards like a regular cooking pot.

"Did you make that little pot yourself?"

"Yes. It took me a long time, but it came out all right, I think." Ernst winked at Paul. "I'll let you borrow my snips and show you how to do it. I was a sheet-metal worker at home."

Paul nodded his thanks, then asked, "Tell me what are those scratch marks on the outside?"

"You'll see that on all the cans in this camp. Each mark counts for a day we spend here behind this awful barbed wire. At night we make the mark, because then you know for sure that you did the day. Tomorrow you might not need to make another scratch." He studied Paul's haggard face. "You've been there, you know what I mean."

"Yes, I know."

"Listen, Paul, I've been here for some time. We were shipped here from North Africa. They fed us well there, nothing like your hunger camp. I have seen many men come from those camps in Germany. Quite a few guys did not make it here for long. They ate their first meals too fast. Some ate the grass that grows along the fence or the dirt they slept on. The ones who did the grass died in terrible pain. Don't do all that. In a few minutes you'll have some sort of soup in that can of yours. Don't, don't wolf it down. Your gut will not take it. Go slow, okay?"

"Okay, thanks. And if you see me do stupid things, hit me. Deal?"

Ernst nodded. "Deal." Ernst stayed close to Paul as he crawled toward the kitchen. When it was their turn, he helped Paul to his feet.

"Hey, cook, give him just a little. He came in yesterday from Kreuznach. Look how thin and weak he is." The cook took a long look at Paul and gave him half a ladle of watery mashed potato soup. The chowder was hot. Paul drank some right away and he could feel its warmth burn all the way down to his stomach.

"Oh, is this ever good! My first warm food since April. Thank you," he said to the cook, who merely shrugged.

Another prisoner-cook handed him a slice of hard, white bread that was rimmed with green mold. As he and Ernst walked slowly back to Tent "A," Paul dipped the bread into the potato soup and swallowed it. Although it tasted awful, he did not care. This was food, warm food, and it looked like there would be more tomorrow.

Slowly life sneaked back into Paul. His first few days in the camp were hazy, not quite real. The temperature climbed steadily in the late August days, and the heat inside the tent often reached over a hundred degrees.

On the third day, when Paul needed to go to the latrines, Ernst showed him a row of outhouses without walls or partitions. No log to fall off—just a typical French toilet, a square concrete plate with a hole in the middle and raised foot-sized pads placed on either side of the hole. That was it.

To squat down was not an easy thing for Paul to do in his weakened condition, but he managed and waited patiently till his churning innards let go. It had been more than a week since the last time. After a painful delivery, a stool emerged, hard as a rock and black as coal, leaving him torn and bleeding. In time, his digestive processes would return to normal.

Slowly Paul became acquainted with the other fifty or so men who lived with him in Tent "A." He marveled at how life here was so much better than in Kreuznach, even with the meager food and shelter offered. Their tent, long and rectangular, had two doors, one on either end. A narrow path stretched between the doors, next to which the men lay perpendicularly.

The guards were dark-skinned Moroccan soldiers. Paul had never seen people of another color before, and he felt a nervousness around them. When one guard tried to touch his face during a morning muster, an intense fear coursed through his body. The guards counted the camp's prison population every day. Often they had to remain outside for long hours, herded together on the adjacent field, because the disorganized sentries could not agree on the total number. About six hundred prisoners were held in the camp, but the number would fluctuate as prisoners died or new ones arrived.

The inmates often were assembled into small work platoons. Nearby villages sent their delegates to collect these groups of prisoners to work in their quarries, to help farmers in the fields, or to build roads.

Friendliness pervaded among the men most of the time with one exception: the hour of feeding. Mealtime was wartime, when human beings turned into silently roaring animals. They ate in silence in that tent, the only sounds the clicking of homemade spoons hitting pots and teeth. The tension tightened here—more than it ever had at Kreuznach—because the many prisoners ate together in the tent, crowded into an elbow-touching closeness. They slurped soup from their scratch-marked pots, just inches away from each other. In Kreuznach the hungry had been more scattered, separated by the earth berms that rimmed their shallow holes. They had eaten in groups of just ten, with the open sky making them freer from one another.

Here, too, some people played the game of not eating until all the others had finished. In Paul's tent, about five men tortured the rest. At those moments, the other faces seemed chiseled into pure hate. Lips spoke without moving: "I want to kill you for this..." When the five finally ended the ordeal, had licked their cans clean, everyone began to lean back a little and the tension would slowly ease. Soon the tent would be awash again with conversation, many of the men bragging about how life had been.

"We had a big house and every fall we'd go to Italy, to Rome, and see the Pope..."

They bragged about where they came from, how much money they had made at home, how well they ate, how many maids took care of their houses, how many roses bloomed in their gardens, how many crystal wine glasses and pieces of silver adorned their tables. They boasted of what great things they had done before the war had taken them, had destroyed their families, had burned their homes.

These were lies, but unconsciousness lies, for these hapless men had convinced themselves that all that they said was true. They had lived for so long at the edge of life, so near death, had been hungry day after day for months on end, they hardly believed anymore in a tomorrow that would end all their pain. They did not know where their wives were, their children, mothers, and fathers. They longed for compassion and love, which would not be forthcoming. To cling to sanity, to hope, they needed to make up a world that was better than the one in which they found themselves warehoused.

At Rennes, the prisoners indulged in a most unusual diversion: the invention of grotesque cooking recipes. The daily work commandos had smuggled writing paper and pencils through the gate, and the tent bosses saw to it that the sheets were distributed equally among the men. The pencils, essential to recording those peculiar culinary fantasies, were traded back and forth for spoonfuls of the noontime potato soup. The sharpness of those pencils determined their value, and Paul used to freshen them up by chafing the wood against a sliver of brick he found during a walk along the fence. His Kreuznach knife would have come in handy.

Paul soon joined in. He liked apple cake, so he devised a recipe. He started with ten large apples, a jar of honey, a pound of butter, yeast, and seven eggs. As time went on, his recipes became more extravagant. He used different flavorings, like vanilla or hazelnut, added more butter, or included as much as two tablespoons of cinnamon. He "baked" one cake every day, sometimes two. At nighttime he would, like all the others, fold up his creations meticulously and then hide them under the cardboard he slept on. This cardboard, his one "luxury," had come from Ernst, who had found a large piece of it somewhere. Ernst had traded part of the cardboard for a slice of green bread and let Paul have a smaller piece free of charge.

At night in their dreams they ate what they had cooked up during the day. The gritty grinding of empty teeth, awful sounds to the ear, kept at bay the rats that chewed on the leather soles of their brittle shoes.

Paul had learned from Ernst that the Moroccan guards in this camp forced younger prisoners to be their whores. "Try not to be alone with these homos. Stay out of reach. Don't take candies from them, and when you are on the barracks-cleaning detail, stay away from the ones that are in bed. Most of them are drunk. They have done real harm to some of the younger boys around here. In the tent across from us a man—just your age, Paul—had been molested and abused so badly and by so many that he no longer could hold his stool. He died not too long ago."

"Are they all that way? And how come they can keep doing it?"

"I really don't know. The rumors say that women in Morocco are in the minority by a ratio of ten to one. Over there the homosexuals are probably much more civilized. You know, these soldiers here come from the fringes of society. You see how sloppy they dress. They are filthy, they smell, they piss right outside their living quarters. They probably were drafted away from prisons and the dark streets of Casablanca."

"I remember learning in school that there is no such person as a native Moroccan. Our geography books had them coming from Spanish, Turkish, Berber, Arabian, Portuguese, and French mothers, their fathers being professional pirates."

"Yes, and they've been at war nearly forever. All that leaves footprints on people, bad ones. And on top of it, war like the one we went through unleashes the worst in man. From what you told me, I know you've been there, seen it, felt it. You and I, we will wear that for all time to come. We may never be freed from it."

One day Paul asked Ernst about his home.

"Home? I don't know anymore where home is. We had a small house in Leipzig, at the outskirts of the city, almost in the countryside. It took me forty minutes to go to work on my bicycle. We had two children, both girls. It was a happy family. Sybille, my wife and I..." He hesitated, wanted to say more, but his voice failed him. He looked away from Paul into the distance, through and beyond the fabric of the tent. His eyes were like glass balls drained of the warmth that usually shone from them. His lips twitched. No other part of his body showed life.

Paul remembered that day in the autumn of 1944. The sky was clear and blue. A light wind coming from the sea carried the unmistakably chilling hum of invading bombers. The Allied planes came in from the Baltic Sea, heading south. The air-defense battalion's listening disk had picked up their roaring engines a few minutes earlier. And then four ten-centimeter guns ripped the sky open. Yellowish-white puffy round clouds exploded among the oncoming planes, the Flying Fortresses, as the American Air Force called them. But those planes were out of reach. They flew higher this time, higher than usual. In their wake a rain of radar-foiling tinsels glittered in the morning sun.

Paul sat in the steel saddle of his twenty-millimeter Oerlikon and watched wave after wave of planes. There seemed to be no end, hundreds of them. The first reports of destruction came in over the radio.

"Leipzig, they are leveling Leipzig and Jena..."

Many women, children, older people fried to crisps in the firestorms of that day, torn into tiny bits, suffocated in bomb shelters, suffering deep and fatal wounds from shrapnel biting into flesh. Thousands succumbed.

As the first wave of aircraft made its way back from the killing fields, a few planes limped along, engines afire and trailing black smoke. Desperately trying to reach the open sea, they had lost altitude and fallen into Paul's range.

Paul aimed. The barrel of his gun turned a hot, purple-blue as round after round sought its mark. The tracers showed that he was on target. Two of the planes did not make it to their destination, but began a perilous dive just beyond Swinemünde, near the shoreline of the Baltic, exploding on impact.

From that moment on, the sixteen-year-old Paul was no longer a kid.

"Thou shall not kill." *But I have killed.*

Talking to himself, he kept staring at the two smoke balls that mushroomed above the sea.

Paul knew why Ernst stopped suddenly, unable to continue. He knew there was no home anymore in Leipzig, no loving family waiting for him to come back. It was all gone.

Paul wanted to hug that man, but his mother never had taught him how to do that. Instead, he got up and went outside to walk and to cry.

Time moved sluggishly, uneventfully. Occasionally, a prisoner would die, and after he had been carried out, a shuffle took place among the men. Spaces were traded and new neighbors replaced the old.

Green bread got whiter as the weeks went by and Paul slowly gained back some strength. But the process was slow, as they still received only one meal a day. Hunger plagued them day and night. As Ernst had predicted, a few could not resist filling their bellies with grass. Their faces would take on a greenish pallor, and shortly thereafter they would die. Paul had carved some forty marks into the side of his homemade soup pot. Ernst looked after him, much as Wally had done, but in a more fatherly way, for he was older than Wally by some thirty years. He had been under Field Marshal Rommel's command in northern Africa until General Montgomery overcame the Germans in 1942.

He spent two years in an American prison camp in Morocco where English soldiers guarded them.

"They treated us like human beings," Ernst told Paul in one of their many conversations. "The food was good and plenty. Yes, they took care of us."

In 1945 he had been shipped to Nantes in France. The Americans had outfitted the departing prisoners well with new clothes, heavy topcoats, socks, and sturdy boots. When the prisoners disembarked from the ship, about two thousand of them, the American commando passed on their authority to a horde of French soldiers. Within the hour, they had stripped the prisoners of their clothes and anything else they had on them, including their underwear. The prisoners then were herded into large dock warehouses where they were given old, torn, filthy German uniforms that Ernst believed came from dead soldiers.

Throughout his stay in the tent city, Paul had remained at his spot by the door, unable to jockey for a new position whenever one opened up. He wanted to move to a different place to distance himself from his nearest neighbor, a man who claimed to be a university professor from Freiburg. Herr Egor von Ebenhorst, as he had introduced himself, had a habit of putting on airs, always talking above Paul's head. Egor "knew" from his "reliable sources" that Hitler, Hermann Goering, and Wernher von Braun, together with Siemens and Halske, the giant electrical manufacturing company, still were working on the weapon that would "blast England completely off the map."

Egor was involved in a violent exchange that Paul would never forget. The barracks-cleaning detail had brought a Rennes newspaper back with them. A horrifying picture leapt from the front page: a mass grave filled to the top with terribly mangled bodies, some partially clothed, many of them stripped naked. No one could read the French headline. The paper finally made its way to the professor.

He studied it for a minute, then explained, "This says that Hitler has killed hundreds of thousands of Jewish people. They died in gas chambers, built by the Gestapo-man Heinrich Himmler.

This shows one of the many mass graves. It also says that as many as a million were beaten, raped, and poisoned. Then they were burned in large ovens in Auschwitz and Birkenau. The paper calls it genocide."

The men in the tent had fallen silent, shocked by this unbelievable account. Some of the prisoners had heard rumors that the Gestapo had committed atrocities in Poland, but nothing like this. So many people... The professor paused and looked with disdain at the hollow faces staring back at him.

"Do you believe this?" he sneered. "Propaganda, a lie, that's what this is. Hitler would not, no. Not one word of this is true." He turned away, his contempt for his "ignorant" tentmates palpable.

Suddenly, a man named Wolfgang sprung from his place in the middle of the tent and ran down the aisle. The other men quickly pulled back their feet so they would not trip him. He spun Egor around and tore the paper from his hands.

Through bared teeth, Wolfgang seethed, "You bastard! You godforsaken idiot! You dumb piece of shit! They took my wife there! She was a Jew. One more word from you and I kill you!"

God, did you let that happen? Did my father know about it? What if he did?

This was the first time Paul had heard about Auschwitz and what Hitler had done to the Jewish people there. The thought of it overwhelmed him, so cruel, so shameful, so incomprehensible. He could not think of a word that would even come close to describe these awful, brutal killings.

How could this happen? Why did nobody do anything about it? How was it possible that his mother, his father, his friends, teachers, and neighbors could let this go on and remain silent?

But it had been possible to shield these horrible events from the view of the German public. Paul wondered if the people of other countries knew this horrible secret. He could not think his way through this news at the moment. Later he would know more, but many of his questions would never be answered.

Several prisoners had ushered Wolfgang back to his spot. Ernst came over and held him tight until the sobbing stopped. The tent did not go to sleep that evening until the wee hours of the morning.

Paul complained to Ernst about Egor. "I don't want to be next to this man anymore. Besides what happened the other day, the guy never washes himself. He stinks. And he's one of *those* 'Five Late Diners,'" Paul reminded Ernst, alluding to the prisoners who tortured their tentmates by saving their meals until the rest had eaten.

"Give me some time, Paul. Please."

But there was little Ernst could do. Nobody wanted to live next to that monster.

Everyone in the tent had lice. Paul was no exception, but the bugs didn't bite him for some reason, so he remained unaware. One day Ernst said, "Paul, I never see you scratch your head or under your arms. Don't you have these filthy bugs?" When he had Paul take off what was left of his shirt, they could see shiny silvery spots along the seams inside the sleeves.

Ernst whistled. "You know what those are? Man, you have lice eggs by the thousands! But I can't see that any of these green mothers have sucked on you. That is strange. You sure your blood isn't blue?"

Most of the men in the tent took off their shirts or jackets on a regular basis and de-liced themselves, flattening the little critters between thumbnails. But although Egor scratched incessantly, he never preened himself. He flatly denied that he could be infected.

"People like us have no lice, no. Those are mosquito bites." Soon, not just Paul but others began complaining to Ernst.

"This pig makes me barf in my dreams."

"Get him to take care of himself or kill the son of a bitch. Somebody must have forgotten to do that anyway."

The complaints got so bad that Ernst finally called the tent city boss for help. The chief, a German army sergeant, brought two men with him. When Egor refused to take off his reeking clothes, they did it for him.

Paul and Ernst gasped at what they saw: thousands of disgusting green specks, moving in all directions, giving the appearance of an industrious anthill. The shirt seemed to crawl on its own as it lay on the ground.

The two soldiers dragged Egor outside to the long wash trough next to the latrines and scrubbed him vigorously. The professor screamed and fussed, indignantly protesting at this brutish behavior. The show attracted the attention of dozens of onlookers, and other tent bosses saw the opportunity to clean house too. Soon Egor had company in the bath, and the crowd cheered as the washing ceremony went on for hours.

Afterwards the "baptized" stood together as though in a line-up—naked, thin, skin revealing shrunken rib cages and knobby knees and ankles. Ironically, there wasn't much difference between the pictures of concentration camp inmates and these poor souls considered to be among the "upper ten thousand," the cream of German society. The chief officer warned them, "If you do not want to take care of yourself, I will ship you out of here and into the isolation bunker. The rodents there will rid you of your lice, and maybe of more."

Hardly a week had gone by when the tent boss made good on his word. The camp police came and took most of those same men from their tents, sequestering them in the isolation bunker until long after Paul had moved on to his work platoon.

Paul found it strange that the most educated people, those with seemingly good names and high positions at home, were the dirtiest of the prisoners. Throughout the coming years behind barbed wire, he would find this to be true over and over again. They never took care of what little they had, never mending a shirt or repairing a shoe to make it last a little longer. They were the ones who thieved and lied and snitched. Later, when the first American CARE packages arrived from across the Atlantic, it was these "hoodlums," the "Egors" of the camp who got the new shirt, pants, and socks, because otherwise they would be forced to walk naked down the streets of the village where they worked.

Paul, as did many others, tended his few possessions as best he could. When the boots he had taken from the dead man on the train began to fall apart, he traded one half of his piece of cardboard for a length of rusty bailing wire. By bending the wire back and forth, he broke it into two long pieces and then wound one piece around the front part of each boot, which kept the sole from coming off completely. Yet, when it came to deciding who would get new boots sent by a family from Pennsylvania, Paul lost his bid. After all, he still could walk in his wired ones.

Paul bitterly resented that his resourcefulness kept him from enjoying any small improvement of his lot. He complained to Ernst.

"Why is it that the people who take care of their clothes and themselves don't get a new shirt or socks? Is it because those assholes don't give a shit? Why don't we let the bums rot in their stuff? And why are they still alive? Why didn't the bullets find them? Why did they not burn up with the others in Leipzig?"

"Paul!" Ernst's cry sounded like a shot from a pistol. He sat there, holding his head in his hands. "Do you need to inflict hurt? Will that make you feel better?"

Jesus, what did I just say? Leipzig. Oh my God! I never in my life before ever wanted somebody to be dead. I am becoming an animal. Is that all that is left in me?

Ernst lay back on his cardboard and after a while tried to explain.

"I understand how you feel. But, you see, the world is not all that pretty and the people living in it are not either. The ones you are angry about have different priorities. At home they lived affluent lives, moved in upper society. Pretentiously, they took credit for the good things that happened in the past. They created a make-believe existence around and among themselves that has little to do with your or my reality. Being truthful, honorable, clean inside and out, was not, is not on their list. Others mended their things, straightened out their messes for them—their maids and butlers. This seemed natural to them, that they should be privileged. They had two sets of rules, one for themselves, and one for everyone else. "This bare life here, the watered soup, the absence of featherbeds and audiences—they cannot handle that. They do not know how. Shakespeare has spoken to them, Goethe and Schiller, but they have not understood the real message. You see, once Mozart hums lullabies in your ear at night, you—"

"Stop it, Ernst. I like Mozart. Besides it is Schubert who is the guy with the night songs. You sound so...so..."

"So communistic? You think so? No, I don't believe in the preachings of Karl Marx."

"Who's that?"

"Were you sick that day in school when the teacher told you about Marxism?"

"They talked a lot about Stalin and Bolshevism and so on."

"Well, okay, so you like Mozart. But boy, look at us! Was it your doing that we marched into Poland? I wager that Mr. Krupp who made the guns for that excursion is not hanging out at a prison camp right now. You told me that your father was a high-ranking army officer. What do you want to bet he is home already, while you are still in the dark not knowing whether or not your family made it at all?"

And what if he is right?

That question would keep bouncing through his mind.

A week or so later Ernst negotiated the relocation of Paul's space, arranging it so they could live next to each other. Paul parted with one of his prime cake recipes, and Ernst promised his old neighbor a new soup pot. The deal was done and Paul "moved in."

September 1945. Summer, on its way out, slid into autumn with many days of rain.

One Monday morning, after shivering through a cold night, Paul asked Ernst, "In Kreuznach they told me that I would work for a while rebuilding an airport somewhere in France. After that I would be shipped back to Germany with or without a home address. What'd they tell you?"

"Pretty much the same."

"Well, don't you wonder what's going on? Whom can we ask?"

"I don't know, Paul. I really don't care when they let me go or to where. You might not understand that, but that is the way I feel. Wolfgang will tell you the same. You only lost your home, maybe not even your parents. We lost the ones we loved, our wives, the children we had together, everything we cared about. There isn't anything to look forward to."

Paul did not, could not answer, knowing anything he said would only hurt Ernst more.

The Moroccan guard banged the tent door open with his foot. Too tall for the door frame, he had to stoop to enter the barrack. The American army coat he wore made him look bigger than life. Strolling down the narrow pathway, slowly, arrogantly, looking right and left, he gave the impression that he was searching for something special...perhaps someone special.

"You!" The guard had stopped short of where Paul was sitting on the ground and fixed his eyes on him.

"Watch out, Paul," Ernst whispered under his breath.

Paul looked straight ahead as though he had not heard, as though he did not realize the guy meant him.

The guard kicked Paul right above the ankle, nearly knocking him over. Everyone froze. This seemed to be different from the usual Monday-morning shit-bucket selection process.

"Me, Abdul. You! Come you!"

He grabbed Paul's arm, tore him from his cardboard bed, and shoved him toward the door at the other end of the tent.

Powerful and devastating fright strangled Paul. He felt as though he weren't there, that all this was happening to somebody else as he sat watching from a safe distance.

Was this another lieutenant like the one in Weimar, cruelly counting down...9...8...7? Perhaps. He could not tell.

All of a sudden he was very weak. The Moroccan steered him toward the guards' quarters, but he felt like he was walking through deep water, moving in slow motion. His feet did not seem to touch the gravel beneath. He was aware of nothing else.

The husky guard put his arm around Paul and delivered a kiss that sent a piece of razor-sharp steel through him.

Why don't you run away, Paul?

But where could he run? Prisoners had been beaten unmercifully when they tried to escape the paws of these animals.

Entering the cabin, Paul and the guard were greeted by a drunken racket. Most of the guards sat around tables, smoking and eating some sort of porridge with their bare hands. The rotten smell, the noise, the grinning faces jarred him into tremors. Paul did not understand their Arabic words, but he knew what the shrieking screams he could hear meant.

They gathered around him, grabbed him between his legs. The ones at the back of the table laughed and waved at him like they were greeting, even welcoming an old friend. Paul pushed away their searching hands, but he could not escape. One of the filthy thugs stood up and hugged him, forcing Paul's face up to his for a foul-breathed kiss. Paul wriggled out from under with a scream so piercing that the room fell silent.

Run! Run!

But before he could move, Abdul snatched him in by the collar and shoved him toward a set of bunks in the far corner of the cabin. He kept a tight hold around Paul's shoulders. With his free hand he searched and dug up a bottle of cognac and a bar of chocolate from under his pillow.

"You eat, drink cognac. We make fun, you!" Paul tried to push the man away, but he was far too weak. The monster roared with laughter as his right hand closed around Paul's throat, an implicit threat.

The Moroccan peeled the wrapper off the candy bar with his stained teeth and forced the sticky chocolate between Paul's lips.

"You fuck me with you..." While he was growling these words, he stuck his thumb into his mouth. His head moved back and forth. "Oui, fuck with bouche. Ha, oui, yes, yes!"

The guard took a shot of the cognac without swallowing, then, burping, he threw himself onto the bed. Still holding Paul by the neck, the drunken man unbuttoned his fly and pulled Paul closer. What Paul saw made him shake even harder. The man's organ, erect, was huge.

"Oh, please, no, please don't. No...no...no..please, no..." The smell was unbearable. Paul stopped breathing for as long as he could hold the air. The man turned sideways a little, grabbed him by the ears and forced himself into Paul's mouth. Another guard who had followed them into the corner ripped down Paul's trousers to suck on him.

When Paul came around, Ernst and two other prisoners were bending over him. One held Paul's head in his lap, and stroked his sweaty head. His clothes, which had been fouled by the Morrocan's spilled liquor and sticky semen, had been removed, and he had been covered with a piece of newspaper to keep him warm. Fierce spasms shook Paul's body as he lay in shock. He did not quite know where he was or what had happened to him.

"Hey, man, how do you feel? It's over. You've been lucky. They threw you out the door. They don't like to play with boys that are out cold."

The pictures came back, sporadically. Paul spoke with slurred words.

"Did he, did they... I don't feel anything. Did they... I am numb all over. Ernst, will I die?"

"Did you ever hear of guardian angels? You must have more than one!"

"Did they? Tell me, did they, this man, did he..."

"No, Paul, he didn't. We checked your rear end. It's okay. Come, we're here. It's okay now. Try to forget the whole thing."

"What if he comes back?"

Ernst had alarmed the chief, who had spoken to the French commander of the camp. It had been the commander who, with another French soldier, had picked up Paul from outside the Moroccan's quarters and carried him back to Ernst.

"He won't, Paul, and for a while they won't bother anyone."

"So help me, I'll bite his thing off! I will! I don't care if he kills me!" The fierceness with which Paul spoke took its toll on his frail body, and he vomited.

Two French German-speaking MP soldiers paid a short visit to Paul and Ernst. They shook their heads as if in disbelief after they heard Paul's story. Upon leaving, one of them gave Paul a package of Lucky Strike cigarettes and some matches.

They moved on to the guards' cabin where they arrested two Moroccans, chained them to their jeep, and left the camp. Wolfgang, who had watched, later reported to Ernst that he did not think that either of the men taken away was Abdul. The MPs had gone in the Moroccan barracks and probably handcuffed the two most inebriated guards. Abdul, most likely, had hid to escape detection.

A few prisoners came by the next day and visited with Paul. One had a recipe to share. Another one offered a small piece of bread. Two others gave him bits of charcoal.

"You can eat that," one said. "It fills your stomach, but does not kill you. Beats chewing raw branches or eating sand." Everyone carefully avoided mentioning what had happened.

It took some time until Paul was with it again. His throat hurt for a while and the deep scratches on the backside of his ears took several days to heal. His will to survive crawled back out of the darkness, and hunger once again covered his landscape. Nothing, nothing was more important than that warm potato soup.

As severe as the assault on his body and soul had been, his system recovered fairly quickly. His mind, however, handled the shock the only way possible—by blanking it out, storing those minutes in hell at a place deep inside where he could not touch them for a long, long time.

It would take more than fifty years before those ugly moments would surface again. And even then, the event would be more like a story he remembered hearing long ago. And although this particularly sordid episode remained in his memory as the most distorted aberration of war, the years that passed defused its power and finally made it possible for his heart, his soul, his mind to forgive.

Another month went by. As autumn took hold, the French soldiers handed out blankets. Used, torn, and smelling of mold, they still warmed better than plain old newspaper and cardboard.

A "new" rumor came down the tube: The camp would be closed soon. The prisoners would all go for a short time on work platoons and then be discharged whether or not they had a home to go to.

How many times had they heard that before! Yet their minds clung to this phony news. It didn't matter that they had been fooled time and again by stories like this one. They heard what they were longing for, and their hopes climbed anew.

"Going home? You believe that?"

"Well, yes! It's got to become true one day soon! A half a year has passed since the war ended!"

But no one knew for sure what was going to happen or when. Then, soon after that rumor had rattled through the tents, part of it became reality.

It happened on a bright sunny afternoon, when two men, French civilians, came to the tent. They seemed friendly enough, nodding their heads and smiling a lot. One of them spoke some German.

"Der Burgermeister...the mayor of Trois Boeuf needs a few people to help us repair our country roads. He asked me to tell you that he will have good food for you and that you will be sleeping in real bunk beds. We need sixteen altogether; we have a truck outside with eleven of you already. Who wants to join them?"

Paul shot up and raised his hand so fast and high, it nearly went through the canvas ceiling. His quick movement, however, made most of his blood rush to his feet. He became light-headed, a bit unsteady, though he tried mightily to stay on his feet.

The men from Trois Boeuf had instructions not to select the ones who looked weak and fragile.

They peered at Paul skeptically. "What's your name? How old are you?"

"Paul. I am eighteen. I would like to go with you."

The two huddled. One raised his shoulders a little, but the other one gestured with a smile. Approved!

"Okay, boy, get your things together and wait till we are done here."

What things does he think I have?

Just as Paul moved toward the truck, Ernst returned from a barracks detail. He immediately saw what was going on. He looked at Paul, and then to the ground.

When their eyes met again it was Ernst who shouted, "Go, Paul, go for it. Get out of here. No, you don't cry, you son of a bitch. Get! Good luck, you'll make it and so will I. Now move! Get going!"

Paul often wondered what ever became of Ernst, for they never saw each other again. But Ernst's image kept on living with him throughout the years, along with Wally's, never fading. He would pray for them and sometimes, in his way, would ask for their silent nod.

Paul gave away all but one of his recipes—keeping that one just in case they had value where he was going—the cardboard, some toilet paper, and a few leftover charcoal crumbs to an older man across from him. He had wanted to give those things to Ernst, but his friend had gone outside and could not be found.

The two Frenchmen, Bienne and Avreau, selected four more people, among them Wolfgang. He walked to the truck with Paul, who still swayed a little.

"Don't let go now, Paul. Walk straight...be strong...they will not take you if you let them see that you can barely make it. Okay?"

Bienne helped Paul get in the truck bed, which sat quite high off the ground and had nothing but a rope across the back, fastened to the sideboards.

"Attention! Fall off, you kaput," Avreau gestured, talking with his arms and hands. He unpacked the food they had brought to feed the hungry prisoners.

"Do I see butter, I mean real yellow butter and bread?"

"Look they brought apples!"

"Hey, smell the meat! Wow!"

"They have wine for us!"

"Hey, we're living again!"

Everyone talked at the same time, loudly, boisterously. Pedestrians watched as they motored through the streets of Rennes, seeing what looked like a bunch of guys going on a picnic. Kids waved at them. Paul thought how different this was from the train stop in Paris.

Wolfgang sat across from him. Their eyes met and they laughed and shook hands. Had this moment occurred a few decades later, they would have exchanged high fives.

"You know how I feel?" shouted Wolfgang. "Like I am almost a free man. I just can't believe all this yet. Kick me!"

Avreau had made galette rolls so large that the prisoners nearly choked on the abundance of cheese, butter, and meat.

"Slow down," he cautioned them, albeit in French, "don't eat too fast. We have enough to fill you up."

They would learn later that Avreau, a Jew, had survived Auschwitz. How he got there as a Frenchman was never made clear. Maybe he was part of the French Underground. His eyes were hard and he walked as though carrying a heavy load.

Yes, Avreau knew what hunger was, and he knew that too much food into a very empty stomach could kill. He had seen men killed this way intentionally.

Watching the prisoners, Avreau began to worry. Again he spoke his warning in French, waiving his arms frantically. But the prisoners took this as encouragement, as though he were saying "Eat, eat, eat!"

It was as impossible to tell them not to eat too much as it would be to ask a person dying of thirst not to drink the water. In the minds of those in that truck, dying from too much food proved a more attractive death than dying from not enough.

The truck headed northeast, following streets that left the city and turned into country roads. Rennes faded from view, but the prisoners did not care. They laughed, they sang, they joked and jostled each other in their glee.

Then it happened.

Suddenly, one, and then two, and then seemingly everyone in the gang began to shout, jumping up from their seats and gesturing wildly. "Stop! Stop! I need to go! Now! Stop, please, stop!"

Avreau hammered the roof of the cab with his big, hard fists. Bienne screeched the truck to a halt almost swerving into the ditch. Neither Frenchman carried a weapon, and they were not sure whether this might be a premeditated attempt to escape.

They knew better soon enough. For some the truck had not stopped quickly enough, and as they jumped off the side, they left behind a trail of smelly, slushy waste.

Even in his pain, Paul realized that anyone viewing this situation would have found it funnier than hell. Sixteen arses blasting away along the ditch. Neither Avreau nor Bienne had thought to bring toilet paper; even if they had, it surely wouldn't have been enough. Three or four bites into those fabulous sandwiches had triggered the onset of diarrhea so immediate and so severe that undigested food shot out the other end. Then the cramps began.

But all in all, these prisoners were happy. They were touching real life again and freedom was moving ever so much closer.

Trois Boeuf

Trois Boeuf

Villages passed and disappeared into the dusk as the narrow road meandered toward the small town of Trois Boeuf. They had to stop often, for the prisoners had indeed fallen ill from so much rich and heavy food. The two Frenchmen worried. What would the mayor say when he saw this pile of literally "shitty" people? Could the men die of the cramps and diarrhea? What would they do then?

Darkness had fallen by the time they drove through the rough, unlit streets of the village that would turn out to be their new home for more than a year. The truck finally stopped in front of a two-story house outside of town.

"Venez...Come, we are home. Hurry up! It's late."

Bent over in pain, the sixteen prisoners crawled off the truck and struggled to follow Bienne. The mayor and the schoolteacher welcomed them at the door. Avreau engaged in animated discussion with them until the mayor finally threw up his hands. He seemed angry, though he managed a smile as the prisoners passed by him.

A lone lightbulb lit the hallway that led to the stairs in back. They ascended to find three rooms on the second floor, two furnished with double bunks. A long table with wooden stools on either side stood in the third and largest room, which would be their mess hall.

Paul saw that all the rooms had windows, and he couldn't remember the last time he had looked through one.

It took a while until everybody found a bed, which were actually wooden boxes on stilts. They were filled with loose straw held down by a sheet of sorts stitched together from cloth used to make flour sacks. It didn't matter, for it was so, so very much better than the tent city in Rennes.

Paul, who had been assigned to a top bunk, tried to climb in, but had to get a leg up from the bearded man who would sleep on the bunk beneath his.

Jesus, is that ever comfortable! Ernst, I wish you be could here too. This is so very much out of this world!

Paul lay on his back, very still, afraid that someone may put an end to this, would take away this softness, this moment of comfort. Hardly did he dare to breathe. He stretched out his legs and tucked his hands underneath his body, feeling the straw through the sackcloth beneath him. The straw crackled and buckled, giving way to the contour of his body. His warmth coaxed a whiff of harvest time, of fields and summer days. The pain in Paul's stomach subsided some, and he drifted off to sleep.

When Paul awoke the next morning, he realized that his sleep had been so deep that he hadn't moved at all. He sat up and swung sideways, his feet dangling from the bunk's wooden frame.

"Hey, buddy, get your stinking feet out of my face, will you!"

This came from his bunkmate, the man "with the hair in the face," as Bienne had called him.

"Sorry," said Paul, looking down. "I'm Paul, Paul Berck. What's your—"

"Johannes," the man said, cutting him off, "just Johannes."

Bienne entered carrying a large bucket.

"How do you men feel this morning? Better, oui? Doctor say you drink much to get all well. I brought water and cups."

They were thirsty and drank deeply of the cold water.

Later, they gathered in the room with the long table and the stools. Avreau and Bienne stood by the door.

"Now, listen. The mayor will be here in a few minutes to welcome you. Until then let's talk about what we are going to do today. First, did all of you find a bed? Are you next to the one you like? Oui? Well, you might want to move around later."

Bienne looked the men over. As the mayor's right-hand man, he had to make sure this risky venture would not disrupt the community. His first task was to find someone whom he would make the leader of this little outfit.

"We will not go to work today. You will have time to get to know one another."

Avreau also studied the men who would be his crew. While they would start out building roads, as he and Bienne had told them at Rennes, he knew their main work would be at the nearby quarry, pounding rocks into aggregate.

As the supervisor at the quarry, he would be at work with the prisoners, teaching them how to mine that hard, blue basalt at the site some five miles to the west of the village. He judged each man's build, and decided where he would station each prisoner. The strongest prisoners would break large blocks from the wall using heavy pry bars, sledge hammers, and long-wedge chisels. Others would split those blocks into one-man rocks. The youngest and weakest men would sit and make fist-sized ballast from the blocks with small rock hammers on long hazelnut sticks. Avreau's goal was to produce ten to twelve yards of rock in a ten-hour shift. Although he knew he might have to change this plan, one thing was for sure. He'd make them work, and hard.

He wondered about Paul. He was so thin, looked so fragile. They should not have taken him. Well, they could always send him back.

Bienne was laying out work schedules when the mayor walked in. He grinned from ear to ear.

"Messieurs, bon jour, bon jour! Mon Dieu! Comment ça va?"

Bienne translated this friendly burst of greetings into German.

"The mayor, Mr. LeCarte, welcomes you here. He says that he will see to it that you will have enough to eat."

Bienne barely could keep up with the translation, so very fast did the mayor speak.

"Mr. LeCarte has spoken with the people of his village and has asked them to accept you as helping hands, not as their enemy. He wants you to know that it has not been easy to convince the farmers and the townspeople of that."

Trois Boeuf, only a dot on the map, had been a strategic location for the German army. Heavy fighting close by destroyed many houses. Fortunately, none of the villagers had been killed; still, some of the farmers had not come back from the war.

Before the prisoners had arrived, the Catholic priest had taken up a collection of clothes, which were waiting for them at the local schoolhouse.

"They have shirts, pants, jackets, and maybe even some blankets for you."

A prisoner stood up and asked Mr. LeCarte in fluent French if they would get cigarettes.

Avreau burst into laughter, relieved to find that someone spoke French.

"Mon Dieu, someone in the quarry can pass on my directions in plain old French," he said to himself as he pulled out a handkerchief to wipe his brow. "It's going to be okay."

The mayor, who understood the question, spoke to Bienne, who translated.

"Mr. LeCarte says he will talk to his clerk and ask her to make a deal with the local grocer for tobacco and cigarette paper. Just be patient."

Cigarettes! I haven't had a smoke since April this year.

All applauded, and the speaker, Dieter Lehmann, sat down next to his younger brother, Hugo. The Lehmanns, the heartiest of the men, also could pass as the best dressed "PDG" (Prisoner Of War).

Dieter had been a school principal and Hugo had owned a sporting goods store. Both came from Danzig in East Prussia. Their speech and good manners marked them as highly educated and well-bred.

Bienne moved over behind Dieter and announced that he was promoting this Lehmann to be the leader and spokesman of the group.

At this announcement, Avreau scowled inwardly. He had a bias against educated people, feeling that most of them did not know what work really was about. And they used words in their conversation that he did not know what to do with. But he knew how to level the playing field. He would make Lehmann one of the pry bar men.

The mayor, a naturally gregarious, friendly man, stayed for quite a while, talking, laughing, shaking hands with everybody at the table. Paul, the youngest of the bunch, had been placed at the far end of the table. When Mr. LeCarte came by, he took Paul's hand into both of his. He shook his head and motioned Avreau to come over to him. Putting an arm around Avreau's shoulder, the mayor said, "Regardez...jeune, trop jeune...Avreau, he is too young to have been in the war."

Avreau didn't say a word, but gave a slight nod. Inside his thoughts burned. He hadn't been too young for Auschwitz, had he? He turned abruptly and left the room.

The mayor, sensing Avreau's thoughts, turned to Paul and gave him the okay sign.

"Avreau also had a hard time a few years ago, in Auschwitz. But he is a good man."

Bienne chose two men for the job of cooking. One was Franzl, a tall Bavarian who walked with a stoop. Paul could not understand him very well, especially when Franzl droned on in an obscure Bavarian dialect very different from the Pomeranian flat German Paul drifted into once in a while.

Franzl's helper, Gruber, came from Munich, also in Bavaria. He felt he needed to make an acceptance speech for both of them.

"Franzl here and I will cook the best lunches and dinners you've eaten in a long time. We'll find a way to serve lunch warm at the quarry every day."

Gruber waited. Although that was good news, no one clapped as he had expected. Instead, everyone imagined how pleasant a job cooking would be, even though nobody knew yet what breaking rocks was all about.

The men sensed something strange about Gruber, too, for he never made eye contact when talking, but looked away or focused on some spot above the other person's head. The gang found out later that he had done time for armed robbery before the war. And while they did not hold the crime against him, they never quite trusted him all the way.

Paul was one of the few who knew that Gruber was all right. If it hadn't been for Gruber, he might have bitten the dust.

The men had been working for a couple of weeks, and some progress had been made. Everyone had regained his strength—everyone except Paul. His diarrhea had not stopped; in fact, he was weaker now than he had been when he first arrived. It got so bad that Paul began to discharge completely undigested food laced with blood. Whenever he ate, he would have to go to the bathroom within a few minutes. The others began to worry about him.

The walk to and from work became his way of the cross. Each night, they would carry their tools home so that the blacksmith could sharpen and reshape the picks, the chisels, and pry bars, which they would carry back to work in the morning. Wolfgang, seeing that Paul could barely carry himself, hauled Paul's pick to and from work for him. On the long walk home, Paul could not keep up with the gang, straggling in nearly an hour later. Avreau let him trail behind knowing that he couldn't possibly escape.

It became clear that Paul needed medical attention. Because the closest doctor resided in the next town, Bienne waited until Sunday to load Paul in a wheelbarrow to take him there. Wolfgang had asked if he could come along and help with the pushing, and Bienne gratefully acquiesced.

Though the day was warm, fall already had painted the leaves of the apple trees in the orchards with yellow, brown, and red colors. Paul felt every little grain of sand the steel-banded wheel of the cart ran over. The going was rough, and Wolfgang and Bienne rested often.

In Broons, five miles down the road from Trois Boeuf, the doctor first took Paul's temperature. When he saw the mercury climbing, he whistled. He pushed into Paul's stomach, who let out a scream. Wolfgang took his hand to still the shivering. The doctor gave Paul a shot of morphine; he felt better instantly. The pain subsided, as did the shaking.

The doctor motioned to Bienne to follow him into the waiting room. When he returned, his face showed grave concern, but he said only that it was time to return to Trois Boeuf. Wolfgang helped Paul back to the wheelbarrow, and they began the long trip home. Bystanders stared; some laughed, assuming the two men with the white letters painted on their backs must be criminals.

At the first farmhouse outside of town, they stopped and Bienne went in. He came back with a sack stuffed with hay Paul could use as a pillow. The farmer's wife followed him with a bucket of water and a piece of bread, which they snacked on.

Paul felt drowsy as Gruber and Dieter carried him upstairs. Gruber looked at him with concern.

"Bienne just told us that you are very sick. Maybe you have typhoid fever. He said you can stay home tomorrow. Now sleep."

His words came to Paul from far away, as though spoken through a veil. He sank into sleep, exhausted from the day's journey.

The next morning, after breakfast, Gruber came up from the kitchen to check on him.

"How are you feeling? Still hurts?"

"Razor blades are dancing inside me. Do you have a little water? I am so thirsty."

Gruber brought a small bowl, and with some effort finally got Paul to sit up and drink.

"Now listen to me. I heard years ago when I was in the tank that salted butter can help heal what you might have." He pointed to a dish he had brought up. "The butcher at the slaughterhouse who brings lungs and kidneys for our meals gives Franzl sometimes real butter. I brought you a thin slice. Try to eat it. It can't make you worse."

Paul no longer cared, but Gruber insisted.

"Come, lift your head, I feed you. Let it melt in your mouth, slow. You almost had it, kid. You know that, don't you?"

Yes, Paul understood that, but how many times had he almost died? It had become a way of life.

He stayed home the next several days, and Gruber cared for him, feeding him butter twice a day. Whether it was the butter, the doctor's shot, or simply Paul's will to survive, he began to recover. After a week the pain was gone, and his food no longer traveled through him without stopping.

As he slowly regained his strength, he would try to build up his stamina by walking around the buildings. One day he ventured into the kitchen, where Franzl peeled potatoes and Gruber diced beef kidneys.

The kitchen actually was a lean-to at the backside of the house. Prior to the arrival of the prisoners, the town's bricklayer had constructed what looked like a walk-in fireplace. The opening was some eight feet wide and at least four feet deep. Every house in Trois Boeuf used this kind of a fireplace for warmth and cooking.

A large black kettle sat on a steel grate above the fire Franzl was blowing to life. To the right, adjacent to the fireplace, stood a long table with a rough-hewn wooden top. A couple of cow lungs, some onions, and a bunch of fresh-cut nettles sat upon it, waiting to be prepared for the evening meal.

Franzl and Gruber tried their best to put flavor in the unusual dishes they came up with day after day. The prisoners were always surprised, never sure what their culinary team would concoct for supper.

As Paul entered the kitchen, Franzl called out to him, "Paul, is it ever good to see you walking again! Come in, man.

Sit down." Franzl made a point of staying away from his Bavarian slang so Paul could understand him better.

"Franzl, thank you for the butter. I don't know why but it did the trick." Paul pointed to the nettles. "What are these for?"

"Oh, you haven't lived if you never ate nettles," cried Franzl. "I cook them like spinach, and they taste like it. There are plenty of them around here."

"But they sting like hell. How do you keep from being bitten?"

Franzl shook his head. "Naw, where do you get that? They don't sting me."

"Don't sting, huh! I did not shit out all my brains, you know."

Franzl laughed at this. "No, you're right, they can sting. But there is a trick. In the moment before you touch them, you breathe out, and they won't sting."

Paul doubted this, but said nothing more.

Although Gruber retained his odd habit of never looking directly at anyone, he was a friendly fellow whom others instinctively liked. He struck up a friendship with the local butcher, and because of this, real beef or pork sometimes found their way into Franzl's kettle. The meals also benefited from the gang's growing familiarity with farmhouses along the road. Chicken, an occasional turkey, even a newborn, cute-looking goat would be smuggled in, which Avreau and Bienne pretended not to notice.

Avreau and the crew had settled into a routine, finally learning to accept one another. The first couple of weeks had been difficult; the prisoners felt that Avreau worked them too hard, and they resented, even hated him. Although deep down in his soul he was a man who wanted to do the right thing, to be fair, Avreau had taken an oath in Auschwitz never to forgive the Germans, to avenge his friends they had taken to the chambers. That was the reason he had taken the job to supervise the quarry gang.

But on the day Bienne brought Paul back from the doctor, something changed in him. He saw himself again in those black-and-white-striped cottons and remembered how he had hung onto life from hour to hour.

Without realizing it, he became more tolerant, more outgoing, more talkative, and he began to smile a little. He changed the noon break from fifteen to twenty minutes. More often he helped when a particularly large boulder posed a problem.

Some of the prisoners responded to this change, especially after Bienne had told them Avreau's story, how he had fought for his country in the French Underground and had been captured and taken to the concentration camp in Poland. They began to understand why Avreau had been so hard on them. Yet many of them still harbored bitter feelings toward him.

One evening after their meal, Dieter asked all of them to stay for a bit.

"Johannes has asked to say a few words to you."

All eyes turned to Johannes in surprise. He was not one to talk; in fact, he had been aloof, saying little during the weeks they had been together.

Johannes stood and, after a moment, began to speak.

"I need to tell you, to share with you what I've been thinking over the last few weeks. First, I must apologize. I should not have pulled that stunt with the rattlesnake. It could have bitten Avreau, even killed him. I am sorry for that, and I know you who helped me must be too."

During the time when Avreau had ridden the prisoners especially hard, he had been rewarded with little acts of anonymous sabotage. One of these had been the placing of a live rattlesnake in his jacket, which had thoroughly shaken Avreau.

Johannes paused as though uncertain of how to go on.

"But to be sorry is not enough. There is more."

Some looked with surprise at this man with the big beard. They had figured him altogether differently. Did he not feel the way they did? Many of the men wished every day that the wall of basalt would collapse and bury Avreau. They prayed that the Lord would take that son of a bitch away and never let him come back. So what was happening to Johannes? Did he get soft all of a sudden?

"I think we have heard enough, seen too many pictures in newspapers, to ignore what has happened. You, Dieter, have translated story after story that tell of the terrible, horrible time people like Avreau had to endure. And just because they believed in a different God."

"I know we doubted these reports. We did not believe the pictures to be real. We did not think that one human being could do that to another. I know I did not."

Paul, who sat staring at his empty plate, heard Johannes call his name.

"I know you told me they raped you, but by God they let you go, they did not gas you and throw you into the fire. You are here; so is Avreau. Both of you made it. We all are making it. If you had met Avreau in times of peace, you would not have had hate in your hearts. That hate came with the brown uniform they made you wear so very proudly.

"Yes, all of us here were pressured to accept and trust in unbelievably grotesque ideas. But it is time for us to leave those ideas behind, to move on. We must start over again. Hate is not getting us anywhere. We need to forgive. That is what I want to do, and I ask you to do it with me."

The men stared at Johannes in silence, dumbfounded. This was not the Johannes they knew. What got into him all of a sudden?

Paul looked up and said, "I know what you say is true, but how do I do that, forgive? I don't know how, yet I will try with you."

The hour was late when they went to look for their bunks. Something good had happened that evening. Listening to Johannes had opened their minds, their hearts, unleashing emotions that been buried for so long. They had become more of a family, had gotten closer to each other. When Johannes asked that they forgive, he had struck a chord that had not been plucked for some time. They felt lighter, yes lighter, less burdened, even happier. Johannes had given that to them.

As Paul went to his bunk, he found Johannes there, bent over, sobbing deeply.

"Johannes," Paul said, putting his hand on the man's shoulder, "what is it? Please...you should be proud. You have given us hope."

Johannes quieted a bit, then said, “I want to be a priest again. I want to go back to my parish, which I abandoned.”

Paul could not believe what he was hearing. “You? You are a priest?”

“Yes, and I betrayed God.”

It was around that time, too, when Paul started to pray again, saying the rosary as he marched to and from the quarry.

“... You who died for us on your cross...” Often he would add an extra *Hail Mary*, sometimes two—one for Johannes and one for Ernst.

One day in the fall the butcher and his wife had to leave town suddenly, as the wife’s sister had fallen ill and needed their help. Gruber had come up from the kitchen after dinner and given the sad news that they would have no real meat for the next week or so, just lungs and kidneys and liver.

“We know that you pass by several farms on your way to and from the quarry, that you have all paid visits to the henhouses and clotheslines there. We ask only that you visit these farms a little more often and pick up ‘supplies,’” he said, “for I don’t want you to eat too often what Franzl came up with tonight. How’d it taste?”

A man sitting near the door, Heinz Gutemann, the oldest of the group, said, “If I didn’t know any better, I would say that this here tasted like dog, or am I wrong?”

Gruber’s stare reached higher than usual above the man’s head, and he threw up his hands.

“If I hadn’t said anything, you’d have thought that it was a tough chicken, yes?”

At least half of the men had eaten dog before, and stories of unusual meals—frogs, porcupine, rattlesnakes—poured out of them. But Bartholomew topped them all.

“I caught a rat once...”

Even for these men, who had been through so much, the thought was almost too much.

The prisoners had a problem with rats. The rodents crept into the sleeping quarters every night, and seemed to own the building. Paul often felt them jump onto his legs as he slept.

One morning after a particularly strong invasion, Dieter Lehmann took up the subject.

"Our doors and windows are closed overnight. How do they get in?"

He suggested moving the bunks away from the walls; what they found answered his question. Behind the head frame of Karl's bunk were two fist-sized holes. The rats had gnawed their way through the plasterboard. They found similar holes in the other room.

Now, how to get rid of them? Dieter told of a farmer, a kind man who sometimes came by the quarry with a jug of apple wine for the men, who knew how to get rid of rats for good. First they must catch one, wrap it in a single layer of paper secured with a string, and then set the paper on fire. As the thin paper burned away, the animal would feel the heat, even get its fur burned a little, and would take off screaming like the devil himself was chasing it. When it returned to its burrow, the other rats would smell the burned rat hair and take off in all directions never to come back.

The room erupted in debate after hearing this story.

"How in hell can we catch one of those bastards?"

"If you asked me, that's a crock of shit. The guy is pulling your leg, both legs."

"Burning a rat alive? That's cruel."

"Cruel? You die if one of those filthy animals bites you!"

They all had something to say about the rat burning.

Finally, Dieter said, "Wolfgang, why don't you take a vote. What's the worst that can happen? Set this place on fire?"

"Don't forget the wine barrels in the cellar. It would be a shame if we lost that." Karl, the wine chef, though "thief of wines" would have been more fitting, brought that up for consideration. "But you are right. I'm sick of those ugly beasts too. Never mind a vote. We don't know anything about democracy in the first place. Paul, you and I will catch a rat tonight."

After a while they came up with a plan.

"When we hear at least one rat come in the room, we stuff something in each hole. Then we corner it, and Paul and

Karl will catch and hold the thing. Have a sack ready to throw over it to hold it down."

Hugo offered to let Bienne and Avreau know that they understood that the prisoners were not trying to escape or staging a protest, or, worse, setting fire to the building.

The rats must have listened in on the men's discussion, for they did not show up that evening. It took three more nights until one no longer could stay away from the stolen bacon that hid under the straw. After being chased for almost an hour, the exhausted rat finally fell into Paul's clutches.

The farmer had been right. The rats cleared out, but eventually would return, making it necessary to repeat the burning ceremony about every four months.

The house where the prisoners were quartered was the town's municipal building. It sat at the rim of the village, a neglected garden strip separating the entrance from the street. A fence of waist-high, white-washed slats leaned around the house and the meadow in back; fields stretched beyond the fence.

On the first floor, just to the right of the entrance, were the living quarters of the schoolteacher, a single man. The left portion housed an office and a large gathering room, where the city council members met once a month to drink apple wine and discuss the complaints of their constituents.

Way in the back, under the stairwell, was another small room, where Avreau slept. On the second floor to the right and left were prisoners' rooms.

The cellar of the building was stocked with barrels and barrels of apple wine in various stages of aging. Hundreds of bottles of wine and apple liqueur lined the shelves along the walls.

Nobody noticed that Karl had taken to managing their supply of wine. He described the cellar as a terrifying place—dark, dank, cold, decorated with spiders and their webbing. Karl not only had his hands on the wine, but, unbeknownst to his fellow prisoners, he had found a way via the cellar into the schoolteacher's wardrobe and kitchen, where he helped himself to soft Camembert, twenty-year-old cognac, and money.

Karl developed his own little black market, secretly trading with Gruber, the butcher, and even Bienne. It all came to light when Karl drank himself drunk and blabbered all about his exploits.

When Dieter, who had laid down the rules about drinking, got wind of it, he took Karl aside and threatened him.

"I don't care if you steal and deal, but don't you ever get drunk again. That can hurt all of us, and before I let that happen, we will hurt you. I mean that!"

Karl managed to shape up, and no one else dared get drunk.

One morning Bienne came upstairs early and shook Paul from his sleep. He would be taking Paul with him out to the mayor's farm, a couple of miles to the south.

Paul slipped into his wooden clogs Holland-style and picked up his walking stick. Although Bienne had told him they would be leaving early for the farm, Paul had no idea why they were going.

"What will we be doing there?" he asked once they had set out.

"Mr. LeCarte plowed one of his fields the other day. Whenever we plow the soil around here, we dig up small rocks by the thousands. He wants you and me to pick those rocks off the land."

The mayor had asked Bienne especially to bring Paul, for he could not forget the moment he first saw the young prisoner. Thin, pale, with hardly any life left in him, Paul had rekindled the memory of Mr. LeCarte's own son, who had been a bit older than Paul. The war had taken him, but no one even knew where he was buried.

When Mr. LeCarte saw Paul, his heart went out to him—so young, someone's son, suffering because of this war. That first day the mayor had taken Paul's hand into his own, he promised himself to see to it that Paul would be well cared for.

Often he checked with Avreau, asking, "How is Paul doing? You think he is well again? Did he get stronger?"

And the taskmaster would reassure him. "Oui, monsieur, he is okay. The other prisoners seem to like him, acting as though they are his big brothers. They help him. Yes, I think he is fine."

"Ah, good. Please, do not be too hard on him."

The town of Trois Boeuf found the prisoners a mixed blessing; they labored hard at the quarry, but they also worried the townsfolk. The local priest and the mayor took on the responsibility of making the strange arrangement work.

One Sunday after church, Mr. LeCarte stopped by the town hall to have a talk with Avreau. Just that day in church, the priest had mentioned the prisoners in his sermon. The farmers had been complaining about the prisoners stealing from them. Shirts were missing from clotheslines, the hens didn't lay as many eggs as they had, and most of the nests in the berms were completely empty.

From his pulpit, the pastor implored his congregation.

"So, you people kneeling in your pews, celebrating Mass with me, you tell me you want the prisoners punished. I ask you to think for a moment. Do you eat good food? Do you hang more than one shirt in your closet? Do you have enough eggs?"

He paused, trying to read his audience's faces.

"Does it ever occur to you that our prisoners may be in need of those very things? Perhaps if you would give them clothes, bring some eggs, some good meat to them, they would not have to steal from you. Have we forgotten already what we did when the Germans were here? We not only stole from them, we killed a few, didn't we?

"These men, working at your quarry, are people like you and me. We work them pretty hard. They behave, they do their job. Aren't they of God's creation too?"

At the end of his Mass he gave them his special blessing.

"In nomine patris...ite, missa est!"

Avreau answered his door, surprised to see the mayor. They exchanged pleasantries, and Mr. LeCarte asked Avreau to arrange for Paul and Bienne to come to his farm during the week to pick stones. Then he moved on to his real reason for coming.

"Avreau, I have something else on my mind. We all know that the prisoners take things from those farms you march them by every morning. The priest just spoke about it in church. I ask you not to punish them for that. Of course, I ask that you not encourage it either."

Avreau eyed the mayor with new respect.

"Yes, I am aware of that. I have looked the other way, because they don't take more than they can use. I am relieved that you feel the same." Avreau paused, then continued in a low voice, "You see, I've been thinking what I would have done in Auschwitz, if I had had the chance."

"Yes. I know they treated you like an animal. I confess, when we hired you, I was not sure you were the right man for the job. You were very bitter. I sensed that you were looking for revenge. I worried that you forever would nourish hate, that you never could forget, forgive, and start over again. Yet something in my heart told me that beneath that roughness lived a gentle soul."

Avreau seemed confused at this revelation. "You are concerned about me, my life? But why..."

"Avreau, listen, I have watched you. So have others in our village. I want you to know we feel you are doing the right thing with our prisoners. I am a simple man, but I understand, we put up shields to protect our souls from being hurt. If we let that wall grow all around our hearts, it will stifle our life. I know people who have allowed this to happen. They are not happy. And that is so very sad because life can be so beautiful."

Shaking his head, Avreau interrupted, "Those are very big words. How can you know what is in me?"

"I don't, Avreau, I can't possibly know how much they've hurt you, how big the scar is you are wearing. But I can see it is healing.

"I never had the chance to talk to you about those terrible things. And that has bothered me, because to ignore them will keep us living in an awful past. When we talk about it, we have a chance to walk away from it into a new tomorrow. One day, maybe, we might be able to forgive. I think we must, or we will not make it.

"One more thing, Avreau. I want you to know that I trust you. I know you are a good man, that underneath you are a gentle, kind person. I would like you to be my friend."

Avreau stared at the mayor. Then tears streamed down the unshaven face, the first tears Avreau had let go since he had stood at the grave of his mother and father when just a boy of seven.

As the mayor embraced him, Avreau said, "You have believed in me when I didn't believe in myself. Yes, I would be honored to be your friend."

Johannes, who also knew some French, shared this exchange with the men during dinner that night, having overheard the conversation as he was washing his shirt—stolen off a clothesline near the quarry.

As Bienne and Paul walked down the road toward the mayor's farm, Bienne struck up a conversation with Paul.

"Where is your home? I know you have not received any mail since you came here."

Paul smiled resignedly. "I don't know where my home is any more. We used to live in Eastern Germany, close to the Polish border. My father was in the war *(I'd better not tell him he was an officer)*, but I don't know if he still is alive. I filled out the Red Cross questionnaire, but that's been a long time ago. So far nothing has come of it."

"I'll mention that to Mr. LeCarte when he comes back to town. How do you feel today? You look so much better, you know. A couple of weeks ago we all thought you would die on us. Even Avreau, who usually doesn't like anybody, even he worried. He told me that he felt sorry for you."

"Yes, I was sick all right. But to tell you the truth, I didn't really realize it."

"The morning after we came back from the doctor, I went to the church and got the priest to come and see you. He did his thing, you know with the oil and so. Perhaps that's why you made it."

"Do you believe in that?"

"Oui."

"But why did you do that for me, a German prisoner?"

Bienne's eyebrows wrinkled into a frown.

"I'm not sure, for I do not like you German folks. But, you...you are just a kid. It's different." Then, a smile crossed his face and a sly look came into his eyes. "There is something else you should know. One day, while you lay there sleeping, I had the clerk from downstairs—she is kind of a Gypsy woman—read your palm."

"You what? She read my palm? Funny, that reminds me of being back home, the day my mother once took me aside and told me a Gypsy woman had assured her that my father would come home unharmed. Of course, I was not to tell anybody about that. We were Catholic." Paul looked at Bienne, curious but a little afraid. "What did she say?"

"Well, she took her finger and followed your life line in both of your hands. And then she let out this little cry. 'Oh!' she said, 'I have not seen a pair of hands like this boy's in a long, long time. He'll never die. Really, look!' And then she showed me how your life lines go up right into your wrists. She was so astounded, she hurried home to tell her sister what she had seen."

"And do you believe in that too?"

"Oui, I do."

This man who does not like Germans tried to save my soul. Lord, you must be looking out for me! What else do you have in store for this prisoner?

The fall weather had turned misty. They strolled at a slow pace, as Paul's feet still were not accustomed to those "wooden canoes" they had to wear. Without any socks to cushion and comfort, Paul's feet had become blistered and had not yet healed.

Bienne did not want to tire Paul before they reached the farm, for he knew a difficult task awaited them—bending down to the ground for hours on end, gloveless hands thrust into cold, wet soil.

Farmland bordered the road on both sides, sectioned into small parcels of two or three acres. Apple trees, randomly and widely spaced, branched above harvested earth that yielded corn, grain, and potatoes in the summer. The fields were rimmed by high berms, topped with narrow-trunked, knobby willow trees planted closely together, giving the feeling of high walls fencing in the view.

The mayor's farmhouse sat back from the road by a good stretch. It looked more like barn than a house, with its long side parallel to the thoroughfare and no windows. They followed a rutted driveway that led toward the back of the building.

Bienne pointed at the rocks on the fields as they passed. It looked as though they had been strewn there on purpose, shiny as marbles from the rain, many, many more than Paul had imagined.

The yard was a mess, and the smell of manure hung in the air. Goose droppings were everywhere. Close to the house a couple of piglets dug in the mud. Countless chickens, brown, red, black, and white, blotted the scenery, making walking difficult. Black-and-white-blotched cows and their little ones, motionless and staring, stood by a large, long water trough fitted with a hand pump. Close by sat the outhouse.

A long shed extending from the right side of the house covered a great many sheafs of branches. These bundles, taller than Paul, were held together with twigs twisted into a thin rope. Every house, every farm seemed to have these strange bundles.

"Bienne, what are those?" Paul asked. "They look like the branches from those funny-looking trees growing on the berms."

"That is our firewood. We have no other trees around here that could be used for this purpose. The people harvest the branches frequently. That is why these trees have so many large knobs on their trunks. The more often we take their branches, the faster they grow those round burls from which again and again new growth sprouts."

Talking of trees made Paul think of another question. "Bienne, will we have a Christmas tree?"

"Oui, the one you will be making from a broom stick."

Paul wasn't quite sure if this was a joke.

The whitewashed building had several windows on its back side, affording a view of the backyard, field, and gentle rolling hills beyond. Splattered mud decorated the side of the house. Paul was to find out later that all of the farmhouse were built this way, with none of their windows facing the road, as those that did were taxed.

Bienne knocked on the Dutch door, and soon the lady of the house opened the upper portion. Paul could see she was a beautiful woman, much too young to be the mayor's wife. And she did not resemble what Paul imagined a farmer's woman should look like—she was not worn and weathered from the hard work of farming.

Mrs. LeCarte leaned out and greeted Bienne with astonishing friendliness, a kiss on this cheek and a kiss on that cheek, a kiss for the lips too. Opening the lower half of the door, she invited them in.

"Is this the young fellow who had been so very ill?" she asked Bienne. Evidently, Mr. LeCarte had mentioned Paul to her.

"Oui, this is Paul."

Barefooted she stepped forward, her feet sinking into the poop and clay mix, and took Paul in her arms. He felt the casual yet distinct pressure with which her hands held him. She then stepped back a little and looked him over. Her eyes lit a fire inside Paul. Bienne could see that Paul was blushing.

"Je suis Yvonne. Entrez-vous, mes amis."

In the anteroom, they cleaned their shoes and feet with straw and threw it outside. A goat came jumping after it. Yvonne then ushered them through the main entrance door into the house.

All the while, Bienne and Mrs. LeCarte chatted away. Paul marveled at the beauty of the French language. It reminded him of orchestrated music, the speakers singing it, their voices rising to peaks and gliding into valleys. Paul had learned some French in school, but what Yvonne and Bienne spoke was the dialect of Bretagne. Paul recognized a few words only, not enough to get the drift of what they were saying.

"Paul, Yvonne says for you to feel at home here. Have a seat at the table. We'll get a bite to eat before we start working."

Paul couldn't help but see that Bienne had a funny look on his face.

What's happening here? The way they look at each other goes beyond how a city employee should look at his boss's wife.

It would not be long before Paul would find out.

He sat on the bench at the table and looked around. The living room was huge, with two large windows that let in plenty of light. Long, dark beams held up the ceiling that had been in need of fresh paint for quite some time. The floor was not wood, but plain compacted brown loam. Only the giant fireplace and its hearth were bricked. The plasterboard covering the walls had warped into wavy unevenness. No chairs could be seen, but a box and a trunk sitting under one of the windows and topped with two hay-stuffed pillows were used for sitting. On either side of the fireplace a closed door guarded two rooms. A spacious pantry, partially hidden behind a colorless curtain, covered nearly the whole windowless street-side wall.

The room smelled of burned wood and smoked pork, though no fire burned in the hearth. It was barely warmer inside than outside.

Paul had a hard time keeping his eyes off Yvonne. She had stooped down to blow a pile of ashes into a hesitant little fire. Bienne, standing too close to her, helped with a hand blower—a folding leather bag squished between two flat pieces of wood, reminiscent of the accordion. Yvonne added more willow sticks from an undone bundle standing upright in the corner.

Bienne sat down across from Paul, listening intently to Yvonne's chatter.

"Mon chéri, it would be better if you do not come tonight. I am not sure when Leon will return from the convention in Rennes. I will let you know...some other night, or perhaps next week some afternoon." As she said this, she smiled at Paul. "You are sure, Bienne, that the prisoner does not understand our language? Oui?"

Paul could see the wrinkles on Bienne's forehead underlining his disappointment, but he did not yet fathom what was transpiring between the two. All he knew was that he felt uncomfortable.

Yvonne served freshly buttered galettes on an oval plate with a few slices of salted pork she took from a covered stone jar. Bienne took a pocketknife which unfolded into a long, sharp blade. He picked up a galette with his left hand and a slice of meat with his right, which he held between the ring finger and the little one.

Skillfully he used his fingers and the knife to cut off bits of meat and galette.

Paul couldn't help but stare, so different was it from German table manners.

Yvonne sat next to Paul, waiting for him to start eating, and then realized he had no knife.

"Mon Dieu, Bienne, I forgot. You don't allow your prisoners to have such a tool. Pardon, Paul. I get you one." From a drawer in a tall cupboard that decorated the wall opposite the fireplace, she fished out a knife. "Ici, I'll open it for you."

The knife was similar to the one Bienne used. He explained to Paul that this was the way people of the region ate their meals, with fingers and a pocketknife.

"It does the butter, the jam, chicken, beef, goat, the bacon and the fried eggs. What more do you want?"

The galettes were delicious. Paper-thin, made of flour and water, they were baked on an upside-down twelve-inch flat pan. Paul ate with a hearty appetite.

Yvonne was talking slower now, her voice low, sensuous. Here and there she paused. Her dark-brown eyes played with Paul. At times Bienne looked at Paul while he answered her, so he sensed that she was inquiring about him.

They finished the early lunch with a water glass of apple wine and then it was time to get to work.

The rain had stopped, but the wind was still gusty. Yvonne showed them two large baskets by the shed. They were made of thin willow twigs and had a handle at each side woven into the rim. The mayor had asked Bienne to gather the rocks and pile them along the edges of the field. Paul filled his first basket, but then found out that he could not lift it, so they divided the labor: Paul gathered the rocks in the baskets, and Bienne carried the baskets to the edge of the field, where he piled the rocks.

Paul found the bending down and up and down all day to be fatiguing. He slowed considerably as the day wore on. His mind drifted, and he tried to find a pleasant memory to soften the day. But this bending over, the pain in his back as he burrowed into the cold soil for rocks only triggered another time in his past he kept trying forget.

Fall break at school. Every boy in the Hitler Jugend had to spend their vacation helping the farmers bring in their potato harvest. Pomerania, a northeastern province of Germany, harbored potato fields so large that their furrows touched the horizons all around.

It was hard work for twelve-year-old boys. Their days went from dawn to dusk, rain or shine. Sundays brought no respite, for these, too, were working days. The harvest had to be brought in before it started to freeze. Early in the morning, the fog would be so thick that Paul could not see the end of his stretch that had to be picked clean of potatoes. Only the clicking of the hoofs from the horses that pulled the rotary rakes would tell him that he was not alone out there.

First he tried to pick by bending down to gather. After a day or so he no longer could stand it, so he went to his knees. Although picking was easier that way, the soil worked itself through his pant legs, and the skin of his knees became raw. Paul fashioned himself kneepads from a piece of a potato sack stuffed with hay and some string. It was not perfect, but it was better than the thin cloth of his pants.

One morning Paul had it up to his nose and above. He decided not to take that any longer and went to the train station for a ride home, arriving late in the evening. The door of the apartment house on Wasserstrasse #4 where he lived was locked. He rang the bell and after a while a window opened.

His mother looked down on him standing there in the dark.

"What do you want here? Why are you not with the others?"

Her cold greeting would pain Paul's little soul for some time to come. His mother was a harsh woman, living by an unforgiving set of rules.

Paul had turned to walk away, then hesitated, hoping that she would call after him. Maybe she had only said that because she was sleepy. But she did not call him back. Paul had no choice but to return to the station where he caught the early milk-train back to the potato farm.

Bienne's angry shout jarred Paul out of his reverie.

"Hey, man! We are not done yet. What are you doing, just hanging out? Mon Dieu! Get down and pick!" And for himself he added "you little bastard."

This son of a bitch is even worse than my mother. Jesus, all that was so long ago it seems. I hope that life has other things to offer than picking potatoes, going to war, gathering rocks in a foreign country and being guarded by a moron.

Now, now, Paul you are judging, you are looking down on people. We don't want to do that. No. This war was the second one your mother had to live through. If you want to have a better slice, okay, go get it! No one is going to bring it to you. But don't you forget, it won't be free of charge.

Paul could hear his inner voice cautioning him, and he knew he should listen. Whenever he tried to ignore it, he always regretted it afterward.

In the afternoon Yvonne brought some dry white bread and a jug of apple cider. They rested for a while. She wore an ankle-length skirt and a black, knitted throw that covered her shoulders and her head. Gentle gusts played with its folds.

Paul found her so beautiful, reminding him of the Madonna. Her complexion, unblemished, featured a soft face that could not belong to any woman who had worked in the fields and barnyard. Though the bulging shawl hid her lines, Paul could see the mounds of her small breasts. A cross hanging on a silver chain rested between them, but her fine hands wore no jewelry.

Darkness fell, and Bienne waved his flat hand by his throat, his sign to knock off and go home. They had made a dent. Many "marbles" were piled up along the berm. Mr. LeCarte would haul them to the backyard to stabilize his mud.

They left without saying goodbye. As they walked home, Paul could see that Bienne was angry.

"Anything wrong, sir?"

He took a long look at Paul.

"You know, the gypsy woman said something else after she had read your palms that day."

"What?"

"That you not only will live forever, you will also be a man with many women. I can tell, she is right. You twisted Yvonne's neck already. God, you are a prisoner! Just a short while back, you were our enemy. Some of us feel you still are. Mon Dieu, a boy, a boy wants to steal my woman, a German boy on top of it!"

"And how do you think I could have 'twisted' her neck with you staring at me every moment?" To mock him, Paul held up his cane with both hands and pretended to unscrew the handle from its shaft. "Like this?"

Bienne's face by nature was always red, and his eyes seemed too large for their sockets. The short haircut he gave himself on an irregular basis made his head, which apparently sat on no neck, look as though it were square. He usually wore a jacket at least one size too small. He had no ass and no hips, which was why he wore only bib coveralls that at one time had been of a green color.

When he was angry, he began to stutter, spit escaping his mouth as he shouted.

"B-b-boy, don't you shit m-me! You know darn well w-w-what I mean. I saw you operate. Your hands w-were shaking w-w-when she was sitting n-n-n-next to you. And I noticed her left hand not being on the t-t-table!"

Is he bluffing or did he really see her touch me under the table? I tried very hard not to make a funny face. But he is right, not only my hands were shaking.

Bienne, his sleeves so short, looked like a clown does in the circus as he waved his arms about. Paul mantled his laughs by coughing out loud.

"I am a prisoner. What chance would I have? I'd be shot in a second. No, you're just jealous, jealous of a German, a cochon!" Rubbing it in felt so good, for Paul had not felt any sense of power for a long time. "I, too, have eyes, you know. In my country guys like you don't look at their bosses' wives the way you did at Yvonne. But, rest assured, I am much too tired to...well, you know."

Bienne snorted. "I need to watch you, I can see that." He simmered down some, but when Paul tried to change the subject,

Bienne cranked it up one more time. "If she gets involved with you, I will kill you! So help me. She is my concubine, my girl, you hear? I don't know w-w-why I am t-t-telling you th-this. And don't you ever say anything t-t-to nobody! We are in love. It's too b-b-bad both of us are married. It is very sad. But you are still too y-y-young to understand all this."

Paul did not reply, but retreated into his thoughts.

How could Bienne possibly think I could mess up his mess, though I have to admit, Yvonne is a woman I could easily be with. It would be my very first time. I have never even seen a woman without her clothes on. I wager she could teach me a lot. Yes, Paul, you keep on dreaming. It isn't going to hurt you.

At "home" on the second floor his comrades were eating dinner already. Paul joined them.

"Well?"

"Well what?"

"Baby, give us the scoop, come on, let's have it. You got promoted to the mayor's deputy? No. He let you take his woman and... Come on, we need to know! It is important. If you want us to keep being nice to you, you better start spilling it."

They laughed, joked, teased Paul mercilessly because they liked him and were glad they had not lost him to the illness.

Sitting down to his empty bowl, he waited for Gruber, who was standing by the door next to the kettle, the ladle in hand.

"Hey, little boy, they told me not to feed you until you give us the details, tell us what fun it was to pick rocks."

Even Franzl had come up from the kitchen to listen. He had learned from Avreau that the mayor, in his late forties, had a very young woman for a wife. She was not from around here, but had come back with Mr. LeCarte when he had attended a farmer's conference in Paris the summer before. She was brand new, maybe pushing twenty-five, and came from a well-to-do family. The two of them had gotten married right there in Paris in the church of Le Sacré Coeur, against the wishes of her parents.

But the townspeople had come up with a different take. And right away they had a nickname for her.

"They call her Mona, you know like Mona Lisa, the one with the dirty smile on her face, hanging in the Musée du Louvre."

Avreau had said some vicious tongues in town claimed she really was from somewhere around Place Pigalle below Montmartre, where the ladies of pleasure plied their trade, certainly not from the high society enclave of Rue de Rivoli.

But since the mayor was going to run for reelection soon, Avreau concluded that the rumors could be of a political nature.

"Hmm, I don't know why all this expectation. Picking rocks sucks, you know that. If not, you will find this out next spring. We all will pick rocks then. Bienne told me."

"So you even have privileged information about our future. Wow! But there must be more, Paul. You want to sleep tonight? You want to eat before you go to bed? What about Mona?"

He enjoyed their exaggerated interest. Somebody must have filled them in. Paul decided to string them along a little.

"You really want to know? You're sure?"

"Quit stalling, boy!"

"You know I'm afraid if I tell you what really happened to me today, it is going to be *you* who will not sleep, and not only for one night, but a few! Okay, okay, I will share. You promise though, you won't say anything to my mother, Oui?"

Gruber whistled. "Look, she has taught him already to speak French! Maybe we should strangle him now? Wrap him in paper and light it..."

"Don't you scare him. He might run away like the rat did, and we'll never know."

Dieter, who had taken a liking to Paul and would keep the others at bay, put on a serious face.

"Now what could a little fart like you tell, never mind do, that possibly could excite us?"

"Dieter, she hugged me. No, no, just a kiss. Ja, on these lips, yes."

"You little bastard, you are teasing me. Tell me more."

He had them going and he was enjoying himself. But, the reality was very sad. These men had not been with a woman for more than two, three, maybe four years. Most of that time they could not think about physical desire, for hunger had shut down those thoughts and emotions, done away with any other physical want. Keep living, everything else can wait. They hardly dared to think of their own wives, because beyond sex, the longing for love, so much stronger, hurt them very deeply.

Their hearts ached because they could not be with their people, be home with their wives and children. They were denied humanity. Not enough that the war had torn their lives apart. Not enough that friends had been blown to pieces. No, all that was not enough. And many of them did not know what was waiting for them once the French would let them go. Some would never find their way back into normal life.

Paul did not know it yet, but his home was gone forever. He would never have a chance again to walk the streets of his city, talk to old friends, visit the house his family had lived in. Why? Was it because they were German, people of a nation that had committed inhuman crimes far worse than any war, any prison camp ever could have? None of those working in the Trois Boeuf quarry had anything to do with Birkenau. Still, Germany had to pay her debts, had to amend, had to console. But seeking revenge, turning prisoners of war into slaves, keeping them from healing, that did not seem to be the right answer either.

While Paul was gone to the farm, Franzl inadvertently had lit the fuse of the other prisoners' interest. Franzl and Avreau often talked, with Dieter interpreting for them both. But Dieter had not been present when Franzl talked with Avreau about the mayor's wife, so he repeated what he thought he had heard.

"She's a loose woman, sort of. He said that Bienne would know more about her."

That's why they hung on Paul's lips. Even if he had just seen her close up, it would have been enough of a picture for them to take into their dreams. And now it turned out that this little jerk may have done more than just look at her. No boy is too young for that. Somebody ought to warn him that if they caught him, he'd be history.

"Well, then we went to pick rocks, and..."

But no one was listening. He had lost them. They got up, busy caressing their imagination on their way to dream of unveiled beauty, fragrances, and the soft hands of a woman.

Paul ate his dinner and hit the straw. His back hurt like hell. He kept feeling the touch of her hand on his right thigh.

His return to the quarry brought hard work. Avreau had put him with the other five men who were making ballast from one-man rocks. Johannes, Barth, and Karl had hammered them from the big ones Dieter, Hugo, and Wolfgang were breaking off the terraced walls.

Paul sat on a flat slate with his legs folded in yoga fashion. Like the others, he wore protective eyewear, some wire mesh that had been pressed into a goggle-type shape. The device obstructed his vision, but kept out fine splinters that buzzed from his small rock hammer.

The six ballast-makers were positioned in pairs, opposite one another. An ever-lengthening pile of fist-sized rocks separated the men. Heinz Gutemann raked and heaped the broken stones into long trapezoidal mounds, resembling those in old graveyards, sitting about three feet high, three feet across the top, and six feet wide at the bottom.

Around noon, Gruber, Franzl, and Bienne would come with a lunch cart to dish out warm soup. Sometimes they would steal apples on their way and bring them too. The cart was Gruber's invention, with a cushion made from hay and wet loam held in place between the sides of the wheelbarrow with bailing wire. This same "machine" had taken Paul to the doctor when he was sick. The loam had hardened into a firm form exactly fitting the bottom of the kettle, and the carpenter in town had fashioned a wooden, tight-fitting lid after Gruber had shared a half bottle of Karl's apple schnapps with him. It was a nearly spill-proof system.

Franzl and Gruber enjoyed those trips for several reasons beyond bringing comfort and food to their associates. Bienne let them smoke his Lucky Strikes, swearing them to secrecy because the rest of the men had to roll their own from the awful, biting French tobacco. And, on the way back from the quarry, Bienne frequently stopped at the mayor's house, making the two cooks wait for longer than half an hour before he'd return. Sometimes he would bring a few goodies Yvonne wanted Franzl and Gruber to have: a piece of good cheese, smoked pigs' feet, a small jug of apple wine. Once in a while Gruber thought it necessary to pass some of those treasures on to Avreau, wrapping them in newspaper and putting them under the pillow on Avreau's bunk under the stairwell.

Franzl and Gruber would use the half hour outside the mayor's house to their advantage. One would stay with the kettle. The other man would scout around nearby farms and bring back a shirt or two or a pillowcase from the clotheslines, and always some eggs. Those hens loved to lay them in the dense undergrowth on top of the berms.

It was no small wonder that they wanted to leave the quarry the moment the kettle was empty. That return trip was their reward for driving the soupbarrow for so many miles every day.

After the rock gang had slurped up Franzl's cooking, each man napped wherever he happened to be. Paul usually got up from his hard, uneven, cold stone seat and stretched out on top of his pile. The hard rocks did not bother him a bit and he usually fell asleep in an instant. So deeply would he sleep, that it took Avreau sometimes two or three hard punches to wake him.

December 1945. Paul's first Christmas in captivity loomed on the horizon.

All but Johannes and Paul received some mail, a parcel, a letter, or a postcard. The Lehmanns received a large package. Their parents and their families had fled from Danzig before the Russians had stormed the city and were living with relatives in Cologne on the Rhine River. The Red Cross people had found them early on. Since the Lehmanns had a home address, no one knew why the French still kept them prisoners.

One night after a dinner of calf brains, Karl put some white candles in front of his bowl.

"Lehmann, how do we get a hold of a Noël tree?"

"Around here there are none. But if you really need to see one, you have to go and ask the mayor."

According to Bienne, the mayor's wife, whom the prisoners always referred to as Mona, had visited Paris and brought back a Christmas tree.

That was all Karl needed to know. After dinner, he tried to go downstairs to see Bienne, who was still talking to the Gypsy woman, but the upstairs door was already locked. Undeterred, Karl leaned out the window and yelled.

"Bienne! We need to talk!"

"Demain. Tomorrow."

"No, Bienne, not demain. Now! I want to come down to you, okay?"

Bienne felt a chill up his back. The prisoners knew so much about his ways. One word from any one of those PDGs could get him in a lot of trouble. Of course, the townspeople might not believe the Germans, but he could not be sure of that. He let Karl come downstairs.

When Karl came back up his grin stretched between his ears.

"You, Dieter, and you, Paul, come. We discuss my plan."

"Hey, why all the secrecy?" the others complained. "Aren't we a family?"

"Jesus, simmer down. It is a surprise for all of us. Now shut up!"

When Dieter heard Karl's idea, he laughed, shaking his head.

"Karl, I got to hand it to you. You are criminally smart. Okay, do you want to do this Paul? If not I can ask someone else."

Paul jumped on him. "Of course I'll do it! It is right down my alley. You know she already sat next to me. The rest ought to be easy."

"Hey, you," growled Dieter, "didn't you tell us the other night that you not only sat next to her but also kissed her? Yes?"

Paul's face turned crimson. He hadn't realized that Dieter had bought that line. Out loud he said, "As a matter of fact...naw, never mind," and hoped Dieter wouldn't press him for details.

A week or so before Christmas, the mayor, Avreau, and Bienne had a meeting in the conference room downstairs. They discussed among other things the weather and how it affected the production at the quarry. Several prisoners had come down with rather severe cases of the flu and the common cold. Though they were made to go to work anyhow, their output was minimal. The wind blew very hard, and daily rainstorms turned the mining operation into an extremely hazardous place to work. Gruber and Franzl no longer could ferry the noon soup because heavy gusts swayed the wheelbarrow all over the road, and most of the soup washed overboard.

The three Frenchmen decided that it would be in the best interest of the mining program and the health of Trois Boeuf's prisoners to shut down the quarry. The sick men would stay in their bunks and recuperate. The healthy men would help the mayor and other farmers with their work. Some would shred the partially fermented harvested apples; others would operate the big city-owned cider press the villagers used to squeeze the juices from their potent apple mash.

The press was housed in a special shed next to the school building in town. It had been destroyed by German SS troops during the war. But wine was important to this community, its exportation raking in a substantial income. So when the Germans were driven out, the town blacksmith, carpenter, and mason were immediately commissioned to fix the press.

Bienne explained the juice-to-cider-to-wine-to-liqueur production.

"First we harvest the corn, grain, and vegetables and whatever else we grow on the land. Later in the fall the apple trees drop their crop in plentiful quantities."

"But we saw apples on the ground rotting away. Did you have too many?"

"There never can be too many. No, we leave the apples on the ground on purpose, to let them ferment. Then the farmers mix them with earlier picked ones. This is what we call around here the 'art of blending,' and each farm comes up with its own taste. Around the middle of November the distiller arrives. He sets up his machine down by the creek, and people from as far away as Broons come and have their best apple wine evaporated into a heavy liqueur."

"Apple schnapps?"

"Yes. And it's a very potent type of gin. A lot of 'tasting' goes on during those distilling days. People are drunk for weeks on end."

Paul was among the ones who would go to Mr. LeCarte's farm. The flu so far had spared him, but sometimes he suffered from long coughing spells, bad enough to worry Bienne. He did not want Paul to get sick again. Yet he did not trust Paul, for he was sure Paul would steal Yvonne from him if he could.

Bienne was so in love with the mayor's wife that his judgment was clouded, blind to all reason. Later in life Paul would find himself in this same state, and he would think back to Bienne in Trois Boeuf.

It was easy to see why Bienne was so enchanted. Not only was Yvonne a beguilingly beautiful woman, Bienne endured a hellish life at home. He lived with a shrew of a wife, but no children to bring him joy. He longed to divorce her, but as a Catholic, he could not. At forty-five, he was a man without hope, knowing he could never turn things around.

Distraught, deceitful, feeling sorry for himself, he escaped to Yvonne. Paul wondered if Bienne asked himself how he could justify betrayal of his marriage vows, when his morality could not accept a divorce. And what about Yvonne's betrayal of her husband? How could Bienne be sure she wouldn't betray him as well? His jealousy of Paul showed that he was not.

The night before the new work assignments would go into effect, Johannes took Paul aside. He squinted at him, his clear blue eyes boring into Paul.

"Listen, you villain, I want to know what's up your sleeve. You are avoiding me, like a boy with a guilty conscience. Every night Dieter teaches you French. What for? And how did you manage to be chosen for the mayor's farm team?"

Paul ignored Johannes' question, turning the tables to probe the older man's secret.

"Johannes, when will you tell the others about your priesthood? They know there is something special about you. I knew it that first day, and later when you talked about forgiving. Perhaps it is possible for us to help you carry your load."

"Man, this war has ripened you in a hurry. I guess that's how you have come this far. Maybe on Christmas Eve I will read the story for all of us."

Paul nodded, and got up to leave. Johannes let him go without protest, but he could not shake the feeling that something was very fishy. Still, he gave Paul his "ego te absolvo" and threw in the sign of the cross for free.

Bienne seemed to be one of the stumbling blocks of their plan, and so Gruber and Karl decided a little blackmail was in order. They told him Avreau had assigned Paul to the mayor's farm project team, but he was not to interfere. In his charming way, Karl pointed to certain alternatives Bienne would have to face if he did. The rat had been trapped.

Gruber and Karl intentionally forgot to tell Bienne that the butcher in town had given them new information about Yvonne. He regularly delivered meat at the mayor's farm, and being a man who could have his way with any woman of his choice, and with a reputation to preserve at the bachelor's tavern, he had seduced Yvonne with little effort. In return he had to promise that he would arrange for Paul to service her.

"I want him to sleep with me," Yvonne had said. "He is young, a virgin. He needs to be taught. And I have the time and the expertise to do so."

The butcher had protested. "My God, he is a prisoner! It could cost him his life. And your husband would land in jail after he had beaten the living daylights out of you."

But Yvonne had shrugged. "Listen, garçon, I've handled far more difficult situations. Just do it or find yourself some other woman."

Karl and Gruber thought the man was full of bullshit. But then again, maybe he wasn't.

After dinner, Bienne yelled for Paul to come down.

"We have to go to the pharmacy and buy aspirin for Hugo and Wolfgang. They have a bad fever."

"Why do you need me for that?" Paul asked, but he already knew that Bienne would try to find out what Paul planned to do while at the mayor's.

"The Bayer Aspirin comes from your country. You know how to read the label." Although the aspirin was sold all over the world, these bottles had come with several other kinds of medicines the pharmacist had "acquired" from a German field hospital.

On the way back, Bienne took the scenic route.

"Paul, is there something you want me to know?"

That was polite.

"Oui, not want to, but I guess I have to. You tried to save my soul, and maybe you have, at least for a while. You held a candle while the priest gave me the Last Rites. I owe you for that. It's this simple: We prisoners need a pine tree on Christmas Eve. We know there is one at the mayor's house."

"Mon Dieu! You want to steal it? You can't..."

"Now, Bienne, that would be a stupid thing to do. How can you think we Germans are that dumb? No, we want the mayor to invite all of us to his house that night. Dieter has asked him, but he said no, since it is Yvonne's first Christmas at the farm, and they wanted to be alone."

"Jesus! Why did you people not talk to me about this? I couldn't get a tree, but I could have asked Yvonne to persuade Leon to invite you."

"We have come up with a plan. You see, you were right that miserable day we picked rocks the mayor's. I have since received a message from your girlfriend that she wants to see me sometime soon." At the sight of Bienne's reddening face, Paul held up a hand. "Bienne, simmer down. Remember what Karl had to say to you." It was odd talking to a guard this way, as though to a child. "While we are doing chores for the mayor, my comrades suggested that I undo the mayor's decision. We need to be around that tree for more reasons than one. I will do my best to have that happen, whatever it takes! That's the end of it."

Bienne was beyond stuttering. He looked like a gnome, with his square head topped by an oversized hat. What a miserable creature he was! He could not have been more hurt.

They returned to the duplex and Paul dispensed the medicine to the sick men. Dieter went through his last rehearsal in French, giving Paul a smile of approval when they finished.

"Paul, you have a gift for languages. Yvonne will understand you. Don't worry, and remember you will use your hands and other things to help you to get your message across."

Paul began to blush, thinking about what he planned to do. "Thank you for overlooking that I never...I haven't..."

"Hey, man, it's about time. I'm sure even your mother would agree."

"Oh, ja, you are quite a clown!"

The next day at the farm, the mayor gave out the work assignments. Paul drew the job of cleaning the sludge out of the long water trough.

The weather was clear but cold. The curtains in the farmhouse were drawn, but the chimney spilled good tidings. Any Santa Claus would have loved the smell of what Yvonne was preparing for Christmas Eve.

The prisoners joked and laughed, a happy bunch of people. All this felt like freedom to them, and Christmas still bore the magic of little surprises, of gifts, of warm flickering candlelight, and the fragrances of cookies and pine needles. There might even be some peace under that tree. Ja, there was something about that night in Bethlehem.

Paul felt apprehensive about what he would try to do if given the chance. He wanted to convince himself that Mary's child should look the other way today, for just a short while. He tried to figure out a way betrayal, Christmas, lust, and dishonesty would mix, would be acceptable under these circumstances, to lessen his guilt.

Karl came around the corner, his wooden shoes caked with manure.

"Paul, did you know they have a horse back there? A nice stallion that might just help us out later."

Paul looked up nervously. "I didn't. Do...do you think it's time?"

"Yes! Go!" came the command in a loud whisper as Karl worked on his wooden clogs. The ooze made a sucking sound as he slipped them off.

Paul brought a bucket of water to Karl so he could wash off all that shit. As he returned to the trough, he started to cough. It sounded hollow, coming from deep within. The coughing seemed to gain momentum, turning into a severe spell. Paul grasped the handle of the water pump for support and bent over, his body jerking back and forth until he finally fell to his knees.

Karl yelled for Mr. LeCarte. The door opened, and Yvonne sprinted toward Paul just as the mayor came around the corner and saw the boy wiggling in the mud.

"Allez chercher le docteur! Vite! (Call the doctor! Fast!)"

Yvonne hurried back into the house. The mayor's farm was one of the few that had a phone, an item Karl had failed to consider. But it made no difference since the butcher, proving to be true to his word, had slipped Yvonne a message outlining the coming events.

Mr. LeCarte and Dieter brought Paul into the house. Yvonne picked up the phone and went through the motions of calling the doctor, a bit of play acting on her part.

The men set Paul down on the bench by the table. His coughing seemed to be less urgent now.

"Okay, Paul? Oui?"

"Merci, Monsieur LeCarte, oui, okay."

Dieter was proud of Paul. His lessons had taken.

Yvonne poured some boiling water into a cup with apple blossom tea leaves that had been waiting for this very moment. The mayor asked him to breathe in the steam escaping from the mug. Paul inhaled deeply, and raising his head, he smiled and eased the tension by giving the okay sign.

Dieter translated that the mayor suggested Paul stay inside until after lunch.

"Oui, you must all eat with us," invited Yvonne.

Then she ushered the mayor and Dieter out the door, closed it slowly, and turned to Paul.

"Good show, my boy. You did well!"

"I beg your pardon?" Paul looked at her, perplexed. "Did I just hear you speak German? Maybe I'm sicker than I let on." She gave him a devious smile. "Hell! Yvonne, you speak German!"

"You're surprised, oui? Well, let's just say I learned it in school. But you're the only one around this town who knows of this secret of mine. Keep it! I know I can trust you."

"Mrs. Mayor, I just work here. I am a prisoner, a German one at that. Nobody would believe me anyhow. You are safe."

Yvonne quit smiling and leveled her gaze at him.

"It would be better if you'd cut the crap. What is your end of the bargain?"

Paul looked at her uncertainly. "I'm not quite following you. I was led to believe you wanted to seduce me. I have no problem with that except that the outcome could be an insult to your husband and to your lover."

"Only those two? Well, you are off some. But, never mind. The butcher implied you wanted more than just to bed me, yes? What would that be? I warn you, I do not do anything strange."

As Paul watched, she was unbuttoning the upper snaps of her blouse.

Paul, you remember the script? Follow it!

"You see, we people want to celebrate Christmas Eve the old-fashioned way, with a tree and candles and nuts and raisins. Avreau had told us if we wanted a tree, we would have to make one with a broomstick and apple tree branches."

Yvonne moved to the windows and parted the curtains a little to check the yard outside. Karl waved, letting her know that Mr. LeCarte had left for one of his fields. If he returned unexpectedly, Karl would scare the horse out of the barn, and the mayor would certainly run after it, giving them time to put things back together.

Yvonne came over to Paul, her every step laced with sensuous movements. She sat next to him, and Paul felt his body, his soul vibrate beyond his control. She staged in him an uproar of unprecedented enormity. He could not resist falling into this abyss. Its vortex sucked him over his boundaries, away from what they had taught him was right and good, and swirled him into gardens that had been forbidden until now.

He tried to continue with the negotiations.

"We would like you to change your husband's mind, to have him invite all of us on Christmas Eve. You see, we would feel more like we did at home, safer, not so lonely. For a short time we might even forget our bunk beds, the quarry, our wooden shoes. In return, we would sing for you and one of us would read the Christmas story."

She had moved closer. Paul could see that she was not wearing her bra and he felt himself go hard. Inside him, an argument raged between reason and passion.

Paul, listen to me! You don't have her answer yet. Don't you blow it!

Do you have any idea how I feel, what is going on inside me, how tempting all this is?

And you shouldn't now! You want to get shot? Do you want to spend Christmas, and not only this one but also all of those to come, in a wooden box surrounded by these dirty marbles and deep under the roots of an apple tree?

"Tell me what's in it for me. Non! I'll tell you what I want out of this.

"I think it will be easy for me to change his mind. I have long levers I can use. He is constantly afraid that I will leave him and run back to Paris. My pimp there wants me to do just that soon. But I despise the life around Moulin Rouge on Cabaret Street. It is not life, but a hollow existence thriving on perverted moralities. I thought I could forget, erase what I have done there, but I can't.

"This Leon, he is a good man, so fucking honest, so damned sweet. His values sparkle in the darkest night. They are so high up there. I cannot reach them."

Her story was by far more painful than the one written on the pages of Paul's life. Paul felt his organ go to sleep again. This was no time for sex, but a time for soul searching. He wished he could do something, could ease her burden. Everything inside him reached out to her. He could see that there were some things worse than hunger and death.

"But you can change, start out new, forgive yourself, be his wife, his woman. Bienne means nothing to you. You don't love him, yet that is what he wants from you so desperately. You think this is fair to him?"

Paul that is nice, very nice. But it's not on your script. What are you trying to do here?

Yvonne looked at him with surprise.

"Kid, you don't have a clue. Shit, why do I tell you all this? Forget it. Here is my deal. I want to teach you how to make love to a woman. I'd like to feel your hands all over me. I want you to kiss me, to caress me, tell me that I am beautiful."

Don't, Paul, don't.

"Yvonne, business first. Will we celebrate Christmas Eve here with you and him?"

"Oui, I can promise that. Now, let's get started on my part of the deal."

Now what? There was nothing in the plan about making love to her that same day. I'll have to write my own script.

"Yvonne, why me? I am a prisoner, a green one at that. I have never even had a girlfriend. I became a soldier when I was sixteen. You must have noticed when you touched my leg a moment ago, I came right into my pants. No, I'm not your man. Besides, I cannot do this to your husband. So help me, I cannot."

"Why you? I tell you why. You are clean. You are missing those infamous qualities of these egotistical hypocrites that only take, but never give. You are so young and yet you seem to understand what life is all about. I can sense that you have walked through hell. Pain has shaded your innocent eyes. When I saw you standing by the water trough this morning, I saw hurt all around you."

She got up to check the curtain and saw from Karl that all was okay.

"And that is why I want to give to you something precious, not as a whore, but as a woman that for once would like to do a good deed. I wish that you could understand that."

Paul saw tears clouding her eyes, and he reached for her hand. He thought of the mayor who had not spoken the truth about her past. Had he met her reaching out to him from the gutter? Had he taken her out of pity and then fallen in love with her? Will he be strong enough, tolerant enough to forget where she came from?

He kissed her hand, and while she held her blouse closed, she leaned over to him and let him kiss her eyes, her face, her lips. She embraced him, clung to him with an urgency that pierced his soul.

What a fool I was to judge her. I believe her heart is longing far more than mine. I could imagine her life, harder than mine and with less hope than I carry in me.

The alarm sounded, followed by Karl knocking and storming into the room. Her husband followed close behind. He could not help seeing the Yvonne and Paul close together as they hurriedly broke from their embrace.

"Is he all right? I did not see the doctor coming down the driveway."

Yvonne lowered her eyes. "Leon, I could not reach him," she lied.

He looked at her more closely.

"You are crying? Girl, why? I see he is shaking. Is he unwell?" He looked from one to the other, a look of concern rather than suspicion on his face. "What is it? What is wrong?"

Yvonne met his gaze then.

"Leon, yes, this boy is hurt, but not in the way you mean. His pain broke through and so did mine. We tried to console each other. Can you understand?"

Karl held his breath as he watched this drama unfold. Then the mayor did something that shook Karl all the way through his thieving shell.

Leon dropped his heavy jacket onto the earthen floor and went over to Yvonne and Paul. He knelt down and took both into his arms.

It was noon. Mr. LeCarte shouted through the open door.

"Venez, come, we have a drink. We eat. D'accord. We celebrate!"

Dieter, Barth, and Heinz came in after they had shaved the mud off their clogs. The smell of manure they could not leave outside. But soon the flames in the fireplace and a little smoke undid that. They took a drink from the bottle Leon was passing around. Paul took two heavy swigs of the thick apple schnapps, which warmed him up in a hurry.

The mayor was beaming, happy for a reason they couldn't have guessed. He got up and fetched Yvonne by her arm, catching her by surprise. The prisoners fell silent, waiting for the mayor to speak.

"C'est ma fille. I want you to meet her."

The prisoners looked at Dieter. "What did he just say?" Dieter, however, stood with his mouth open, shocked by the mayor's words. When he finally recovered, he said slowly, "Guys, Jesus! The mayor has just introduced his daughter to you."

The room became very still. Only the willow branches spoke as they crackled in the fire.

Finally, Yvonne broke the silence.

"Merci, merci mon pére! Oh, mon papa! Thank you, my father, thank you!" She sobbed with joy, relief, hope. "Thank you, my God, my gracious God! Am I finally home?"

The moment held them all spellbound. They were moved by her emotion, but confused too.

Seeing the questions in their eyes, the mayor spoke. "Why I did not tell our people the truth? You might ask that; I know the villagers will. They have a right to know, as do my friends. It will be difficult to talk about it, to explain. I might not ever have said anything, but when I saw you, Paul, my prisoner, my 'enemy' and my daughter cry together, here in my house, I knew things needed to be straightened out.

"But give me time, please. This hour for me is so filled with joy that I do not want to dwell on the past." Then, to break the tension, he called out in mock gruffness, "Girl, what are you waiting for? Is our lunch ready? Bon, let's eat."

Galettes, pork, butter, cheeses, hardboiled eggs, hot apple wine, turkey legs, and steaming peeled potatoes. Yvonne put on a record—dance tunes played by an accordion, a fiddle, and a trumpet. Parisienne!

Leon had broken out different makes of pocketknives, and Paul showed the others what to do with them.

The occasion was festive, like a reunion of a large family with many sons but one daughter. The three white-painted letters on their backs seemed to be part of their costume.

Karl asked Paul, "What about Christmas Eve? Yes? No?"

"Isn't there any way of turning you off, even only for a short while? Man, what better Christmas do you want?"

At the end of the day, Bienne came on his bicycle to pick them up. The mayor offered him a drink. He took it, his eyes drilling into Paul's as he drank. Yvonne had disappeared into another room and did not greet Bienne.

Shortly before Bienne arrived, Dieter had sworn his people to an oath.

"We never talk about this. Do we understand one another?"

Yes, they would keep this secret, hold it, and protect it like it was a precious stone.

On the way back the wind blew through their threadbare coats. They marched without their usual chatting. Only the clatter of their wooden slippers penetrated the swishing of gusty air. They had just witnessed life in a different lane, a lane they had been bounced off and kept from. Yet something comforting had happened. They took the glimpse of family love they had seen as confirmation that the lane was still intact, being used, and they, too, would walk it once again.

The next morning Bienne got a phone call from the mayor.

"Have the prisoners stay in their rooms. Lock them up and come out to my house. I need to speak with you."

Such a summons threw a scare into Bienne, triggered by his guilty conscience. What if...

He biked to the mayor's, but was not gone long before he returned. The wind had spanked his face into the reddest color they had ever seen on him. His voice sounded hoarse as he explained his errand.

Mr. LeCarte had let him know that the prisoners would not have to go back to work until after Christmas. Bienne, too, could have a holiday, so he could celebrate the Holy Night at home with his wife. They cheered and hollered and stamped the floor.

Bienne interrupted their joyous noise.

"Oui, I almost f-f-forgot! You jerks, all of you have been invited to his house tomorrow night. He'll light the t-t-t-tree for you." The mayor would pick them up the next day around noon, taking complete responsibility. Bienne was not to worry. "Don't you d-d-dare to run away! We'll shoot you on s-s-sight!"

He *was* mad. And a few of the prisoners thought they knew why. But they could not have known what else Bienne regretted to have been told. He wondered for a long time if Paul could have had anything to do with it. He swore if that boy, that prisoner, that *German* had his hands in that, he would undo him, yes.

Yvonne had asked him not to come by anymore.

"Try, please, try to make a new life together with your woman."

They had brushed and brushed their hands until all the black had disappeared from under their fingernails. Wolfgang had given the men a shave with the razor blade Karl had borrowed from next door, the kind that needed to be drawn over a wide leather belt to be sharpened.

Karl had found a pair of scissors in the teacher's bathroom cabinet, and Hugo, who had boasted that he was good at cutting hair, set up shop. Paul volunteered his head to be the first for Hugo to demonstrate his skills.

Hugo started out by explaining that he had always cut his children's hair, though he admitted that his career had only lasted for a couple of years. His brother Dieter filled them in as to why this moonlighting had come to a sudden halt.

One Saturday morning, Hugo's clippers had slipped and accidentally sliced a piece off his son Bruno's left ear. Screaming bloody murder, the boy ran to his mother, trailing blood all over the not-so-old carpet. Hearing Bruno's screams, a neighbor called the fire department to the rescue.

The firemen arrived moments later, saw the bloody apron Hugo's wife was wearing, and assumed she was the victim. The medic forced her down on the ground and pulled up her skirt to find the wound the "burglar's knife" had made. By this time she, too, was screaming to high heaven. Siren blaring, a police car joined the scene, which did not help the situation. Neighbors peering out from their blinds expected to hear shots any minute.

The medic, not finding what he was looking for, finally gave up, but took with him a bloody lip.

"Dieter, you are awful close to being called a dirty liar."

"Fellows, bear with me. The best part is yet to come. The policeman, being a Catholic, suggested the family pray. In so many words he implied that Jesus might stop by and put the slice back onto Bruno's ear. The man mentioned that the carpenter had done this once before to one of his apostles in the garden of Gethsemane. But, of course, that had happened quite a while back."

"You can see why I hate my brother," complained Hugo in mock anger. "Have mercy on me. I guess I will be suffering Bruno's pain and disgust till the day I am gone."

"Well, Hugo, my friend," said Paul, "that could be soon. Even if you only nick my tender scalp, you will be walking around here playing ghost. Do we understand each other?"

Much laughing, clapping, and stomping accompanied this banter. They were in a festive mood. They giggled like school girls in an ice cream parlor.

While Paul was being sheared, Gruber came along and planted himself in front of him. He fixed his sight at about Paul's hairline, and said, "It is good that you did not bite the dust, kid. Thank you for the tree." Then he pulled Paul down and hugged him, his eyes fixed at the lightbulb dangling from the ceiling all the while. Given that Gruber could not look anyone in the eye, the rest of the group was astounded that he could hug someone.

At noon the haywagon drove up. They were ready. Everyone had done his best to look sharp, clean, respectable. The work had gone on nearly all night. Dieter had asked Bienne not to turn off the light at the regular hour of seven, and despite his dismay about this whole situation, he obliged.

Paul had mended his torn pants, working late into the evening, and had scraped the maplewood clogs until they shined.

Using pieces cut from barely recognizable old shirts Franzl had collected to clean his kitchen, Heinz had tailored sixteen narrow ties just long enough for the men to tie a double knot holding them in place. They looked good with those shreds around their necks.

Hugo had shared good-smelling soap he had been sent in a large Christmas package from home.

They were filled with expectations, just like children at this time of the year. For some of the prisoners it was their third Bethlehem Night behind barbed wire.

As they filed out the door, Johannes brushed their fronts and backs to clean off the ever-present straw splinters from their bunks.

The two-wheeler, drawn by Mr. LeCarte's stallion, teetered its way through the village. Pictures came into Paul's mind from his history class years ago of citizens carted off to the guillotine in just this kind of haywagon.

During the previous week's town meeting, the mayor had asked the villagers to think of the prisoners while they were prepared for the Christmas feast. He had appealed to them to share their good will. Now, as the cart passed the modest homes, women came to the road with little packages and small bundles of clothes. The cart stopped often. The men cheered, waved their hands, blew kisses and shouted, "Noël, Noël! Merci, merci!"

Yvonne welcomed them excitedly as they turned into the yard. Mr. LeCarte jumped off the wagon and got a big hug from her. Turning to the gang that was getting down from the cart she almost shouted her greetings.

"Mon Dieu, you guys look nice! Clean-cut kids and older men, what a mixture. Did you bring Paul? Where is he? Did you lose him on the way or did some other girl snatch him from the wagon? I will have to break her bones!"

Paul hid behind tall Franzl as Dieter pretended to be concerned.

"We had to make him walk. He had not been a good boy..."

"The hell, I am always a good boy. I don't know how to be bad. Yvonne, these people don't like me. Come, be nice to Paul!"

As she opened her arms to him, Paul fell victim to her charms.

How beautiful she is! I think I need to kiss her. Am I ever glad that Bienne is not around. And there is no script covering this evening!

As the other men went inside, Paul hung back to embrace Yvonne. She looked into his blue innocent eyes, and holding his head with both of her fragrant hands, she said, "I missed you. I am so happy that you are here with me tonight." She hooked her arm under his, and they followed the others in.

Mr. LeCarte wore a spanking new, white shirt. A gold-framed sapphire closed his collar. Red suspenders held up his black corduroy pants. Unlike on other occasions, this afternoon his hair was combed. He walked in wooden shoes painted light blue, with a yellow rose carved into each side of them.

Yvonne had prepared the room for this festive event. The rough-hewn tabletop was covered with a white cotton cloth and a blazing fire streaked dancing shadows over the dim ceiling. Two large candles, one on each sill, mirrored themselves in the wavy glass of the window. Fresh straw covered the earthen floor. Though the room wasn't all that large, the eighteen people had ample space to move.

Leon had brought in several bales of hay to act as benches to seat his guests with comfort.

Yvonne welcomed them all, saying, "Come, please, feel at home." Then she hesitated, covering her mouth with her hand. "Oh, I'm sorry, I wasn't going to use that word. I just meant for you to feel good and safe, cozy and warm. This evening we share with you our food, our house, and the peace of this night."

The men had found places to lounge. Some had taken off their jackets. Yvonne poured apple wine into clay cups, a smile on her face for each man. The mayor mingled with the crowd. He shook hands, patted shoulders, told some jokes. He seemed to be enjoying himself, smiling and laughing.

The French had always been shortchanged in German textbooks, with the possible exceptions of their artists. Peasants, plebeian farmers, commoners, European troublemakers—that was what the arrogant German middle class thought of its neighbor.

Mr. Schulze, my teacher at home in Schneidemühl, should meet the mayor. I would have to walk for quite a stretch in my town to find a person like Leon. What makes us Germans so conceited, so uppity, so fucking overbearing? Paul! It is Christmas time. Let it go. There is enough peace and compassion in this room to wrap around the world many times over. Let it go.

Wolfgang chatted away with Gruber and Barth when the three suddenly looked at each other and jumped from their seats, excitedly waving their arms. Something had just rung their bell, and very loud.

"Yvonne, hey, beautiful! Young lady, over here!"

The others turned to look at them, perplexed.

"Yvonne, I just realized, you have been speaking in our language! This whole time, I understand all you say, yet I do not ask myself, hey, how come? You speak German? How..."

Everybody began talking at once.

"How could we not have noticed?"

"Dense, we have become very dense!"

"I must be blind in both ears!"

"This is great! This really frosts the cake!"

"Yvonne, you barely have an accent. Where did you learn to speak our language so well?

Yvonne laughed, but demurred. "Another time I will explain. Not today."

She put out some food for the men to nibble on, then went to the record player, cranked the arm, and lowered the needle.

"Stille nacht... (Silent and holy night...)" They had known this song since they were born, had sung it so many times, yet tonight it sounded new like never before. Each word had a new meaning, carried new messages. Each chord reverberated deeply through their longing souls. Paul, the youngest among them, couldn't stop the tears running down his face, and Johannes put his arm around him for comfort.

Mr. LeCarte brought a wooden box from the pantry and opened it. Cigars—dark, aromatic, long cigars! He personally offered them around and quite a few men took one.

"Thank you, papa mayor, thank you." He smiled at the "papa." Franzl stood by the fireplace with a flaming willow twig in his hand lighting cigars right and left. Soon blue smoke wedged itself between the smells of straw, wine, cheese, bread, and roasted meat.

Every so often Yvonne's eyes searched for Paul. He could feel it. Her fleeting gesture found him like the beacon of the lighthouse that guided lonely ships to shore. He would look at her in awe time and again.

You are so very beautiful! Am I in love?

Her smile told him that she had read his mind.

Yvonne wore a long flaring skirt of maroon velvet with a short matching vest over her beige silk blouse. A crocheted brief scarf covered her dark hair which she had loosely teased into some sort of a ponytail. Her feet were dressed with comfortable street slippers, their red leather blending softly with the velvet. The small, golden cross dangling from her silver chain sparkled whenever the flirting light of the flames caught it. Standing there on the straw-spread loam she resembled more a Madonna than a woman from Trois Boeuf. No, the lady standing before him had just returned not from the fields, but from an afternoon stroll down the Champs Élysées in Paris.

Paul saw Papa LeCarte's proud smile. She had come to sit with him at the table and they talked and laughed happily. Several times he took her hands and put his lips to her fine, long fingers.

Yvonne motioned to Dieter to come over to them.

"Monsieur, Dieteur, s'il vous plaît," she said, then translated for her father. "Papa asks that you light the candles on the tree. It is a special moment for my father, and for me. Long time ago, when Mama still was with us, our family, my brother and sister and my grandmother, we would gather around the tree, and he would light the candles, then read the story of Joseph and Mary and the shed near Bethlehem."

Dieter, honored by this request, took a branch from the fire and lit the dozen or so candles on the tree. The men gathered closer to the tree, admiring the symmetry of its branches, which Evonne had decorated with tinsel and stars she had made with thin twigs.

Heinz, Franzl, and Barth, started to sing, "Oh Christmas tree, oh Christmas tree..." and the other prisoners joined in after clearing a few rusty bars. The song died, but they remained spellbound. Only the crackle of the fire could be heard.

Johannes stood up and walked slowly to the end of the table. He bowed to Papa LeCarte and Yvonne, who sat on the old chest by the window.

"Mr. Mayor, Yvonne, we thank you for inviting us to this celebration. It was very kind of you, especially since I'm sure some of the villagers will criticize you for doing so. But you show us the true spirit of Christmas.

"Christ, Mary's son, was born on this night in Bethlehem almost two thousand years ago. You all know the story, we've heard it many times. We all are touched by it tonight; even the ones among us who are still searching for their God feel moved.

"The flames of these candles, our memories and expectations, awaken us and brighten our hope for a new, better tomorrow. Our world today is no longer as simple as it was when the shepherds saw that bright star. Nowadays it seems harder to see Christ. Our own suffering and that of so many others, the slaughter of men and women and children fog our view."

Johannes looked around the room. The straw, the fire, the simple furniture and the shabbily clothed crowd—all this was much like the very place where Mary gave birth to her son. He went on.

"We might ask what in hell is there to celebrate? This Jesus, where is He? Where was He when we stepped over so many dead people as we walked through those hunger camps? Where was He when His own kinsmen suffocated in gas chambers, when His brethren fell to ashes? Where was He?"

Johannes hesitated. "My saying *'Friend He was there then and He is now here with us'* probably is not going to cut it. I cannot give you the answer. Myself, I am not humble enough to understand. I left the priesthood because I could not believe any longer that Bethlehem and Golgotha were more than just stories."

Barth shot up from his seat.

"Johannes? Are you making this up? You are a priest?"

The room broke into commotion. Doubt. Anger. Incredulity. Him? A priest? Some wanted to confess to him, others thought him a traitor. Johannes a fallen priest? What else could the Lord have in store for them? Did He have to break everything into pieces, even His own messenger?

Paul, though he had known it, was moved beyond expectations.

Johannes, you are a tall man, I think taller than any one of us here. Your God at this very moment must take you back, must forgive you. Yes, that is what we need to celebrate tonight!

Paul got up and clapped for attention.

"Johannes! You are a great person. Forget the Wise Men, we celebrate your rebirth tonight and tomorrow!"

Yvonne was the first to embrace Johannes, followed by the rest, much like a team falling on its hero who had shot the winning goal.

Cigars were lit again, the earthen wine cups ran over, and tongues wagged loosely, creating a joyous din.

Johannes struggled free, held up his hands and yelled into this tumultuous scene, "People, prisoners of Trois Boeuf! Please, my friends, I've not finished, hear me out!" After a few minutes of frivolity, they quieted down and once again gave him their attention. "Here is my Christmas message, my wish for all of you and for myself. Nobody can bring God to us. We ourselves must search for Him, want Him and love Him. Keep Him and never let go of Him!"

He then took four candles, three in his right hand, the fourth pressed against his chest.

"I still have the power to bless you." The candles flickered and dripped as he made with them the sign of the cross. "In nomine patris...Lord come, be here with us, forgive us, and help us now and tomorrow." There wasn't a one who did not put in his "Amen!"

Papa LeCarte offered Johannes a cup filled to the brim, then he raised his own.

"I never knew that Christmas Eve could bring so many presents to me, so many new friends into my life. God bless you all." He bowed and then drank from his cup.

The people in that room would part from each other before the new year 1946 would finish its course. Some would escape. Two would die. The rest of them would be made to work in the underground coal mines in western France. They would never see one another again, but all would, as Paul still does to this day, remember this Christmas Eve in Trois Boeuf.

It was late. Heinz licked his fingers and squeezed the wicks. Franzl helped to put away the food. The good time had worn them out and the wine had made them sleepy. Gruber and Hugo, per the mayor's instructions, cut the hemp strings and spread the bales out over the floor. They would all sleep right here in this room tonight.

Yvonne whispered to Paul, "Viens, come, I want you close by me. I'll bring you a pillow." The glow from the hearth faded into the dark as she pulled her quilt over the both of them.

The weather had turned nice again. Spring was to come early this year. Soft winds floated new rumors, new hope through French prison camps.

"The government is working on a huge prisoner discharge plan that will have everybody home by October." October, maybe, but what year?

The Trois Boeuf quarry gang kept marching, month after month after month. Before they would leave Trois Boeuf, they would have broken some 96,000 cubic feet of fist-sized basalt ballast, creating a towering pile that weighed 3,000 tons. Road-building contractors would use the rocks sometime in the future to repair streets and country roads throughout the village district.

Nothing much changed at the "duplex." The honeymoon had ended right after Christmas. Avreau had returned from his vacation, unsoftened by the holidays. He drove the gang as hard as ever, upping their daily production requirement. Still, Paul thought Avreau seemed a little friendlier, that he did not shout quite so often.

The crew became more proficient, having learned how to split rocks using the basalt's natural fractures. Paul considered himself a professional hammerer, having developed a technique that harnessed the inherent spring of the stick to make it work for him instead of vice versa.

The gang's outfits looked as worn as their faces did. The menu, lunch or supper, never changed beyond calf liver, hog ears, pig brains, and lungs from slaughtered cows.

The prisoners took fewer words to communicate. Smiles no longer lit their faces beyond brief moments. New jokes were hard to come by. Laughter was rare and tempers were short. Dieter had to intervene quite often.

Bienne and Avreau let it be known that acquisitions from clotheslines would no longer be tolerated; instead, punishment, such as working all day without food, would be imposed.

They all wore their hair much longer now. Johannes had let his beard grow to cover his entire face, which fit his new nickname, "Jez," their word for Jesus. Johannes had become their counselor to whom they brought their heavy thoughts, their hopes, their disappointments. Dieter, too, consulted with Johannes before he announced any important matters.

The memory of the last Christmas began to fade. The shine of that evening had drifted beyond their reach. The ugly fact that they still were prisoners foamed to the surface and devastated their hearts.

Occasionally there were brighter moments. One Saturday afternoon Paul picked nettles for dinner, remembering Franzl's promise that if he breathed out when he grabbed the nettle's stem, they would not sting him. But, of course, they did.

I knew he was pulling one on me. Look at my hands! Feel how they sting! I will mix some of these nettles in with the straw in your bunk, you bastard.

That evening when Gruber dished out the nettles, he mentioned that they should all thank Paul for this delicacy. "Oh, by the way, Paul, Franzl is deeply dismayed. He remembers telling you about the breathing procedure, but he feels terrible at having forgotten to mention that it only works when gloves are worn at the same time."

The rest of the gang had a long and much-needed laugh at Paul's expense, and it took weeks for him to live it down.

Paul kept praying the rosary every day walking to and from work. He asked Mary to take care of Wally, Emus and Ernst, he prayed for the souls of Bauer and the dead man who let him have the boots, he wished for Wolfgang to heal from the loss of his wife who would never come back from Birkenau.

Sometimes Paul would close his eyes and reincarnate the night under the warm quilt, when he fulfilled his part of the bargain with Yvonne. She had given herself, heartening him to take the pleasures she was offering. He had been shy at first. But she unshackled him, letting him realize the intense delight their colliding bodies and souls unleashed. She asked him to touch her breasts.

"Paul, you kiss them..." Timidly he stroked her back. "Yes, I want you to. Here, I help you..." She led his hand up between her thighs and made him gently fondle her mound. Raising her hips she urged him to explore her wet inside.

"Yes, Paul, I want you to touch me all over. Yes...yes..." He trembled. She took him between her two hands and drew him in, slowly and deeply. She paced him, let him rest in the cradle between her legs, and then kissed him back to take more and more of her.

Paul had seen Yvonne only once since that night. The gang had been on its way home from the quarry. She had waved back at him and blown a kiss. No red slippers or velvet vest, just a cotton skirt and wooden clogs. Elegant? Yes. And beautiful in a simple way that told Paul she had left Paris forever. That made him feel good.

One day, Paul sought out Johannes.

"I want to ask you something. Do you have a moment?"

Both lay in their bunks, and Paul had leaned over the frame to look down at Johannes.

"You know that Yvonne and I made love that night on Christmas Eve."

"Yes, the people sleeping next to you said they heard you talking in your sleep. Karl..."

"Johannes, I want to be serious about this. It was the first time in my life that I had come so close to another person. No one ever told me how beautiful life is at a moment like that. You people taught us how sinful, yes, how dirty this act of love is if it is done out of wedlock. You inserted guilt into our minds, shameful feelings. To frighten us you invented the story about the snake and the apple, and dramatized God's rage and punishment.

"Paul, slow down a bit..."

"I am not talking about you, Johannes, but the Church which you still seem to represent. Don't tell me that making love is only pure when it is done to make children. I have been mulling this over and over for some time. God installed powerful forces in both woman and man, just to be sure they would keep making love. Why do your Cardinals brand this first deed of love between the first man and woman as something bad? You call it sin. Worse than sin, it's the "Inherited Sin." You think that God gave us something that was dirty to start our lives with? Is that what you are saying? God is not stupid. Never ever would He have thrown them out of his garden. You did, and you keep doing it. Why?"

Johannes did not answer right away, but the thought went through his head that, though Paul was unorthodox, and perhaps even a heretic, he was closer to Him than Johannes had ever come. He scratched his bearded chin and got up. Leaning against the neighbor's bunk he looked at Paul for some time.

"I cannot answer your question."

"Paul sat up, his feet dangled over the sideboard.

"Well, try this one for size. As much as you advertise grace and faith, so do you plant the seeds of fear into your flock. You are herding your sheep with dogs that answer to names like Hell and Guilt.

"What did they tell you when they threw you out? Might they forgive you, let you back in after you say fifty thousand *Our Fathers* for penance? Johannes, your clergy wedged itself between people and God. Your confessionals block their way to Him. I know we will be forgiven whether man says so or not."

Paul jumped down and grabbed Johannes by his shoulders. "Yes, He, God, is forgiving us. That I believe. He will again and again and again."

Two of the mayor's cows had calved. The old hog had brought on another litter of some ten naked pink snouts. The fields sprouted with new growth. The apple trees blossomed, their heavy fragrances filling the air with anticipation. Summer was getting closer.

The villagers committed to four more years of mayor LeCarte's reign. During one of his town meetings after his re-election, he explained why he had not told them the truth about Yvonne.

"My fellow citizens, at the time I could not have told you about Yvonne and myself even if I had wanted to. My daughter had joined our underground movement. She was taught to speak German and was sent to the streets of Paris to go to bed with ranking German military personnel. When the Germans surrendered the city, the Allied Forces used her as a spy in Russian occupied zones. Last year in May I received a telegram directing me to come to Paris to meet 'someone close to me.' I cannot tell you how moved I was when I saw my daughter, Yvonne, sitting in this sidewalk café at the Les Halles. She ran to me and both of us were shaking with unspeakable joy. 'You are alive! Yvonne, my child, I love you.' I screamed so loud that the bystanders first wondered and then began to applaud.

"She was going to come home with me, though not yet as my child. She was to retain her cover as prostitute. The story they had invented was that I would fall in love with this street girl and we would get married. I did not mind. I would have done anything to get her off this Rue de Paris. In time they would 'bring her home.' She would be safe then. If necessary, they promised to help me straighten things out around here."

Some in the room felt deceived. Before his death, the mayor's father had lived in Trois Boeuf at the farmhouse, but Mr. LeCarte and his family had lived in another village. He alone had moved to Trois Boeuf to take over the farm after his wife had died and his two children had grown and left home, the son off to war, the daughter to fight in the French Underground.

Someone in the back got up and asked, "LeCarte, we did not know you had children. What else do we not know about you? Are you a man to be trusted?"

The city clerk, the gypsy woman, raised her hand.

"Louis, you sit down. All of this is really none of our business. Understood? Mr. LeCarte is a good man, and a good mayor. We all agree?" The rumble in the hall indicated reluctant concurrence.

In August, 1946 the city council discussed the possibility of dividing the prisoners into small groups of two or three to have them help with the harvest. Some men had not come home from the war. Farmers tried to help those in need of additional hands, only to see their own fields being neglected.

There was, of course, the risk of flight. Other villages around had experienced prisoners escaping under the same conditions Trois Boeuf had in mind. But those incidents were rare. The distance to the next friendly border was rather great and it was said that the French people were highly suspicious of strangers walking their streets and roads. Still, escaping prisoners would disguise themselves as nuns and priests, even as French soldiers. One day in the future Paul would leave that way.

Mr. LeCarte pointed out that good food, some new clothes, and a comfortable place to sleep could be offered as incentive for the men to stay and work.

A few days after the meeting, Bienne met with Dieter and laid out the plan. Dieter assembled the men after supper to discuss it.

"I do not know when they will let us go home. Some day they will have to. Until then I suggest we make the best out of our stay here. We probably are not cut out to milk cows or slaughter pigs or run a plow, but look, none of us knew how to break rocks. We learned and we are good at it now, aren't we?"

The men discussed the matter for some time.

"What have we got to lose?"

"At least the work could not be as dangerous and hard as it had been in the quarry."

"Being with people who need us would be a welcome change."

"We really have no say in the matter."

The gang agreed, and with that to look forward to, their mood switched to an upswing again. Better times were ahead of them. Living at a farm with people other than their bunk friends, and away from Bienne and Avreau, meant being one step closer to freedom.

Only Gruber and Franzl were not as pleased as the others. The men had always been jealous of them, yes even suspicious. Swinging a wooden cooking spoon never would come close to hammer-milling granite-hard rock. Occasionally, one of the men would ask Dieter to rotate the duty of preparing their meals. But he felt it would not have been in the best interest of the gang and managed to avoid it.

Poor Gruber, never confident, always wondered whether the men were friendly to him simply because he determined how much meat he dished out with the soup spoon. He asked himself often whether or not they counted him as a friend. Franzl felt that cooking for them gave him a certain amount of control. He had seen himself a centerpiece, a team member of importance. Now, these two would lose their status and return to being as common a prisoner as the rest of them. And there were a few soldiers around the table who enjoyed the thought of the two cooks finally putting their asses to the grindstone.

Sunday night the mayor showed up with Avreau and Bienne. Johannes and Hugo, Gutemann and Gruber, Karl, Dieter and Wolfgang, Franzl and Barth, were dispatched to farms around the village. Hans, Jacob, Ortwin, Leo, and two other prisoners were assigned to work at a larger homestead nearby.

Paul waited to hear his name called. Then a thought struck him.

Ah, they'll send me home. Sure, I'm the youngest.

Not home, as it turned out, but almost as good.

"Mr. LeCarte wants you to work at his farm. You think you can handle that?" Avreau asked. He couldn't help glancing over at Bienne, whose fingers behind his back were making something other than the okay sign. Avreau started to laugh out loud, then turned it into a cough.

Paul stood there in awe.

I am going to Yvonne's? My God, what is it you want from me so bad that you bribe me with this job?

Across the table, Johannes shook his head and said to the group, "Friends, we will lose this child for ever. His soul will slosh in sin. Dieter, should you not intervene?"

Since Christmas, Dieter and Paul had become close friends. Paul thought of him as his big brother, as though he had found a new Wally, another Ernst. He shared with Dieter his thoughts, his longings, and the pain of not knowing where his family was.

Now Dieter shot back at Johannes, "Why? Do you want to work at the mayor's farm? You know 'they' might not ever take you back after that!"

"No more blessings for you, man!"

The room emptied as people went to pack up, but Barth hung around. Deadly serious he said, "Paul, you think the quarry was hard on you!" He could not help chuckling. Dieter and Johannes grinned widely, showing their teeth. "At least you had the night to rest! Man, I do envy you. Keep me posted, will you? Details, I need details."

Another flip of the finger, this time from Paul, and not behind his back either.

Yvonne taught Paul to milk the cows. Mr. LeCarte showed him how to trim the willow burrs, sort the cut branches, and tie them into bundles. The horse liked Paul. It nudged him when he brushed him down at night after work. One day a butcher from Broons came to slaughter one of the pigs. Paul watched how he cleaned the gut and prepared it for stuffing. Yvonne had been cooking, mixing, and spicing sausage meat all day long. At the end of the day, the butcher loaded some meat into the trailer he pulled with his bicycle, to be brought back after having smoked it at his shop.

The LeCartes owned a buggy, and Leon taught Paul to harness the stallion and make him trot around the yard. From then on Paul drove them to church each Sunday. Yvonne and her father would sit in back like royalty. Paul would show off in his clean white shirt, the sleeves partly rolled up, the wind ruffling his long blond hair, which Yvonne loved. He sat up straight, holding the reins like a jockey does, snapping his short, black whip in the air every once in a while.

Before they left for the first time, Yvonne had taught him a few words the horse had been brought up with.

"Droit, gauche (right and left), and huee and aarrrr. Mind you, never say 'huee' to me."

"And why not?" said Paul to tease her, then took off for the back of the stable as she came after him. Their horseplay was cut short by Leon's whistle.

"Venez, vite, Paul, Yvonne. Church starts soon. Hurry, we don't want to be late."

Yvonne grabbed Paul's hand and whispered, "Paul, I am falling in love with you."

He looked at her with deep affection. "Moi aussi."

Dieter was in church, so was Johannes, Hugo and Franzl. After Mass they exchanged their experiences.

"Mr. LeCarte bought new working pants for me. See, no white painted letters anymore on them."

Franzl did not seem happy at all, but Dieter looked well.

"My farmer, or should I say my master, Mr. Deboire, said to me last night that he would bring Wolfgang and me to your master's house next Saturday to visit with you. Tell me, will that fit in with your schedule?"

Without blinking a eye, Paul, with all the arrogance he could muster, replied, "I think so. I will have my woman make something special for you to eat." They exploded into sobs of laughter.

Johannes reported that the widow who owned the farm where he worked, a fairly young woman, had asked him to stay. They could get married, have children, and have a good life.

"But, I am married already. My spouse is God. There can be no divorce. Do you guys understand that? How can you, if I can't?"

With a cheery goodbye, Paul climbed into the buggy and drove to the big portals of the church, where he waited for Yvonne and Mr. LeCarte to finish exchanging pleasantries and shaking hands. And then they were out of town, under a clear, blue sky, a warm afternoon breeze frizzling the stallion's mane. The clappe-de-clappe of its hoofs lent soft percussion to match the song Paul was humming.

"Es geht alles vorüber, es geht alles vorbei. Nach einem Winter folgt wieder ein Mai (All will pass, all will go by. After any winter comes another May)."

In the back seat Leon had his arm around his daughter, happy and at peace, as was Paul. The work at the farm was hard but it revolved around life, animals and plants that grew and bloomed. The piglets became pigs and apple blossoms turned into delicious fruit.

Paul liked his life. Mr. LeCarte commented often on Paul's adaptability and praised him for his initiative and good ideas.

"You would make a good farmer," he would say, but that was as far as he would go. Mr. LeCarte knew that Yvonne loved Paul, but he was still so young, just nineteen. When Yvonne asked her father one day if he would allow Paul to sleep in her room, in her bed, he did not say no.

Paul and Yvonne worked side by side, deepening the trust, the admiration, the attachment they had for one another. Terrible things had happened to Paul during the last two years. Now, Yvonne was giving him new life, and more, much more. She fed his starving soul, letting him draw from her the salve to soothe his hurt. And he shared with her his insatiable desire to become whole, to live, to be. Making love to him cleansed her of the humiliating stigma the war had tattooed on her heart. Paul did not know much about what it meant to love. But during those days and nights she taught him that love is sharing, giving of oneself completely, the essence of life.

One night after they had eaten, Paul asked her to come with him to the narrow creek that ran through one of the fields. They went there in silence, listening to the soft chafing of their wooden shoes as they walked over the loose soil. As she snuggled up close to him, Paul kissed her hair and touched her face.

"Love, why do you cry?"

"Paul, so many, many times did I cry without someone holding me. Tonight my tears run because you are with me. I listen to your heart, and I know that both of us will make it. But why did you ask me tonight to go with you to this brook? You seem sad. Are you?"

He did not speak. The water curled by some rocks and rippled the stillness. He put his arm around her.

"Yvonne I am afraid of that moment when we have to bid farewell to our time together. You have become part of me. What will happen to us when we can no longer touch each other?"

"I am afraid as you are. I do not dare to think about it. I doubt that you or I will ever be this happy again. But I know our stars will shine their light long after we are gone. Come let's live the hour high, as if it would be our last one together. Come and take me home. I want to hug your soul."

Two days later a French officer came walking down the driveway. Mr. LeCarte had sent Yvonne to pick up the smoked meat from the butcher in Broons, so just he and Paul remained at the farm.

The officer briefly spoke to Mr. LeCarte, then both came over to Paul who was standing at the long water trough. The officer, in very cultivated German, greeted Paul.

"Mr. Berck, I need to inform you that your stay here in Trois Boeuf has come to an end."

Oh my God it is over. Yvonne! It is over. Did you know this was coming? You were so sad, so wild last night. You never cried before when we made love. Did you know?

"Well, what will happen? Are you letting me finally go home?" His voice sounded strange, distorted, like someone else was speaking.

"You will be shipped to eastern France to work for a while longer for my country. The train leaves from Rennes tonight."

"Tonight? Sir, I have made friends here, and I need to say goodbye to Dieter and all the others..."

The soldier allowed himself a brief smile.

"Don't worry, they are waiting in the truck out in front. Come, we need to go." Quickly, efficiently, the officer handcuffed Paul and led him away. "Sorry, but I have to follow instructions. We don't want you to escape now."

It is two years after the war, and he talks about me running away? Who gives them the right to keep me?

"Mr. LeCarte, Mr. LeCarte, what am I going to do?"

The mayor could barely speak. His hands shook violently.

"Bless you, Paul!" he cried.

With that he went back into the barn.

Merlebach

Merlebach

The French officer had Paul climb into the waiting truck, an army vehicle driven by a young soldier.

"Sit over there," he commanded.

Dieter, Wolfgang, Hugo, Franzl, Barth, Heinz, Ortwin, Hans, Jacob, Thomas, Ed, and Emil sat in the truck. Paul saw faces as hard as the basalt they had hewn. None of them did as much as even look up when Paul took his seat near the tailgate. The officer undid one of Paul's cuffs, but quickly shackled him to the wire rope connecting each prisoner to tie-down links on the sideboards.

They got into Rennes late in the afternoon. Not a word was spoken during the journey.

I wonder what happened? Why did they come so suddenly, without any notice?

Certainly these prisoners wanted to go home. They longed for their wives and children, for the little piece of the world that was theirs. But they also had been in Trois Boeuf for over a year, made friends, built trust, fused into a special family that had allowed for new bonds to grow.

Doubts plagued Paul. Had they been betrayed after all? Had Mr. LeCarte known that this was coming? Had Yvonne gone to Broons because she knew? Had her love made it impossible to watch him leave? Or had she just played with Paul, as she had with so many others?

It does not make any difference to me. She gave me back my life. I believe when we made love, we did love, it was love. Yvonne, you opened the door to my tomorrows. You always will be beautiful, and I will remember you that way forever.

The truck delivered them to a different camp. No Moroccan guards, but French soldiers in decent uniforms. The tents had cots to sleep on, lightbulbs to read by. They were served three meals a day, and the bread they ate was white and soft, with margarine spread thickly upon it.

There must have been more than five thousand prisoners in the camp. By design or by accident, the men from Trois Boeuf were separated from each other. A steady stream of people coming and going confused their attempts to find each other in the camp.

Only thirteen of the quarry team had returned to Rennes. Johannes had decided to marry the widow he had talked about several Sundays ago. Gruber and Karl got away, escaping after church the weekend before.

For the rest, it appeared that, even if the French government knew where their families were, they were not going to be allowed to go home. And now, after many of the prisoners had found a bit of real life, even happiness, living among the people of Trois Boeuf, the French authorities had uprooted them. Paul felt such despair, he came close to wishing he could run at the fence and draw the fire of the prison guards, just like Leo's friend in Kreuznach had.

On his second day, a civilian and an officer entered the tent.

"Your attention, please. Tomorrow the occupants of this tent will be checked out. Recruiting teams from the Saar District coal mines will look you over. You will receive a medical examination and we will judge you to be fit or unfit to work at the mines. In either case you will not return to this tent. Take your belongings with you. Trains will bring you to the eastern mining camps or to German prisoner discharge locations in the occupied zones. Please understand that we have to find you rather ill for you to qualify to go home. Remember, the old rules apply. We shoot on sight at anyone trying to get away."

Paul was among the youngest of the men in the tent, with the oldest in his late forties. All fifty of them had come from various places in the Bretagne and Normandy regions where they had worked in villages and small cities.

Somebody said he had heard from the German medic in the examination tent that smoking damp cigarettes would make for a fast and irregular heartbeat. However, there had been cases where not-so-healthy hearts had stopped pumping altogether. Paul had been told when he was drafted that he had a heart murmur. The doctor had joked, "Berck, you are leaking. You need to watch it." He wondered if wet tobacco smoke might do him in. He tried it anyway, but with great difficulty, as lighting damp tobacco was not as easy as it looked. The first draw shocked his lungs.

He did not die, nor did the smoke do the trick, and Paul found himself traveling once again across the French countryside by train. His mind drifted to Yvonne, and an intense feeling of loss came over him. He remembered an old Nordic saga, in which Brunehilde mourns her husband Siegfried's death. "It is better not to own than to lose," she says, and Paul finally understood what she meant.

And yet I'm not so sure that this is so. Had I not met you, had I not loved you, I would be a pauper now. No, you gave life to me. I will cherish it and not throw it away. I promise!

The train stopped in St. Avolt. The heavy sliding doors opened wide, and the prisoners stumbled from the boxcars. There had been no riots on the way, no dead people had to be pulled from the straw.

The September sun was still very warm as the prisoners disembarked. Most men carried some sort of luggage, boxes with string tied around, bundles wrapped in plastic, gunnysacks, wooden crates, backpacks, even real suitcases. Standing on the tarmac, waiting around, the disenchanted prisoners began to let go of the things they had brought—coats, clothes, blankets, paraphernalia. Paul had nothing to dump. (After the prisoners had left the bunkhouse at Trois Boeuf, Avreau and Bienne had shared whatever they'd found of value. All other things they burned—even the bunks.)

French sentries marched the five hundred or so prisoners toward Merlebach, a small coal mining town in the Saar River Valley. The guards carried guns, barrels down, hooked over their shoulders. Security was tighter here. The camps were much closer to the border, closer to home. It was more tempting to escape, more achievable.

"Merlebach 23 kilometers" said the sign by the roadside. As they walked, the prisoners let go of more and more of their belongings, pieces at a time. Shoes, shirts, towels, underwear, whole suitcases were tossed into the ditch. The heaps left a wake that became wider and thicker as the miles dragged on.

Several automobiles followed the procession. Women and children gathered what they could of the things left behind. Still, the trail of litter stretched for miles.

All Paul carried was on his back, which included a coat Yvonne had given him. As the day wore on, as the march got longer and the temperature warmer, he realized he would have to part with his one treasure. *I've got to let go of this heavy jacket, Yvonne, even though you gave it to me just a few days ago.*
Late in the afternoon they arrived at the first of five mining camps. The column halted and the men collapsed wherever they stood.

The guards shouted, "Carpenters step to the left!" Nothing happened. "If you are a carpenter, step out to the left! Come on, get your asses going... vite, vite!" A hundred people or so picked up what was left of their gear and moved to the left side of the road—some actual carpenters, some just tired of the walk. The rest of the marchers hiked on. Four more camps were waiting to swallow the remaining four hundred prisoners.

The man walking next to Paul said, "What are you? I am a butcher. You think they need butchers around here?"

"They might need cooks at the camp ahead. Just pretend you are a master of cuisine."

Mining camp number two was coming up. Paul decided it looked pretty good. *No matter what they call for. I am it! I don't want to go any further. This marching is for the birds.*

The guards passed down the word. "Mechanics, maintenance people, blacksmiths, plumbers, step to your right, to your right."

Paul decided he would be a mechanic and stepped to his right; the rest kept on going. He looked for Dieter and the others but could not find them. He and some other forty men walked through the wide-open gate.

The butcher-turned-plumber admired, "Man, how clean this place is! Look, all these guys are wearing decent clothes. I hope they need a cook here." The place did look clean. The buildings had been arranged in the shape of a U, with the open side facing the gate. Twelve barracks, wide spaces in between, lined up to the right with their gables facing toward the center of the camp. Two barracks sat on the left side. The one that housed the camp's medic and his six-bed hospital displayed neat curtains through the windows of the first aid room. Red geraniums bloomed along the front walk. The second building, sitting amidst a small patch of lawn, was the home of the guard force. Three barracks made up the bottom of the U. The one in the center was a store of some kind, with a cafeteria on one side and a kitchen on the other. Flanking this center building were washing and shower facilities and restrooms. Graveled pathways wove throughout the complex connecting the buildings. The center of the U resembled a town square with benches, bushes, and a few trees. And at the back of the camp climbed a high cliff that glowed each evening with the setting sun. Paul had to admit the place did look inviting. But, still, a razor-bladed barbed-wire fence surrounded this peaceful setting.

The camp chief was a German officer, whom they called "Professor." He welcomed them while some three hundred inmates lingered around and inspected the newcomers, looking for familiar faces. "Hello, men. This is no hotel. Barbed wire still surrounds us and keeps us from being free. But it is a good place.

Our guards here are French civilians. They are reasonable people. The food is good. Our life is peaceful here.

"Work in the mines is hard work, and dangerous. It will take time for you to get used to it. We get paid by the month. The store here in back of me, The Franciscan Buvette, will extend credit to you till your first payday, but you need to negotiate your limits. I doubt you will spend much, for there are no women within twenty miles.

"Disputes will be settled by the foreman of your barracks. I get involved only in severe cases.

"Let me say it again. We live in a peaceful place here. We are a large family. All of us like it and we want to keep it that way. I will do whatever necessary to assure that it does. These twelve fellows to my right are our barracks foremen, our 'apostles.'" The crowd laughed, some clapped. "No, I didn't say saints. But these apostles carry the master's message to you and make sure you understand it. They will take you into our homes. If you want to bunk with someone in particular, let them know.

"I hope you will match the friendship we offer you. Good luck." The apostles mixed with the newcomers and picked whom they liked.

"Hi, my name is Luke, I live in Number 9. Wait here, I have to fill three more empty bunks." As Paul waited, he worried about how he would pass himself off as a mechanic. Although he had no real training, he had always had an itch for mechanical things. He had tinkered with gismos and gadgets since he could crawl. As a young boy he had picked up all sorts of "how-to" tricks from the shoemaker and the cabinetmaker. He also had spent countless hours disassembling and then reassembling his toys, particularly after Christmas and after his birthdays, much to the chagrin of his mother. She could not understand his fascination, as Paul's father had no interest or aptitude when it came to mechanical devices.

Paul remembered one truck in particular that challenged his talents. He had been given a pair of pliers and a beat-up screwdriver by his two mentors, and he was determined to see how this truck worked. He was only five. His workshop was under his bed. Because he had very little light to work with in that cramped space, and had to avoid attracting the attention of his mother, he worked during the noon hour, when the light streaming in from the windows was strongest and Margarete took her nap on the couch in the living room. Although he usually did not disassemble the spring-driven transmission, which was made of hefty sheet metal, this time it had to be done. He wanted to know just how the spring was anchored to its key-winding shaft.

The freed narrow steel band missed his face, not by much. But on its way to flatten out, it shot into his thumb, lodging itself deep between his nail and the bone.

His scream woke his mother her from her nap. She pulled him and the spring and the transmission from under the bed. Paul in all his life had never experienced such pain, shrieking each time the spring moved the slightest bit. Although she could not remove the imbedded spring, she finally stabilized it by banding it to his right wrist.

They had to walk to the doctor's office, an hour of pain and suffering for little Paul. The people sitting in the waiting room took one look at the child and agreed he should be next in line.

Grete, her usual unsympathetic self, said, "Look, Doctor, what this child did. I am sorry to bother you with this, but my husband is at work and I did not know what else to do." She left out that Paul's father very likely would have fainted had he seen it.

The doctor asked Paul's mother to hold his arm, and then, with a pair of surgical scissors, he made a deep cut to extract the barbed end of the spring. Novocaine had yet to be invented, so Paul nearly bit his lip all the way through.

The doctor asked, "Shall I throw the spring away?"

But Grete shook her head. "No, he took it apart, he will have to put it together again." The doctor stared at her in disbelief at her lack of compassion, but she took no notice, paid him, and they walked home.

She did buy the pills the doctor had prescribed, which lessened the pain after a while. The bandage was impressive and the wound took six weeks to heal. In the meantime, Paul learned to do things with his left hand. That ambidextrous ability would enhance his mechanical aptitude.

Why do I think of this now? What does this all have to do with me wanting to become a mechanic? Man, Paul, you really have the jitters, don't you? Me, afraid? Naw. You liar, I know you are! Yes, I guess I am.

Luke, apostle Number 9, had found three more men who would mix nicely with the family. He led the way to Paul's new home. Bystanders waved hello. They wore real clothes, nothing like the rags Paul had on him.

The entrance to Number 9 led into a spacious area, similar to a foyer. Bunks, stacked two high, lined both walls with a table and two benches on either side between them. The window at each table was trimmed with colorful valances. A few men crawled from their bunks, others interrupted their card games. They shook hands with the four new arrivals and welcomed them. All of them talked at once.

"Need anything, let me know."

"Do you have a blanket? I can get you one."

"I have a towel you can borrow."

"Have you eaten yet?"

"What's your name? Where do you come from?"

Luke called somebody sitting at the table in the far corner of the barracks.

"Hey, Martin, why don't you take Paul here and let him have that top bunk above you."

The man ambled over and introduced himself. "Paul? I am Martin. Come meet the other two of our gang. You have no things, nothing? That's fine. Don't worry, pretty soon you'll be a packrat again, like all of us." Paul followed Martin to where two other men sat talking. "These two characters here are my fellow inmates. Otto and Knute."

"Come sit down. You must be all walked out," invited Knute, indicating a chair next to him. "At least you had good weather. When we got here it was snowing, the wind blowing like hell!" He leaned forward, steamrolling into his story. "We'd been shipped in from North Africa. The Americans had outfitted us with brand new uniforms, good boots, and so on. When we landed in Cherbourg, the first thing the French guards did was to take all that away. They gave us their stinking rotten French khaki outfits, including the lice."

Paul suddenly found himself back in Rennes, in the tent city with Ernst, who had told him the very same story.

"Knute, why are you telling him all this right now? There'll be time enough later for that kind of shit. I bet the kid is starving." He pulled out a bill and handed it to Knute. "Here, you can atone for your sins by running over to the store and buying him a sandwich. When you get back, we'll have a toast. This occasion needs to be celebrated. Right, Paul?"

Paul felt overwhelmed by this friendliness. *These people are so nice and easy, so relaxed. I feel like a different person, more civilized. I am safe here, that's what it is. Safe, yes! It is so reassuring. No Moroccan guards trying to screw me. God, I want to forget that camp in Rennes!* Knute returned in less than five minutes with a ham and cheese sandwich. Paul unwrapped it greedily and took a huge bite. "You guys have no idea how good all this is!" Martin had put four small glasses on the table, clean glasses.

"Otto, come, break out some of that Pernod you smuggled in the other night." Otto obliged, rummaging in his trunk for the small bottle and then filling their glasses. "Okay, Paul, be slow with that, it hits bottom pretty hard."

They lifted their shots.

"To Paul!"

Paul took a sip and made his own silent toast. *Ivanovich, here is to you. This is better than your torpedo juice, by far! I hope you have made it home by now.*

Night. A wayward harmonica weeping the song of the Volga filled the empty spaces between the huts. Faint lights from the barracks windows lit the quad where people strolled about, smoking, talking. All was so tranquil, so at rest. There was peace. Before bed, Paul went into one of the wash houses, took off his clothes, and had a long shower, his first since he left boot camp in Weimar, twenty long months ago. He dried himself with the leftovers of his shirt.

The next morning, Martin, Otto, and Luke left early for work. "Enjoy sleeping in. Someone will let you know when the dispatcher wants to talk to you. See you tonight."

Later in the morning, Paul awoke refreshed. He got up and made his bunk. The mattress, a large gunnysack filled generously with straw, was much more comfortable than the loose weeds he had slept on in Trois Boeuf. He made his way over to the store to arrange some credit with the storekeeper and to buy a few things he needed.

"Good morning," the man greeted him, "you must be one of the newcomers? Am I right? You need some things? Right again? Yes, Martin stopped by this morning to let me know. We will take good care of you." Paul was struck by how friendly he was.

"My name is Paul. I arrived here yesterday, and yes, I need a few things."

"Sure, sure. Whatever you need. Ordinarily, you can get credit for toothpaste, soap, that sort of thing. But Martin said to get whatever you wanted and he would cover for you until you can pay me back. By the way, I'm Gustaf, with an 'f.' Do you know yet where you will work? What's your trade? I mean, what will you tell the dispatcher you can do best?"

This man wasn't born yesterday. Is it written all over me that I'm nothing but a quarry laborer?

"Well, I had just started my apprenticeship as a mechanic when they took me away and taught me how to kill."

"I bet when they took you, they didn't tell you about being a prisoner. They told us to shoot ourselves. 'Don't even think of becoming a prisoner,' they said to us. I am twice as old as you are, and for my part, I had a hard time believing all the shit they made us wade in up to our necks. You'll be hearing more. We talk a lot about it one way or the other. This barbed wire becomes thicker as the days go by, crowding our space. You know what I mean?"

"Gustaf, yes, I understand how you feel. Often I wonder myself how much longer I can take it."

"I put a few things together here for you, Paul. Toothbrush and paste, two towels, a plate, cup, fork, knife, spoon, hand soap, and a nailbrush. You'll need those bristles. That coal dust fills every crack of your body. You comb your hair? Okay, I throw in a hairbrush. A gift, okay?" Paul looked at the toiletries as if he had never seen them before.

I wonder how it will feel to brush my teeth again. I haven't done that in years. And a hairbrush! Holy, holy! Life is coming back at me with giant steps.

"Gustaf, I think I need to take lessons from you on how to act in this new civilized world. How much do I owe you?"

"I can give it to you for seventy-five francs. You probably will get fifty per week. They claim that they put an equal amount into a separate account so that you have some money when they let you go home. No pun, but don't bank on it."

As Paul picked up his treasures, he said, "Thank you, sir, not only for these things, but also for being kind to me."

Gustaf reached over the counter and grabbed Paul by the shirt, catching him by surprise.

"Paul, this is a prison camp. It may be a better place than the one you came from, but don't you forget for one minute we still are prisoners, self-centered, out only for ourselves. Mind me! You cut out all this crap, this soft stuff. Don't drop your guard, or all of us will take advantage of you. No shit, I mean it! We still are the same animals. We fleece whenever we can. We betray to get ahead. We will step on you if you let us. Nothing in this world has changed, and neither have we."

He sure knows how to pop balloons.

Paul carried his things back to the barracks, where he put them under the blanket on his bunk. A note on the door had greeted him.

"Newcomers living in Number 9 need to see the dispatcher at two o'clock at the guard's quarters."

He sat down on one of the benches and lowered his head until it rested on his hands on the table. He prayed his first *Hail Mary* in a long time, then added, "Forgive me for my silence. And I ask you to please help me to become a mechanic."

Slaving in the quarry, marching in those wooden shoes that blistered his feet, suffering through typhoid fever, sleeping with rats—then he had needed Mary.

At the mayor's farm, life had been a little easier. No barbed-wire fence, no hunger, no lice. His days had been filled with fruitful labor, his nights with passion. He had not found it necessary to pray for help. And what would Mary have had to say about him biting so deep into Yvonne's apple? Prayer would have invited uncomfortable introspection on that part of his life.

Paul's mother often said that he should pray not only in bad times, but in good times as well.

"Let them know up there how thankful you are for the good things you never deserve."

Now Paul prayed for the people he had shared this horrible war with. "Wally, Emus, Leo, Max, Ivanovich, Dieter, Ernst, Johannes! Please have them be in heaven with you or give them a hand with their lives. Oh, and I hope you let another in, the one who knocked at your door with bare feet."

He had skipped breakfast, preferring to sleep in, so he did not visit the canteen until one o'clock, time for the midday meal. The server loaded his plate with boiled potatoes, stew, and a slice of buttered bread on the side.

"Your first meal here? Wash your plate after you are done and stack it back there."

He ate feeling more like this was his last meal rather than his first, so worried was he about the meeting with the dispatcher. He tried to get his mind going in a different direction.

Somehow I've got to get me a watch. I see others around here wearing good-looking timepieces. Well, I need to get a whole lot of things. My shirt is falling apart. I have mended my socks so many times that I now mend the mended patches. My pants look like a quilt. They have become so stiff, I don't need to hang them, they stand by themselves. My shoes are worn, their soles have holes. If the camp would ever have a worst-dressed contest, I would not even have to show up to win first place.

His anxiety would not let go of him.

What could the dispatcher do to me that hasn't been done already? I suppose he could send me to the mine. Then I would look like the men in the pictures I've seen, the ones who carry acetylene lanterns, their faces blackened with coal dust. Yes, he could do that to me, and I would have to take it. As he passed several barracks on his way back to his new home, some men waved at him,.

"How do you like it here?"

"Good luck to you."

At first he couldn't figure out how they knew he was a new recruit. Then he remembered how he must look—a raga-muffin next to them. As he brushed his hair with the new brush he looked at the distorted image the warped window glass reflected back at him.

Yes, that's the way I feel.

The door to the guards' barracks was wide open, and Paul stepped inside. A few guards played poker, the room gray with their cigarette smoke. Rifles leaned in the corner between a bunk and the window. Candy wrappers and newspapers filled the waste basket, and empty milk bottles with green bottoms sat on the bare, wooden table rimmed by cigarette burns. Hash cans, cut in half, overflowed with stubbed-out butts, and fine cigarette ash seemed to have settled everywhere. The coffee-stained plywood floor had not been swept in weeks. Pictures of undressed girls decorated the banged up doors of three lockers. A foul smell hung in the room.

"Entrez, monsieur. You are looking for the dispatcher? Over there, in that room. And check back with us on your way out. We need to know which mine you will be at."

Paul knocked on the door indicated and heard "It is open, come on in." A man seated at a desk, got up to shake Paul's hand.

"My name is Fritz. Yours?"

"Paul, Paul Berck."

Fritz was in his thirties, tall and well built, wearing clothes that Paul wished he had in his closet. Fritz shuffled some manila folders, then found the one he wanted and open it. The sheet he pulled out was covered with scribbled notes. A wrinkle appeared on his forehead as he squinted at the piece of paper, and Paul's heart beat a little faster.

"Luke, your barracks leader, listed you here as a mechanic. I am sorry to say I don't have a job opening for you. I will put you next on the list if we need a mechanic in the near future."

Then he looked Paul straight in the eye.

"I am assigning you to shaft Number 2. You will work underground, mining coal. Don't be discouraged, things can change overnight. But be prepared, you might have to work at the nine-hundred-meter tunnel. Steiger, the mine's superintendent, usually sends newcomers down there."

Fritz thumbed through more paper. Paul did not move; he hardly breathed. Did he hear the man say nine hundred meters? Twenty-seven hundred feet? He never knew there was such a deep hole anywhere on this earth.

"Paul, I see here that Martin in your barracks, and Otto too, worked at the nine hundred meters. So talk to them. They have been here for a while. They'll fill you in." Fritz laid down the folder and gave Paul what he thought was a reassuring smile.

"I'm sure everything will work out fine for you. Soon as I know of a place to put you in, I'll let Luke know." With that, he sent Paul back into the reeking room where the guards played cards.

"Well, what did Fritz say?"

"I will be working at shaft Number 2 at the nine-hundred face." Silence. One guard shuffled the cards, another one lit a cigarette and let it dangle from the corner of his mouth, fanning away the smoke that curled into his eyes. Paul waited. Finally, the shuffler looked up and said, "Could be worse. He could have sent you to be a timberjack. Okay, the shaft Number 2 crew leaves at five in the morning. You will be with sixty-five others. We search you—better be clean. A guard detail marches you to the mine about half an hour from here. The foreman at the nine-hundred tunnel will outfit you. Might as well throw all your clothes away. With what you are wearing, you couldn't stand in for a beggar. You begin the day after tomorrow. Questions?"

No, no questions. As Paul left, one of the other new men in Number 9 came in. *Will Fritz do his little tap dance for him too? Send him down into the bowels of the earth? Or will he get to he get to stay topside?* Paul went back to the barracks, crawled into his bunk, and fell asleep.

By five in the evening the camp came alive with the returning shifts. The Merlebach prisoner camp supplied a sizable workforce that dug for coal in four deposits located within a few miles from each other. The underground tunnel network extended far beyond their shafts. Some miners had to travel underground for an hour to reach the faces they were working. Small engines pulled very low-profile carts and transported people within a complex rail system. Mining carts carried coal endlessly to the elevators. Export had priority over any other traffic. Under no circumstances, barring major accidents, would this rule be violated. Once the men had arrived at their job site they would stay there until the end of their shift.

Paul got down from the bunk and greeted the guys. He was surprised to see them looking so clean after a day in the mines. "Did you have a good day?" Paul asked. "What kind of mines are these that you come back looking so spit and polished?" Martin laughed. "We get plenty dirty, but we clean up there. If nothing else, the mines have great showers." He gestured to Knute.

"Come, show him."

Knute fetched a package from under the blanket on his bunk behind him.

"Here, Paul, this is our welcome gift for you. Ja, take it. We hope you like it."

Paul unwrapped the box and opened the lid. Inside he saw a brand-new, blue cotton shirt with long sleeves. He touched it. It felt so soft, and blue was his favorite color.

"Jesus, guys. You really did that for me? I don't know what to say. You are so nice, I can't believe all this yet. Thank you, thank you! This is the first new shirt I've had since I became a prisoner almost two years ago. Do you know, of course you do, how good all this is!"

Paul! Cut out this soft shit. Remember what Gustaf said this morning? Naw, I don't care. He is bitter. I'll try not to be that hard. This moment is beautiful, and I'll take it.

"Try it on, go ahead!"

For the last time, he took off the rag-shirt. Delicately, he unfolded the new one and slipped into it, first the right arm, then the left one. The sleeves were a little long, but they would be just right after the first wash.

Martin gave him a fatherly smile.

"Kid, you look good in it. Now tell us the good news. You've been to the dispatcher, haven't you?"

Knute had poured Pernod for the four of them. "Celebration. The new shirt and they have not sent you away to another camp. Good, good. Shoot!"

Paul let the burning warmth of the liqueur fade before he started to speak.

"Well, first I want to thank you for talking to Gustaf at the store. He gave me credit, and I got me a few things. Would you believe I have a brush for my hair and a brush for my teeth? Yes, life is really picking up." He set down his glass. "I have been assigned to shaft Number 2. The dispatcher had no place for me where I could work as a mechanic. He said I probably will make coal at the nine-hundred-meter tunnel. You worked there for a while, yes?"

Knute and Otto both swore, and Martin sat there looking at Paul, not saying anything at first.

"Knute, move over here. I want to sit with Paul." Knute, shaking his head, switched with Martin. "All newcomers, the young guys and the fellows who've done something wrong at their job, are being sent to that deep tunnel. When Otto and I came here, we worked there too, yes. Knute was lucky; he hired out right away as a carpenter. He works at one of the above-ground mine maintenance shops. It is good for us to have him around. Without him you would not wear this new shirt, and we would not be drinking that expensive liquor. You see, when a guy works topside, he has access to the outside world. Knute builds things for the guards and people who work with him. They pay, bring booze, buy things for him. Not bad, huh?"

Otto, a scowl on his face, added his two cents about the nine-hundred-yard face.

"Yes, Martin and I worked there for about six months. I'll give it to you the way it is. The nine-hundred faces are about four miles north of shaft Number 2. The shuttle carts brought us within a hundred yards of the face. We crawl-walked the rest of the way. The ceilings down there are only four, maybe five feet. The face is wide enough for three guys to drill, pick, and load."

"Is it very cold down there?"

"Hell, no! It's warm, very warm, around 110 degrees Fahrenheit. But the weather in the tunnel and at the faces is good, because the coal mines in the Saar River Valley are well ventilated. You'll notice the strong wind. Outside air is blown through the tunnels at a rate of seven to ten miles per hour. Yes, it's quite drafty down there. And there is water everywhere. The humidity is what got Martin and me."

Martin put his arm around Paul.

"You mustn't be scared. Being scared does people in before they get there. You need to look at it as a temporary job. Six months is the longest they have prisoners work at nine hundred. I know mechanics always are in great demand. You will make it.

"Now let's talk about you getting down there. That's something you want to be prepared for, or it will get to you. After the first few times, it'll be like riding an elevator in a department store. Knutie, you tell him, you've been through this a few times yourself."

Knute gave Martin a withering look.

"Martin, you give me that 'Knutie' shit one more time and I cut you from my liquor list. Got that? Okay, I had just gotten here like you, when they said they needed carpenters. I'm a carpenter, so I raised my hand. Big mistake! They needed a timber crew.

"The lumber is used to build roof frames that keep the tunnel from caving in, and the timber crews worked on the weekends, between the regular shifts. It was Easter Sunday. I complained that I needed to go to the chapel. Didn't matter. As it turned out, I did plenty of praying in the mine."

Otto poured another round from Knute's bottle and added his story.

"A miner once told me that he feels safer working in wood-framed tunnels than in excavated drifts that have roof-bolted ceilings. 'Otto,' he said, 'the wood talks to me. I hear it moving!' Whenever it stops 'talking,' it's time to get out. It means the pressure is too much and the tunnel is close to collapsing.

"The father had learned this lesson the hard way. I guess he didn't 'listen' to the timbers one time, and the mine fell in on him. Took a rescue crew two days to dig him and his buddy out.

"So, Paul, when you're down there and hear the wood creak, you know it is safe. But you have to listen very carefully to hear it. It's loud down there, with running water, the wind blowing through, and the compressed air drills going all the time." He glanced at Knute.

"Sorry, but he should know this. You keep going now."

"Okay, back to that Easter Sunday. The logs, about thirty feet long and some ten inches in diameter, are hung to the bottom of the skip. That's the coal elevator cage, a three-decker that brings loaded coal carts to daylight and returns empty ones to the filling stations. At those times the cage runs at a speed of about thirty-five miles per hour. But at shift change the miners travel only about twenty miles per hour, still fast enough so your ears have no time to pop, no matter how much you swallow.

"When I arrived at station nine hundred, I was completely deaf, and my ears were hurting like hell. You know, when the cages started to go down, my guts wanted to come out my eyes."

Martin squeezed Paul's arm. "He is right. The first few times I puked out my soul. And on the way up I peed into my shorts. No kidding, I did."

"How long does it take to get down there?"

"It takes about a minute and a half to get to the nine-hundred-yard tunnel. Now listen, no matter what, you stand upright, straight up. Try not to be at the center of the elevator. It is better to stand close by the frame of the cage. There are no walls, just the steel structure to hold onto. You see the shaft casing flying by. Your arms want to leave your body. You feel that everything in you rushes to your head. And then when the elevator stops, the gut you were wearing in your mouth now wants to shoot out of your ass. If your legs are not straight you will slam into the floor with at least an extra 'G' or so. Also, at 2,700 feet, the hoist cable stretches like a rubber band. It yo-yos the cage up and down almost fifty feet either way. You need to practice that and learn to like it. "Okay, enough for one lesson. You know there is no charge this time for the valuable information we volunteered. Next week it might be different." Paul did not like the sound of any of this.

"Otto, Martin, and Knute, thanks, but I can't help feeling that I don't really want to do this. I'm going back to the dispatcher and try to persuade him to come up with something else."

"Sure, it's worth a try. But don't kid yourself. Fritz is a tough cookie." Paul left to take a walk, thinking what angle he could play.

I'll tell him about my heart—my heart murmur. Yes, ever since I had rheumatic fever in Swinemünde, my valve has been leaking. It just might be the right moment in my life when I turn the ring on my finger and say my first wish. Tomorrow, first thing.

"Hello, I would like to talk to the dispatcher one more time. Is he in?"

"Where else do you think he would be? Yes, go right on in."

After hearing Paul's story, Fritz asked one of the guards to get the medic over to the dispatcher's office.

"Willie, listen to this man's heart and tell me what you hear."

Paul unbuttoned his new shirt and let the medic place his wooden stethoscope on his chest. Willie, an older prisoner, wore some shrapnel in his right leg, which did not want to bend anymore the way it was supposed to. He always limped, and he complained that the pain never left him.

"Hold your breath a minute. Okay, let it go. Hmm. Fritz, make him run around the shed a few times."

While Paul was running outside, Willie looked at Fritz and said, "Sounds to me like he has a leaky heart valve, no kidding. But I'll be sure after his running around. Where did you have him going?"

"Well, he's new and you know where Monsieur Steiger has those guys working. He'll be at one of the nine-hundred faces." Paul came back. He had done the shed three times. Might as well put on a little show for Fritz. Breathing heavy can't hurt the situation. Willie, listening again with his wooden stethoscope, exchanged a worried look with Fritz and shook his head.

"This guy here won't make it at nine hundred meters. I recommend you put him topside somewhere and away from coal dust."

Fritz did his looking-through-the-files routine. Once again, he pulled out a sheet with lots of notes scribbled all over, perhaps the same piece of paper he had consulted yesterday.

It seemed as though a miracle had happened overnight. Like someone who could not believe what he was reading, Fritz gave his face a serious twist. He turned his head a little to underline that he was puzzled. He even asked his right index finger to help him read, though the notes were not written in Braille. He seemed to wonder why he did not see it the day before.

"TEGH Company needs a mechanic, as soon as possible, three exclamation marks, and underlined heavily with a black pen."

Willie, who took his time putting his equipment away, saw that Paul was falling for it. The medic thoroughly enjoyed Fritz's act. He had seen it many times and always marveled at it. Fritz deceived new arrivals, and for that matter, he deceived everyone who crossed his path.

Before the war Fritz had been a bouncer on Place Pigalle in Paris. After a while, looking for a better life, he promoted himself to pimp. During the German occupation he herded French "escorts" through the bedrooms of Hitler's upper echelon. Here is where he polished his manners, learned how to dress, cultivated fine speech, and handled sizable amounts of hush money. Things had gone along fine for quite some time. Then the day came when one of his girls left a bacillus at the bedsite of an influential customer. Pimp friends helped him to get out of town in a hurry. He surfaced again when the French government began to hire men for supervisory positions at Prisonniers de Guerre camps around the country. Eventually he ended up in Merlebach, where he applied his skills to collecting compensation for good deeds he did for the inmates. As the new dispatcher on the block—the old one had boozed himself into the coffin—he also was in charge of the The Franciscan Buvette. When he and Gustaf met, they instantly realized that they were reading from the same book. They devised a positions-for-pay scheme and established a cover for Gustaf. He would be the "good guy," helping the prisoners with their problems. Credit was one of them, another was a promotion or change in work location. Willie made the third member of the club, for it was Willie's stethoscope that often made the difference. He listened to hearts, lungs, and bowels, and rendered above-the-table opinions like the one in Paul's case. In the absence of other clinical procedures, his diagnosis always seemed to hit the nail right on the head, and he was smart enough never to exceed established and generally accepted medical parameters.

Later that day, Gustaf struck up a conversation with Paul when he came into the store alone.

"You know, Willie told me your heart is not in that bad a shape. He just tried to help you out of that nine-hundred hole. And Fritz, he took a liking to you. He realizes that you are still so young to be dealt such dirty cards. You should know he had to juggle names and positions to give you that opening at TEGH. He even told me to take good care of you."

"Yes, I am very thankful for what he did. For a while I was kind of scared, because I did have rheumatic fever years ago. Well, I am glad to hear I'm really okay." *I get it. This guy's middle name isn't "confidential," it's "crook."*

"Paul, you'll be going to a good company. I know a few guys who work there. And, you can make some dough on the side building things for the guards and the people who work for TEGH. I hear there is money to be made out there by guys like you."

The dispatcher wants to get paid for giving that job to me. I bet that's what this is all about.

"Oh, and Willie did you a great favor too. So after a while, you know, after a while when you are collecting out there, you could, well...you get the drift. I trust you. By the way, congratulations!"

Man, this guy is full of it. A few days ago he was trusting no one. I should have known then. I better ask how expensive it is to get the drift.

"How much?"

"Now don't be pissed. It's only fair. I think a couple of two-hundred-franc bills would not be so hard to come by. But it is up to you. I don't get anything out of this. I'm just the middleman."

"Tell him I'll do it, and thank him for me, will you? And I'll have something for Willie also."

"Well, you see, I knew you are an okay guy!"

"Well, I am not going down the nine-hundred-meters," Paul told his new friends after they returned from work. "The medic examined my heart. It did not sound all that good, so Fritz gave me a job at TEGH."

Better not tell them the truth about Gustaf yet. Later maybe.

"How much?"

"What do you mean, how much?"

Otto gave him a knowing smile.

"I had to shell out three hundred francs. I bet Gustaf suggested the same to you too."

"So everybody knows? Well, you're wrong—it's gone up to four hundred."

"Ja, inflation! Good to hear he got you a better job. That's what counts. I didn't think your heart would do the trick, but that goes to show you what kind of a doctor I am."

The next day Paul started his new job with the construction firm TEGH. The outfit manufactured prefab homes made completely of concrete components—floors, walls, roofs, and siding. The plant coordinator introduced him as a mechanic-welder to the French shop superintendent. Four other prisoners worked in the fabricating shop and one Frenchman in the forging department. Mr. LaTone managed it all.

Heinrich, the oldest of the prisoners, acted as the foreman. Paul would find out that Heinrich was an excellent and very experienced mechanic, smart and inventive. Lucky for Paul, he was also a very kind person. Heinrich knew from the beginning that Paul could not spell "mechanic," much less be one.

After the first day, Paul felt he'd better have a little talk with him.

"Heinrich, I need to tell you something. I am not a mechanic. Halfway through my apprentice they drafted me. Please, don't let anyone know. I can still work very hard and help the crew, I know I can."

Heinrich gave him his direct but bemused look, one that Paul would come to know very well. "Yes, you didn't fool me. And I believe the others are no dummies either. But I will teach you the ins and outs of our profession. You'll do fine."

Boy, do I feel sneaky. But I'm not going to lose this job here, no way. Paul thought it wise not to mention that he went to the Gymnasium and had been chartered to go to a university later. If they knew, he was afraid they would not accept him. And he was right.

In Germany, society worked along strictly defined borders that guarded a hierarchy of social standings. The "lower class" did not want to mingle with those who were "educated." And it was worse the other way around.

When Paul's father had worked at a bank in Stettin, Paul never knew exactly what he did, only that he could have been in middle management. During that time, Paul became friends with Petrus, the boy from across the street. They were in the same grade at the same Catholic school, rode together on the streetcar, and played at the nearby playground after they had done their homework. Petrus was outgoing, friendly, and had good manners, and Paul enjoyed him. But, his father worked as a conductor on the railroad, a working-class job.

One evening after dinner, Paul's father said, "I saw you playing with that kid, Petrus, the one who lives in the cellar across the street from us."

"Yes, Vati, I like him. He is—" Georg cut him off.

"Listen, you do not play with him any longer, understand?"

Puzzled, Paul asked, "Why not? I don't understand. Vati, I like him. We are good friends." Even though he was afraid of his father, sometimes Paul dared him.

"They have lower standards than we have. His father is just a railroad man. They live in the cellar because they are poor. That is why!"

Paul looked at his mother for help, but she was busy brushing up breadcrumbs from the tablecloth and pretending not to hear.

That was the class system. People judged others by where they lived, how their furniture looked, what kind of curtains framed their windows, what they did for a living. Craftsmen were "below" men with a middle school education. Those with less education lived on a lower rung than those who had gone to a university. Even among those who had a higher education, a class system developed depending on which university had given out the degree for life. When Paul would work with the cabinetmaker and the shoemaker, Georg gave his grudging consent, only because he thought Paul would learn some skills. Grete was constantly on alert, however, so that Paul did not adopt their "common" manners and speech.

As young as Paul was, he felt embarrassed. *How can he do this, forbid me to play with my friend? Vati, I never liked you as much as I like Mutti. But now I really do not like you at all.* This moment left a deep, deep hurt in Paul's mind.

The men in the shop watched him suspiciously. They could not put their finger on it, but Paul seemed different than the usual cast of a craftsman.

"Where did you come from, Paul?"

Günther wanted to know. He was from Berlin, where people spoke a fast and sloppy northern German. At first Paul had a difficult time understanding him. *Well, the time has come. I better get my "story" out there, otherwise they never will let me come close. They won't share with me what they know. I like all of them, so I better do it.*

"Actually, I am from all over. My parents are circus people. They take care of the elephants and tigers. And sometimes they fill in as clowns."

The others looked at Paul with blank faces.

"You don't believe me, do you? Okay, let me show you what the dwarfs taught me. It was part of their act. They entertained the crowds while the stagehands changed the arena for the next event."

Paul stuck a cigarette into his mouth.

"Günther, I need your help. Yes? All right, take your lighter and lay it down on the floor, close to your left foot. Now, get off your chair, stand behind it, and hold it fast. I don't want it to turn over when I do my thing on it. Please, don't let go of it. If it tips, I'll break my neck and you guys will be short a mechanic. This here is a concrete floor. The 'tiny people' usually do this on sawdust. So, I'm taking a chance."

Günther looked at him worriedly. "What are you going to do? You're sure?"

"Well, hell, how else can I make you believe that my blood is not blue, but as red as yours?"

Paul had the others move a little to make room for his show. He took off his sandals and his shirt and checked the floor for metal chips, nuts, and bolts. The area needed to be clean for his performance. He put his hands on the concrete floor and did a handstand. On his hands he waddled over to the chair Günther held. Paul shifted his weight over onto his right arm, grabbed the lighter with his left hand, and lit his cigarette. Still balancing on one arm, he placed his left hand onto the seat of the chair and slowly moved his body over to the left. With his free right hand he clutched one leg of the chair and pushed himself up till he was handstanding on the seat. Then he folded down and stood upright, facing the small crowd that had gathered.

At first they just stood there, then Günther gave Paul a hug. The others began clapping.

Heinrich, who never used four letter words said, "Holy, holy shit! Paul you are something. Jesus, I never thought of you as a man from the circus, no. Wow! I'll buy you a drink tonight at the camp."

I hope it worked. It is the only "circus act" I can do.

Paul had always been a good athlete. Of course, he had not learned this hand-walking in the circus, but from his physical education teacher, Mr. Engel, who had a knack for special tricks. He would make the kids walk upstairs on their hands to the second floor of the gym, the only way he would let them go to the bathroom.

News of his feat spread through the camp like wildfire.

"There is a circus boy in Number 9!"

In the morning marching to work, he noticed Günther right next to him.

That's a new thing. He never even came close to me before. I got to remember this, walking on my hands makes people like me. I feel sad that I needed to lie to be accepted by the guys I work with, share the same barbed-wire home with, the same hours longing for freedom. Gustaf, you prick, I hate to admit it. You are right. But it really hurts.

This morning, Günther was downright chatty.

"Hey, Paul, how are things? Heinrich told me last night that he will see to it that you become a welder. He's already spoken to our boss, Mr. LaTone. You no longer need to worry. LaTone is quite the guy. He understands. I think he'll talk to you today. And listen, I am sorry we were such a bunch of assholes. We thought you were from an upper class family. I don't trust upper class people." He lit a cigarette, which barely slowed the flow of words. "At the camp in Cherbourg," he continued, smoke spewing out his nose, "the man next to me let everyone know that he was a lawyer. Further down the tent lived a banker and a professor. Now, mind you, we all had lice, and plenty of them. We common people, we preened ourselves and our clothes twice a day. We pinched lice and their eggs so they would not eat us up overnight. Do you think these educated bastards did anything like that? No, this guy said to me he never had lice in his whole life. 'Who do you think you are,' he says, all indignant when I brought it up. 'I don't have any lice!' "Finally one day we made him take off his rags. He had no lice—no, they had him! I had never seen a thing like that. The sleeves were..."

Paul thought back to Egor at Rennes. Same story. It was a fact that educated men, professionals, were the filthiest. They never mended anything, but thieved from their neighbors. Those guys were the ones who wore the slogan stitched or painted to their caps: "Ubi bene, ibi patria...Where it is well with me, that is where my country is."

At the shop that day Heinrich took Paul aside.

"We need a welder in this here outfit. I talked to Andrè—Mr. LaTone—and told him your story. He wants me to help you.

You know I am doing this already, but it is nice for him to say so, to have his blessing. We no longer need to worry. He listed you as a welder-mechanic, and you will get paid accordingly." He fixed Paul with his bright, blue eyes. "I am happy for you, not just for the new job, but that you convinced Günther and the others. You're now one of us. I personally think you are a good actor—and probably a good man—who by chance knows how to walk on his hands. I will keep this a secret."

Heinrich, you are special. Man, thank you, I owe you not just one, but many.

"So, here is the torch. This is how the flame must look. Take the filler rod, melt the material, stick the rod right in, and puddle while you keep moving forward along the seam. See? Never use too much oxygen. It burns the steel and makes the weld brittle."

Günther came over a little later and adjusted the oxygen pressure by a tiny bit.

"Man, you are doing great! Hey, I have to go to the mine supply house soon. We need a few things—acetylene, welding rods, a roll of sheet metal... Why don't you come with us? François, our truck driver, wants to meet you. We'll go on Monday, right after lunch."

How different things became. Even Noël, the Frenchman in the forge, said "Bonjour" to him.

"Viens, I show you something," he motioned to Paul one day. "You walk on hands. I hit cold steel so hard that it will start to glow. No kidding, you can light your cigarette with it. Watch me."

He took a piece of three-quarter-round steel, held it flat on the anvil, and started to beat it with his four-pound hammer. The round bar got thinner and thinner as he kept turning and hammering, turning and hammering. After a couple of minutes it became dark cherry-red. He held it up to Paul's face, who felt the glowing heat of the rod when he drew smoke through his tobacco.

"Noël, you are one strong blacksmith. Look how the sweat is pouring down your neck. Tell you what, I'll include you in my next circus act. Deal?"

They both laughed, and when they shook hands, Noël almost crushed Paul's.

In time Paul learned not only how to weld, but he became a very good welder. Heinrich had also taught him how to braze cast iron. Paul was in demand. A steady stream of manufacturing people from the plant, managers, and guards wanted him to weld broken machinery, gadgets, bicycle frames, and the like. He could do marvelous things with his welding torch, and his customers were very appreciative.

One day Mr. LaTone came to Paul with an unusual request. At the site of a large building complex in St. Avolt that TEGH was constructing, they used a tall, free-standing, hammer-head crane to lift concrete buckets and building supplies to the upper floors. The sheave bearing at the tip of the crane boom had broken loose from its mounting, and Mr. LaTone wanted to know if Paul could weld that support bracket back into place without having to take the crane-boom down.

"It's possible," said Paul. "Let's go take a look."

LaTone, Heinrich, and Paul went to St. Avolt in the company's Peugeot. Paul wore a new pair of coveralls and a canvas jacket with TEGH written on its back.

"They don't need to know you are a prisoner. Heinrich, you better change too."

The boom was about seventy-five feet long, with the broken sheave bearing support at the tip, some ninety feet up in the air. There was no walkway, just the angle-iron structure of the boom. Paul looked up as it swayed in the crosswind.

Did I say it could be done? Paul, who in hell made you do that? Are you out of your mind? Yes, you are.

"Well, Paul, what do you think?"

Heinrich, usually very positive about what could be done, looked up in dismay.

"This stinks!" he said.

LaTone laughed. "Merde et merde encore!"

Paul heard himself say, "Mr. LaTone, I believe I can do it." *Idiot!!!*

The next day was Saturday. Heinrich and Paul gathered the necessary tools, changed the cylinders of the portable welding outfit, donned their TEGH uniforms, and climbed into François's truck.

It took two hours before Paul started the actual repair. The boom was of an open triangular construction. Paul crawled inside the unforgiving angle-irons till he reached the sick cable wheel-bearing. In his mind, he felt pretty safe; his stomach, however, did not agree. The boom tip, way, way above the ground, swung up and down and sideways whenever the wind barely kissed it.

The coffee and sweet rolls he'd had for breakfast fell out of Paul's face, and not only once. But the wind carried the mess away and no one noticed.

He took his time. If this broke again, it could kill somebody. When finished, he checked his welds. They looked perfect. He reinstalled the wire rope, and waved the operator to run the hook. After adjusting the sheave guard a little, he signaled his approval.

Now came the hardest part of the whole affair. He could not turn around in the tiny space and had to crawl backwards through the boom on his hands and knees from angle brace to angle brace, seventy-five feet, with a welding machine on his back weighing eighty pounds. He had a hell of a time. When he reached the operator's cab, he took a break. The guy there offered him a cigarette.

"You must be out of your mind. I don't know of anybody in town who would be crazy enough to do what I just saw you do. You saved them a ton of money. They should pay you something extra."

The ladder down the mast was easier for Paul. On steady ground again, he realized he hurt all over. Still, it felt good to dare fate, to take on a challenge and beat it.

Some of those sparkling, liquid, white-hot steel pearls that had not wanted to stick to the overhead weld had burned their way through the TEGH jacket. They had left small, painful craters in the skin of his throat and chest. Because he had not worn any welding gloves, his right hand looked like it had a bad case of the chicken pox.

François, of course, knew how to heal all that in a hurry. He pulled a pint of Pernod from under his dilapidated coat.

"Viens, Paul, here, have a drink!"

When Mr. LaTone showed up and saw Paul's burn marks, he went over to the construction superintendent, grabbed him by his shawl, and barraged him with thundering expletives. His words shot out like bullets.

"You dirty son of a bitch, you shithead, you asshole! Look at that man! Why did you not give him some gloves? I will report you to the master, you—"

"Andrè, mon ami, calm down, think of your weak, stinking heart. Keep on shouting, and it will quit beating. Your miserable corpse will litter my construction site. Don't do that! Tell you what, you take them out for dinner and send the bill to me. How's that?"

"You rotten bastard, you pay for the drinks, too, alors!"

Then they offered cigarettes to one another, pulled out their lighters, and gave "du feu" to each other's smokes.

"À tout à l'heure...See you later! By the way, you there, welder, thank you. Good job! You saved my ass."

They drained the pint and threw the bottle onto one of the piles of rubble that littered the scene.

Andrè drove Paul and Heinrich back to Merlebach where the three had dinner at one of Andrè's watering holes. En route, Mr. LaTone summarized his dispute with the construction super. He wanted them to clearly understand that this guy was the biggest jerk in and around St. Avolt.

"At least we got the little son of a bitch to pay for our dinner!"

The bartender came from behind the bar and gave Heinrich and Paul a bear-hug so strong that Paul's burn spots woke up.

"I lost my brother in this terrible war. I am glad you guys made it."

Paul thought that no one was to know they were prisoners. *How come he does?*

But Mr. LaTone had bragged many times about what a good bunch of people those prisoners were who worked for him. He introduced Heinrich and Paul. "Yeah, they are my heroes, oui! Paul, here, risked his life today!"

The bartender interrupted. "Paul, you're still a kid. I want us, you and me, to live in peace. I want to dig for my potatoes in my backyard without hearing sirens and bombs. Andrè, it is good that you brought them here. Promise you'll take good care of them. Yes?"

The man had tears in his eyes. He had meant it! He took off his Basque beret and wiped his face with it.

Back behind the bar he poured Pernod and Aquavit into four tall glasses, added a few drops of water, and wiped the rims with a slice of fresh lemon. Lifting his drink he said, "Here, boys, salut, it's on me. I drink to your health, and to peace! Oui!"

The dinner was very good, though Paul seemed to have some difficulties the next day remembering what he had eaten the night before. He did recall, though, that Heinrich had held him steady under an icy shower in one of the camp's washrooms, and that Martin afterwards had bandaged his right hand.

At the mine on Monday afternoon, the supply clerk, also a prisoner, handed the shipping list to Günther for his signature. Paul did not see the silent communication between the two. The clerk nodded. Günther blinked. He counted the acetylene and oxygen bottles on the truck to make sure the number jived with the one shown on the invoice. He pursed his lips and from nowhere produced a small wad of bills.He folded the money into the shipping papers and handed them back to the clerk.

"We appreciate your expediency. Have a nice day."

Sitting in the cab, they took a swig from François's always-full metal flask. It was close to quitting time when they arrived back at the shop. Paul and Günther unloaded the sheet metal, the supplies, and five bottles.

"What about the other ten? Why did you buy so many? The shed is still full of them, and we have plenty of acetylene." Günther put his arm around Paul and walked him to the welding shop.

"Yes, I thought you'd ask. Well, we have friends who need those ten bottles. They buy them from me because I don't charge as much as the store does."

"You what? You sell TEGH's welding gas to your friends?"

"Yes. And here is your share. Put these bills into your boots under your feet. You'll be walking on money on your way home tonight. How's that?"

Paul was speechless. Then he considered the risk and convinced himself that it was okay to take it.

What the hell, I've got nothing to lose. Ha, I've been suspicious for some time. Knute's expensive liquor, Martin's new dress shoes, my blue shirt... I'm beginning to get it!

On the way to the camp, Paul walked between Heinrich and Günther. Heinrich gave Paul a slap on the back.

"Hey, you are in now, Paul. It's okay. We have a good and safe system. The guards know about it, so you need to share a little of your take with them. They like a bottle of booze once in a while. You get it? See, with being a prisoner come some fringe benefits. We are allowed to steal, to be corrupt, to favor a little the crooked side of life."

"Paul, you told us about Trois Boeuf," Günther said, "where you broke into the schoolteacher's cellar and helped him consume his apple wine, took his butter and money from under his carpet. Man, this here is the same. It's just more organized, more efficient, safer, and much more profitable."

"Why are you telling me all this?"

"We think you are uneasy about what happened today. Right? Your conscience needs a shove to get clicking with the real world. See, Merlebach is a fun place to live, especially for people who can light their tobacco while upside down and standing on their hands. Oui!"

Yes, they have a point. I need to buy new underwear, a watch, socks, nice-smelling soap, lotion for my tender body. Yes, I like to live in Merlebach. I'll do my share and then some!

"Okay, guys, I'm in. Thank you. I'll do my share to keep this operation prospering. You just let me know where and when and how."

When Paul got to his corner in Number 9, he found Martin sitting on the bench. His elbows were planted on the table and both of his hands held his head. He was staring at what seemed to be a letter.

"Hey, Martin, what's cooking? Did you..."

Martin did not look at Paul, but slowly stood up and leaned into his bunk. His whole body was shaking.

"Martin, Martin, what is it? Tell me, please! Is this a letter from home, from your wife?"

He tried to speak between his deep sobs. "It's...it's just...I am so homesick. It hurts so...so much. I don't want to live anymore. I want this to be over. Oh my God, I can't anymore..."

Paul was struck dumb. Martin, the strong one, always clear-headed, always there to help others, wanted all of a sudden to give in? Paul dropped his bag, leaned with Martin on the bunk, taking him into his arms.

"Martin, please, you need to let that idea go. Come, this life here stinks, we all know that, but we can't just give up. We must handle it, we must be strong. Man, we have come so far. We have won so much. Look, soon it will be over and we'll be home. Come, Martin, sit. Come, dry your face. Look at me. Yes, come and put your head on my shoulder, yes, yes..."

It took a while for Martin to get a hold of himself. He sat there, tortured by loneliness, hurting so much he no longer wanted to live—another fragile human left over from a war that had killed so many people and still kept on killing their souls.

"Guys, what's going on?"

Otto had come in, with Knute trailing behind him."Bad news from home? Paul, what is it?"

"He is homesick. Knute, fix him a drink."

Otto reached over the table and took Martin's hands.

"Come on, boy. We are in this together. We all know how much it hurts. We know it is bitter when we can't say the word 'hope' anymore. We are here for you. You are not alone, Martin. Here, drink this and tell us what Mama wrote to you. Yes, let that smile light up a little." Gratefully, Martin took the glass and threw the shot down his throat.

"Well, Maria, my eldest daughter, had brought home a boyfriend for the first time. Marsha writes that he is a well-mannered young man. A picture of them will be in her next letter."

Knute poured another round.

"Martin, man, so be happy. Be as happy as they are."

Paul, Otto, and Knute were young. They missed their parents sometimes, but that never brought the pain that Martin felt. Martin missed his wife, his family of three sons and a daughter. That was hard. The kids in barracks Number 9 could not know how heartsick Martin really was.

They raised their glasses.

"Martin, this is to you! We live one day at a time. Let's all take a walk. Maybe Gustaf will sneak us beer from behind his lunch counter!"

This acute homesickness could have hit any one of them, in any barracks, in any bunk. When would the French let them go? It seemed as though the answer was to be "never."

Christmas came and went. Only Paul and two other men in Number 9 received no mail; Martin, Luke, and Otto kindly shared their gifts from home with him.

The dreary days dragged on and on, time passing as slowly as molasses dripping from a clogged bottle. They hardly noticed when the budding flowers and trees announced that spring had arrived; the summer that followed seemed endlessly long and hot. Nothing brought relief to the daily routine, no hope of release, not even a rumor that hinted at their going home. Every day they lived added years to their time.

"Paul, bonjour. Comment allez-vous? How are you?"

"Merci, I'm fine, Mr. LaTone. What can I do for you?"

"Well, I'd like you to do me a favor, please."

"Of course, what is it?"

"Last night I took delivery of a large load of logs. I want to ask you to come with me to my house and split them to fit into my fireplace."

"Sure, sure, I can do that. You've done so much for me. It feels good that I finally can do something for you." When Paul told Heinrich where he would be for the day, the older man broke into a wide smile.

"Why do you wear that grin on your face?"

"Me? Oh, it's nothing. Just be careful, Paul."

Andrè and Paul drove off north past the mine shafts, climbing uphill as the road meandered through thick forest. It was a beautiful, warm day. Only a few clouds here and there hushed shadows over the peaceful landscape. The smell of fall was in the air. Leafy trees had been painted with a touch of gold, brown, and red.

"Mr. LaTone—"

"Paul, please call me Andrè."

"Thank you, Andrè. Do you have any idea when they will let us go home?"

"Non, mon Dieu, non. Have they found your parents yet?"

"No. Maybe I have no parents anymore. It's been nearly three years since the last time I talked to my father." LaTone did not know what to say.

It took them twenty minutes to reach the house, which was tucked in between trees at the end of a quiet cul-de-sac. A white-washed lattice fence with a narrow gate framed the garden in front of the home, and a roofed sidewalk connected the adjacent garage. Smack in the middle of the driveway sat a huge pile of hemlock logs. The wooden mountain was taller than Paul. The smell of the fresh resin hung in the air. As they drove up, a stunningly beautiful woman came out to greet them. Although she was around thirty or so, she wore her long, brunette hair in a style that made her look younger than she was. A beige turtleneck sweater painted her small but shapely breasts, which she had partially hid beneath her tan pig-leather vest. She wore a brownish calf-length skirt. A thin golden chain banded her left ankle. This woman seemed out of place, not matching the scenery, someone with extravagant tastes for such simple surroundings.

She came bare-footed through the gate and greeted Andrè. Her toenails wore the color of lilac and complemented her narrow long feet. As they kissed hello, Paul looked away and inspected the wood pile.

"Sash, meet Paul. He is going to make this mess into a neatly stacked wall of firewood."

"Hello."

Her deep, husky voice made Paul shiver. With distinct grace she offered her hand, and he caught the seductive fragrance she wore to match the look she gave him. Something about her reminded him of Yvonne. At first things had not seemed to fit there either.

A few weeks before, Paul had received a letter-card that had been previously opened by an inspector. It was the first mail he had received since he had left Weimar more than two years ago. He opened it and saw her handwriting. "I will love you forever! Yvonne."

Yvonne had pulled some strings to find out at which camp Paul was working. She had to promise them not to come near. She had agreed, but she had still sent her love.

When he read her words, one of those enormous basalt boulders rolled over him. Paul drank himself unconscious that night. Otto found the card on the table. He shook his head and shoved it under Paul's pillow.

"Sash-baby, you fix him a good lunch, please. Paul, the ax is in the garage on the left side right behind the garbage can. Be careful. I'll pick you up around three this afternoon."

After giving Sash a hug, Andrè drove off. She waved as he turned onto the main road, and then, without a word, went back into the house.

Paul found the ax, took his shirt off, and went to work.

She can't be much older than thirty, give or take a year. LaTone must be around sixty. What a deal.

While he was splitting away, he had the feeling that he was being watched. It bothered him, and finally he looked over to the house just in time to see the curtain move.

Yes, it's true, I'm much closer to her age.

God, this is hard work. There are so many knots and the wood is soaking wet. It'll take me a while. Maybe I will ask her to help me stack the stuff. Ha!

His ax swished down hard, piece after piece falling to the right and left of the big stump he used for a cutting block.

I wonder if... Paul!

She must be his wife. No daughter kisses her father the way she did. I thought you looked the other way when they did that half-open mouth thing, no? Don't even think of it! Don't! Yes, but remember, I've been there before. Perhaps it's time to practice what I was taught.

"Viens ici, Paul, la soupe à la maison."

By now Paul spoke French nearly fluently. Yvonne had finished Dieter's lessons, and although Paul understood the language, he could not read or write it, and he was often confused by the idioms the local folk would use.

He looked up at her call, admiring how she looked in the short, checkered apron she wore. Suddenly self-conscious, he put his shirt back on.

Sash pointed to the bathroom, and Paul went to clean up. Refreshed, he found his way to the kitchen. She had her back to him pouring red wine into some short-stemmed glasses. She turned when she became aware of his presence and, holding the glasses in front of her, she beckoned for him to come closer. Paul could not move. He looked at her as she stood by the sink with not so much as a stitch of clothing on her.

She was very beautiful, very.

Mr. LaTone arrived shortly after three.

"Man, you got a lot done! Very good! Probably one more day and the pile will be all gone, oui!"

He went inside and came back dragging a cloud of scotch behind him and a glass for Paul.

"Here, this is on me. Yes, drink up, we got to go."

Paul's conscience began to kick in. What if Mr. LaTone found out? More so he felt that he had betrayed Yvonne. Their two stars collided in the sky above Trois Boeuf, yet the impact had not changed their orbits, no promises had been made.

The road in front of them wound through pastures and forest. The coal mine head-frames loomed in the distance.

LaTone turned to Paul, a small smile on his lips.

"Did she make love to you?"

Paul suddenly wished for a head-on collision.

"I...I beg your pardon? Mr. LaTone, she, I mean your wife..."

"Paul, she is not my wife. My wife died years ago. I am living alone."

"Then who is that woman? Your daughter? A friend, maybe a neighbor?"

"She is a girl from the streets in St. Avolt. I hired her to be with me for a while. I needed to drown my loneliness. I asked her to wrap you up in her net. Paul, you deserved to be treated to something special."

"Why?"

"You remember when you fixed that crane in St. Avolt? That improved my reputation, and eventually I got a raise because of that. I did not know how else to share it with you. And I wanted it to be a surprise."

Jesus! I know I should not use your name in situations like these, but you allow very strange things to happen to me. He mentioned that it will take one more day to finish the work. Will that be okay with you?

"Mr. LaTone, did you tell Heinrich about this? He couldn't keep from grinning this morning when I told him that I was going to do some work for you."

"Mon Dieu, I do not remember."

When Paul came back home to his corner in Number 9, Martin and Knute looked at him with faces made of question marks.

"Why are you looking at me that way?"

Martin cleared his throat.

"Well, if I didn't not know better, I would say that you are wearing that I-just-got-fucked expression."

"And you have a certain...aroma about you," Knute added.

"Okay, okay. Now you two tell me what you are going to do about it. Knute here isn't the only one who has a license to sow his wild oats."

Otto had come back from the wash barracks. Towel around his neck, ignoring Paul, he sniffed the air.

"Hmm, Knute tell me, did you again have one of your 'screwy afternoons'?" It took Paul two more days to finish the job at Mr. LaTone's house. The hard work showed. He looked very tired. But nobody felt sorry for him, least of all himself. When he had said goodbye to Sash, she remarked that whoever had taught him had done an outstanding job.

The trips to the mine supply store became routine. Still, the siphoning of gasoline from François's truck remained the most profitable transaction. Paul had paid off Fritz some time ago. He had also given a few francs to Gustaf and Willie. Gustaf had assured him he would be there to help whenever the occasion would arise.

Paul wore good underwear, had bought a nice watch and expensive after-shave lotion. The soap he used was spiced with lavender. He now had five new shirts and on Sundays he wore a pair of striped slacks he had fashioned that went well with his black leather shoes—a farewell present from Sash.

Paul had written a letter to the LeCartes thanking them for the life they had allowed him to live in their home. He never knew if it ever arrived there. It was better that way.

Life went on. In the evenings Heinrich and Paul repaired broken watches for the guards and people on the outside. Paul learned from Heinrich how to make rings and other jewelry from silver coins. They made earrings prettied up with the colored plastic from splintered toothbrushes and sold them to the villagers. On weekends they manufactured sandals, satchels, and pouches from chunks of a new conveyor belt the clerk at the mine supply store had let them have for a bottle of cheap perfume. All that work brought in good spending money.

The camp had a band now that played on Saturdays after dinner. Gypsy songs, told of men longing for kisses, drifting clouds that bring messages from home, and rivers that carry freedom from mountains to the sea. The saxophone wailed until deep into the night and touched their hearts with its longing calls.

Life in Merlebach was good, better than Paul had ever hoped it would be on the day he had decided to be a mechanic. But it was still life behind razor-bladed barbed-wire fences. The Merlebach people were not free. Some of them had been prisoners for over four years. And their inability to be free began to outweigh everything else in their lives.

One day a French government official showed up at the TEGH repair shop. Mr. LaTone introduced him.

"Mr. Boseur here needs to talk to you."

Shit! I knew one day we would get caught, one day they would find out. Paul looked over to Günther, who stood in the corner by the drill-press wearing his stone-faced expression, the same one he displayed whenever a situation turned iffy. Paul raised his shoulders slightly as if to say, "Hey, what about it?" Günther ignored him.

LaTone spoke, his speech was hoarse. It sounded like he was running low on air.

"Boseur would like to present a...repatriation program the French government is offering. Many prisoners are...are considering staying here to become citizens of France. Paul...it is for the young...young men like you. I know...you said that...you still don't know where you parents are. And it is now more than two years after...the war has been over..."

Poor Andrè! He was clearly distressed by what this man was offering.

Paul had heard about the program earlier. They had discussed between themselves the pros and cons of such a deal. He knew of some men in the camp who had signed up, Knute being one of them.

No, not for me, baby. I like you, Mr. Mayor, you, Yvonne, but your government is doing harm to me. Yes, I admit I am not particularly proud of my German Land. But I want to go home. I want to do something else there other than marching and wearing the swastika on my brown shirt. Naw, this here is not for me.

Paul had his mind on something else. He had carried it in the back of his mind for a long time, but lately it had come to the surface more and more. He often talked to himself about it.

I don't yet know how to do it and when. Whom would I tell and not be betrayed? Heinrich? Yes, he will help me, and maybe Otto who had tried it, though they had caught him, and had brought him back to this camp...

Ja, I want to go. I want to leave here. That barbed wire has halfway threaded itself through my heart and my soul. Ja, I want to escape. What do I have to lose?

Boseur was afraid Andrè would steal his thunder. He interrupted him.

"Yes, fellows, I have something for each one of you that would make you instantly a free man. If you sign on today, you would not have to go back to your camp tonight. I mean it. The French government means it."

The man's German was nearly perfect, only the fact that he could not make the "h" sound, which no Frenchman can pronounce, gave him away.

He turned to solicit Andrè's concurrence, and LaTone nodded. Paul could see that the man was hungover, suffering from a bad headache. Sash had left him the night before, something she had told Paul that she would do sometime soon.

"I am paid to make love, not to baby-sit" had been her exacts words. She had used other hard language, and quite a bit of it. Paul felt sorry for Mr. LaTone, knowing what was coming. Then she had handed Paul a card. "Paul, anytime, when you are free, look me up, baby. Here is where I live. You're a sweet boy. One more time, no?" He had given her card to Knute.

The French official's presentation dragged on for an hour. The government would pay room and board for the first six months. The men could choose where they wanted to work, earn good wages, receive two thousand francs for new clothes...the list went on and on.

Boseur looked at Paul.

"Well, young man? Would you—"

Paul stopped him short.

"I don't think so. I must still find my parents. I will go home someday. But thank you anyway."

Günther made a happy face, and Heinrich held up his two fingers in victory like Churchill used to do.

It was late that night when Paul went over to Heinrich. Both of them sat on a makeshift bench outside barracks Number 9. They talked far into the night.

"Yes, Paul, I will help you."

The Escape

Paul had made his decision to flee when he finally found out where his family was.

Coming home from TEGH one afternoon, he found a letter on his bunk. His heart had quickened. Yvonne? Instead, it had been from the Red Cross. After two years, they had finally located his mother and his sister. The letter explained that the two had fled from the Russians to Simbach, a small village in Bavaria.

Paul had been so relieved and happy he had written right away. *Finally!* Over the years there had been times when he feared them lost forever. His mother's reply came back just as quickly. His father was with them, having come home from an English prison camp near Hanover. They were living on a farm in a small room above the milking stable.

The letter held news about the fate of others they knew.

"Frieda Mortz also got away from the Russians. She lives in Stukenbrock, on a farm, with her youngest son, your old friend Mieschel. Her daughters, Geela and Inge, are studying in Bonn and Heidelberg. They come to visit from time to time. Frieda's husband, Max, did not make it. The Russians had gathered up all men in Schneidemühl and marched them to a prison camp near the Polish border. Max's heart was weak. When he collapsed, a guard shot him execution-style in the back of the head."

Ivanovich, your people are so cruel. Does war do that? Or is man that way to start with? Does war allow these things to happen with God looking the other way? Does war free man of his social oath not to kill, not to torture? Is war the virus that God put in the apple at the time when he planted his trees in Eden?

Hitler had the idea that only the fittest have a right to prosper. War is justified as a way to weed out the ones that do not fit. God, are you listening?

Wolves only will kill weak caribou. But something must have happened at the time when we left the ape sitting in the forest. Something we can't fix. A decadent link in the spiral of our ancestral inheritances. The wolf does it because he is hungry. We do it—murder, mangle, twist, burn, rape, shoot, tear apart—because we enjoy it!

It is not war that makes us that way. We are that way. It is us who make war.

Max, you were such a good man. I liked you. You had faith. You were gentle and humble. You played the big pipe organ in the Familien Kirche, our church back home. Mieschel and I worked the air bags during midnight Mass. We helped you to burst that "Hallelujah" into people's souls. Max, you know, Ivanovich reminded me of you. I wonder if he made it home.

Paul waited for word that he would be released now that he had an address, a family waiting for him. But nothing was said, no orders given. They must have forgotten their promise to send him on his way.

So, he would do it himself.

Otto and Paul sat on a makeshift bench outside barracks Number 9, their home.

"Well Paul, you know, I tried to get away from here a year ago."

"Yes, Hoffman told me. Can you talk about it?"

"I still hear that thump the bullet made when it hit Eddie. He fell right on top of me."

Paul saw the pain in Otto's eyes and had a change of heart.

"Look, that's okay, let's talk about something else. You want a cigarette? Here, I'll light one for you."

They smoked in silence. Paul had listened around the camp to the men's stories of their escape attempts and being caught. They had been sent back to camp, most of them within hours of their break.

A large forest stretched from Merlebach south to St. Avolt, some five miles wide. Several country villages lined its eastern rim. Many of the men told him that they had used noises for their orientation, noises originating in Merlebach behind them and from St. Avolt to their right. But that did not work. Wind and the forest itself made it impossible to distinguish the sources and their origins.

"You know, a person is prone to walk in a circle in the absence of reference points," one man named Bucholz volunteered. "Furthermore, it turned out to be more difficult to walk away from a noise than toward it. I did not know that until it was too late."

Bucholz told Paul about the bounty-seeking headhunters who patrolled the forest and collected sizable rewards for the capture of a prisoner, dead or alive. They shot on sight and without warning.

"If I ever try again," Bucholz continued, "I'll go all by myself. And I would only clue in my best friend and nobody else."

"Why? Prisoners turn in prisoners?"

"You bet your boots. Maybe not directly, but little hints like 'He is tired of this place here, but don't say anything.' And within a few days the guards know who will try to escape. It happened last year to a friend of mine."

Otto and Paul tossed their butts, and then Otto put his arm around Paul's shoulder.

"Here is the way it went. Eddie and I were good friends. Both of us worked in the mine down there at the six-hundred-meter tunnel. He couldn't stand it anymore. The face we worked was narrow. Crawling was the only way to get there, because the ceiling stood only four feet high. Water trickled out of every little crack at the boundary layers between rock and coal, and the heat was unbearable.

"One night Eddie came to me and said, 'Let's go.' I was ready too. We told no one. We had tobacco stashed away inside our bed sack and some good shoes."

"How about clothes?"

"We didn't bother about that, because they would have been hard to come by. Paul, it is not that easy to get the things you need when you work in the mine. In your job you can deal and steal and get things. We couldn't.

"Anyway, we took off. We did not get very far. We saw the two men with their rifles walking in front of us some fifty feet away. We hid in the underbrush. They had already passed us when Eddie sneezed. Both of us panicked. He jumped up. I screamed for him to stay down. There were two shots, one missed, the other one went right through his chest. I should have run. They would have shot me too. But I froze. It probably will never let go of me, being a coward." He paused, and then gave Eddie his epitaph: "He was my friend."

"Otto, you and me, we've gone through very hard times. We lost friends. For many of them the candle ran out of wax before they even came close to being free again. Leo, the kid, I met in Kreuznach that first night, said to me that I should dream of summer. The next morning his dream had taken him to where summer lives. Him and all the others left a message for us. We, who are still making it, must pass it on. We must keep on living every second, every hour, knowing it could be our last. I am sure your friend Eddie would agree."

"I am beginning to understand that. It is good that we talked. Talking out things always helps my grieving heart. Thanks, Paul, for listening."

They hugged each other and went inside where Schuster had already started his weekly dance lesson.

"Guys, tonight is the night. Find your partner! It is fox trot night. Ernst, play your fiddle."

"Otto, want to dance?"

"Naw, not tonight."

Before Schuster went to war, he had been a dance teacher with his own studio. He was older than most who lived in Number 9. Paul had never had a chance to learn how to dance. Hitler kids did not do ballroom dancing. So he took lessons at Schuster's "Club 9." Men danced with men. That was okay, except for the two "Antonios," as Paul called them, after the homosexual guard who took pleasure in patting Paul down every morning. He did not dance with them.

At one time Schuster surprised his students. The lesson was about half over when the barracks door opened and a guy came in playing a mouth harmonica, followed by a young woman. The men instantly came unglued. Everybody was after her, and she danced with all of them, even with the ones not in the dance class.

After an hour or so she introduced herself by pulling off her wig.

"Hello, guys. I am Jacob. I live in Number 15."

Everyone in the room froze. One could have heard a needle dropping to the floor.

How could I have not noticed that? She had his cheek to mine. Man oh man!

After that Paul no longer frequented "Club 9."

Paul told only Heinrich and Otto that he was planning to take off. But he did not tell them the exact day he would leave, so they could give nothing away accidentally.

"Heinrich, if I want to make it, I must have a compass. Can you help me to make one?"

"I thought you would need such a thing. Yes, I know how to build it."

One night after they had eaten, Paul and Heinrich got together and started to make the world's simplest compass. Taking a razor blade, they broke it apart lengthwise, trimmed one end, and shaped it into an arrow. The opposite end was heated with a candle till it got cherry hot. They kept the arrow portion cooled with wet toilet paper to prevent annealing beyond the middle of the blade.

"Heinrich, why do we do that?"

"The heating softens the steel and rearranges its magnetic make-up. Since this is not the metal's natural state, the blade tries to correct that problem by aligning with magnetic field lines that stretch between north and south. But it needs a pin so it can pivot freely."

"I often wondered why a compass needle looks silver at one end and blue at the other. Ha, you are one smart fellow. Tell me, how do we balance this small thing on a pin?"

"Paul, I've done all the thinking I'm going to do for one evening. You work on it. I'm going to bed. Let me know tomorrow night how we can do that. That is your homework."

They continued to work on the compass in their spare minutes in the evenings. Paul had figured out that the blade needed a hole-bearing, similar to those in the watches they repaired. They tried and tried to indent the blade in the middle between shiny and blue, but used up several razor blades before they got one that did not split when they punched a tiny hole in its center.

"I should have bought a compass. We've spent two weeks on this thing, and we still are not there yet."

"Simmer down. The word 'patience' wants to be spoken very slowly. You will learn that as you grow older."

It took another week to balance the blade and make it stay on the pin. But on that Friday, the compass blade showed them where the North Star would rise that night. It worked. When they tried to push it around, it always came back pointing north.

"Heinrich, you are one genius! If I hold the needle in front of me, and it points to the left, I am walking straight east. Hallelujah! And I will outsmart the city noises that led so many others right back to the camp."

For weeks Heinrich and Otto helped smuggle things out of the camp—tobacco, shoes—one shoe at a time—a shirt, socks, and the like. Martin and Knute did not have a clue. The TEGH guards did not notice either. They were civilians, and since most of them were heavy drinkers, mornings were not their best time. Paul found it fairly easy to sneak things by them.

Each prisoner was frisked before they went to work. Somehow Paul always drew Antonio, no matter which line he chose. The guard would smile while his filthy hands slid over Paul's body, his face lighting with excitement when he "searched" Paul between the legs.

My God, will this ever end? I will use this bastard to help me get away from all this. Antonio, you will think you're doing me a favor. I'll bring you booze, money, and cigarettes. And when I carry out my stuff for the last time, you will think only of the bribes I brought to you.

The morning Paul chose to go it was raining, not much, but enough to keep the guards in their shacks. Paul told Heinrich that he had to finish up a job on the hill in Building 17. He shouldered his portable welder, took a few tools, and left.

At the main entrance of the TEGH complex Antonio stood guard. As Paul passed by he asked, "When will you be back?"

Paul blew him a kiss and threw a pack of cigarettes through the open window of his guardhouse.

"Soon, a couple of hours, maybe three."

All of Paul's senses were on high alert. He felt his legs tremble. He had to stick his hands into his pockets to still them.

He wondered if Heinrich knew that this was good-bye day? But of course Heinrich knew. He had been standing next to Paul in the morning in line, and he could see that Paul was excited, his eyes darting about, unable to stand still even for a moment.

Otto must have known, too, for he gave him a little help. Standing a few rows ahead of Paul in the line, he had turned around and yelled, "Hey, Paul, play cards tonight?"

"Yeah, will do. See you later."

Paul went up the hill and entered Building 17. The house was unoccupied. During the past week he had brought his civilian clothes, a brief case, tobacco, and money, hiding the loot in the crawl space below the living room. He pulled the items out from the space and changed into the new civilian garbs.

Heinrich had helped to prepare his trousers and the new cotton shirt. He and Paul had stuffed the shirt collar with money. Paul had sewn the lining of his pants into a sack that fitted around his hips. It stored cigarettes and loose tobacco in watertight bags. Heinrich also had stitched a pouch to the inside of Paul's pants, way up in the crotch.

"You may want to hide your pay stubs in it and some extra francs. I heard the stubs could be used for identification, so don't forget to take them with you."

"But why should I need identification? They'll know that I am a prisoner. Besides I will be in my own country, Heinrich."

Heinrich shook his head. "You know how we are. Without papers, we are nobody. Think, Paul!"

On his way out of the subdivision he dumped his coveralls into a garbage can, folding them so that the white letters PDG on the back would not show when the can was collected the next day. He had rolled up his work boots into his jacket and would carry this bundle with him for a while.

He walked quickly, the going a bit better now since the rain had let up some. An hour had passed since his talk with Antonio, but the guard would not get suspicious for another two hours, maybe even longer.

The road to shaft N2 was crawling with civilians going to work or coming off shift. He fit right in, with his worn briefcase and a bundle under his arm, both similar to what the workers carried. After a bit, he jumped over the shallow ditch at the side of the road and took a leak, as did others along the way.

Then he was out of sight. No one had seen him disappear as the forest swallowed him. He ran for a while to get away from the road. Then he halted to be sure nobody was after him. He tossed the bundle and took off his watch. The compass needle was hidden inside the leather watchband. The pin he took from under the collar of his shirt. But his hands were shaking far too much for this delicate balancing act. He took a deep breath and tried again. After several attempts, he had it. Finally, the needle pointed north to his left in an angle of about 45 degrees away from his body. He turned to his right till the needle was wiggling parallel to his chest. He walked on due east.

Wow, there is noise all over this forest. I wouldn't know which way to go. No wonder they all got caught. Without a compass I would be lost already. Mary, please help and tell me when to duck.

By now it was two in the afternoon. Antonio began to feel a little uneasy. But he did not worry yet. He knew Paul sometimes got involved in extracurricular activities. First Antonio had not understood what that meant, but then Paul had explained it to him and given him a bottle of booze to keep quiet.

Antonio wished Paul would fool around with him instead of with these women up on the hill. He decided that when Paul got back, his lateness would cost him another bottle.

At this same moment Paul saw something moving. He couldn't quite make out what it was because of the many trees that stood in his path of sight. Whatever it was would be at least a hundred feet away.

Is it a deer? Why does it not move on? What is that there to the right of it?

Paul froze. He saw now that it was a man. Paul could see part of his face and the gun hanging from his shoulder. Slowly, without cracking a twig, he slid behind a tree into the underbrush. A second man crept into view, well camouflaged by his green raincoat. He held his gun by the barrel like a walking stick.

Headhunters! Holy shit. Now what?

Heavy raindrops from the trees above splashed onto the leaves of the undergrowth. It broke the silence like the ticking of a large clock in an empty room. Some drops fell onto Paul's bare neck and started a small river down his back underneath his shirt. He hardly breathed. His heart pumped in double time. His left leg began to tingle. It had fallen asleep. Nothing moved.

Then, all of a sudden, the guard on the left started to speak. Paul could hear clearly what he said, for the French people always spoke loudly, whether they were angry or just bidding good night to one another.

Thanks to Dieter and Yvonne, Paul could understand what they were saying.

"See, most of them come this way." He pointed in Paul's direction, almost right at him. "I've caught quite a few right along here. I hide behind that fallen tree. Since this is your first trip, I will fill you in. Let's go have a drink where it's dry. I don't like this fucking rain."

Paul peaked around the tree and saw them leaving. He stood up and stretched, shaking his leg fiercely to wake it up. He went over to the fallen log to have a look.

I would have walked right into this guy. Man, that really was close!

He looked at the compass needle again. He could see that he had walked too far to the right—not very much, but enough to bring him back to camp if he'd continued.

He changed direction. Walking through this dense forest and underbrush was not all that easy. The shoes he wore were city-slicker footware. They were soaked and provided absolutely no support for his ankles. A kink in his foot would have been a disaster.

What in hell was I thinking when I bought these flimsy things? I should have kept my work boots on and changed later into these saloon slippers. Not thought through well enough. Next time... Don't touch that thought. Just keep cool, Paul. You are making it. Quit being so nervous. Watch out for more men with guns.

He kept up his stumbling walk over the rooted ground. At one time he lost one of his shoes in a mud hole. The legs of his pants had turned into wet, muddy rags. He took a break and ate the sandwich he had brought along in the briefcase. Raindrops on the leaves around gave him water.

After Paul had been underway for about four hours, the forest gave way to flat land and roads.

Looks like the end of the tunnel is coming up. Okay, next move.

Staying back between the trees, he surveyed the landscape in front of him. Wagon tracks wound between pastures and disappeared farther down into a village. He followed the rough road.

It was mid-afternoon, and not a soul could be seen, the village street empty. He walked towards the first house, not sure whether or not he had crossed the border. Rehearsing his plan, matching time with distance, he figured that he must by now be in what used to be Germany. But because the borders had been rearranged after the war, he couldn't tell for sure.

A man came out from a barn and saw the stranger walking toward him. He waited till Paul had come closer.

"Hello. You look like you could use some help. You are not from here, are you?"

"Not really. I am on my way to St. Avolt to see my brother."

"Ja?" The man raised an eyebrow as he looked Paul over.

Paul could see the man did not believe him and decided to keep on walking.

"Wait," said the man, holding up his hand. "I'm not one of those headhunters you may have seen back there in the forest. I am German. I'll guess that you just escaped from Merlebach." He gave Paul a smile. "Trust me, I have helped others who came from there."

Paul tried to remember his script, looking for a footnote that would cover this situation. He could not find one in plan A, and there was no plan B.

Jesus, Mary, what do I do now? Otto said not to trust anyone. I've got to think fast here. Should I run?

"I guess if you are a crook, it would be too late for me to run. So what do you want me to do?"

"Come in the house."

Paul followed the man into the house where his wife met them.

"Oh, Maria!" she greeted him as she surveyed his haggard appearance. "You look so tired, you are so wet and your pants are so dirty! Look, your hands are blue from the cold. My God! Well, you are safe here, yes you are."

Paul shivered as she helped him out of his coat. She took the briefcase from his hand and showed him into the kitchen, which was cozy, warm, pleasant. A red-and-white checkered tablecloth covered the table, and the chairs offered flowered cushions to sit on. The wooden floor wore a glossy coat of brownish paint, and yellow-toned half curtains decorated the two windows.

Paul's nose filled with the inviting smell of cinnamon and Christmas cookies. In one corner stood a woodstove with a kettle on top, its steam escaping with a faint hiss.

The man came back from another room and handed Paul a pair of pants.

"Take your shoes off. Mama will wash and dry them. The bathroom is over there. You can change into one of my shirts and these trousers. It might not all fit, but it will do till your stuff is clean and dry again. Please, don't worry. I am not turning you in. Really, I am not!"

Otto, there is no other way here. I need to trust these people, so help me God.

Mama poured some of that steaming water through a sieve heaped with tea leaves and into a large mug.

"Here, young man, warm your hands and your insides. Where do you come from? Have you eaten anything today? We'll have fried potatoes and bacon tonight for dinner. Can you wait that long? I'll bring you a cookie anyway. I made them for Christmas Eve next week. The grandchildren will come over, and we will go to midnight Mass together. Here, have one."

The man stacked the stove, building a roaring blaze. Only when Paul was warm did he realize how cold it had been outside.

"Hans, come sit down. You have some tea too."

The two of them sat across the table from him, their faces inquisitive. He guessed they were of the same age as his parents.

"My name is Paul...Paul Berck. I must thank you for being so kind to me, and I hope you forgive me for not trusting you at first. Yes, I escaped this morning from Merlebach. At the camp I heard many stories from men that got caught and were sent back. Is it true that German people turn in escaped prisoners for money?"

Papa cleared his throat.

"Yes, son, you heard right. It is such a shame, but nothing new. You know how it was during the days of the Third Reich. Children told on their parents, and friends betrayed friends. I am embarrassed to remind you of that.

"Listen, we will drive you tonight to the train station in St. Avolt. Our neighbor has a car. He is okay."

"We have to go through St. Avolt?"

Holy hell, I don't want to do that!

"Yes, you are not yet in Germany. Look, I am a retired railroad engineer. I used to work out of St. Avolt and I still have real friends in that town. My neighbor and I have done this sort of thing before. We've helped many prisoners to go home. Please, don't worry."

"But you must understand that I am afraid. What if the officer at the border..."

Paul knew that to get to St. Avolt they would have to cross from French-occupied Germany back into France again, and that guards would be looking for people just like him, escapees trying to make it to the station to hitch a ride on a coal train.

"I know some of those people too. You will have to travel in the trunk for half an hour, until we cross the border. Berthold next door has cut a hole through the back wall, so there is no problem with air. You also will hear what is being said. Trust me, it will be okay. I know how uncertain you feel and how hard it is for you to believe me. Just think, if I were hunting guys like you, the police already would be here to take you in. Right?"

"Let me ask you, Hans, when you saw me out there, what made you think I was an escaped prisoner?"

"The way you walked. You have been behind barbed wire for nearly three years. It shows. Besides nobody in this neighborhood carries a briefcase like yours. That alone set you apart from people around here. The police station is right down the street. If they'd seen you with that satchel, you would have been a goner. I am glad I saw you before anyone else did."

He is probably right. But I'm still not one hundred percent sure that this not a set-up. I need to find out how much all this is going to cost me. I have five thousand francs and about two pounds of tobacco in bags—ten tobacco cubes and twenty-five packs of Guillards. I need to be saving as much as I can. The trip has just started.

"Well, that makes two of us. By the way, sir, what do I owe you for all this? I would like to reimburse you for the good things you are doing for me."

Mama looked at Hans.

"Be gentle with this man," her eyes were saying, "he does not seem to have much."

"Ja, you know, I'm glad you asked. I have to slip the chief of police a little something. He is a Frenchman and always has his hand out. He knows what we are doing. And Berthold needs to buy gasoline..."

"Tell you what. I will give you a pound of French tobacco, five packs of Guillards, and a thousand francs. Yes?"

Both Mama and Hans tried not to smile too much.

Must have hit it on the high side, but that's okay.

"That is fine. That will do. I hope you have a little left for the conductor. He will get you to the coal train, that'll bring you to Mannheim in real Germany."

Paul looked at his watch, worth six bottles of oxygen. He saw Mama sliding her elbow over to Hans. Again, she silently communicated that she wanted her husband to ask for the watch.

But Hans, barely noticeably, shook his head, as if to say, "No, he has given us too much already."

I'll give him the watch after he has dropped me off at the railroad station. Yes, they deserve that. After all, he saved my life, and he is helping me to become a free man again.

Mama got up.

"I will clean your things now. We'll hang the pants and your shirt close by the stove. They will be dry in no time."

"I'd like to do my pants myself, if I may. Tobacco is sown into them. I don't want that part to get wetter than it is."

He stood up and Hans's pants slid down right off him. They laughed, but it was not funny for Paul.

He noticed his shoes, which Mama had cleaned earlier, drying on the chair close to the glowing stove.

"I'd better put those on before they shrink too much."

But he couldn't get into them, as they had become too small already. He went into the bathroom and dipped the shoes into the toilet bowl to make them wet again. They soon began to feel better on his feet.

A good cook, Mama served a delicious dinner that satisfied Paul. Hans even offered him a beer, but Paul wanted to stay sharp and politely refused. By now it was seven in the evening and pitch dark outside. Berthold came over to shake hands and explain their plan.

"We will drive with you in the back seat lying down until we are out of this town. Near the border you will hide in the trunk. Hans here told you about the hole, yes?"

I am sure these people are real. They mean well. It sounds like they have done this kind of thing before. I just have to quit hesitating and second-guessing them. Paul, they know and you don't. You are the man they are laying out the carpet for. Asshole, start walking on it.

"Yes, Hans told me about it."

"It is the week before Christmas. I think the men at the border will be boozed up and happy. Should there be a problem at the border, I will give the officer a bottle of cognac. That has helped once before. I would need some extra money from you to cover that, okay?

"After the border crossing Hans will walk you to the station. You go in, and wander over to the window farthest to your left. It will be around eleven by that time. The place should be nearly deserted. Hans, you tell him the rest."

"The ticket clerk will ask you where you want to go. Lean close to the glass partition and say 'Kohlenklau.' The railroad people help prisoners from all over to get home. But don't ever misuse this word. Speak it only to a railroad man and only when there is no one else around. This code word will get you to the conductor. He will brief you. Some times the locomotive engineer hides men in one of the empty water tanks inside the coal trailer behind the engine. It all depends on what shape you are in."

"What do you mean by that?"

"Well, frequently prisoners come from as far away as Brest or Rennes. Some of them are very sick, some arrive with frozen feet and hands. My brother-in-law, Arnold, who works for the railroad, tells me that three men had survived riding on top of the car's axle stays on a train that came from Bordeaux. So, actually, you got it pretty good. You are young, healthy, strong. It will be a short trip for you. I am sure you will scale the wall of that boxcar like there is nothing to it."

Berthold put his hand on Paul's arm and looked at him. He wanted to make sure Paul would understand what he was going to say.

"There are, I believe, twenty-three tracks at the St. Avolt railroad yard. Coal trains are staged on at least half of them. This is a dead-end yard, so all the trains have their locomotives pointing in one direction, east. Departure times are staggered, and not all of them will go to Mannheim in Germany. Some of them go west or south to other cities in France. If you get mixed up with the track numbers, you may travel farther away from home than you ever have been. The conductor will ask you not to climb into the car until the train has started to roll."

"Why? That is going to be tough."

"Paul, the whole thing is going to very tough. Listen, the train is inspected before it leaves the yard. Two armed guards and two railroad maintenance men, a pair of them to each side, walk by each car to check the brake shoes. They also shine their powerful searchlights all over the place, looking for people like you."

"Man! All that sounds like today's events have just been a mere walk through the park."

"You got that right. Now, Paul, pay attention! The conductor will tell you on which track you have to wait till your train starts to move. Got all that?"

"Yeah, I see a lot of things can go wrong. But I can do it. I am sure."

Berthold and Hans, I am scared shitless. You probably can see that. I won't ask you what the odds are. I can figure that myself. Paul, we really need to talk this over, so we don't fuck up.

On the way to St. Avolt it started to snow a little. The car had no heater to warm them, which might have been just as well as the car smelled like a Molotov cocktail before it explodes. In the distance the halo of the city began to dawn. Paul climbed into the trunk and Hans closed the lid.

"Good luck, Paul. You know if they catch you, they also will have our asses. We don't want that to happen. Hang in there!"

Paul had given his watch to Mama before they left the house. She kissed him for it and dipped her fingers into the holy water bowl. Her thumb carved a cross into his forehead.

"I'll pray for you, for all of you. Here is a sandwich. You might get hungry on the train. If you ever come back here, please come to see us, let us know how you are. And, have a merry Christmas."

The officer at the border was stone sobber. Paul could tell that the man's flashlight searched the back seat, for the air hole lit up. Paul stopped shivering and held his breath. The hole got dark again, and the car motored on.

Mary, thank you!

Paul crawled out of the trunk and sat in the back again. Hans convinced him not to take the briefcase with him, arguing that it only would be in his way, which of course was true. But the briefcase was full of tobacco cubes.

Son of a gun, I wonder if Hans had known that. He might have opened the case back at his house while I was changing clothes. It was just one of those things. Think of this as a gift horse, Paul. No time for checking the teeth!

Now, as they neared the station, he opened the case. "Okay, Berthold, have a few of these cubes here. And you, Hans, take some too, please."

Paul saved five cubes and twenty packs of Guillards for himself. He stuffed the cubes into the empty pockets of his coat. The cigarette packs went into the lining sack of his trousers. He would have them ready for the ticket man and the conductor.

"Right over there. See? Go in the main entrance, turn to the left, and do your thing. Good luck, Paul, and thank you."

The man behind the glass partition wore gold-rimmed spectacles way down on his nose. He had lost most of his hair. Patches of white, right above his ears, still dressed the sides of his oval head. The top was as shiny as a polished apple. He looked over his glasses and raised his white brows.

"Looks like you want to talk to the conductor. Am I right?"

Paul leaned close and spoke the K-word in a low voice. But the man waved his hand.

"I know, I know. Everything is fine. Go to the side door there and knock. That is his office. Take care."

How could he possibly know? Is there something like a "prisoner-look"? Or are those infamous letters PDG still shining through my coat? On the other hand, I am the only one here wandering through this monstrous big hall without a suitcase. Dumb shit, it is written all over me. A nearsighted person can spot me from a kilometer away.

He pushed two cubes through the half moon opening at the bottom of the window. Though there was nobody around, the ticket-man suddenly seemed to be worried. Someone may have seen the transfer. He nervously took the tobacco cubes and stuffed them into his pockets. He beckoned Paul to leave.

A brass plate on the door he was about to enter read: "Eingang Verboten" and larger letters below said the same in French: Authorized Personnel Only. He knocked.

"Come on in. Sit down. Relax, I know where you are coming from. Everything is okay. Where do you need to go, north or south?"

"I want to go to Bielefeld."

"Good choice, the English don't send escapees back. Is your home up there?"

"Ja, sort of. You say that I will be safe up there? That is good to know. It confirms the stories I have heard back at the camp."

He does not have to have the whole truth. Otto had mentioned not to leave a trail behind. Otto, Heinrich, I did not forget about you, but I have been kind of busy. The shit still might hit my fan any minute. I hope you are all right.

"By the way, Siegfried, from the ticket booth called to let you know that he liked your gift." He gave Paul a smile and then stood up. "Okay, we have a coal train leaving for Mannheim in about an hour. Come, look here." He pointed to a large, yellowing map on the wall that showed the entire layout of the yard. "You are lucky. Tonight we don't have many trains leaving around midnight.

"Now, please listen carefully. Ask if you don't understand something. You are here. You go through that door in the back of my office. It takes you out into the terminal. Go to the end of the tarmac and turn left. Walk over three sets of tracks and cross a concrete walkway. The first track after that is Number 22. Go on over five more tracks, and you will be on 17. A train sits on that track. Be close to the ground. Hide behind a set of axles. Number 16 is empty. Your train sits on Number 15. Got that?"

"Hmm, yes, I think so."

"When the engineer on the locomotive gets the green light, he will blast the whistle three times. Three times! Don't miss that! After the third blast you hurry over to track 15. You have only a very short time, a minute or so, and the train will start rolling. At either end of the car is a short ladder. Use it. The box-cars are fully loaded. There may be a foot or two of freeboard, empty space between the coal and the top of the car. Dig in and cover yourself completely with coal. You have about five minutes to do that in. After that the train passes under a bridge. It is manned and outfitted with machine guns and powerful search-lights. The guards fire at anything suspicious. Sometimes they fire just for the fun of it. That bridge is your last hurdle. Once you pass it, you can undig yourself. Did you get all that?"

"Yes, I got it."

"Let me warn you, it will be awful windy and very cold on top of these open cars. There are reports that at this time of the year men have frozen to death doing this journey. Why did you pick December to do your running?"

"Why?" The words flowed from Paul with unexpected emotion. "You heard of the story about the camel and the straw that broke its back? The barbed wire started to grow around my heart. It began to slow my walk. It became so dense that I no longer could see the sky. It ripped through my dreams. I couldn't take it anymore. I picked this day in December because I felt it was the last deadline for my tomorrow. Can you understand that?"

The conductor shook his head. "I can only guess how you feel. Summer or winter, it probably wouldn't make a bit of difference to me either. The Americans and the English had to keep the trains running, so I worked here instead of going to a camp. That spared me from what you went through. But listen, if you have been a good boy, you'll make it. Maybe some time you come through here again. Look me up. Good luck for now!"

I know he has a name, but my not knowing it will protect him, should I get caught. Mary, please put an extra gift under his tree and charge it to me.

"Would you let me look at this drawing a little longer?"

"Sure, you still have some time. It takes about ten minutes to get to the tracks from here."

Paul could see it snowing outside. He stepped closer to the window to check the thermometer. It showed a couple degrees above freezing.

Holy shit! This is not going to be easy. I wonder if he has some gloves. I need a shawl too. I'll offer him a couple of cubes for it. Let's see what he says.

"Say, could I buy from you the pair of gloves over there?" Paul held the tobacco in his hand gesturing towards the man.

"Ja, you can have them. I have another pair at home."

"Do you like this French tobacco? Here, have some of it. I want to thank you for your help."

"Well, that's very nice of you. This is worth quite a bit. Thank you!" The conductor, obviously impressed by Paul's generosity, pulled out a towel from a bottom desk drawer. "Here, take this too. It'll help to keep your ears from getting numb...Ah, listen, before I forget. You are not the only one who is using this train tonight. There are four other guys traveling with you. I don't think they are escaped prisoners. Black-market men, you know, smugglers. I never can tell, but they paid good money. These people usually hide in the cars towards the end of the train. Don't tangle with them. They cut throats, no questions asked."

Paul nodded. "Thanks." He picked up the gloves and the towel. "I guess it's time to go. You have a good Christmas." As he walked toward the door, he remembered one more thing. "By the way, how long will it take to Mannheim?"

"Somewhere between two and six hours, depending on the traffic. The train will stop several times. Don't get out before you are on the other side of the Rhine River. You will know when you are there. It is a very long bridge. The chatter of the train will change into a hollow singing, the sound of steel on steel."

This is going to be a hell of a trip. I hope the coal is not frozen together. Man, what a deal. But I will make it!

As Paul left the warm office, a cold blast of wind hit him. Snow prickled his face, but the towel, wound tightly around his neck, kept it from creeping down his shirt. He made it over to the train on track 17, where he hid behind a set of wheels. The ballast gravel on the ground was spotted with ice.

Voices drifted over from 15. He heard the banging of hammers, as inspectors hit the brake packs of the axle sets under the cars. He could see the crew. It was just like Berthold had said. Paul decided on the fourth car after the loco.

But where is the ladder? I don't see any on that car or the cars in front or behind. What else can I get a hold of? I can't jump that high. But I am scared enough. I will get up there.

Paul was worried that the gloves, which were too big, would make him lose his grip, so he took them off. The poor lighting made it difficult to see what else he could use to climb into the car. Then he saw that the box wall was reinforced with a vertical T-bar structure with horizontal angle irons attached to it. He could climb up on those.

He tensed up. His body was a compressed coil spring ready to pop on the count of three. The inspection crew had finished. From far away down the train on 15, a long, drawn out "Ready!" cocked his trigger. Eternities went by. The first whistle burst jarred the silence.

One...Two...Three! Come on, run, run you bastard!

He dipped under the car and shot over to 15. The top rim of the box was five feet beyond his outstretched hand. The train started to roll. He took a running jump and flung himself at the side of the boxcar, grabbing onto the angle irons. Within seconds he was scaling the wall and hoisting himself over the top and into the inky depths of the coal.

The briefcase wouldn't have made it. You were right, Hans. My knee hurts. One of those bolts sticking out, must have taken a piece out of it. No time now, Paul dig!

The gloves! He had forgotten to stick them into his pockets. The coals were not frozen in big lumps as he had feared. He moled into the black anthracite and covered himself completely. The locomotive passed under the signal-bridge. The engineer let go of one more short blast, letting off a thick cloud of white steam that billowed out over the first ten cars. Paul saw it through a crack in his "roof." He was safe.

After some time he wiggled himself into a more comfortable position. There was a rip in his trousers. Coal stuck to his bare skin and his right knee must have been bleeding a little. But he did not feel a thing. It was too cold for that. The stormy draft turned the snowflakes into streaking dotted chalk lines. He arranged his bed in a way that made the coal protect his head, like the hood on a sleeping bag. He wound the towel turban-style around his head, and it kept his ears from freezing despite it being damp.

It took quite some doing to light the first cigarette. Too windy and too many snowflakes. When the first one finally took, he had almost used up all of his matches.

He had been up ever since Merlebach, twenty-two hours crammed with gushes of adrenaline, new friends, unbelievable experiences, and brushes with capture or worse.

Paul, hey Paul, you and me made it. I want to cry. Do you mind? I love this ride! But you and me, we must stay awake, and we have to keep from freezing. I am sure glad you and me are alone. Somebody might think, we are nuts, talking to each other all the time.

At first he pushed it out of his mind. But it came back, stronger and stronger each time.

What, if this is the wrong train?

The diamond-shaped needle came to his mind. It had survived the washing and drying of his shirt back at the Hans's house.

Father, I knew it. Between the two of us, one always has the answer. You even saved the pin for me! I hope the bills in my collar survived Mama's soap too.

The swaying and the bouncing, his freezing fingers and high winds, all made it impossible for the blade to do the balancing. He waited. After his twentieth cigarette, the train slowed and stopped. Paul heard another one swishing by in the opposite direction.

He took his hands out of his pockets. They were warm enough to feel and hold the pin. The blade finally danced on it. Paul was lying with his back to the loco. The shiny arrow of that homemade wiggling thing pointed to the right. That was where north was supposed to be.

Wow, this son of a bitchin' train is going east. Right! Told you, I grabbed the right one!

It took three more packs of Guillards and about three hours to reach the big river. The bridge echoed the rush of the seventy-five-car coal train.

The Rhine!

He de-coaled himself, then tried to get up, but he could not bend his legs. His feet did not want to move. He righted himself and saw the sign: Mannheim.

The train had stopped at the passenger terminal. Stiff and sore, Paul found it more difficult scrambling out than it had been than getting in. But the terminal was well lit, he had more time, and the train wasn't moving. He could see where to grab and where to step. Once over the side, he saw the ladder he was sure had not been there. It climbed up the cross wall of the boxcar, just above the couplers, a spot he couldn't see from his hiding place in the railroad yard.

The toes of his right foot felt numb and two fingers on his left hand were as white as toothpaste. His lungs were raw and his throat hurt like hell. The white towel had turned into a black soggy mess. Otto had told him that Mannheim had a Red Cross nurse on duty right at the station. Maybe he could find her.

He stumbled between the tracks towards the locomotive. The engineer gave him a cheery hello.

"Did you have a nice trip?"

"Hell yes, I did. Here take this and thank you!"

Paul tried to toss him the last two cubes of tobacco, but his arm did not obey. The engineer came down and put his arm around his shoulder.

"Thank you, man. You might see the railroad police walking up and down on the other side. Don't let them shit you. Ask for the Red Cross nurse. If you need to, say the code word. Wash your face as soon as you can. You look like you just came off shift. You'll scare the stationmaster." He laughed a deep laugh, then said, "Don't worry, I know him. He is a good guy. Good luck!"

Paul staggered around the front of the engine and clambered onto the platform of the station. The train rolled on. He became aware of his throbbing knee and wondered how badly it was hurt.

A policeman spotted Paul and walked toward him. Young and aggressive, even arrogant, he had a voice that was harsh, bark-like and unpleasant.

Be careful here.

"You've been on that train?"

"And?"

"You know, it is against the law to be a stowaway on a freight train."

He called and waved over another officer for help.

So here we go. My legs are shaky. I need to sit down soon before I hit the concrete.

The second officer came over. He was older, about fifty. His left foot dragged a little as he walked, and he was short of breath.

"What's cooking, Helmuth?"

"This fellow here rode that coal train. And I..."

"What coal train? I don't see any."

Officer number two looked at Paul. His gestures were fatherly, sympathetic. His eyes met Paul's, and Paul felt a bond of trust between them. His manner said, "Let me handle this."

"You are lucky to be alive. You couldn't have been on a coal train with those clothes? Don't you know it is winter? Where do you come from? Helmuth, let's bring him to the nurse. He looks like he will fall over any minute. You are a prisoner? You escaped? Shit man, welcome home. Hurry up, Helmuth, let's go!"

They took him into the nurse's office and laid him onto a cot. A nurse with a white bonnet had taken off his shoes and officer number two was massaging his frozen fingers. Helmuth cleaned Paul's face with a warm wash rag. They had removed his coat and pants and covered him with blankets. The nurse tried to trickle some hot tea into his mouth, but he was shaking so hard, she spilled every drop.

"Helmuth, hold him still. He must get this tea down. His body needs fluid. I don't want him to shock out right here under my hands."

Warm. He felt the warmth thawing his blood. No bouncing around anymore, no more wind, no snow, no coals. Paul came to and saw the anxious eyes of the nurse gazing down at him.

"We were worried. You passed out twelve hours ago. What did you think you were doing? One half hour in that weather with the stuff you're wearing kills people. Boy, you had guts. Mr. Schiller, the officer who brought you here, wants to talk to you later. But first you must spoon down this soup. Slowly, please." She handed him a piece of buttered bread to go with it.

"How does your foot feel? I cleaned your torn knee. Who took a bite out of it? Your French Madame? Was she that angry that you left her?"

"Very funny. Frau, please, I can't think that fast. Slow down." Paul tried to pull himself up into a sitting position, suddenly feeling the aches and pains he incurred while riding the rails. "I thank you for taking care of me. I am hungry, yes. My foot is on fire. My fingers hurt. I don't feel anything wrong with my knee. Am I okay otherwise?"

"Yes, you seem to be. And my name is Kate. I am Fräulein, not a Frau. Got that?"

Okay, okay! Must be important, sorry gal. Yes, she is good-looking, all right.

Mister Schiller arrived and spoke with the nurse. He turned to Paul.

"I've ordered some flowers, just in case, red ones. I thought you might like red. How is your knee? Looked like somebody had taken a good chunk out of it. Does it hurt? I know, that is the dumbest question I have come up with today, sorry. Please, talk to me, tell me what you have been through."

Paul gave the man a big grin. "First let me thank you for saving me from that Helmuth of yours. He must be new, or else I looked like an alien. The engineer on the locomotive had warned me that my black face would scare the bravest man."

"You did look like the devil whose fire went out. Yes, he is new. I had a talk with him. By the way, is your name Paul? You blabbered in your sleep. You asked questions and gave yourself the answers too. That was nervy. We didn't know who you were as I did not want to go through your things without you. Kate locked them up in that locker over there in the corner."

"Paul, ja, that is me. I know, I am very smart when I am asleep. I guess you want to know from where I escaped and whether or not I really was a prisoner of war. I'll tell you my story, because I like you."

After several minutes of listening to Paul and his escapades, the officer asked, "Why did the French keep you that long? Were you in the SS, or did you pull some shady things in France?"

"I was not in the SS. Here look under my arms, no tattoos, see. I think the French kept me because I did not have a home address until about three months ago. My mother with my sister fled from the Russians and landed in Bavaria."

"Paul, let me warn you, be careful. The Americans occupy Bavaria. Are you aware of the sad fact that they send escaped prisoners back to their camps?"

"Yes, Mister Schiller, I am. We had quite a few prisoners who got away and were brought back from the American-occupied zone. Yes. That is why I am not going to Simbach, where my parents are. I will stay for a while with a family that had been our neighbors back home in Schneidemühl."

"Damn, it must have been rough. You were just a kid three years ago. Well, you don't want to hear my story. Compared to yours, I have none. Listen, I talked to Kate. We suggest you stay another night. That will give you time for a complete thaw-out and warm-up. She tells me that neither your feet nor your fingers had really frozen. And your knee is okay too. You got here just in time. If you'd stayed on that train any longer, you could have been in a lot of hurt. What do you say? The knee, too, will be better in a day or so. I was trying to get you to a hospital in town. But you don't have any real papers. Some other Helmuth could mess up things for you."

"When is Christmas Eve?"

"In four days. Where do you have to go?"

"The family I told you about lives nearby Bielefeld. I would like to be there by Christmas Eve."

"That can be done."

"Okay, I take you up on your kind offer. Tell you the truth, I feel like shit, real shit."

Kate had brought Paul's pants over to his cot. He opened the Heinrich pouch and took out the stubs and the letter from his mother.

"You know, Paul, I don't need to see all that. I believe you. I had a chat with the stationmaster. The engineer on the train you came in on is his friend. I also read somewhere that crooks look different than you do."

"It is not the easiest thing to come home after three years and be nobody, with no identification and no place to go to. I do thank you for your trust. When I saw you coming towards me out there, I knew I would be fine. You have no idea how good that felt."

Paul asked Kate for a pair of scissors. Kate, the Fräulein, was beautiful.

Very nice, and my age. Hmm.

He cut the lining of his trousers and took out the pouch filled with loose tobacco.

"Here, please take this, Mister Schiller. Do you smoke? No?"

"You don't have to do this, really. No, I don't smoke, but I am hooked on coffee. Tobacco is a good commodity to trade with. Guess what a pack of Ami-cigarettes costs on the black market—twenty-five marks! I buy one pack per week with my ration card. I pay two marks for it at a regular cigar store, then I trade the cigarettes for coffee."

"What's a half-kilo of coffee worth?"

"It varies, between sixty and a hundred marks. Paul, you sure you want to give me that? All right, thank you. For that I will help you to get a free ticket from here to Bielefeld. Yes, I can do that.

"You have to excuse me now. My shift starts in a few minutes. I wish I had a different partner. That jerk Helmuth thinks, actually says it right to my face, that Hitler wasn't all that bad. And then he brags about how smart he was, avoiding the draft. I look at you, the many other men coming through here, and I could kill that fucking son of a bitch. Sorry, but shit like that really steams me. Forgive me. So you stay?"

"Yes, thank you again, Mister Schiller, thank you for saving my ass. See you in the morning. Tell Helmuth to go and help clean up Auschwitz. Have him ride a coal train in the wintertime. Then ask him what he thinks of Hitler!"

After the officer left, Kate sat down next to Paul.

"That Schiller, he is such a nice and gentle man. The Russians let him go a couple of years ago because he had some sort of cancer. He says he is okay now, but he lost his wife and two of their children during an air raid here in Mannheim. His house just exploded. He lives now in an underground air raid bunker the city has converted into living cells, yes cells, not rooms. It is an awful way of living." She eyed him critically. "How old are you Paul?"

"I'm twenty, and you?"

"I can see we have to send you back to school and teach you manners. Did you lose them over there in Frankreich, or did you never have any?" But she smiled as she said this. "I forgive you. Guess."

She stood up, and with her head tilted a little, slowly turned around, keeping her beautiful eyes on him all the while. She was an elegant woman. She wore her hair combed straight back. A green ring of some sort held it until it flowed into strands of golden spun silk. It tinseled with every move she made. Her face was delicate, like soft velvet. A smile played with her lips and gave her the looks of one sweet rascal. No rings, no bracelet, no golden chain marred her fine hands. Yet, beneath all that beauty, a soul tinted with pain seemed to linger.

"I'll wager to put you into the barely nineteen bracket."

She laughed and tossed her hair.

"Paul, will you marry me? You are so sweet! You know how to talk to a lady. Those French women tutored you, yes? I am sure glad that you did not freeze out there riding the train."

"I am too. Listen, Kate, I have a little money stashed away. I want to share some of it with you. But my fingers still hurt, so I need your help. You see the seam right under my collar here? Okay, take your scalpel and cut it open."

"No, no, no. I don't need your—"

"Look, I want you to have some. I have enough left. Now cut the seam, Miss Kate! A nineteen-year-old woman should be able to follow this kind of a simple instruction!"

"I'll have to cut your throat for that. But first I do this to you."

Sitting next to him on his cot, she leaned over, reached for his face, and kissed him. He kissed her back gently, but with rousing passion.

"Welcome home, man."

"You are some woman!"

Earlier, she had put up another cot for him in the next room.

"Get in there and go to sleep. The stationmaster told me that a train is bringing home three more prisoners tonight. They come from Le Mans and are in better shape than you. The engineer hid them in one of the empty water boxes in the engine trailer. There will be a lot of commotion. Here, eat that potato soup and then be gone!"

Paul lay on his cot, tingling all over. Kate's kiss lingered on like a wonderful dream.

The next morning she shook him awake.

"Here is your ticket. Schiller brought it in this morning. He also wanted you to have his address. Your train is leaving at three in the afternoon. Come and say hello to the others. They got here after midnight. They are up and will be going on to Hamburg, leaving at the same time as you."

"Do you ever go home, Kate? Don't you need to rest at all?"

"Paul, this is my home. I live here. I have no other place to go." He could see tears begin to fill her eyes. "We lived in Danzig. The Russians came...they broke into our house. They raped my mother and forced me to watch."

"Did they hurt you too?"

She shook her head.

"One soldier ripped off my clothes and made me dance naked in our living room. My little sister was hiding in a closet and saw all this, but at least they did not find her, thank God. They left with our money, our clothes, our silverware. I remember my mother on the floor, beside herself with grief, screaming..."

She broke. Paul cradled her head onto his shoulder and held her tight. He took off her bonnet and caressed her hair. After a while she stopped sobbing.

"I don't know why I am telling you all this. You have enough to carry already. It's just that...sometimes I want to run out there and...and let a train run over me."

"Where are your mother and your sister now?"

"We were loaded into boxcars, going west, they told us. In Stettin we got separated. We had to change trains. I went to find something to eat and came back too late. The train had left without me. I don't know where they are. I don't even know if they are still alive."

I thought I had it bad. What can I do? I have nothing to give. I am new in this world. I am nobody, still fleeing and not sure of tomorrow. I can hold her, yes, but that is all I can do. If I had a place, a real place to go to, I would ask her to come with me. Both of us are lost. We may never find ourselves, never mind the others we have lost.

"Paul, you must let go of me. You must keep walking into your freedom. You do not need to take my pain with you. We need to go on, need to live, need to forgive. I can do that, you see, as long as you guys keep coming home on coal trains."

"Here, this is for you. Please take it. I mean it!"

He put a small roll of francs into her hand.

"Thank you so much, Paul. You just may have bought yourself one more kiss."

"Hey, girl, I don't buy kisses. I give them away. See, like this one!"

She was smiling at him when he dried her tears.

"Now hear me. Promise you will forget what I told you. When you were out the other night, you talked in your sleep about Mary, 'Hail Mary,' you said. Will you pray for me? And I will for you."

"Yes, Kate, I will pray for you. And I thank you for just letting me hold you, to be close to you, if even for a moment. I will not forget. This moment between us will live in my soul forever. In a way I take you with me. I need you to become free again."

He had a tough time keeping his own tears to himself.

She needs a laugh, a bucket of hope, and a strong man with no shit in his bag.

"Don't worry, you will find a girl soon enough. She will help you to forget those three years. You are not so bad looking, Paul, even if you have red ears, a busted knee, and tired eyes."

"Now look who needs to go back to school!"

"Never mind. Now, on the train, be sure you get out in a hurry up there in Bielefeld. The compartments are overcrowded. Try to stay close to a door. The train stops for only a couple of minutes. Don't fall asleep or you'll ride on to the next stop, Hannover. That would be out of your way a bit. They may not have a Schiller there. The folks up north aren't all that friendly."

"May I write to you here at this station?"

She squeezed his hand.

"Oh, Paul, that would be so nice. Yes, let me give you the address here." As she moved to a drawer to get a piece of paper, she gestured to some shoes on the floor. "By the way, I got you some new shoes. The old ones wouldn't have lasted for another kilometer. Try them on."

"You think of everything, do you? They fit, even with my swollen toes."

She handed him her address and a clean, white bandage.

"Here, an extra-thick bandage for your knee. Put it on when you do your walking to Stukenbrock. It'll keep out the cold a little."

Too bad I can't stay with you. We could fall in love. Okay, you say I must let go, so I let go.

He shook hands with the other three, who were older than Paul. They spent the day by talking about how they had been treated, where they had worked, and how thankful everybody was to have made it.

In no time three o'clock arrived. Kate hugged all of them.

"I am so proud of you men! Good luck."

As they walked down the platform, Paul turned to wave his goodbye, but she was gone, the door with the red cross on white already closed.

His fingers still hurt a bit, but the foot and knee were okay. He felt good and ready for another step into freedom.

She had been right about the train. He had to wedge himself between people who did not want to give an inch. He stood close to the door, but could not see out. Others had pushed in after him. Dark descended, and the dim cabin light painted people's faces into masks. He had to fight the sleep that wanted to take him away, although he did doze off a time or two. He dreamt he was talking to the guy next to him, trying to keep him awake. He was in no danger of slumping over during these naps, as the passengers were tightly packed, like asparagus in a can.

When he awoke, his head snapped upwards so hard that his neighbor almost got into a fight with him. How could theyhave fought? They would have had to grow new very short arms.

You are a hero, Kate. Schiller, what a good man you are. Such good people who have gone through hell. And then there is Helmuth, and the people like him, and I can see the reason my country is not well. Mary, please, let them borrow your hands so they can find peace and love. Please let them be safe and help them to forgive. Help me too. I want to be me again.

The train slowed to a stop. Paul could not see the terminal.

"Bielefeld? Is this Bielefeld?"

The woman next to him nodded. People finally gave way, relieving the crush as some of them exited. Still, he had to push and shove to get out.

Kate's words rang in his ears.

"Don't fiddle around. Get out fast. Ask the man with red cap, he'll help you to get where you want to go. Careful, always be careful. The people up north are tough customers. Be mindful whom you trust. There are people out there, Judas-people, who will turn you in for just a few thousand marks."

It was around midnight. The station was well lit. Black letters on a white board a little ways off in the distance spelled the word: BIELEFELD.

God, I'm getting closer. Thanks, but don't leave me yet. I have no idea how to get to Stukenbrock. You know. Share it with me, please. You want me to use the code word? You think they know about it up here?

Paul had just gotten out when the stationmaster raised his signal stick with the green disk, blew his whistle, and the train slowly pulled out of the station. Most of the passengers who had gotten off with him had left the station already.

Paul approached the stationmaster.

"Sir, excuse me. Would you know how I could get to Stukenbrock?"

The stationmaster turned to look at him, mentally matching Paul's face with the mug shots that were posted in his office. Paul knew immediately that he had asked the wrong person.

The man's face hadn't worn a smile for a long time, if ever. His uniform was impeccable, the shiny golden buttons recalling an era long since forgotten. He wore his fire-engine-red cap squarely on his head, and soft, brown, leather gloves covered his hands. He held his signal stick straight down and close to his right leg, clenching it as he would a whip.

He belonged to the same ilk as Helmuth. Though shorter than Helmuth, his broad shoulders made him look taller, more menacing. His demeanor gave the impression that he was a professional, important, not to be taken lightly.

"Now, at this time of the night?"

Paul wondered once again if there was something suspicious about him. Yes, his darting eyes gave him away. Laced with fear, they were always searching for dawning signs of danger.

"Where do you come from?"

Why does he want to know?

"I came from Mannheim."

"Let me see your ticket."

Paul handed over his ticket stub, remembering Kate's warning. Stationmasters were railroad police officers. They had the power and authority to make arrests.

"Where do you live? Where is your home?"

Not in Stukenbrock, Lord, what do I tell this jerk? This is beginning to smell bad.

"Sir, three days ago I escaped from the prisoner of war camp in Merlebach in France."

"You got proof of that, papers, anything?"

Kate had certainly been right. These northerners were cold, unfriendly. There wasn't a trace of a smile, a friendly gesture, a "glad you made it, welcome home." Nothing! This definitely was not Schiller country.

What Paul did not know was that a steady stream of smugglers entered West Germany via Mannheim. The black market was booming out of control, and criminals and crooks flooded the country at an alarming rate. This was life in Germany in December 1947, almost three years after the war had ended.

The stationmaster was simply doing his job. After all, Paul might have been one of "those" guys.

"Well, yes, I do, sir."

As Paul reached into his pants to get the stubs, the railroad man jumped back and raised his signal straight up in the air as a signal for Paul to stop.

"Stop! Don't do that," he commanded and reached for something behind his back.

He has a gun on him. Careful, Paul.

"Mister, trust me, I am not armed. I am an escaped prisoner. I am tired. I am hungry. I am in my own country. We both are German. Why don't you want to help me get on my way?"

The stationmaster looked at Paul with contempt.

"You have no idea how many guys come through here these days, humming that same tune. How do I know what you are telling me is the truth?"

Paul got the stubs from inside his pants, a tightly wadded roll with a rubber band around it. Silently he thanked Heinrich again for making him bring them along. He also handed over his mother's wrinkled letter.

"The pay stubs are from the TEGH Company, where I worked as a prisoner. You can see they did not pay a lot for what they had us do. The letter is from my mother in Simbach."

"How much did you have to pay for all that?"

You are *a son of a bitch!*

"Why don't you go to your mother in Simbach? Come, we talk in my office."

This at least seemed better than being interrogated on the platform. The stationmaster pointed Paul in the right direction and then followed a few safe steps behind.

The office was small, overheated. The man took off his cap and motioned for Paul to sit on the stool by the desk. He lit a cigarette and unrolled the stubs. The rubber band snapped at his hand as he tried to undo it.

As he waited, Paul rolled a cigarette.

"Strong stuff you have there."

I bet you'd like some of it. Ha! Man, you got to wait a long time for one of those. And it won't come from me.

"So, let's hear your story.

The stationmaster undid a few of the golden buttons and leaned back in his squeaky chair. His right arm rested on the desk, his hand playing idly with the cord of the telephone. Paul began to feel like this was just a sport for him, that the stationmaster was the cat, with Paul as his mouse. He fought to quell rising fear and anger inside him.

"All right. I worked as a prisoner of war for the TEGH Company in Merlebach, a coal mining town in France. I was a mechanic at the firm's repair shop. Sometimes I was dispatched to fix things at the miners' housing complex, a subdivision built by TEGH. It was just up the hill from the yard, a fifteen-minute walk. At first when I worked there, a guard would go with me to make sure I wouldn't bail out. After a while, though, they began to trust me. I did favors for them, fixed their motorcycles or their kids' bikes. From then on they left me pretty much alone.

"One of the woman who lived in these houses up the hill that had taken a liking to me. She would buy things I needed, things I could not get in the store at the prison camp. I paid for some of it."

"But your wages sure weren't enough to buy much."

"You are right, Mister..."

"Schneider. Erwin Schneider."

What if he has a hidden button close to his phone that calls the police? Would they believe me?

"Yes, Mr. Schneider, I didn't make much but I saved a lot. Where could I have spent it anyway? I did things in the evening after work. I repaired watches and made rings for girlfriends of the men working at the company. I hammered them out of coins and dressed them up with inlays of colored plastics from toothbrushes. See, like this one I'm wearing."

"Young man, you sure talk a good line, but I still don't believe all this. The stubs and the letter you could have bought, as I'm sure you know."

Sure, I know what you mean. Would you like to know how we really got the money? I could tell you, Erwin, how we prisoners did it. But I don't trust you either. What would you do with me if I told you that I stole a lot?

You see, Mr. Schneider, everyone was corrupt around that place. How about you? Are you straight? Would you forget about me if I greased your palm?

Schneider glanced at the clock.

"You stay here! I have another train coming."

He buttoned up his coat, fitted his red cap onto his crew-cut head, grabbed the signal stick, and slammed the door.

Did he lock it? Why do I have this funny feeling this guy is not okay? I better get the hell out of here. I found Bielefeld. I'll find Stukenbrock.

Erwin Schneider had walked up to the locomotive to talk to the engineer. If he had looked back, he would have seen that his guest had left the office. Paul disappeared like a puff of smoke, the black night swallowing him up. Before leaving the place, Paul had searched Mr. Schneider's cupboard, where he found a piece of bread and an apple, both wrapped in newspaper. He grabbed his pay stubs and Erwin's gloves.

Schneider you are getting sloppy.

He crossed several tracks, jumped over a cyclone fence, and walked the deserted street like a man coming home from his night shift. He had a slight limp to his right foot. The fence had stretched his knee a bit too much.

The cold hit him hard. He nibbled on the bread, which was hard and dry, but the apple tasted ripe, juicy. Half of the bread he put back into his pocket for later. Under a street light on Max Reinhard Street he halted and retrieved a map from a kangaroo pouch Papa Hans had given him.

The paper was warm and damp, and traces of steam escaped from it into the cold night. Clumsily he unfolded it, searching the map for Stukenbrock. It took a while for him to get oriented, but he finally found it, a small dot southeast of Bielefeld.

He kept on walking and turned right on Teutoburger, and then again on Hanse Weg. The outskirts of the city faded into flat farmland and distant forests.

Though he seemed to be on his way, Paul still felt nervous, jumpy. The cold began to crawl under his clothes as he moved along the sleeping streets. A bus came up from behind. The driver stopped and opened the door, motioning for him to get in. He waved him off, and the bus kept on going.

He took a break and checked the map again, wondering how far he had to go. But he couldn't tell from the map.

Still the same. They draw those things only for people who already know where they are going.

Heading south, he finally ran into a sign pointing to a country road. The light patches of fresh snow took the pitch out of the black night, but still he had to get very close to the weathered letters on that slanted wooden shingle before he could make them out.

STUKENBROCK 22km.

Jesus, it didn't look that far away on the map. What would I have done without Erwin's gloves? Kate, those shoes walk good! I better put on that knee patch you gave me. I miss you!

Paul buried his hand with the semi-frozen fingers deep in the pocket of his coat. He leaned against wind, which seemed to be getting stronger. Telephone wires, sagging between their posts, hissed creepy tunes as he marched past.

An hour came and went before he stopped, sitting with his back to the chilling bursts of winter. He scraped snow from the ground to quench his thirst as he ate the last bit of bread, which tasted like crumbly ice. Erwin's gloves stiffened, not fit to take that kind of weather. Beyond a shallow ditch along the road stood cow fences bordering snow-covered grasslands. The night covered the distant horizon beyond.

How much farther do I have to walk? I am so tired, so cold.

The ditch, the culvert, the creek...

Soldiers chained me up like an animal... Ja. When was that? Yesterday? No, long time ago. Hey, Berck, forget that. Think! We are walking away from all that. We are almost home! We will be free. Yes. Free! We are free already! Don't you screw things up! A few more hours only, Paul! Get your ass in gear, now ! Mary, are you around?

Paul got up. Bracing against the wind he stumbled along. His legs did not want to walk anymore. The icy night numbed his dwindling senses. Deliriously he drifted from one side of the road to the other, swaying like a drunk.

Man, I'm tired. I hope this is over soon. I could sit down. Schiller would find me...

Snow dust from the fields drifted in white sheets across the road. Was he walking on clouds? He had to rest more often now and longer. His knee began to hurt badly. In the distance a set of headlights bounced up and down between road and clouds. He got up.

Idiot, down into the ditch! It might be the stationmaster wanting his apple back.

An old farm truck rattled by him. It was storming now and pieces of *"Hail Marys"* came faster off his lips. He tried to run at a slow pace, zigzagging all over the road.

I don't want to freeze to death. You know this here is much colder than it was on top of the coal car. Do you hear me, Mary?

Paul remembered praying the rosary every day when he was carrying the heavy pry bar to and from the quarry in Trois Boeuf. Seven days a week, four miles each way, the painfully uncomfortable wooden shoes clacking the pavement like cattle hooves, the twenty-pound bar denting his shoulder, thirty times "...the Lord be with you..."

Paul, you hear, let that go now. Quit the stumbling. Do it! You have to do it! We are so close. We can't give up now, no! It can't be much longer.

Half of a moon tried to outrace the clouds. The farmhouse in the distance seemed huge. A giant blob silhouetting against the faint sky. Between gusts the wind carried muffled stable noises to the road. Wooden rails rimmed a narrow driveway. Frozen wagon tracks led uphill to the house, not far from the road. Smudges of snow blotched out the dark soil of the fields. There were more houses down the road.

Am I seeing things? Is this the place? Is it over? I'm not lying somewhere by the side of the road, dreaming myself into death? No? Stukenbrock? Where is Frieda Mortz! Did I make it? The stationmaster can't get me anymore. Or can he? Why are there no lights anywhere? They must know Frieda!

He leaned heavily against the frame of the door, head down, eyes closed. He knocked. Paul had no watch; Papa Hans was wearing it. But it must have been around five or six in the morning. The moon had outrun the clouds, and the shadows had become harder. For a while nothing moved inside. Then a dim light came on right above the door.

Through a crack a woman's voice hushed, "Who is it? What do you want?"

"Hello, I am looking for the Mortz family, you know the refugees from..."

A gasp escaped from the woman. "I am Mrs. Mortz, Frieda Mortz...who..."

"Frieda, it's me, Paul, Paul Berck!"

The words came out slurred, drunken. The door opened another two cracks and the light inside shadowed her face. Could that be Frieda? She looked straight at him for a moment.

"Paul!!!"

He was gone.

He came to, sitting on a couch in a small living room. He cried, deep wracking sobs that shook his body. He tried to stop, but the tide could not be turned.

Mieschel and Frieda were crying too. Finally, after a long while, he calmed as the warmth of the room soaked into his iced body. They gave him soft bread and warm milk. No one said a word. Mieschel led him to a bed in the next room. He handed Paul a nightshirt, but he already had fallen asleep with all his clothes on.

Mieschel took off Paul's shoes and undid his filthy wet pants. When he saw the bandage seeping with blood, he called Frieda.

"Mother, come here and look. See his knee?"

"Here, I will take the bandage off. You get some towels and a bowl of warm water, please." When she saw the hole in his knee, she covered her mouth with both of her hands. "My God! How could he ever have walked with that wound?" She fetched some new bandages from her bedroom. "That will do for now. Tomorrow we have to get him to a doctor. I am worried that it might be infected already."

Both of them peeled him out of his coat and covered him with a thick feather blanket. They left the door ajar so as to hear him when he woke up.

A full day and night passed and still Paul did not awake. Frieda asked Mr. Hellwig, the farmer, to come up and check on him.

Hellwig shook his head.

"He must have been deadly tired. Let him sleep. Call me if you need help. Did you say this is the same Paul who used to live next to you back home?" He shook his head in disbelief.

Later that day Paul finally came to and made his way to the kitchen table. Frieda pushed a large plate over to him. He did not trust his eyes: country bread, butter and raspberry marmalade, and milk. He still did not know for sure where he was.

Christ, I hope it's not a dream. Maybe this is what heaven looks like. But, Paul, you know you would have to go to hell first. And in hell, I don't think they get milk to drink.

"Eat and tell us. Please, we would like to know. Tell us how, what, where do you come from, how did you know? Gosh, you look so thin. What did you do to your knee? It must hurt you. You need to see a doctor."

He looked at them, and ever so slightly shook his head.

"Frieda, please, I can't just now. I will talk later. I want to go outside and breathe this new free air. I need to walk for a while without a guard. Walk without being whistled back, without others choosing for me which way to go, how slow or how fast. I want to make sure all this is real. I need to hold this moment and caress it with both of my hands. I need to look in back of me and only see trees, meadows, and sky with no one following me with a gun under his arm. The knock at the door still scares me. I need to lose that. Please don't ask me when I will be back. I promise it won't be long. And don't worry about my leg. It looks worse than it is. It is healing."

Mieschel helped him into a warm winter jacket. It was loose on him, but it was much better than the windbreaker he had worn all these days. The good Frieda had not quite understood what he had said, what he had meant. She had no time anyway to think much about it. Her girls, Geela and Inge, would be arriving in a couple of hours. It was Christmas Eve, and Mieschel still had to go and cut a tree.

Frieda pulled a woolly hat over his ears, and with her right thumb she drew a cross on his forehead.

"Bless you, Paul."

Paul walked out the door into a brisk winter day with gray clouds sailing the sky. The pockets in Mieschel's coat were deep and warm.

Man, I made it! Did I really make it home? Am I free now?

He felt kind of sad. It would have been more whole if he could have been with his family and shared with them these first precious hours of his new life. But that would have to wait.

The narrow-tracked path led him to a corral with horses daring the day. He leaned against the fence with both arms and watched the snowflakes chasing their wind-brushed manes. He listened to the snorts they let go as they came nearer, hesitating now and then. The mare nudged his elbow. Paul scratched her gently between the ears. He inhaled the musky odor of her skin. She snorted again, lifted her head up high, and bolted to find her friends.

He felt life growing back with new, beautiful colors spanning a rainbow into his tomorrow.

Heinrich, I made it. How are you? I hope they did not harm you when they found out you helped me to get away. And Otto, I'm okay, don't worry anymore. Holy Mary, please, help them with their days.

Paul thought about his mother. Over three and a half years had passed since he had seen her last. He wondered how it would be once he saw her again.

Two wars had forged the German people into harsh images. His father had been there twice. Paul had escaped once. Could that be done a second time? Could values and souls be betrayed so many times in one life? Would this blood be dry before another fight?

He turned away from the horses and walked on. The farmhouse was shrinking back into the hills' distances yonder. Once in a while he looked back. Nobody was following him. He still was afraid that this new freedom could be undone on a minute's notice, maybe without any notice at all.

Back in 1941, after dinner one evening, his mother had taken him aside from his sister to tell him that his father had not written for some time. He was fighting the war in France. She was worried something had happened. Paul was surprised she confided in him, as she usually kept everything to herself. For once she had allowed him to look beyond her face.

"Paul, at times it has to be taken away from us, so we know how beautiful it was, when we had it." Cryptic as always. Now, walking this frozen trail, he understood. Before the war he had been free. Freedom? What was it, what did it mean? He really did not know then. But when it had been taken away from him, when he had become a prisoner, when he had to live behind barbed wire, then he came to know what freedom meant.

"Don't worry, Mutti," the young Paul had reassured his mother, happy to be the one to offer solace. "He will write soon. He will be home with us again after we have won this war."

She had just sat there, still, looking at him so very soberly. He could barely hear her speak.

"I don't believe that. Paul, God is not with this Hitler. Never tell your father—or anyone—I said that."

"Oh, Mutti, we *will* win. Yes, I know that. We will!"

The wagon tracks had disappeared under his feet and had changed into a narrow, well-trodden trail that led uphill. Large boulders sat around, lonely. The receding ice cap thousands of years ago had forgotten to grind them up into sand and soil. Now they were a nuisance, standing in the way of plows, seeds, harvests.

Paul leaned over the slanted back of a granite boulder. He embraced the vast expanse of the valley beneath and beyond.

This is so very beautiful! It feels so mighty, wide and far, so very immense and so very tranquil. What I feel must be peace.

He had dared death, but now he hardly dared to touch this moment. He could not handle all this, his new freedom, the stirrings in his soul, the friendly nudging of the mare down by the fence. He felt so unimportant, so small, so lost, as lonesome as the stone next to him.

He did not feel ready yet. The new day could not penetrate the clutter inside him. First he had to face what was haunting him, let the past go to where it belonged before he could trust again, risk new beliefs, make peace with himself. It would happen step by step as he slowly took charge of his own future.

Tiny flakes from nowhere twirled around him and the speckled rock. A flock of white-crowned sparrows skipped over the meadows below, their flight changing abruptly like the Northern Lights shifting colors above the horizon.

The dance of the snowflakes became more crowded. Frieda's farmhouse had disappeared, and the mares huddled nearly invisible at the far end of the pasture. No wind—it had gone to sleep. The flakes, heavy now, fell to the ground weaving a blanket with crystals and glitter.

Kate, I prayed for you on the way up here. I am longing for you. I wished so very much that I could hold you. I wished, oh, how I wished I could kiss you.

He did not want to leave yet and go back to the house. They will have questions he might not want to answer right now.

But they took me in, and I must tell them in a way they will understand. So I better go. I'll be back, though, you igneous-pebbled friend of mine, and share with you my freedom, my new peace.

Paul walked back in the silence of the heavy flakes carried down from up above. His boots left deep tracks. Soon snow would fill them and smooth the trail again. Tomorrow maybe he will leave new spoors striding a little faster into the day.

As he passed the barn, someone came out to greet him, a man so strong and wide he could have been built of the same granite from which Paul's newfound rock had been hewn.

"Good morning, Mr. Paul. It is nice to see you walking around. For a while we thought you'd never wake up. Frieda was worried and so was I. It was rough, wasn't it?"

Paul looked at the man with a question in his eyes.

"Oh," he laughed, wiping his hand on a bloodied towel, then extending a handshake to Paul. "I'm sorry, you don't know me yet. I am Rudi Hellwig."

"Hello, Mr. Hellwig," Paul replied, grasping the massive hand.

"Please call me Rudi, it feels better."

"Okay, thank you, Rudi. Yeah, I needed that sleep. It was a long walk from Bielefeld. If I would not have been so lucky in finding Frieda right away, you might have seen me dead out there somewhere along the road."

Rudi hesitated, looking at Paul and making room for what he just heard.

"Come, we have a new life in here. Come and see."

It was warm inside the barn, and humid. Dim lights took on the gray winter day outside. The air was heavy with the smell of hay and dungy straw. Cows were munching and grinding their second meals. Here and there the tinkle of a chain, the stomping of a hoof spiked into the stillness.

"Over here, see? Mozy just gave birth to her calf. I've been with her since midnight, helping her. I had to pull pretty hard. Finally she let go. I'm so very thankful. On Christmas Eve we have new life in our stables. It is not a child like then, only a cow. Yet to me it is more real than the Holy Night and all the lights and tinsels on the tree."

Paul nodded in awe, not taking his eyes off the calf. It could barely stand. The legs spread awkwardly were not so sure of wanting to take the first steps. Mozy comforted her young. Sniffing and licking it, she somehow managed to make it take her milk.

"May I stay here a while, please?"

As a schoolkid, Paul, like hundreds of other boys and girls, had worked at potato farms during the three-week fall break. In the evening after dinner, Paul would go and watch the farm hands milk the cows and feed the pigs. Often he crawled up in the hayloft where he would sleep till the next morning.

Rudi squeezed Paul's arm.

"Sure, as long as you want. Go on in. Rub the youngster with some straw or with your bare hand. The mother will like that. I need to go, it's milking time. Later, if you like, I'll show you around. Okay?"

Paul took off Mieschel's coat and hung it over a pitchfork leaning against the wall, then watched the calf continue to suckle its mother. The barn suddenly came alive. A woman spread fresh straw in the stall across the way. Anton, Rudi's son, watered the troughs and forked hay into the racks above. Rudi milked a Holstein in a pen close by. Paul could hear the swishing streams hitting the metal pail. Handles clanged as they fell back on the rims of their buckets.

Paul felt tranquil, at peace. With every moment he became more and more aware of his freedom. Many times he said to himself, "I'm free. I'm free."

He went into the crib and sat down in the straw close by the calf. Its fur was still damp from the birthing. He rubbed its back with his bare hand, then lay down. Rudi found him asleep, stretched out on the straw, hugging the newborn animal while Mozy looked on. Rudi would not forget this moment, this Christmas Eve, this true sense of peace.

It was nearly dark when Geela and Inge arrived. Paul had walked to the road to surprise them. But they were so excited to be home, they hurried by without seeing him. He turned and followed.

"Hey, girls! Am I made of glass? Yes, I must be. Can't you say hello to a stranger?"

"Oh my God, I know this voice!"

Geela spun around, stared, let her suitcase drop and ran toward him.

"Paul, oh my God, Paul, is this you? Yes, really? Paul, oh my God, Inge, it is Paul!"

Frieda, leaning out the window, shouted, "You down there, I want a hug too. Let that Paul go. Bring him up here. He's been away all day sleeping with the cows. Come on, it's late. I am so glad you are here safe and sound."

Up in the small living room they settled down a little. Frieda, laughing happily, took them into her arms. Mieschel was hanging tinsel and stars he had woven with straw. The fir filled the room with the smell of Christmas. To make space, Paul shoved the suitcases under the couch and hung the girls' coats up by the door.

Frieda had spent her day baking cookies, rolling almond paste and ground hazelnuts into small balls she dipped in cocoa dust. Mieschel had helped, shelling walnuts and stuffing the goose they would roast on Christmas Day. The Christmas presents Frieda had wrapped the day before. She had no gift for Paul, but she trusted he would understand.

Times were still tough. They were even tougher for refugees. Frieda had been fortunate that the farmer, Mr. Hellwig, had taken her in. He had picked her and Mieschel from a list he had been given by the mayor of Stukenbrock.

The Hellwig family had farmed their fifteen hundred acres for over two hundred years. When his father died, Rudi, the oldest son, had been given the farm. He had two brothers. Egon had become a carpenter and worked in Bielefeld. Willie, the youngest, had gone to sea and traveled all over the world. The war made him into a U-boat man. Somewhere deep in the Atlantic Ocean a torn shell marked his grave. Rudi and Egon did not have to go to war. They produced food for the soldiers fighting on all fronts. Now Rudi, his wife Susi, and Anton, his only son, ran the farm and bred horses, cows, and pigs.

"Paul, come tell us. How did you get here? How did you know to find us..."

Paul looked at Geela and Inge with new eyes. The girls had grown up. The Mädchen had become junge Frauen. He had definitely felt the changes when they hugged and kissed him.

Mieschel ran interference for Paul.

"For now, let's just say Paul got here and save our questions for later. It is Christmas Eve, time to be happy, time to celebrate."

Frieda lit a candle. It flickered at a picture of Max, her late husband. She told the story of the day in 1941 when she had taken it. As she often did, she had brought Max his lunch at his place of work, which was in the public works department in Schneidemühl. Max, the city accountant, had been sitting at his desk adding up the month's utility billings. He looked chipper in his white shirt with the green bow tie.

But Max had come home early from work that afternoon. Like always, he washed his hands over the kitchen sink and then sat down at the table in the living room. He asked Frieda to sit with him. Turning to her, he took her hands.

"Frieda, he won't be coming home."

Shortly after Frieda had left the office that day, an officer of the Army had come to see Max. He had a letter for the Mortz family. Gerhard, their first son, fighting the war in Poland, had stepped on a mine. He had died instantly, the letter said. The country and Hitler himself thanked Max and Frieda for giving their son to the Third Reich. At the bottom of the envelope Max could feel the tag Gerhard had worn. The tag was the only thing that was left of him. And it was badly bent.

The children sat silent, thinking of their lost brother. Then Frieda led them in the *"Our Father."*

There were tears when Mieschel pinched the flame.

"Where are the suitcases? Our presents are in there."

Soon the table was buried under the wrappings of their small gifts, most of them handmade. Knitted gloves for Frieda, socks for Mieschel, a cap for Inge, and a shawl for Geela. Frieda had a leather purse for Inge. She gave a book to Geela, Cornelis Jansen's *Augustinus*. For Mieschel she had a pair of flannel pajamas. Everyone was talking, pointing, trying things on, thanking each other, and hugging. The radio hummed Christmas melodies.

Paul had slipped out. Nobody seemed to miss him. After some time, Inge noticed and went to look for him.

She found him walking towards the road.

"Wait, wait up, Paul!"

A bright moon threw long shadows. The Big Dipper twinkled above among hundreds of thousand of stars. The ground glistened and sparkled in the light that escaped from the windows of the farmhouse.

When Inge caught up with him, she hooked her arm into his. They walked in silence. Paul had always liked Inge, ever since they had been neighbors, living on Wasser Strasse, 3 and 4. She had gone to school at the Lyceum for girls, he to the Tertia at the von Stein Gymnasium. Paul had been a lousy student, while Inge brought home one A after another. Both had been in the Hitler Youth. Paul had sometimes felt like he had a crush on her. But she was a year older than he, and had always considered him just a kid.

At the road Paul halted, searching in the half-light of the moon for her face. He found it hidden under the woolen scarf she wore over her hair.

She almost looks like Kate.

Paul felt her cold hands and rubbed them to get warm. She let him do it, and he even caught a glimpse of a smile. They strolled over to the barn to check on the calf, who stood much steadier now as it suckled its mother. Again Paul looked at Inge, searching, this time wanting. Inge took his arm.

A maple tree had grown tall between the stables and the house. Its barren branches reached into the sky and laid black shadows onto the glittering snow. Paul brushed off the old wooden bench under the tree, and they sat down.

"Are you sad, Paul? You miss your parents, your sister?"

"A little, yes. More so, I miss my friends I left behind. I want to share my freedom with them, the peace of this night, this moment that is not fenced in by guards and guns and barbed wire. And I miss a woman I met a few days ago, a woman..."

The front door opened. Frieda called, "You people, where are you? What are you doing out there in the cold? Come on in. We want to light the candles and sing. Come."

As they stood up to go in, Inge laid her hand on Paul's arm.

"Paul, I am missing someone too. The man I loved and believed loved me, let me go. It happened just before I came here. I feel as though my heart is broken."

Paul took Inge into his arms and, cradling her head, kissed her. She kissed him back. For a long time they hugged and comforted each other.

Mieschel had made a crude nativity scene: the manger of cardboard and paper, white cotton balls made into sheep, two pieces of bark for Joseph and Mary. He had taken a small piece of torn cotton, formed it into a little crib, and stiffened it with flour paste. Frieda held a tiny bundle of wool and yarn, the Christos, and laid it into the crib on the straw. As simple as this scene was, it portrayed perfectly the night in Bethlehem in its deepest meaning.

"Paul, could you read to us Matthew's story?" asked Frieda, handing him the book. Inge came to sit next to him.

"...there was no room in the guest house. Joseph found a shepherd's shed, a stable outside of town..."

Rudi rang the bells on his sled to let them know it was time to go to midnight Mass. Susi had invited Frieda to ride to church with them.

"Please bring the children. This is truly a special Christmas. We have a new calf and your Paul found his way home. The sled is big enough for all of us, and we'll have warm blankets for everyone."

The two horses were waiting impatiently for the smack Rudi would make with the whip, telling them to go.

"All right, go, Marley. Zug, you too."

The polished brass bells on their halters jingled as they trotted toward the village down the road. Loose snow curled in their wake. Inge found Paul's hand under the heavy blanket and leaned her head on his shoulder.

Kate, I feel that I am betraying you. And yet you told me that I would find someone. I just didn't think it could happen that fast. What are you doing now, at this moment? Are you alone, lonesome, longing and sad? I will pray for you, your mother, and your sister. Leaving you that afternoon in Mannheim was harder for me, much harder than leaving Emus or Leo or Wally back in Kreuznach. God, is this life ever going to be a little lighter, not so littered with painful memories? Freedom is so thorny. Others are not free. Is this why?

"Paul, Inge, come, what are you waiting for?"

There was something in Frieda's voice, something in the way she looked at Paul, as though asking herself, "What goes on here? Paul from next door, the kid Geela tutored in Latin and Greek, him? The boy who'd get Mieschel into trouble time and again. I hope not."

The church was filled to the brim. The priest invited them to sit on the floor and on the steps of the altar. Frieda had gone to play the organ. *Te Deum Laudamus!* The Mass was festive. Four altar boys in red with white short gowns brought wine and water. They rang their bells three times at the mea culpa: It is my fault, it is my fault, it is my fault.

The father spoke of forgiveness, of giving, of peace. And then Frieda, as loud as the organ could do, accompanied by trumpets and drums, played *Silent Night*. Paul put his arm around Inge and they sang together.

On New Year's Day, Paul took Inge to his rock. The new-fallen snow gave it a tall white cap. It had taken them some time to get up the hill, with the snow on the trail knee-deep. Paul trampled snow into a bench in front of the boulder for them to sit down.

No horse had greeted them along the way, as Rudi had taken them all back to the stables. The pastures, now white blank sheets, were empty, their fence posts dotting the snow.

Inge, looking down at her iced gloves asked, "Paul, when you kissed me, what did it mean? Where do we go from here? What are your plans? Will you go to Simbach to see your parents and Ingrid? Will you go back to school?"

"Ho ho, Inge, please...I am a man without papers, no certificates to say that I am Paul Berck. I have escaped, you know. The stationmaster in Bielefeld I told you about still might want to have his apple back. I am free, but nobody else knows that, neither can I prove it. I have no money and no place to go, no home. I don't even own a corner somewhere to sleep in. I need to answer many, many other questions first, way before I can talk about us.

"Yes, I kissed you. You did so to me. Do we need to ask why, and what it means? We both are very lonesome people. We hurt. I felt your warmth, your need to touch someone, and I wanted to touch you. My soul is so empty and craving for love. That is maybe why I kissed you and at the same moment I missed Kate, the nurse who saved my life a few days ago when I stumbled off that coal train."

Inge gave him a nod. "Yes, to be honest, when I searched for your hand and hugged you, I wished you were Herbert. He was my first real love. It will be hard for me to forget him. Ja, I hurt, you are right, and I needed you to hold me."

"I like you, Inge, I always have. Maybe we can walk together for a while and try to let the past take and keep what belongs to it. Maybe we could help each other to heal, you from your broken love and me from the war."

"My mother said to me this morning not to tease you, because you are too young for me. Yes, she even said you are nobody, that she never ever trusted you, that I should stay away from you."

Paul shrugged. "Well, then, let's not get too close. I'll go my way and you find yours. Tell Frieda she should not worry about it any longer."

What am I to do now? On Christmas Eve, I offered her my heart. I felt that she was taking it. Yes, I was thinking of Kate. I will always be thinking of her. She pulled me back from the cliff. At moments like those, souls connect, they bond forever. I have to learn to accept that, so must any woman who wants me to go through life with her. Frieda is probably right. I carry too much stuff in my bag. Ugly wounds that fester, keep on hurting, may never get well. Yet, I have lost so much time in my life. I have been without love for so long. It seems foolish for me to wait around. I might never be whole again. I must not wait. I need to go on with my life. I need to find out who I am, what I want, what I need to do to get from here to there. Rock, have you been listening?

The next morning, on the second day of 1948, Rudi took Paul to see Mr. Weizmann, the mayor of Stukenbrock. He listened to Paul's story, examining the TEGH pay stubs and the letter from Paul's mother.

Rudi explained the situation.

"Paul here needs some papers showing that he has been discharged from the prison camp in Merlebach in France. Can you help him?"

Weizmann scratched his beard. He nodded, maybe he could.

"Mr. Berck, I know of an English discharge camp not to far from here. You probably should get your papers there."

Paul shook his head. "Mr. Mayor, with all due respect, I will not go into another camp. I'd rather keep running."

"Yes, I guess I can understand that. Let me think." He sat back in his chair and fixed his eyes on the ceiling. "The commandant of that camp in Münster used to live around here. I know him. I'll give him a call. Mr. Hellwig, please come back tomorrow, yes?"

They rode back to the farm in the small sleigh, with just Zug at the reins. The sky was high and blue, with the sun just peeking over the distant mountains. A glorious winter day.

Inge and Geela would be gone when Paul got back to the house, having taken an early bus to the train station in Bielefeld. They had given him hugs and kisses as Frieda and Mieschel looked on. As the sleigh left for the village with Rudi and Paul, Inge waved from the window above. Paul did not see it. He was sad, very sad. Alone again, yes.

On the way back from the village, Rudi said cheerfully to Paul, "Don't worry. He will get those papers for you without you needing to go down there. He owes me a few favors."

Paul sighed. "Sometimes I think this will never be over. But, thank you, that gives me hope."

Rudi looked sideways at Paul, and seeing his dejection, said, "Listen, I wanted to wait until you got your papers, but I think you need a little cheering up now.

"Susi and I talked about you last night and we agreed. We are happy that you came through and made it home. My brother did not, and I still grieve for him. But, there is something strong in you, very strong. I admire you, and we would like to help. Frieda talked about you going home to Simbach to see your parents, but you have no money for a ticket. Right? We want to buy the ticket for you, and a new wardrobe, as our Christmas present."

Paul stared at Rudi, not believing his ears.

"Rudi, Rudi you are reading a fairytale to me, yes? My God, I thought I would have to hitchhike. I was prepared to get caught again. Do you really mean all that? What did I do to deserve such kindness?"

Rudi gave Paul a smile tinged with sadness.

"See, I cannot go and put flowers on my brother's grave, but by helping you to start over again, I honor my brother. Please, accept this from us."

"How, how can I thank you?"

Although Rudi did not see them, tears flowed unrestrained down Paul's face.

"Come down tonight and have dinner with us. We'll talk some more. We would like to know more about you, your family, your time in the camps, and so on. Of course, if you are not ready to talk just yet, we would understand that too."

"No, I will be there. Thank you! Yes, this means much to me. And give my thanks to your wife too."

Mieschel met Paul at the door.

"Paul, Inge wanted me to give this letter to you." He glanced over his shoulder as he said this, looking to see if Frieda was nearby. "I don't know what's going on. Inge and mother had an argument this morning, and Inge left without a goodbye. She was very upset." Then he noticed Paul's face, which still held traces of his smile. "How did it go? Are you getting your papers?"

"I think so, but I don't know yet." He turned the envelope over in his hands, and his mind drifted back to earlier times. "I'm sorry to hear about Frieda and Inge. You know, I had forgotten it, but I remember now—your mother always was suspicious of me. I think she blamed me for most of the pranks we pulled."

Mieschel laughed. "Yes, sometimes she would tell me I must play with some other boys. 'Forget that Paul for a while,' she would say. But that was all so long ago."

"Well, why all the fuss now? There is nothing going on between Inge and me, though I wished there was."

Mieschel shrugged, not quite believing this.

"Well, she did leave you a letter. Why don't you read it?"

But Paul put it in his pocket. "I think it might be better to wait a while."

Paul avoided Frieda for most of the day and, after dinner at Rudi's, spent the night in the barn. The next morning, he came into breakfast and found Frieda.

"Good morning, Frieda. If you wonder where I've been, I slept in the hayloft last night, right above the mother and her new calf. I needed to be by myself."

She nodded, and set a cup of coffee on the table in front of him.

"I understand, Paul." She paused, then asked, "When do you think you will be going to Simbach? Did you get your papers?"

"I don't know yet. Rudi will take me back to town tomorrow. But, if I crowd you here, Rudi has offered me their spare bedroom downstairs."

"No, no, Paul you are not in the way here. But," she hesitated, "I would like to talk with you...about Inge. You see, she is hurting."

Paul took a sip of the steaming coffee.

"Yes, I know. She told me about Herbert, the man she loves."

Frieda looked surprised. "I didn't know that. At any rate, she is vulnerable right now, and you are desperate for companionship. Inge is still an innocent young woman. I don't know how innocent you are. Do you understand what I am trying to say?"

Paul nodded but said nothing.

How can I tell her about my feelings? What does she know about Inge, about me? I wonder if this Frieda thinks when I worked in the mud for nearly five years that I did not get my hands dirty? She lost her son in that mud, and her husband. So she wants to protect, to shield the treasures the past had not taken away from her. No explaining would help her understand. If her daughter falls in love with a nobody—for whatever reasons—so be it. I need to read the letter.

The mayor of Stukenbrock had telephoned the manager of the discharge camp in Münster and asked for his help in making Paul legal again.

"Well," his friend had said, "we can give preferential treatment to prisoners who have escaped. But I need some proof that it is as you describe it to me. Not that I don't trust you. It's for the records. Everything must be documented."

"I have seen his pay stubs from a construction company in Merlebach. Will those do?" asked the mayor.

The manager of the camp agreed, and after a brief telephone interview with Paul the next day, his papers were prepared.

Three days later, Paul and Susi sat on the early-morning bus rattling toward Bielefeld as snowflakes fell on the countryside.

"Paul, you walked this way just a few days ago. I can't imagine how you did it! God and his mother must have helped you, and some of the angels too." She took his hand. "We so enjoyed our dinner with you the other night. For a little while, it brought Rudi back the memory of his brother, Willie, as he listened to you. He misses him very much, and he has no grave to visit, no place to grieve, to pray."

"I know. Just as I feel when I think about my friends who stayed out there. No cross, no stone tells who they were, whom they loved, who misses them."

"But they have you. You know where their graves are. Paul, your memories keep them alive. You will bring their greetings to the ones they left behind. You have become their messenger. They could not have chosen a better one."

Paul looked out the window at the snow, which was falling heavily now.

If it had snowed that way the other night when I was walking along here, I never would have made it. So much luck, so much help to get me where I am.

"Sometimes I feel guilty being one of the people who made it home, the weight of being the one who must keep on going. Freedom is a demanding gift to carry around."

Paul removed his sunglasses to wipe his eyes. They, along with a hat they would buy later, were to be his disguise to fool the stationmaster.

"Do you really think I will get away with this?" he now asked Susi. "If that stationmaster recognizes me, he will call the police, I'm sure of it."

"You've got your papers now, remember? You are a citizen again, a German one at that. No, I don't think he would, even if he did recognize you."

When Paul had said goodbye that the morning, Frieda's eyes had welled with tears.

"I did not mean to hurt you. Believe me, please."

Paul shook his head. "It's nothing. Thank you for letting

me stay here, for taking care of me. Yes, I will write. And I will not hurt Inge, I promise."

This time Frieda used holy water when she made a cross on his forehead, his lips, and on his chest.

Rudi had walked them down to the road. When the bus came, Rudi kissed Susi and shook Paul's hand, leaving in it several bills.

"What's this?" asked Paul, looking up in surprise.

"Yes, take it. It might come in handy." And then he laughed as Paul gave him a bear hug.

As they climbed on the bus, Paul heard Rudi shout, "Susi, don't forget about the watch!"

In Bielefeld, Susi took Paul to Karstadt, one of the larger department stores that would have everything Susi wanted to buy Paul. New boots, a pair of street shoes, corduroy pants, socks, underwear, three shirts, a woolen jacket, a blue winter coat, and on and on. She selected a good, sturdy suitcase and a satchel made of real leather.

Susi enjoyed herself as much as Paul did.

"Come Paul, let me get you some soft handkerchiefs, and you need these woolen gloves here. Please, try them on. Are they large enough? Oh, and let's not forget the hat. How about this brown one over here? Do you like it? You look charming. Ha, that little Napoleon will not have a clue!"

Their next stop was an Uhrengeschäft, a store that sold watches.

"My friend here needs a good wristwatch that will last him for some time to come. Which one do you like, Paul?"

There must have been hundreds of watches. They sparkled from inside glass towers and from under see-through counters. He pointed at a simple timepiece with a black leather band. A flat crystal covered the golden numerals that contrasted against a white dial.

"No, no, no!" laughed Susi. "Rudi wants you to have a watch that was made in Switzerland. He also wants a good band on it. 'Get Paul a gold-plated wristband, and nothing less,' he said. So, you see, I need to comply. Let's look some more. Don't be so shy, okay?"

Paul felt overwhelmed, undeserving of all the riches that Susi and Rudi lavished on him. He had mentioned giving his watch to Mama and Papa Hans, and Rudi had decided to replace it. Now, as he looked over the staggering array of watches, he just could not select something better than what he had given away.

But Susi saw his dilemma.

"Okay, I'll choose! Here, I like this one, and I hope you will be able to get along with my selection. Yes?"

"Susi, this is a beautiful wristwatch. It costs a fortune! All this is too much for me! I don't know what to say, how to thank you..."

"It's okay, Paul. If Rudi had come with us, he would have filled ten suitcases and probably bought two watches. I had to promise that I would outfit you from head to toe. Not that he really needed to tell me that!"

They staggered under the bags and boxes they now carried.

"We need lunch," said Susi. "Come one, I know where. We have enough time."

Susi took Paul to a fancy restaurant. She ordered for both of them—deer shoulder and white wine. Paul felt elated as he laughed and joked with Susi.

To confuse the waiter, a seemingly very conservative man, they chatted along in French. Susi had taken it in college and, though she was a little rusty, her school-book French went well with the Bretagnese dialect Paul had picked up in Rennes. Since the Germans and the French both wish that the other one would go away, and have fought with each other for centuries, it was only natural that Mr. Waiter wrinkled his nose at these two "foreigners."

After a dessert tart and strong coffee, Susi instructed, "Paul, time to put on the suit of clowns." She handed him the sunglasses, hat, and a cane she had bought to make him look older. She pulled the hat down into his face. "Now let's see how you walk with the cane."

He found it easy to make his limp look genuine.

Susi stood at the ticket window.

"Yes, to Simbach am Inn. What? Oh, let me ask. Paul, do you want to stop over in Heidelberg to visit Inge?"

Now what? Who told her? What does she know?

He cleared his throat.

"Well...if you think that..."

Susi gave him a look of exasperation.

"Listen, young man, it takes a lot to fool me. So don't even try."

Turning back to the ticket clerk, she nodded.

The tarmac was swarming with people rushing between trains. Suddenly Paul froze.

"Susi, there!" He nodded toward a short man in a red uniform walking toward them.

"I see him. Don't worry. Just keep talking."

They carried on their conversation, but had to keep their voices raised to penetrate the din around them.

Erwin Schneider in full uniform, golden buttons and all, passed by. Then, his steps slowed. He hesitated and pivoted to look back at Paul.

Susi, seeing him turn around, quickly hugged and kissed Paul, and shoved him toward his coach.

"Get in there and open the window."

Once seated in his compartment, he leaned out and took her hand.

"Goodbye, Susi and Rudi and Anton. Thank you!"

Schneider raised his green and white disk and blew his whistle. Slowly the train rolled out.

Susi walked along, holding on to Paul's hand as long as she could.

"Good luck, Paul. I know you are going to make it!"

She stood there until the red taillight on the last car disappeared. As she turned back to the terminal, she found herself walking behind the stationmaster.

"Monsieur, could you tell me please, where can I find the bus to Stukenbrock, please?"

Schneider looked at Susi for a long time. Then the real Erwin smiled and said, "I wish I would have had more than an apple and dry bread to give him the other night."

Simbach

Bielefeld—the black letters on white became smaller and smaller and finally disappeared. Paul closed the window. He took off his new coat, folded it neatly, and put it with the suitcase in the net rack above. Sitting down, he let his hands rest in his lap. He tried to wiggle his toes in his new dress shoes that felt so tight.

Well, both of you will have to get used to one another.

The outskirts of the city gave way to snow-covered land. Leaning fenceposts holding onto their strung wires partitioned the loneliness of this cold winter day. Here and there trees stretched their barren ghostly branches into clouded skies.

Paul felt forlorn and alone. He missed the cheerful assurance Susi had carried in her smile, that came with her words. He had never imagined freedom would be difficult to handle, would be a thing he almost feared.

Only a couple of weeks had gone by since he had waved his farewell to Kate, had dared the odds on his walk to Stukenbrock—two weeks of a new life filling his days with tumult and peace, with outrageous joy and deep sadness, and also with fear and doubt.

So help me, I still cannot believe that all this is happening to me. It is so, so immense. I can not embrace it. I am too small for it. My soul is overwhelmed. I do not know what to do.

Paul sat facing in the direction the train was heading. He looked around the compartment, which was only partially occupied. Its wooden benches of shiny, lacquered, oak slats were hard to sit on. Stale cigarette smoke hung in the too-warm air. He began to perspire. The new stuff he wore was so stiff, he began to feel uncomfortable.

The woman across from Paul must have been a school teacher, middle-aged, attractive. Her gray hair was pulled tightly into a knot in the back of her head, a light gray bow sitting on it like a big butterfly. She read from a book she held on her lap, so absorbed that occasionally she would smile or squint in surprise or disbelief.

Paul bent forward a little to catch the title.

Without looking up from the page she offered, "It's from Kurt Kluge, *Der Herr Kortüm*. Why are you staring at me?"

"Oh, I'm sorry. I...I didn't mean to...it's just that...well, you remind me of my mother. I have not seen her in years. I am trying to imagine what she might look like now. You see, I am on my way home."

"You sound worried, yes?"

She looked up from her book and studied him. Her face was soft though not used to letting a smile stay there for long. She closed her book, but kept it in her lap. Paul saw her hands, her long ringless fingers with short, well-manicured nails, like Sasha's. She had polished them without adding any color.
The beige, woolen sweater she wore had a long V-opening in front. It urged the collar of her yellow silk blouse to unfold like the blossoms of a flower. Her dark gray skirt fit tightly, its hem sliding some above her knee. Her soft shoes of light gray leather were flat, seemingly painted to her feet.

Naw, I'm wrong. She's nothing like my mother, no way. How could I have thought that?

Her eyes, dark and cool, kept resting on Paul. Somehow he had the feeling that they were asking questions for which he had no answers.

"No...not worried, anxious... I feel uncertain. Before the war we lived in a small town in Pomerania. Where my family lives now is not our home. I have never been there before."

Why do I talk that way? She is so different from Susi. No, she is not like Sasha. Sasha was less distant, not so made up. I don't know, maybe I'm too tired, confused. I could use a nap. I'll try to sleep a little.

The old man sitting next to her looked over his newspaper. Paul could tell that he was old by the watery eyes behind his dark-rimmed spectacles. Barely noticeably, he nodded at Paul.

"Ja, I know the feeling."

And then he retreated behind his paper again.

The train seemed to slow. Cologne, the sign said; still a ways to Heidelberg.

Paul leaned back into his corner.

The schoolteacher woman kept looking at him.

"You are just coming back from the war, aren't you?"

"Yes, how did you know?"

"There is an air of unrest all about you."

"Yes. Like someone is following me, and does not want to let go of me."

The train rolled on. They raised their voices above the noise that came up from the rails and hummed through the compartment.

"You know, I am hungry," she said, laying down her book. "Would you join me and have something to eat in the restaurant car?"

"Hmm, I have only a few food stamps and I think they are not going to..."

"Oh no, I'll take care of that. Yes?"

"Okay, then." He introduced himself. "I'm Paul, Paul Berck."

"I am Lotte Schröter." In the dining car, she ordered a small bottle of Rhine wine, dry. The waiter swaying with the train filled their sparkling crystals, not spilling a drop. She had declined to smell the cork.

"Just pour it. It'll be okay."

The impeccably dressed steward raised his eyebrows, as if to say, "Ah, one of those."

"Welcome home, young man."

Their glasses clanged together.

"Thank you, Ms. Schröter. You are very kind."

Bullshit, Paul!

"Please call me Lotte."

Paul, what's going on? You've been there. Familiar? Yes.

The sandwiches she had ordered for them both tasted pretty good. Cutting through all the small talk she finally asked, "Paul, when will you be in Munich?"

"Well, I have a stopover in Heidelberg tonight, where I'm visiting a friend. Tomorrow morning around nine I'll be on my way again. The train stops in Stuttgart and Ulm. So I'd guess around noon. Why?"

"Hmm. Since you never have been there, I thought I might show you around München a little. Your family in Simbach, when are they expecting you?"

"Some time this week. When I wrote to them from Stukenbrock, I thought I would have to hitchhike down there. This ride here has come about unexpectedly."

Why do I talk so much? What is the matter with me, with her? When she sat there in the compartment reading her book, she looked so untouchable. And now? I am so much younger. Well, Yvonnette...

The wine had loosened him up. Deep down he knew what she wanted. It seemed obvious now. She had somehow changed from an aloof schoolteacher into a sensuous hunter, well on her way to seducing Paul.

On the way back from the dining car she halted at a window in the passageway. She motioned him to go on to the compartment, indicating that she would follow in a short while. The corridor was narrow, and just as he tried to move past her, the train swayed, throwing their bodies together. Paul felt her warmth. For an eternity the touch lingered on...

Wild thoughts raced through his mind. He raised his arms and—Paul's head jerked up and banged against the wooden back rest of the hard bench. Alarmed, he struggled to get his bearings. The old man slept with his hands folded over the crushed newspaper. The schoolteacher woman, holding her spectacles in her right hand, remained immersed in the *Kortüm* book.

In the corner by the door, a young mother read a story to her young son. The little fellow looked away from the picture book and smiled, giving Paul a "wink-wink" and both laughed. The mother watched Paul for a moment and then kept on reading the story of the prince and the frog. With the confidence of a child, the little boy turned and wedged himself between his mother's legs, using them like the armrests of a comfortable chair. He kept blinking his eyes while he listened to her calming voice retell the fairytale.

Well, I must've been really sleeping. Wow, what a dream! I hope I didn't talk out loud. Jesus! Maybe I did, and they are pretending not to have heard a word. I hope Heidelberg comes up soon.

He relaxed and tried to catch the drift of the story the mother was reading. But the hum in the compartment muffled her voice. The boy continued to listen while he chewed on a shiny spoon that hung from a leather string around his neck.

Paul marveled at how simple and peaceful life seemed to be for this boy. No raging storms in his soul, no doubts or worries about tomorrow. Only the moment counted, the silver spoon, and the story. How wonderful, Paul thought. Yet he could not help asking himself into what times this young human being would grow? Maybe into a time when Jules Vernes' space odysseys would become reality? The atom bomb had already killed, had devastated islands and unleashed molecules that still were poisoning the crust of the earth.

Will this boy have children one day too? What will their values look like? Will there be enough food to nourish them, enough clean water for them to drink? Or will they succumb to untreatable diseases, biological warfare maybe? Or will they deteriorate in galactic collisions that would destroy life on this planet?

Why should I worry about this little boy's future when I do not know what my own tomorrow will bring? When I was a prisoner I did not worry about the next day. Only the moment was important to me. Why does this seem to change now? Why all of a sudden do I feel so lost, so lonesome, so alone? And, yes, afraid! Kate, why is that? Where are you right now? This train does not stop in Mannheim, but I will come to see you soon. Maybe we can be together. I want to. Forgive me about Inge, please!

The prison camp had not offered a hell of a lot of choices. Life or death. Simple. Everything else had been removed from his reach and from his mind. Dreams about being free again, walking without fear, having enough to eat, no longer suffering the pain of hunger had just been dreams. They were mirages skimming along, flirting with a reality that by itself did not seem real.

But now his future was at stake.

Will I learn to survive in this world of free people, this world with its innumerable choices, challenges, and traps? Will I understand that freedom needs to be conquered anew every day, that it does not just happen? Will I comprehend that the rules on either side of the barbed wire are the same? Will I heal from the immensity of pain the war has inflicted on my body and soul? Will somebody be there to love me, help me to become whole?

Paul had read the letter from Inge once right after Mieschel had given it to him. Now he took it from the left pocket of his new jacket. Unfolding it, he looked over to "Lotte." The dream would not let go of him.

In her letter, Inge asked him to wait for her till she could get over the loss of Herbert.

"I like you Paul. I don't know if I ever can love a man again the way I loved him. I want to ask you to be my friend. You said you could.

"I am sorry I encouraged you the other day. I don't know what came over me. I sensed you did not want to. Why? Then we kissed and I made you touch me. No man ever has touched me before. Why did I let you?"

Why did she let me touch her? We never really were friends at home. She is in love with this student, and yet... And why did I kiss her when my heart is aching for Kate? What is the matter with me? I am losing all my bearings?

"It was a sin what we did that afternoon. I will go to confession when I get back to Heidelberg. I do not know what else to say to you. You need to decide which way you want to go, what you want to be.

"My mother says to stay away from you. 'That Paul from next door? You can do better than that. I never trusted him, I never will.' When I left I was angry. She should not have said that. Maybe you want to stop by in Heidelberg on your way home. I have friends there that might be able to help you.

"Do you think you could love me one day?"

He looked out into the black night. The ceiling light of the compartment made the window glass into a mirror. Paul put his forehead against the cold, damp pane. With his hands he blanked out the brightness from above and stared at the toy-like landscape outside. Villages, streetlights of small cities, scattered farmhouses raced by. Bridges crossing frozen rivers and brooks moaned hollowly under the wheels of the speeding train. A pale moon drew freaky shadows over snow-blanketed pastures.

How could she possibly ask me that? She sees no way to feel love for me. She didn't offer any help to soothe my soul. Back in Stukenbrock, up by the rock, she did not have time to listen for what I might have wanted to say. "...decide which way you want to go..." *I barely can understand what is going on inside me. I need someone strong to help me find my way, someone compassionate. Love? I really do not know what that is.*

I don't even know yet what peace is. I have lived without all that for so long. Sure, barbed wire no longer tears at my clothes. Shreds of my soul, though, still hang from it. Shreds I probably will keep missing forever.

He leaned forward and, with both hands, cradled his head.

Just now I am learning to laugh again, to catch and let go of moments filled with bountiful new life. I don't know what I want to be tomorrow other than myself. I don't think I have anything to give that is not tainted with unspeakably horrible memories. Friends I left behind will be walking with me, always. And whoever will be my mate needs to know why. I was wrong, Inge, when I thought that I could help you. I would not know where to begin. No.

He turned from the window with his heart on hold.

Paul saw the large city coming.

This must be Mannheim. Oh God, Kate...

The train made a wide turn towards it.

"Would you mind if I opened the window for just a moment?"

Again, the "teacher" can't be bothered to look up from her book.

"No, go ahead, it's fine with me."

The train did not slow, but raced through the terminal. He leaned out into the cold night. The icy draft choked him. He hoped to spot the Red Cross door. Maybe Kate would be standing there, and he would holler and wave to her. But there was no Red Cross, no white painted door. His window faced away from the station building. He waved anyway.

"Kate! Kate! Kaaaaaaaaate..."

The wind swallowed up his call. His hands became numb. He closed the window and sat down. Nobody seemed to notice him wiping his eyes with a white, neatly folded, monogrammed handkerchief.

Paul got off at Heidelberg to find a nearly empty terminal. A bitter January cold greeted him, complete with biting wind. He clenched the woolen shawl and buttoned up the new winter coat Susi had bought for him.

Why did I stop here? Why, by God, why am I doing this? Is it because I lived next door to her at home, that I've known her since we were kids? Or do I want to drag out the time before my going home, for reasons I don't understand? Is that what it is?

Paul was afraid. He, the boy who had left some three years ago, was coming back as a man, and from a war. He had grown up passing by death, living right at the edge of life. Would his mother and father know that he was no longer a boy? And how will Georg, his father, answer Paul's questions: "Did you know about Auschwitz? How come you came home so much earlier than I?" Yes, Paul was afraid to go on to Simbach.

"Excuse me, Sir. I need to find Werder Strasse in Neuenheim. Could you please direct me?"

"Best thing is to take the tram, Number 2. Get off at Ladenburger and walk west for a couple of blocks. It is not far from here."

This stationmaster was friendlier than the one up north.

Paul deposited his suitcase in one of the baggage lockers and stepped outside onto the street. The tram squealed on the curved tracks and stopped right in front of him. He got in. The black waters of the Neckar River flirted with lights that twinkled down from houses up along its steep banks.

It only took a few minutes to get to Ladenburger. Inge had told him in her letter where she lived. The apartment would be on the third floor.

"When you come upstairs, the door to my room is on the left. My landlord lives behind the door on the right."

Paul looked at his new watch. It was so beautiful, looked so sharp. The numerals glowed in the dark. It was long after eight o'clock.

The apartment house at Ladenburger and Werder Streets happened to be the corner building of a large city block.

Paul, what are you going to say to her?

He checked the number above the entrance. It matched the one given in the letter.

Paul?

He tried to open the narrow heavy door. It was locked. He tried harder. It stayed locked.

The train rattled its way to Simbach at the River Inn, a village some sixty miles due east of Munich. It was a milk train, stopping at every little way station en route. It stopped so many times, Paul could have walked and arrived there ahead of schedule. But that was okay. The longer it took the better.

The benches in those country coaches were harder yet, and the wagons shook from side to side. Four other people traveled with him, an older woman and three men. The men smoked large pipes that looked like huge S-hooks. The tobacco smog was thick and smelled bad. The heat was stifling, but there was no way to turn it down in that compartment. The men talked loudly to each other in their Bavarian dialect, as if they were all alone in the car. What they said Paul could not understand. They wore hats made of dark-green felt and long-linked watch chains that connected the partially hidden timepieces with a button on their leather vest. The pants seemed to be of leather too, shiny in spots with big bulges here and there. Their white socks disappeared halfway up the calves under a colorful ribbon tied below the knee. One man's hands were large enough for a baby to comfortably sleep in.

The woman was dressed in a long blue frock. Despite the overheated compartment, she wore a heavy coat jacket, a shawl, and a woolen scarf over her head, which she had secured with a knot below her jaw. It made her face look very oval as it squeezed her wrinkled cheeks. Every so often she yawned, and Paul saw gaping holes where her teeth should have been. Her chastely folded hands revealed a thin golden ring constricting one of her fingers. The hands were those of a very hard-working woman. Paul decided he liked the woman, although he doubted she would have said the same about him.

Paul must have looked to her like an alien in his new northern street clothes. She studied him, probably wondering whether she could trust him, then she brushed nervously down her frock, as though to assure herself that he did not leave his imprint on her.

The train barely had accelerated to its traveling speed when it stopped again. Two of the men got up and left. They ignored the woman, and, of course, Paul did not count. Their "Grüsst de Gott" was acknowledged by the one who remained and continued to suck deeply on his stinking pipe.

Paul could not squelch a rising feeling of claustrophobia. He wanted to push all this away, to get off the train at the next stop and step into the fresh air.

Kate, I want you to hold me. It is not my knee that is hurting. It is something on the inside, my soul, my heart...

And suddenly he could hold on no longer.

The old woman came over to sit with him. With out turning her face, without a word she reached for his hands and held them. Through his tears he could see her lips move. After a while Paul took her rough hand and kissed it.

In Munich, Paul had called the farmer in whose house his family lived and left a message as to when he would arrive. As the train pulled in, Georg stood on the tarmac, waiting to pick up his son. Paul spotted him first. Georg wore a winter coat and a gray hat. His hair was longer than he ever had allowed Paul to grow it. No red stripes traveled down the side of his pant legs, no golden stars sat on the collar of his coat, no monocle blinked from his left eye.

"Father?"

"Paul!"

"Hello, Vati." They shook hands. Then, Paul picked up his suitcase, and they walked the few miles from the station through town to the farmhouse where the Bercks had a room above the milking stable.

This momentous reunion would forever be a dim, incomplete memory for Paul. Did they hug? Did they talk on the way home? Did he ask about his mother and his sister? The first impression of his mother that Paul carried from that day was that of her kneeling over a washboard by the creek, beating a linen on a board. Later, the only strong remembrance for Paul would be his feeling out of place, wondering whether what he perceived was really happening, and knowing he did not belong nor did he want to be there.

At the farmhouse, Georg led the way upstairs to a large, long room, with a low ceiling. A heavy, black-painted roof beam split the middle of the room, making it necessary to duck when moving from one side of the room to the other. An old couch leaned against the wall, and the two windows faced north. Paul couldn't help but think of his "comfortable" corner in his barracks at Merlebach. But, the barbed wire was missing here in Simbach, and that made this place here a king's palace.

In the evening Grete cooked their meal on a wood stove tucked away in one corner of the sparsely furnished room, with Ingrid sitting nearby at the dinner table. She seemed to hold her body askew, as though she were hurting. When she got up to get the potatoes from the stove, Paul saw why. Her back was hunched.

When Grete and Ingrid were escaping the invading Siberians, his sister had to carry a very heavy knapsack for days on end. The weight was too much for her still-developing spine, and it crippled her back. Now, not even thirteen years old, Ingrid would never go swimming with the crowd, would have to wear special clothes, would forever bear a physical reminder of the hell she had endured. Paul's pains of the past seemed to shrink, to become unimportant by comparison. He was healthy, good-looking, athletic. His scars did not show. Later in life, he would pray to the Blessed Mother for her.

The night darkened the room. Its only forty-watt bulb tried its best to fight against the gloom. The smell of cows and smoked ham covered all else. These are my people. God, what have they done that you make them live in this cage? A general with torn house slippers on his feet? A mother whose eyes were so sad, so despairing, completely vacated of life. A sister left with a distorted body that would never heal. Tell me, what have they done? Their home, their things, their friends—who, if not you, took that all away from them?

But they were free.

Paul, feeling he could not breathe, went out and walked along the creek in back. Ignoring the bitter cold, he watched the water swish around rocks in the narrow river's bed, its gurgle soothing him. He looked up into the starry sky and let Kate hold him.

Before dawn Georg got up, put on heavy rubber overshoes, and wrapped a shawl around his neck. Paul could see the holes in the gloves his father was wearing.

"Where are you going?"

"I must take the train to a farm village not far from here, where I will walk about, talking with the farmers."

"Why?"

"I am a salesman for a fertilizer company."

His mother came and offered Georg a cup of hot milk.

"Ja, your father supports us that way. The farmers know him by now and often let him have an egg or a few ladles of flour, and even some butter once in a while."

That morning, Paul watched the wind pitch the rain against the windows. When it let up, he asked Ingrid to show him the town.

"I saw on the map that the River Inn flows by here, right? I would like to see that."

"Yes, my brother Paul, we can do that."

Although the rain had stopped, the wind kept up its violent tirade as they set out for town.

Grete, no trace of a smile in her voice, warned them, "Now you two remember we eat at five. Don't be late."

"Have fun." Why did she not say that? I have had enough of do not's. I feel so bad. This is all is so terrible. This is not home, not even close to it.

Ingrid, half out the door, turned to Paul, whose feet seemed stuck to the floor.

"I thought we were going to town? So why are you standing there? You look like you are dreaming. Come on."

They had to lean against the gusts on the way to the river. The storm had added to its waters, and it was running fast. Across the river Paul could see Braunau, the place where the infamous leader of the Third Reich had been born.

"How ironic, Ingrid. Of all the places in the country, you and me are looking at a spot on this planet where a monster, a mass murderer came to life. I feel sorry for his mother and father. They must have felt far worse than we ever can imagine. For what they must have suffered here on earth, they should be in heaven."

"Paul, don't say those things. We do not talk about that. We, I mean you and I, had nothing to do with all this, and neither did Mutti."

Paul froze in his step.

"And our father? What about him? Did he not have anything to do 'with all this' either?"

"He was a soldier, Paul. He did what they told him to do. He defended our country. Besides, he is our father, a high-ranking officer—"

Paul stopped that sentence by putting his arms around the little girl. He felt the awkward bulge in her back. It took him by surprise, and yes, it scared him.

Jesus, Mary, Lord, did you hear what I just heard, did you? Don't pretend you were not listening. This is my sister. She is barely thirteen years old. Who told her, taught her to think, to speak that way? Who?

"Come, I'll buy you an ice cream cone. Do you know where the parlor is?"

"They don't sell ice cream here in the wintertime, only in the summer. A man with one leg pushes a cart around. I never have money to buy from him. But I let you invite me for a hot cup of milk. The milk store is not far from here. Okay?"

As they slurped the hot milk, Paul said, "Tell me about how you got away from the Russians, and how it happened that you landed in a town without an ice cream parlor." She laughed. The tension from a while back had flattened.

Her story was heartbreaking, and yet she told it bare of emotions, reciting the events as she would a book report in school.

Germans soldiers had given the order that no one was to leave Schneidemühl, although there was a plan afoot to take the children from their homes and ship them to safety somewhere in the west. The day before that was to happen, Grete ran into an acquaintance, a soldier who remembered and respected Georg. He led her through the barrier at the railroad station and put both her and Ingrid on a train to Stettin.

"What did you do with all the silver we had, the jewelry?" asked Paul.

"Paul, we had less than an hour to get ready and no way to carry anything of value. We left everything there except a blanket and some food."

As she struggled to tell the story, Paul could see that she had pushed the unpleasant memories deep inside her. Grave moments refused to come to the surface, terrible hours did not want to be rerun. In recounting the ordeal, her face did not show the turmoil her soul had endured. Paul did not press her.

"At Stettin we took another train to Schweidnitz in Selesia. We stayed with Grandma and Aunt Mimi for, I don't know, about three weeks." Her eyes seemed to search for something in the distance.

"Once, when our train stopped at a station, we could see a boxcar a few tracks over. As we watched, the heavy doors of the boxcar slid open and what looked like carpet rolls fell off. And then I saw that those were people, refugees like us who had frozen to death during their journey from the eastern border." She stopped, her blank eyes resting on Paul.

God, God what have you done to this child? Was it not enough that I waded through blood and hunger, stepped over death again and again? What more do you want from us?

"Aunt Mimi had a friend somewhere in Bavaria, and they decided we should take the train there. We caught the only train, the last train, leaving. One day later, and we wouldn't have made it.

"The train was so crowded, dangerously crowded. We had nothing to eat for days on end. But, the worst part was that fear traveled with us. People died along the way, and they were simply left at the train stops."

Flashes of the train ride to Rennes shot through Paul's memory. He remembered the dead being discarded like so much baggage at each stop.

"We never made it to the friend's place, because Grandma collapsed, and we had to get off here in Simbach. Aunt Mimi went to the pastor—you know that she used to work for the Caritas, the Catholic organization that helps the needy. The pastor helped us find a place to stay. "Vati came home almost two years ago. I don't know, but I think he has a hard time. He does not talk about the war. I love him. He is doing the best he can. Maybe you can understand, he is a proud man, used to commanding respect, having authority, and now he is begging for an egg, for a couple of potatoes. I did not expect him to be that tall."

Paul and Ingrid left the milk store and walked along the streets of the town. The dark of early evening had crept in, abating the wind somewhat. They ended up at the station, taking a seat in the empty waiting hall. The floor was dirty, the trashcans full, the air tasting of stale tobacco and clothes that had not been washed for some time. But it was warm. The bench they sat on seemed as hard as the story she told. Fleetingly it passed through Paul's mind that all railroad benches must be made to be uncomfortably rigid so no one would linger too long.

"Little girl, you talk like a grown woman. The war took the child right out of you. What went through your mind when you saw the frozen bodies of the refugees from Danzig fall out when they slid back the wagon doors?"

"I really can't remember. Maybe I thought it not to be real. I don't know." She fixed Paul with an unflinching gaze.

"Tell me, Paul, do you love our father?"

There it was.

He took his time in answering, hoping he would not lose her still fragile friendship.

"I suppose I do. But I am not as close to him as you. I don't want to judge him, but he has done many things to me that humiliated me in private as well as in front of others. There were times when I hated him, though I do not anymore. I think loving means giving. But, look, my hand is empty. I have nothing to give. It must be hard for you to listen to this, and very complicated for you to understand it at this moment. Maybe the time will come when I can talk differently about it, more compassionately, less self-centeredly."

The big clock on the wall of the waiting hall said the time was a quarter of six.

Ingrid groaned. "We'll be in trouble, I mean in trouble."

Well, that has not changed, at least.

"Don't worry. You are with me, your big brother. What can she do to us?"

But he returned to his childhood the moment Mutti opened the door at his knock. "I said to be on time!"

The angry words, the bitter rage on her face, transported Paul back to an incident of his youth.

Mieschel and Paul had snuck into Dr. Hart's apple orchard behind the church. They frequently went there to pick a few ripe apples, stashing them in a paper bag and slipping out through a hole in the fence they had made earlier in the year. Their escape route was well camouflaged, undetected by even the custodian, a shrewd and observant man.

One afternoon, when Mieschel had assured Paul that the prelate was hearing confessions, the priest instead decided to walk through his orchard. Evidently he wanted to stew over the sermon he would let loose on the congregation on Sunday.

When Paul first saw him, the prelate was still a ways off, giving them enough time to hide behind the tall pile of compost. But time kept clicking on as he idled in the orchard, and the two boys returned home long past their deadline.

Paul knew he would be in for it. Mieschel would go free, as usual, since the older Paul without question was responsible. This became the standard by which Frieda judged Paul. In her eyes, Mieschel was a good boy whom Paul again and again led astray.

When Paul rang the bell of his apartment, the door opened immediately, with his mother landing a crack on Paul's head and shoulders with her noodle roller before even a word was said.

Now, here in Simbach, he was late one more time. That he had been late coming home from the war did not count. Mother's regulations had remained inflexibly unaffected by the gruesome events of recent years.

Paul sat down to a cold meal. It still tasted delicious. Ingrid, sitting at the other end of the table, hardly dared to look up.

Paul studied his father, who sat on the dented couch struggling to read the paper at forty watts. He thought about what Ingrid had said. He saw the man was worn. Swallowing his pride day after day must have been a nagging pain for him. And then too, Paul believed his father suffered because he could not do better for his wife and his daughter. They had possessed "things" before, as well as stature, and now they were among the poorest, among the ones that no longer were mentioned.

If I ask him how it came about that the "enemy" had let him come home so much sooner than me, his answer would not give back my lost time. Auschwitz, had he known? And what if? What would I do with it? This man is broken whether by his own doing or by the doings of others. It does not change things. His answer, whatever it might be, cannot recall the men from the drenched fields or undo the genocide or heal the cities his war has flattened. It was his war, it still is. It never was mine. He needs to answer to someone else, not me.

All I can do is forgive him. I know that it will take time. I could say it right now though the words' hollowness would ring through. It would not mean a thing. Worse, it would make me a fake. And maybe, in his heart, he would not feel he has to be forgiven. Vati, I know so little about you, so very little. Do you have a God? Two wars have torn on you. Death, too, must have tried to shake hands with you. What do you feel? Why don't I know? Will I ever?

Georg had fallen asleep behind his paper like the old man in the train from Bielefeld.

Do I love you? Do you love me? Both of us have to start mending. You have killed, so have I. In that way, we are no different. Kyrie eleison, we all need your mercy.

The next morning when the family woke up, Paul already was on a train that would stop in Heidelberg. To buy the ticket he had used the last of the money Susi had shoved into his coat pocket when she had hugged him goodbye.

I must write to Rudi and her. And to you, Kate, too...

Ansbach

Ansbach

Paul got off the train in Heidelberg. He had dozed along on the way, uncomfortable and restless, his guilty feelings about his abrupt departure from Simbach disturbing his dreams. Although he had told Ingrid that he was not judging, but forgiving, he knew that to be a lie.

Mannheim, maybe I should go to Mannheim and ask Kate to come with me, but where would we go? Kate, you might not have the answers I need. Both of us are hurt so badly that we probably cannot help each other.

His decision to leave Merlebach had been hard for him. It was not the fear of getting caught, getting shot, but the guilt that made him suffer. As he thought of leaving the others behind, the men with whom he had bonded while death stood watch, he felt a traitor. Heinrich had quieted him down.

"You know, it is you that you have to take care of. Don't wait for others to do it for you. Those who you worry about leaving behind have the same chance, could take the same risk you take. You dare, and so can they. This is your life. You must nurture it, allow it to grow. Only you can enrich it. No, Paul, you are not betraying your friends. You're not a traitor. Not doing what you feel is right—that is betraying yourself."

Hard years had taught Paul about himself. He was finding out that walking the beaten path would kill his chances to explore life, would stifle his growth. Daring would make him a loner later. Daring became his cross. Daring brought him eventual peace.

While riding the train to Heidelberg, he had written to his parents, trying to explain his sudden departure. He knew, though, they would not understand, could not understand. He mailed it and deposited his belongings in the same baggage locker he had used only a few days ago.

It was Saturday, a little before noon. He figured that Inge might be at her apartment. In her letter, she had offered her help and that of her friends. Paul decided to take her up on it. He had not many other choices.

His plan was to apply at the university in Darmstadt. Often, while welding things together in Merlebach, he had envisioned becoming an engineer, learning how to better design the parts so that they would never come apart.

Paul had discussed his intentions with Otto, whose home was in Trautheim, a few miles from Darmstadt.

"I'll help you get started there, if we ever make it out of here." And Heinrich had given his approval.

"Ja, you would make a good engineer." He looked over at Otto and gave a wink. "You may have to walk on your hands for a while before they let you in, but so what?"

Inge was a student at the "Uni" in Heidelberg. She knew what it cost to study and how to go about applying for acceptance. He would ask her to acquaint him with academic life.

This time the outside door to Inge's building was not locked, giving way to his first push. A bare, lonely bulb at each landing lit the hallway. The concrete stairs were narrow. The smell of the old building stuck to the oaken handrail that topped dusty black iron works.

He remembered the door on the left was hers. He hesitated, then he knocked, and from this moment on his new life took shape.

"Oh my God, Paul!"

"Hello, Inge, how are things?"

"What a surprise! Are you coming from Stukenbrock? Did you get your papers? Come on in, come."

The room, which sat at the corner of the building, had two walls with large windows, making the space bright and inviting. A small balcony perched outside. The bed, actually a couch without the backrest, hid on the left side of her room. A large, heavy-looking oval table supported stacks of books. Sheets of paper with handwritten notes lay on the rug that partially covered the wooden floor. Study paraphernalia sat everywhere, stacked in an orderly fashion on shelves along the wall.The room was not very warm. A blanket, thin and very used, hung from the chair at the table. She had hastily thrown it from her shoulders when she had heard the knock on the door.

"You might want to keep your coat on. I am trying to save on my heating bill. Come, sit on the bed. I will go and ask Ms. Baust for some hot water. There is no stove in here. I'll be back in a second."

She wore a woolen shawl tucked into her knit sweater. Its gray color leeched away her womanliness. Her dark-blue bulky trousers further diminished her feminine lines and made her walk ungainly. Her face was a little pale, her lips showing almost no color.

How, how do I start to tell her what I would like to do and at the same time let her know who Kate is?

She came back with two cups of steaming hot water. Pushing aside some papers, she set them on the bare tabletop and sprinkled some malt coffee grounds into the water. Paul tasted the brew.

"I'm glad you stopped by. I have been thinking about our time together up in Stukenbrock. Ever since those days, Herbert has been fading from my mind. More often do I think about you and me."

I should have never knocked on this door.

"But we can talk about this later. First, what have you been doing? Have you decided where you want to go from here, where to start?"

"I've been in Simbach, and seen my family. It was not easy. I did not feel at home there. I want to go to school again, finish my education. Then after that I might want to go to Darmstadt and study to become an engineer."

"Do you have any money?"

"No. I need to find a job right away. Also, I need to find out where I could go to school to finish my education. I don't know how I would fit in with the senior grades at the Gymnasium. I just cannot see myself among sixteen- and seventeen-year-old boys. Can you?"

She did not bother with an answer.

"Last year I heard of a program that offered a make-up curriculum to prepare returning prisoners for matriculation at a university. Tomorrow morning we'll go to church at the university. My mentor, Dr. Richard Hauser, the pastor of the Holy Ghost Church, might know how you can find out about all this." She looked at him uncertainly. "You do go to church, don't you?"

"It can't hurt...can it?"

They kept chatting about all kind of things. It seemed to Paul that she really did not listen when he shared with her his concerns, when he conveyed his difficulties in finding his way back into normal life.

She talked about herself a lot. The university had submitted her application for going to America as an exchange student. She was sure she would be accepted.

"Come, we will go down to the Mensa, the university cafeteria, and have something to eat. I have a student friend who lives there nearby. I'll ask if you could stay with him a few nights until you know more about what you will do. You can not come home with me. Ms. Baust would not approve of us being in the same room alone. She told me her neighbors would start bad rumors."

I want to go back to Merlebach!

After having a bite to eat at the Mensa, Inge took Paul around the University district. Students were everywhere, dressed in clothes that ranged from shabby to chic. The Mensa, the students, the whole atmosphere acquainted Paul with a feeling completely new to him. He felt inadequate.

How am I going to do all this? I don't fit here. I am never going to make it.

They stopped by the church to say a few *Hail Marys*. As Paul entered, he suddenly stopped.

The high stone arches, colored lead-framed picture windows, the rosette above the organ pipes and the wooden pews, all echoed silent madrigals composed of more than four hundred years of prayers.

Seldom thereafter would he ever experience such an enormous, powerful onrush of peace and tranquillity.

It was during those few minutes when he knew, in his heart, that he would make it. On the way out, pretending to sprinkle holy water over his head, he waved back to Mary, who was watching him, as he well knew.

Hubert Kiebel was a medical student who lived in a two-room apartment in the old-town district of Heidelberg. His father, a family doctor in Neustadt, sent comfortable sums of money on the fifteenth of every month.

Hubert did not have to explain all this to Paul. The apartment emitted the fragrance of affluence.

Naturally very outgoing and friendly, Hubert greeted Paul with genuine warmth in his smile and a soft but firm handshake. "Guten Abend, Inge. So this is your friend Paul whom you spoke to me about. Well, it is my pleasure to meet you, Paul. Inge has told me you probably would visit her here in Heidelberg and that you would need a place to sleep. This is my home, please be my guest." He turned to Inge to assure her.

"The sofa is comfortable and Paul is welcome to it as long as he needs shelter. I'll give him a key, just in case he can't make it before ten. That's when the house door automatically locks." He gave Paul a "we won't tell anybody" grin.

The evenings at Hubert's place were a blessing for Paul. They would have long discussions into the night, exploring those things that haunted his soul—Paul on the couch, Hubert in his bed, the ever-present reading-board on his knees. From Hubert, Paul came to learn that, even in Heidelberg, students and professors, no matter how gifted or famous, could not boil water any hotter than anyone else.

"You see, when we are naked, we look very much alike. And after we have made the down payment on that proverbial four-by-ten hole, there is no difference between us anymore whatsoever.

"I believe it to be natural when we occasionally feel inferior. We all have those days, even weeks maybe, when those feelings try to tear us down. For me that is okay. It refocuses my perceptions. There is so much out there that tempts us to be larger than life. We just have to learn that mirages don't count."

Paul had not minced his words about where he had come from, how hard it was for him to find his way back into a society that would not stop for him to get on.

One night at Hubert's place, Paul ranted about Inge. She had told him that day that she was serious about a relationship with him, that she felt his kissing her obligated him to also think very seriously about their future.

Hubert had come over to Paul and hugged him.

"You know, Paul, you have mastered life as no one else I know has. I have no doubt you will handle well whatever comes your way. Come, this is your last night here. I bought a bottle of wine. Let us empty the chalice!"

Sunday after church, Dr. Hauser met with Paul. They sat in the pastor's study, a large room stuffed with books, all of which, according to Inge, Dr. Hauser had read, and not just once. Paul was overwhelmed. He tried to read a few names. Kiarkegaard, Freud, Sartre...all were Greek to Paul.

No wonder when this Hauser looks at me I feel like I'm being x-rayed. He is extremely well informed. His hands show that he is celebrating the daily mass out of conviction and utter dedication. I am in awe. Inge has precious friends.

"Mr. Berck, I found out that the Gymnasium in Ansbach is commencing with a course for escaped prisoners. They ceased taking applications last week; however, the principal there, a Dr. Wagenraht, is an acquaintance of mine. He will admit you if you meet the basic requirements. The course starts toward the end of February. So, you will have a few days to prepare yourself. I suggest you travel there soon and apply in person. Ms. Mortz had mentioned that you are without funds. I have arranged for the Caritas director to advance two hundred marks to you." When Paul tried to refuse the envelope the pastor thrust toward him, the older man insisted. "Please, take it. One day when you are an engineer you might want to pass it on to people who are wearing shoes like yours today."

Nodding, Paul accepted the money gratefully. "Sir, I don't know how to thank you. I came here not expecting all that. In fact, I expected very little. When I first stepped back into my country a few weeks ago, I did not find a soul who would even say "hi" to me. Then in Stukenbrock, a man named Rudi and his family helped me with my first hours of freedom. So did the Mortzes. And now here today you gave to me the opportunity to go on with my life. You will never know how much I am indebted to you."

Paul had not been able to apply in person as Dr. Hauser had suggested, for there was no money for the trip to Ansbach. Luckily, Mr. Wagenraht had accepted him after a brief interview by telephone.

A bright early February morning in 1948 found the Heiligen Berg, where Inge and Paul had walked to say goodbye, bathed in full sun. The morning rush of the city had disappeared, and the streets rested now, awaiting the onslaught that would come again later that afternoon.

The Neckar River below pushed its lazy waters through the city and under the new bridge further downstream. The red sandstone arches of the famous river crossing upstream carried the street through the towered medieval gate into old-town Heidelberg. To the left and above the maze of narrow alleys, the famous castle raised its ruins. They could see The Holy Ghost Church from up there.

"I will come to see you when I can."

"How do you think you can do that, Paul? You have no money."

"Maybe I will. Now, girl, we need to go. The train is not going to wait for me."

On the way down Philosophen Weg, they walked in silence holding hands. The streetcar took them along Brücken Street across the river to the railroad station. He bought a ticket and still had enough money left over to pay the first month's rent for the room in Ansbach.

"Paul, you will need some money to buy food."

"Don't worry. I've been hungry before. I will get a job right away."

Leaning out of the window, he kept waving until the white steam clouds had swallowed her.

Ha, steam billowing back over the train...only a few weeks ago I saw the same thing. Wow, things sure changed in a hurry. Kate, next time I am in Heidelberg, I will stop en route and come to see you.

"Young man, would you please close that window? It is too drafty and I already have a cold."

"Of course, ma'am, I am sorry."

Paul shoved the window upward and sat down. He tried to start a conversation with the elderly woman, but the draft must have been too much for her.

Looking away from the woman's stony face, he turned to gaze out the window at telephone poles flashing by at a fast and steady clip. The white porcelain insulators strobed as they raised the wires above their sagging valleys. Up and down, up and down, Paul's head oscillated in synchrony. Beyond and in the distance, horses, trees, roads, and cows were busy with life. The train seemed to zip along the edge of a slow-spinning disc composed of still pictures seamlessly sliding from one into another.

I am afraid of Ansbach. School? Me going back to school again? How will I get my brain back in gear? I hate Latin and Greek and history, and I'm not so hot in Math. In religion, where everybody got an A, I could barely come up with a B. How will I be able to make it in school with a job on the side? Hubert! I need a shot of confidence!

More houses rushed by followed by fenced fields. Wide roads snaked between them. Ahead he could make out his new city.

Ansbach, a town heavily burdened with history since its medieval birth, sprawled into a late afternoon day.

The family letting him the room had told him which narrow streets to follow to find their house. He found the address in no time and was greeted by Mr. and Mrs. Holzmann with the reserved manner of a smalltown couple.

Mister Holzmann led the way upstairs to the room, which Paul found charming: clean, neat, much like an enlarged dollhouse! A colorful quilt dressed the bed. A small table covered with a red-and-white checkered waxcloth stood right by the narrow window. A large gold-framed mirror hung above a bowl and a carafe filled with water, and a waist-high washstand with its Louis XIV legs stood by. From the center of the ceiling dangled a tiffany lampshade, its iridescent glass absorbing most of the light and dimming the room into a warm coziness.

"Is that all the luggage you brought?"
asked Mr. Holzmann. He had a low voice and spoke slowly, hesitating before speaking words with more than two syllables.

Do more suitcases make for a better person?

Paul's insecurity index increased by several points.

"Yes, that's all."

This seemed to worry his new landlord, or perhaps it was the battered and used condition of the case, Paul could not tell.

"We hope you will like it here. I'll bring up a chair for you later."

There is more. Tell me. Come on.

Holzmann's eyes were searching for help that seemed to be hiding in the corner above the ancient mirror.

"We don't want you to have any parties here, and no"—his eyes pussyfooted over to the bedstead— "no girlfriends. You know, the neighbors, how they are, they might...well you know. The rent is due on the first. Else, my wife, offered to wash your shirts and underwear." His face flushed with this last word.

"Thank you, Mr. Holzmann. Here is my first rent payment, forty marks, as you told me. I like the room, thank you again. I promise, I will behave."

"Oh Mr. Berck—"

"Please, call me Paul."

"Yes, Paul, okay. Our son, Ludwig, well, maybe you could help him sometimes with his homework?"

"I'll try my best."

Just what I needed! Classes, a job on the side, my homework, and Ludwig. No parties? It's superfluous even to mention that.

Holzmann left with a smile, but still troubled by that beatup suitcase. He would have to talk to Else about that right away. Fortunately, he did not know that it was empty, not counting a pair of socks and a change of shorts. Paul, without unpacking, shoved the thing under the bed.

The smell of boiled potatoes and polish sausage crept through the cracks of his new place and right into his stomach.

It's Sunday. The stores are not open. Even if I wanted to buy some bread, I couldn't.

He deadened his hunger with two glasses of stale water from the carafe and then took to the streets. He found his school, which looked just as forbidding as any other school he had ever been in. The Catholic school in Stettin came to mind. It looked like a prison from the outside, which fit the style of his old tormentor, Mr. Macke, and the other teaching guards inside. His memory of his teacher had not mellowed with the distance of time. Instead, he saw the man for what he truly was: a sadistic tyrant who abused his power to physically and mentally harm his students. He, and the others like him, were never reined in, for parents of the time considered severe punishment a necessity in bringing up well-behaved, and more important, *obedient* children. Their *Oliver Twist*–era penal practices were simply considered an essential part of every child's education.

The evening came alive in Ansbach. Streetlights, lanterns atop ornamental cast-iron posts, were being lit by a city worker who carried a long tube with a flame at the end. He pulled the gas valve open and gave the flame to the Laterne. As the man went from street to street, Paul followed, fascinated by the ritual. Only fancy cities had lights like these.

Back in his room he gulped some more water and went to bed. Sleep hushed away the worrisome day.

The next morning he showed up for school, garbed in fresh socks and underwear from the suitcase, but the same shirt from the day before. He'd had no breakfast, which did not worry him, for his body had gotten quite used to starting the day with out any nourishment.

If I don't like it, I'll quit, I'll... The hell you will! You are strong enough now to snap Macke's neck. Look at the others, they cannot possibly all be smarter than you. Go on in.

The classroom filled from the back. Like in church, nobody wanted to sit too close to the communion rail. Paul picked a desk somewhere in the middle. The men grinned at each other. To an outsider, it would not have appeared that these men were ex-prisoners. They looked more like older boys staying after school because they had flipped wet tissue balls at the blackboard. And yet there was something about them.

"What am I doing here?" their eyes seemed to say. "I must be nuts!"

Their faces mirrored their uncertainty. They had survived hunger and hard times, had formed their own thoughts about things. They might, they just might have different opinions about Homer or God. Would that be acceptable here?

Bells shrilled throughout the building. The door opened with a bang.

Alea iacta est...the dice has been thrown, it has started.

Two men walked to the podium. One stood ready to speak, the other remaining in the background.

"Meine Herren, gentlemen, it is good to see you all have made it. Welcome. I am the principal, Mr. Wagenraht. Mr. Schäufel here is your resident teacher. He will be your guide through what will probably be a difficult time for you.

"I would like to assure you that we have thoroughly scrutinized your applications and are aware of what each one of you had to go through. I also must say that our staff never before had to master a task like this one. I want to be honest with you: We need your help to make this a successful event for all of us."

Paul looked around. Heads were nodding here and there. The initial tension seemed to have found its way out of the room. Paul felt more confident, more at ease, too.

"We are looking forward to this new experience. I believe it will enrich our curriculum. I know we, as teachers, will benefit. I envision you leading us into new territory, which we had felt to be off limits.

"Charting this course, we have eliminated many subjects that we usually teach in Primas and Oberprimas, Grades 12 and 13. Believe me, it was not easy to cram two years into six months!" Paul leaned over to his neighbor.

"He does say the right things, doesn't he?"

"Yeah, but I am still scared shitless. How about you?"

Paul answered with a confirming nod.

The principal drew his remarks to a close.

"One more item. We understand, from what you have told us, that only a few of you have financial support. I am very pleased to let you know that several firms here in town have pledged job opportunities for you. To ease your mind, we will hold homework to an absolute minimum. I personally know how hard it is to have a job and go to school at the same time. We will meet with you on a monthly basis. You can check on your progress and voice your concerns. I hope this format will work for you. I wish you success. And now, may I introduce your guide for this new journey, Dr. Victor Schäufel." Turning to Schäufel, he gave a wave of his arm. "Victor, I present you with your class of '48."

A few rows back a couple men started clapping, soon all joined in. Wagenraht had taken the edge off. It would be all right.

Victor took the floor. He began by telling them a bit about himself—where he had been during the war, about his wife of thirty years, Martha. He would be their mentor, together with Father Krause. Science, biology, chemistry, and physics were his specialties, and he would do his best to make them all very interesting for them.

At first glance, Mr. Schäufel seemed a bit odd. His shoulders barely reached the top of the podium next to him, because his hunchback kept his frame tilted. His words, tinted with a slight Bavarian accent, flowed from his mouth with a frail hiss. He saw the world through glasses with thick lenses and old-fashioned horn-rimmed frames. Hair nearly whiter than snow topped his head, and he hid his clothes under a light-blue lab coat.

But Paul saw something he liked, a little of Max and a perhaps a piece of Ivanovich. Yes, Paul decided he could get to like the man. With his help, they would make it.

Each student stood up, gave his name, told where he came from, and what his plans were for the future. The bells rang, but nobody paid attention. They were too busy getting acquainted with each other.

When school let out at one o'clock, Paul stopped at the personnel office to get a list of the firms Mr. Wagenraht had mentioned. A few of those companies only needed gofers, which offered little pay. A few blocks from where Paul lived, however, he found a junkyard company that offered him a job as a scrap cutter, working each afternoon from three to nine. His take-home pay would be two marks per hour.

The foreman, Mr. Wiesel, took a liking to Paul right from the start.

"You, what's your name again? Ja, Paul go to the office and tell the payroll lady I said you need a little money in advance. No, no...don't worry, I know you will come and start tomorrow. You don't look like a loser to me. Go on, do it."

He spat twice, not to be rude, but because he spat on the ground after every sentence he squeezed from his chest. Then he straddled his bike and disappeared between huge piles of twisted steel beams.

Paul received ten marks. Bread, margarine, and some sausage would cost about two marks and fifty pennies at the grocery store he had discovered down the street from his apartment.

HORNUNG'S DELICATESSEN, the sign had read. Sitting at the corner of Eschenbach and Parzival, the store featured two large display windows, one facing each street. These windows seemed to compete with each other, with their elaborate arrangements of food and flowers that invited passersby to come in and visit with the cheeses, to admire the baskets holding dark blue grapes and red apples. Deliciously coarse-sliced liver sausage shared a bed of straw with brown jumbo eggs. Big loaves of flat, round country bread leaned like wagon wheels against a terraced glass shelf, on which sat tall jars bursting with long dill pickles. Hams, smoked at farms in Westphalia, lay in folds of bunched-up burlap. A few bottles of ruby red Cabernet Sauvignon added an exquisite touch to this portrait of specialties.

Paul found the store to be larger than it had appeared from the outside. A curved glass-fronted counter offered cut meats, chops, and fresh fish fillets. Fragrances and smells of smoked chicken, herbs, and fruit lured an empty stomach into surrender. As Paul waited his turn, he checked out the prices.

Yes, two marks an hour will do fine. Better than I had hoped. But I wonder if I am not too poor to become a regular patron here.

The owner spotted him, a new customer! All perked up, he held his hands, one washing the other, in front of his chest. With his head slightly leaning to one side, he was a perfect replica of a squirrel hiding a peanut under its tail.

"Good evening, mein Herr, good evening! What is your pleasure tonight? Have you recently moved to our beautiful city, or are you just visiting?"

Paul mentioned that he was attending a two-years-crammed-into-six-months course at the Gymnasium.

"Ah, you are one of those prisoners that came home late after the war. Yes, yes, I heard about it. Are you living close by?"

"Yes, I am renting a room from the Holzmanns."

"Good, good, good. I know them. Yes, they always buy my sausage and the special cheese I import from France. Nice people, very nice."

His air-washing hands worked faster. "And what can we do for you tonight?"

Mr. Hornung wrapped up everything Paul had bought and handed it over the counter.

"I put an egg in there, free of charge, my welcome gift. Good evening, Mr. Berck."

Now, I did not tell him my name. Must be a small town. Could be, too, that Felix has told him in strict confidence. In a way, it is good the grocer knows me. Ha, one egg! Paul! The gift-horse! You promised no more looking in its mouth.

He was sitting at the table eating when he heard the knock on his door.

"Come on in, it's open."

In walked a boy. Clean, neat, with short blond hair that stood straight up, he did not have to open the door wide to let his thin, wiry frame slip into the room. Paul liked him at once.

"Hey, you must be Ludwig, yes? Here, sit on the bed. I am Paul."

Ludwig stared at Paul's napkin, a double-folded page of newspaper. It protected the wax cloth from the margarine and the sausage he was putting away in big bites.

"Is that what you eat for supper? You have to come and eat with us. I'll tell my mother."

"I'm okay, don't worry about me. Do you have a question about your homework?" "

"Yes, my father said that you offered to help me. But I am only allowed to ask you if I am really stuck, which is quite often, you know."

Paul told him about the new job and his schedule. They would play it by ear.

"All right, let's give it a try. What is it tonight that you do not understand?"

"I have a problem multiplying numbers in my head. Our teacher does not allow us to use our fingers. Is there a way you know of that would make it easier for me to come up with the right answer?"

"I can show you how I multiply numbers without using my fingers." said Paul, wiping his mouth. "Let's take 17 times 15. I think of the 15 as a 10 plus a 5. Multiplying by 10 is easy. So 10 times 17 makes 170. Now 5 times 17 is just half of 170..."

"Gosh, I see, I see. So half of 170 is 5 times 10 plus 5 times 7; 50 plus 35. I got it. I got it! Wow! 17 times 15 is 170 plus 85. 255 right? Paul, come, be our math teacher."

Paul laughed at the boy's enthusiasm.

"How old are you, Ludwig?"

"I'll be twelve next month. I need to go now. Good night, Paul, and thank you. Maybe Saturday?"

Paul did the cat-wash with the carafe and the bowl. The cotton towel was just large enough to dry one arm, and he had to windmill the other one.

What if he comes one day with a problem I can't wing? I would tell him, I guess, and get the answer from the wise men at school. Now, what am I going to do with that raw egg? I know—get hungry and eat it! You know how to do that. Remember, it tasted pretty good.

Yes, Trois Boeuf, 1946. They had been working the quarries for some time. On the way to or from work, the guard let the prisoners sometimes leave the walking platoon to relieve themselves in the tall, loose-brush hedges that lined the road. The farmers' hens laid clutches of eggs in these same bushes, and Paul and others learned how to eat the eggs raw, since they could not carry them home in their pockets. With a nail, Paul would poke two holes into an egg, one at each end, and suck the white with the yolk right down his throat. To inhale three took about thirty seconds, no longer, which still gave him time to pee. The gang never got caught because none of the farmhouses had windows facing toward the road. Paul sucked the gift egg à la Trois Boeuf and went to sleep.

At the next morning, Mr. Schäufel brought name tags.

"I am sure you are familiar with your own name, but I am not. So, please, wear those things until your face and your name have become one for me."

His neighbor's elbow poked into Paul's ribs.

"I like him. The man is a clown, a mentor clown. Hey you, this is Franz speaking. Will you tell me your name now, or do I have to wait for your tag? If so, you have to read it to me, 'cause I am farsighted and can't afford glasses."

"I can give it to you now. I know it by heart. It is Paul. Are you sure you can hear okay? Ja, I like him too."

"You know, they told me that there were enough comedians in this class already."

Victor passed the tags out. Three students did not put them on.

"With all due respect, sir, I feel like I am still wearing my PDG tag. You don't want me to wear two tags, or do you?"

Without hesitation, Victor smiled and said, "Of course, of course, I understand. Here is the deal. I will call you Number 1, you over there Number 2, and you there in the fifth row, you are Number 3."

He had not hurt them, but had shown that he was running the show.

"The first two hours this morning will be filled with biology, unless you fellows want to discuss other more important issues." Silence. "Good. I take this as a vote of confidence. "Biology is the science of life. Gentlemen, that is a mouthful—bios and logos. Two Greek words that describe the basic building blocks of culture: 'life' and 'word.' You probably know that the Greeks were a religious, mythological people back in Agamemnon's time. All wisdom, their gods, judgments, and prophecies were 'logos,' the supreme essence of logic."

Franz shielded his mouth to ask Paul, "Do you know about this shit? What's it got to do with biology? You know the bees and Adam bitin' in that apple. That's biology, or am I..."

Victor had good ears. He walked toward Franz.

"Mr. Franz, yes, I see your tag, thank you. Is there something you would like to share with us? By the way fellows, you don't have to get up when we talk to each other. Another rule we are breaking to make things easier. Well?"

Franz gave Paul the "Jesus!" look. Drumming on the desktop with his pencil, he answered, "Well, if I get this right, you are saying that life has to do with logos, yeah, with God."

"You feel that is too far away from the fundamental meaning of the word biology?"

Franz was grasping for a reply when Number 3 raised his hand.

"Yes, Number 3."

"Sir, I personally don't care about this Greek stuff. I want to find out where life comes from and how we go about finding out what it is. You know, cells, molecules, behavior, things like that." Mr. Schäufel squinted. As time went on Paul learned to associate this twist in Victor's face with a desperate internal call for help.

The bell cut things short. Number 3 would have to wait for his answer until tomorrow.

Third and fourth periods, dedicated to chemistry and physics, passed without Victor mentioning the atomic composition of hydrogen or the anomaly of water. But he discussed with them the atom, its stored energy, and the racing electrons that orbit around the nucleus.

"When I went to school, the word 'atom' described a particle that was so small that it could not be divided into yet a smaller part. 'Atomos' in Greek, means indivisible, actually 'un-cut-able.'"

Paul raised his hand. "Yes, Mr. Schäufel, we were taught that too. Hiroshima, though, was proof that this never had been true."

The bell told them to go and have lunch.

"Paul, I just discovered that I forgot to bring my lunch. Do you think..."

"Franz, guess what? This morning my mother slept in, so I had to leave home without the bread."

"Despite that you are too funny, I'll share a cup of water with you. Yes?"

"And from whom do you think we could borrow a cup?"

Schäufel had retired to the conference room, the safe haven for teachers, where he sat down across from Father Krause.

"Father, take this chalice away."

"Victor, that is not exactly what Jesus said at Gethsemane."

"Krause, I forgive you because you have no idea what is coming your way!"

On his way home, Paul bought a pair of boots from a gypsy who was trolling the streets for customers.

Five marks, not too bad, I can handle that. I'll last till payday on Friday.

He reached for the new shoes and caressed the stiff leather. Boots! Suddenly he felt them burning his hands. Their laces curled like eels in a barrel, slimy and ugly.

The gypsy bent over his cart. His face showed worry.

"You? Boots no good? Why? You give back. Want this pair here, maybe better for you, yes?"

Paul stared at the man unable to move. Boots! The shoestrings that were so tight and the dead man's stiff legs...in the boxcar...at night...on the way to Rennes...

Oh my God!

For a moment the man behind his cart looked like the soldier who had cut the laces, taken off the boots from the dead man's feet, and thrown them back at Paul.

Yes, I wore those for a long time, with the bailing wire around them to hold the soles in place, the shoes I robbed from a dead man, and I didn't even know his name...

Paul slowly turned from the cart and walked away holding his new shoes as a mother would cradle her baby.

The foreman and another scrap cutter outfitted Paul with goggles, a face shield, gloves, and a cutting torch with a lighter.

"Now listen," Wiesel said, then spat.

Paul found this constant spitting mesmerizing. Wiesel's technique—his tongue forcing saliva through a small gap between his front teeth to create pressure and achieve distance—was a new one to Paul. His aim was excellent, consistently hitting the ground about two inches away from Paul's left boot.

"You told me you know about torches. Okay, this here is a three-footer." Spit. "You can reach way into the scrap heap with this thing." Spit. "Cut pieces no longer than five feet. Burning paint on steel smokes and stinks. Try not to breathe it." Spit, Spit. "Watch out, do not burn those hoses, really, don't. The guy who let that happen the other day is still in the hospital, got it? I'll come by in an hour to check on you. Yeah, I asked them in the office to pay you every day after work. I thought that'd make it easier for you."

"Okay, Mr. Wiesel, and thank you, especially for that pay deal."

What a good man this guy is. It sure does not show. The clothes that hang on him are filthy and have large holes in them. One sleeve of his coat is shorter than the other one. It probably caught on fire. I really do not have it bad at all. Mary, please help him, his wife, and his nine kids along.

After a while Paul's back began to hurt. The hot steel made him sweat. He coughed a lot. The water faucet was a long ways off. His torch was blowing tiny pearls of sparkling liquid steel all over the place. Many of them holed his pants.

Like at the tip of the crane in Merlebach. But this here is free-cutting!

Mr. Wiesel came back bringing a pair of leather leg protectors.

"Here, sorry I forgot to give you those." Then he reached into a pocket of his coveralls and handed Paul a wrinkled fiver. "Get yourself some new pants. I know they won't let you study with burned holes in your trousers. Otherwise, is it going okay?"

"Yes, sir, thanks for the five marks. You know, you are very good to me."

Wiesel had already turned to leave. He spit and waved his arm as if to push something away from him.

"Okay, okay, just go to it."

After six hours, Paul's back had stiffened into a hard board and his dry lips had stuck together. He made it to the wash room.

Water, water! Am I ever thirsty! Need to get a thermos tomorrow. Warm shower, wow, like in the coal mine. Great. Hey, I'll wash my shirt here and my other stuff. It will be dry in the morning.

He wore his windbreaker home and his pants with nothing underneath.

A surprise awaited him at home. Frau Else had brought up a real porcelain plate with blood sausage, mashed potatoes, and sauerkraut! He sat down and ate, enjoying every bite.

Before he went to bed, he dressed the back of his chair with the wet shirt. It would finish drying on him in the morning on the way to school.

He dreamed of Kate, and in his dream she made love to him.

By the end of the first week, the men had become acquainted with each other. Mr. Geography, Mr. History, and Ms.

Latin had made their debuts. The first Krause hour was to come on Monday.

Paul worked Saturday forenoon, leaving the site with eighty-four marks in his pocket. Rich! He bought new socks, a new shirt, unmentionables, and a towel, so he would not have to use his shirt all the time to dry himself after the shower at work.

At Hornung's he bought butter, and ham, and half a loaf of country bread. Mr. Hornung also sold cigars. He let Paul have one for half price.

Ludwig was waiting for him at home.

"Hi! Will you have time after dinner tonight?"

"What are we going to talk about?"

"Our physics teacher asked us to write an essay about clocks. You know, since when do we have clocks? And, funny, he said to write a sentence or two explaining what makes them tick. We all laughed about that. Can you help me?"

"Sure, you bring a dictionary, I'll bring my memory, and we will do it together."

Paul was writing a letter to Inge when Ludwig showed up with paper under his arm, a pencil in his mouth, and a covered plate he was balancing with both hands. He spoke in Morse code through the pencil.

"Mmm mosser nts you hu eat siss." Paul took the pencil out of Ludwig's mouth. "Fried potatoes, onion rings, and beef gravy. You'll like it. Eat first."

"How come the dinner?"

"Paul, we like you. At first, my father wasn't sure about you, you having been a prisoner and coming here with nothing. He went to the school and talked with Mr. Wagenraht. Some day you must tell me about the war and the camps that you were in. So, anyhow, Mutti wants me to bring you once in a while some of her cooking. She makes good stuff, you know."

"Ludwig, please tell your mother that I am thankful, very thankful. I also understand your father's concern. You see, Ludwig, I was a prisoner for nearly three long years. Trying to find my way back into normal life is rather hard and often awkward. I still think they are watching me. Sometimes I feel that the barbed wire does not want to let go of me. Yes, I have my freedom. But that's all, nothing else. I have no home to go to when this school is over. What I will do for a living once I start in Darmstadt, I have no clue. One thing is for sure though, I'll make it, just taking it one day at a time."

He finished eating.

"Okay, here is what I remember. We can check with the dictionary. Did you bring it?"

"I got none."

"We'll do without then. You take notes. I am not writing this essay for you, understand? What is the exact title?"

"I made one up: 'The History of Timepieces.'"

"All right. Early on, about 800 BC, the Egyptians used a shadow clock to tell time. A stick in the ground scribed a shadow circle as the sun traveled between dawn and twilight."

"What if there was no sunshine?"

"Ludwig, not so fast, you are way ahead of me.

"As you say, this did not work when it was raining. On cloudy days, the Chinese cut notches into a candle and measured time notch by notch. Later the Egyptians drilled a hole in the bottom of a water pail. They measured time by the gallon of water that leaked out, similar to the hourglass today."

"You should be a teacher. Really, I want my friends to hear how you explain things."

"Are you taking notes? The people used those makeshift timepieces for generations. Around 1350, the mechanical clock was born. It consisted of gears and a weight. A Dutchman later incorporated Galileo's pendulum to regulate the mechanism of the clock.

"In the early 1900's, the Americans invented the electric clock. Someone had discovered that a quartz crystal vibrated very consistently when stimulated by an electrical current. And in 1929 the quartz clock became the most accurate timepiece the world has known."

"Paul, you are an expert in clocks, no? I mean, where do you know all this from?"

"During my days in the Merlebach prison camp, I learned how to repair watches and clocks. A prisoner who lived a few bunks over from mine taught me how. Heinrich and I used to talk a lot about time. How do we count time, what is time, where did it come from, that sort of thing."

"Man, you know so much. Maybe next weekend I'll bring my friend and we can talk about time, okay?"

"We'll see."

"Please don't say, 'We'll see.' My father answers my questions that way. It means 'no' in most cases. Say 'yes,' please!"

Paul had to laugh, remembering how his parents used to answer him with vague responses when he was a boy.

"Yes, yes, we will do that. Now, go, and don't forget to give my thanks to your mother."

It had gotten too late. He would finish the letter to Inge tomorrow.

He woke up late on Monday morning and had to hurry to make it on time for the first Krause class. Rain and wind swept the streets into the gutters. People walked fast with their heads down. The news that the German mark would be devalued weighed heavily on the minds of everyone. It would happen in May. Ten marks on the fifteenth would turn into one mark on the sixteenth.

The government announced that it would give each citizen thirty marks to help start over again. The people would have to pick up the money at the place of their permanent residence. Paul had none in reality, but Inge had added his name to her lease to satisfy the government's regulations. That meant Paul would have to go back to Heidelberg to get the thirty pieces of silver.

All the prices in stores and elsewhere would be adjusted along a ten-to-one sliding scale. Paul's two hundred he had saved would turn into twenty. Despair gripped this sleepy town. But the drastic measure was necessary to get the economy back on track. The black market had gone berserk, with a pack of cigarettes fetching one hundred and twenty marks, and the German currency had lost much of its worth. The devaluation would help to shut down the illicit purchase of goods, and establish a new value to the Deutsch Mark.

The eight o'clock bell tore into the discussion people were having before the Krause religion hour. Bells still meant emergencies for some of them. Three U-boat men in the course turned pale whenever that school rang its chimes.

The door opened, and just as on their first day, Mr. Wagenraht, this time with Father Krause in tow, approached the podium.

"Good morning, gentlemen. Bad news, yes I know. Should the devaluation come about this May, here is what we propose: "First, we will interrupt this course for three days at that time. You can go home and collect your share.

"Second, we advise you to negotiate new rent payments with your landlords.

"Third, we suggest you buy your train tickets now.

"Fourth, negotiate the continuance of the job you are holding now."

Number 2 raised his hand. "It's the same, isn't it? It is always us, the people from the street who have to spoon up the mess."

Wagenraht was prepared, having anticipated something like that right from the beginning of the course.

"Young man, you are right. Nevertheless, let's not forget that we, the people from the streets, let this happen. Millions of us could have said no to Hitler in the thirties. We as a nation made a mistake. We as a nation must right things. If you want to live as a free man tomorrow, yes, you will have to do some spooning today.

"I am deeply sorry you have lost three years of your precious life. I really am. I also am so very sad about the things we let happen to our people in those concentration camps. I wish we could undo the past. We cannot. We can go on, though, and amend. We must. We need your assistance, your help. We as a nation must forgive. We have to do our very best not to let that happen ever again!"

They could see that he was breathing hard as he tried to control his emotion. No one in the room moved. Most of them looked straight down onto the top of their desks. Priest Krause twiddled with one of the thirty-three buttons on his cassock.

Then, in a barely audible voice, Number 2, asked, "With all due respect, Mr. Wagenraht, didn't we prisoners pay back some of the debt? Don't my three years count for anything? Don't you think we here have spooned enough?"

"Young man, how do you suggest we measure that? I do not know if it ever can be enough, I don't."

Wagenraht left, forgetting to introduce the priest. A man in the front row jumped up and held the door for him, receiving the principal's distracted thanks.

He is right. We must learn to forgive. I don't think, we here are ready to do that just yet. I am not. And I feel that there must be something like "enough," but I am not sure when that would be either.

Father Krause started his religion class with only nine men. Franz, Number 3, and the others either did not want to attend or were non-Catholics. Those black sheep talked about a "different" God in a room right across from the chosen ones.

The priest surveyed the souls hovering at their desks. He could not shake off the feeling that they were not ready for the good word he had prepared for them.

Victor Schäufel had given him a word of advice. "Joseph, try not to impress them with big words that have nothing to do with the hard reality of what they have seen, where they have been. I would not tell them outright that God is always right and man is always wrong. Not everything can be fixed by going to confession or by His eternal grace."

"Victor, I must tell the bishop about you. I'm glad we are alone here in this conference room. I might have to excommunicate you otherwise. What heretical garble did you just put on the table? Do you doubt the Lord's grace? What are you trying to instill in those lost men?"

"They are not lost, Father. They come from places in their lives where they left behind dead bodies that belonged to their friends, their fathers and mothers, their brothers and sisters. These men never were lost. They were alone, lonesome, forgotten by your bishop, your cardinals, and your infallible boss.

"I have talked with them. They have led me through their agonies. To save themselves, they became thieves, killed for crumbs, looted the dead and dying and left them naked in the mud. They did not only stumble and fall three times under the cross. They fell many, many times over. No, they do not have nail holes in their hands and feet. They have craters in their souls. The thorns are bleeding their hearts."

"Victor, what is all this? Why do you tell me? What do you want me to do? Don't you believe in our God anymore?"

"Krause, yes, I believe in God. Though I have never been challenged not to believe.

"Listen to them. Listening is what you should do. I have come to like these men. They are hurting. I want them to heal. Don't push them away. You may be safe. They are not. We must help them to find their peace. They will draw you a picture of their God, and it might not look as pretty as your sketch. You need to respond when they tell you that He is cruel. Look what He let man do to His son! Your absolution will not cover their needs by a long shot."

Paul took inventory of the priest. He seemed to be in his forties. The black, snug-fitting cassock made him look taller than the six feet he would measure at the doctor's office. He wore shiny black dress shoes and a stole around his waist, the tassels almost sweeping the floor. He kept his blond hair combed straight back, yet allowed it to wave a little. His hands, mostly hidden in the deep pockets of the cassock, were well proportioned. Paul could see that they were made to hold the chalice and break the bread.

His watch circled his right wrist with the crystal turned under. To check the time, he would turn his right hand inside out, stretching it away from his body to slip up his sleeve. He often adjusted the casing with thumb and index finger of his left hand, questioning just what the white oversized dial told him. The frequency with which he consulted his timepiece depended on the pressure he felt, or on the amount of time he needed to stall before answering a chancy question. In severe cases, he would add to this act his slightly raised eyebrows.

Joseph Krause walked back and forth between the podium and the first row of desks. His left arm crossed his chest. His right elbow rested in his left hand. He massaged his close-shaved chin. Head down, he asked the Lord how he should start this lesson.

With a calculated suddenness he stopped and faced the men.

"Do you know God loves you?"

The silence in the room was numbing, but their blank faces spoke loudly.

"What did you just say?" those faces asked.

He checked his watch and turned to the window. Paul raised his hand. Krause did not see it right away. He was looking out, his hands resting on the sill.

"Father, I am Paul."

Then he saw Paul in the mirroring window glass.

"Yes, Paul?"

"Father, who is God?"

He looked at his watch and wound the stem.

"An excellent question. More yet, it is the essential statement that ever since the beginning of time has troubled the mind of His people.

"God is the great gardener who did not like the snakes to give away His apples for free.

"God is the father of peace.

"God is the magician who creates life and lets it change itself into infinite forms. God is the master of our universe, our—"

"Father Krause, please, I hate to bring this up, but your book has some pages missing."

He checked his watch twice, but no raised eyebrows yet.

"Paul, if you have those missing pages on you, please, share them with us."

Eronimus Franke cleared his throat.

"Father, may I say something? It's not only pages that are missing. It is like our book has been written by a different author."

Krause interrupted. "You mean the devil?"

Nine men booed. Not just a little, but loud and long.

Number 2 shouted, "Hey, you guys, neither is this nice nor does it shed any light on the problem. Father Krause probably never has seen death in any other form than in a bed where the man or the woman or the child succumbed to sickness or old age." He turned to address the priest directly.

"Father, it seems to me that you might think God had nothing to do with World War II, with the gas chambers or the prison camps. Let me just ask you, have you ever been in a bombing raid? Have you ever had strangers shooting at you? Have you ever heard the howling of artillery rounds, smelled the bodies they blew to pieces?"

Time check, a dash longer than usual. He became upset.

"Mr...." Father Krause looked uncertainly at Number 2's chest, searching for the nonexistent nametag.

"Grüber, Heinz Grüber."

"Mr. Grüber, men make war. God doesn't. After Adam and Eve left, He closed the gate of Eden. From then on the world became a hard place to live in."

"I beg your pardon, Father. You are not another Pilate, are you? He too washed his hands telling the crowd that he really had nothing to do with Calvary."

Eronimus took over. "Father, stay with us for a little, please. What if Eve would have had a headache and Adam would not have made love to her? Then what? Would God have continued to take out ribs to keep the garden populated? Whatever was plan A? We are only taught about plan B, and if you—"

"This is bordering on blasphemy! I will not—"

Krause did not have to hear the rest. The bells called him back to his corner.

Victor was eating his lunch when the priest came into the conference room.

"How'd it go?"

Krause sat down. He folded his hands, not to pray, but to keep them from shaking off the table.

"The devil is at work in that classroom. I can feel the fires of hell. These ex-prisoners are blowing the heat to a white glow. You said they are not lost. Victor, they are lost, so lost nobody ever will find them again, not even the Lord Himself!"

"Why? Did you lose your trust in Him? Aren't you supposed to have all the tools to build the road for them to travel back on, to return without their pain? No? They are angry with God, not with you. Don't take it personally."

Victor poured coffee from his thermos.

"Would you like some? It's good stuff. I bought the beans for four hundred marks a half a kilo."

The other man nodded. "Yes, thank you." Father Krause took the cup in both hands, yet he still spilled a little of that expensive brew. "I need to go somewhere and pray."

Mr. Schäufel did not say it, but he was worried. He knew that this was just the beginning and that more, much more would be coming.

May came, the newspaper confirmed the worst scenario.

Paul went to work early to have time to talk to Mr. Wiesel.

"What is going to happen? I need to go back to Heidelberg to get my money. Will that be all right?"

"You have been doing a good job for us..."

Attention! That does not sound at all good. Do I see a big "but" following that compliment?

"My boss told me we will be shut down for a week. You can go to Heidelberg, just come and see me when you are back. If I am still here, you have a job. For how much, I can't tell you yet. When are you leaving?"

"I thought around the thirteenth, my lucky number."

"Okay, Paul, so this coming Friday is your last day. I'll see you before you take off. How in hell can thirteen be a lucky number?"

He spit and kept shaking his head as he walked back to the office.

Paul went to the railroad station after work. Others had the same idea, the long line stretching around the building.

It was two in the morning when Paul finally reached the window. The man at the ticket counter had tired eyes and no smile. His tie hung loosely, partially undone, and the first button on his shirt was missing. The railroad cap he wore disguised unruly, sticky hair. Two fingers on his right hand showed a brownish stain, no doubt from chain smoking.

Paul felt compassion and imagined having a job as a ticket seller for the rest of his life.

That would not work for me. I need something new to do, not only sometimes, but at least twice a day. How different this guy is from the one behind the window in St. Avolt. Tired or not, this one here has no spark left. Mary, you need to take care of him, please.

"Ansbach-Heidelberg, Heidelberg-Ansbach, right? May 13, back on May 16. Student pass?"

"Yes, thank you."

"Your discounted fair is thirty-four marks."

This time Paul did not shove French tobacco through the half-moon opening at the bottom of the window, just worth less money.

He walked home. The gaslights in the streets made the raindrops sparkle like diamonds.

On the day before the devaluation, Number 2 surprised Victor. Heinz Grüber wore his tag! Victor did not blink an eye. He had known all along he would win them over.

During the ten o'clock break, Grüber took the floor.

"Listen up, you guys. You probably have thought of this already. But here it is. Tomorrow the stations will be overcrowded. The check booths will be flooded with people. Everyone will be in a hurry and that spells opportunity for us. We have been trained for situations like these. Sneaking by, avoiding the conductor on the train should pose no problem for us."

Number 1, still with no tag, asked, "What does this give you?"

"Big boy, I checked. The tickets I bought yesterday will remain valid for a year."

"That means I can use the ticket twice and see my wife for free in a month or so?"

"You have the mind of a thinker. I am overwhelmed by your grasp of the situation." Heinz Grüber's speech usually dripped with sarcasm, creating tension at times.

Eronimus, a mild-tempered fellow from Hamburg, filled the delicate gap of silence.

"Fellows, this is not legal."

Twenty-three heads spun around and faced him.

"So?"

Now Number 3 raised both hands ready to speak. He was the senior member, and the tallest of the clan. Without having voted him into that position, the class allowed him to be the head pawn. He wore rimless glasses that highlighted his ascetic face. Paul got the impression that this man made up his mind before he ever spoke, regardless of the situation. He needed no second opinions. He was as arrogant as they come.

One other fact that set him apart from the others was that he had money. He wore a golden ring on his little finger. He manicured and polished his nails. His shirts were tailored, not bought at Karstadt, the department store for the more peasant-like folks.

Number 3, still both hands up in the air, got everyone's attention. All eyes focused on him. The classroom was afloat with anticipation. At that moment, Mr. Salzhammer, the historian, came in to start his lesson.

Seeing the tall man, hands raised, he felt compelled to ask, "Was Number 3 talking to Mecca?"

Victor had prepped Salzhammer to be ready for his students, yet the eminent professor decided on his own course. He thought that his mere presence would turn the class's attention to him. He was used to being acknowledged, instantly recognized and admired by everyone—students, fellow teachers, ordinary people in the grocery store. His physical stature alone commanded a certain respect. Always dressed in a black pin-striped suit, his broad shoulders, eyes of cobalt, and large hands gave him an intimidating presence.

All that might have worked elsewhere. Here it didn't. The troops ignored Salzhammer and his comment and continued their discussion.

Number 3 spoke. "Eronimus, we disagree. Man needs to fend off disadvantages thrown at him by circumstances beyond his control. Special situations require special means to handle them. We did not ask to learn how to take these advantages, but the fact is we know how. And take them we must."

Salzhammer looked perturbed, unused to being made superfluous. Insecurity rumbled beneath his shirt.

Number 3, who sat with his back to the teacher, continued to share his philosophy.

"Sneaking by, reusing the ticket, is really an ethical issue. We know ethics are made of rubber and come in as many colors as our leaders have at their disposal. Handling gray has become our business. We know that right or wrong can be stretched a lot either way."

"That son of a bitch will become a lawyer, don't you think?" Franz whispered to Paul.

Paul got up. "Look, drop that 'we' shit. Speak for yourself. You flunked the test the other day when you walked out on the priest. You handle your stuff. I'll handle mine. Got it?"

Number 3 had not figured on that. While he was searching for a comeback, Mr. Salzhammer defrosted. He took his cue.

"Quite a discussion, quite. I could offer different views, but I am here to lead you into the past.

"History is a science based on proclaimed opinions of today's historians who are judging events that occurred a long time ago that no longer are familiar to us today."

He paused and waited for them to write that down. Twenty-four minds went blank. Pencils dropped onto the writing pads, some rolled down to the floor.

Walter in the next row exchanged amused looks with Paul.

"Another Caesar! He, too, made sentences so long that they did not all fit into one paragraph."

The men started to chuckle, then laugh. Salzhammer looked around the room with chagrin. Never had he been treated with such disrespect.

"Sir, please." Eronimus tried to get his attention. "Mr. Salzhammer, please don't fly so high above our heads. You see, we are people who have forgotten how to read big words. Where do we come from, how did we get where we are? That is what we want to learn from you. You know, the truth, and you don't have to go back to Trafalgar or the Huns."

Salzhammer had begun to freeze again.

The round was saved by the bell.

Grüber's method worked for Paul. The Ansbach railroad station was flooded with people. He pushed through the crowd and passed the control booth waving his student pass. The man punching the narrow cardboard tickets did not even see him. The station was an anthill in turmoil. Paul chose a car in the middle of the train. He knew the conductor would start checking tickets at one end. As he moved down the train, Paul would keep ahead of him, moving from car to car. There would be a stop in Stuttgart. By then two-thirds of the compartments would have been checked. He would simply step off and reboard another car where the tickets had been checked already. It was unlikely he would get caught. And if he did, well, he had a ticket on him, if not validated, but that would be overlooked on a day like this.

He disembarked in Heidelberg and left the station through an unlocked, unguarded gate in the perimeter fence of the station. He felt a little creepy. All this was still so close to what had happened only a couple of months ago in Bielefeld.

At Werder Strasse, Inge opened the door. He had written to let her know he was coming to get his money. They kissed, and she hugged him so hard that he hurt. In one of her letters she had asked him not to tempt her into making love.

"It is a sin to do that before people are married. You need to promise me."

How can I do this? Why can't we make love? She did let me play with her already. I am a human being. I feel passion. I want to make love to her.

He pulled her down onto the bed. She did not resist. He kissed her like Sasha in Merlebach had taught him. It scared her at first. But after a few moments she responded. Her tongue searched for his, and she clamped her legs around him. Paul felt her shudder. Then, suddenly, she got up and scolded him.

"I asked you not to come this close to me! It is a sin!"

"Inge, did you just come? That's good, but what about me?"

"You must not talk to me that way. What about you? What do you mean? If you want me to touch you...well, I can't."

"Well, girl, you were excited and so am I, so excited it hurts. Why don't you help me? You seem to think it was okay for you, why not for me?"

She clamped her hands over her ears to shut him out.

"I did not want that to happen, and I will go to confession. Come, we'll walk down to the river. It will quiet you down."

He had time to leave, to find someone else who would be more considerate, more down to earth, more giving and less self-centered. But Paul did not leave. He stayed, accepting her values as being more pure than his. Yet he would never understand how she measured life with two different scales. He would marry her despite this basic flaw in their relationship that contained the seed of failure.

She had no place for him to stay, for Hubert had gone to Neustadt to get his thirty Deutsch Marks.

When they hugged goodbye, in his mind Paul hugged Kate, not Inge.

It was late. He walked back to the station. People sat in the waiting room, people who, like him, pretended they were waiting for the midnight express. Taking a seat on a crowded bench, he slept sitting up, all of them packed together like sardines, holding each other straight up. When one left, the row tumbled like dominos.

Early the next morning he picked up his money from the post office, three crisp, brand-new ten-mark banknotes. On his way back to the station, he passed the interurban electric train station. Trains from there shuttled passengers between Heidelberg and Mannheim.

Yes! That's what I will do!

He bought a ticket for the next shuttle.

Kate, I am coming. I cannot wait to see you, Kate!

A tram took him from the shuttle stop to the railroad station in Mannheim. He bought a tarmac-ticket for ten pennies and went to look for the door with the red cross on the white panel. But there was no door anymore, just a newly constructed wall with a few windows in it. He looked through them. The cots were gone. People in railroad uniforms sat bent over typewriters with telephones on their desks.

Paul went to see the stationmaster. He did not recognize Paul, who reminded him of the day he met Mr. Schiller and Helmuth.

"Oh, ya, Kate. She helped hundreds of men like you who had escaped from prison camps. But then earlier this year you people stopped coming, and the railroad closed the shelter."

"And Kate, where did she go?"

The stationmaster looked at him. He shook his head, and put his hand on Paul's shoulder. His right foot played with a small pebble, shoving it back and forth on the concrete. He looked up. His eyes searched afar for a way to say it.

"On her last day...we had an accident here. She is in peace now, I know. We brought her to the eastside cemetery. The caretaker can tell you where. Her last name was Sommer. I am sorry. You liked her, didn't you?"

Paul stood there. The blow struck him, tearing right through him, yet he could not comprehend the words. He reached for the man's arm as the tarmac began to sway.

"What did you just say?"

"I asked you if you liked her..."

"No, before that. Kate had an accident? Was it bad? Is she okay now? Where does she live, far from here?" Paul began to shake.

"Young man—"

His face distorted into grief, Paul grabbed the stationmaster and shook him.

"It is not so! It is not true! Tell me it isn't! You tell me! No! Please, please, say it isn't so!"

The people around blurred in and out of Paul's vision. He tried, but he could not focus. With unimaginable force the quake hit his soul. He buried his face in the man's shoulder and began to sob. They stood there for a long time, not far from where the white door used to be.

"You did like her!"

"Why did she do it?"

"We don't know. It was a non-stop train from Hamburg to Munich. It buzzed through the terminal at high speed. The engineer saw her a split second before she ran right in front of his engine."

They had walked over to a bench. Paul had his hands folded, looking down at the concrete between his shoes.

"I fell in love with her right over there in that room. I think she knew it. We were talking about her family. She mentioned that nothing, no one was waiting for her to come home.

"'...sometimes I feel like running out there in front of a train...,' that's what she said to me.

"I held her then, very tight and kissed her, caressing her hair. I should have stayed! Oh my God!"

He took the tram to the eastside cemetery. The caretaker gave him directions. He found a small headstone:

the many you helped
on their way home are praying
for you Kate
January 1948

He knelt close by the stone, bent down, and rested his head on the cold grass that had grown over the mount. Hours later, long after dark, the caretaker helped him up.

"It's late, I need to close the gate now."

Lord, you stop at nothing, do you? Why did you take her? She was so young. She did what you taught your disciples to do. She did not preach. She acted. She shared. Isn't that greater and better than anything else we can do? Now I am more alone than I was in Merlebach that night I sat on the steps of the Buvette, listening to the guy playing the song of the Volga River. Do you know what you have done? I guess you must. Why would you be God otherwise? I loved, I loved this woman. I thought the hard times were over. Ha! You, You don't give up. Soon there will be no soul left in me that you can step on. Mary, what is going on?

Paul bought a ticket, Mannheim to Heidelberg, and switched trains there to go back to Ansbach. He was devastated. Kate's leaving took a piece of him. He never would be able to fill that void in his heart, that place inside him that already missed so many others.

He told the man in the control booth in Ansbach that he had lost the ticket. He waved his student pass in front of the man's nose. He let him through. In this small town, word had gotten out that those older students with that special ID card had less than a mouse in a church.

The bell rang. The following hour was set aside for math. All but one had come back from "May Day." The classroom was alive with stories and laughter.

Victor burst into the room and strode towards the podium. "CHARGE!" was written all over him. He needed no trumpet blare, no banner, no announcement. He was the leader, ready to inspire his students, these men whom he so obviously liked and respected.

"Hello, hello! Good to see you back! I hope things turned out all right for you. You look well and healthy, so let's get this show on the road again.

"First, I have some administrative information for you. Number 3 decided not to attend any longer. I wish I could share his reasons with you, but the matter is confidential."

Paul kicked Franz under the desk. "Hey, Franciscus, I don't know about you, but I like him. He's got something in him the others teachers don't, that I-can-do attitude. I bet he would have escaped, too, hunchback and all."

"Believe it or not, Paul, I missed you. No shit, I did. I like the guy too, better every day."

Victor had launched into his lecture.

"Zero. We want to talk about the zero. What is it, when was it born? Did it derive from infinity or did we, man, invent it? Zero stands for nothing—and yet many zeros can change unimaginably small numbers into infinitely large ones."

Paul felt excitement. This was his thing. The zero often had come up during the discussions with Heinrich when they talked about time, infinity, and the universe.

"We also use the zero to pinpoint the intersection between positive and negative. Multiplication of numbers with zero result in nothingness. And you still remember 'Thou shalt never ever divide any number by zero.' It would produce an undefined expression. We can do a lot in mathematics, but, God forbid, we cannot handle an undefined expression, not even with the help of the natural logarithm 'e.'

"May I pose the question to you again: The zero, did we make it up or has it always been there, hidden from us like the newly discovered elements of matter? I also ask if it is necessary to have an answer to that question at all. For my part, I believe it is more important to query what would we do without it."

Paul raised his hand.

"Mr. Schäufel, what is nothingness?"

Victor squinted. Was this Paul trying to trick him? No, the question was not out of order.

"Mr Berck, I need to confess that I do not know the answer. Maybe it is 'it' into which the universe is expanding."

Franz broke into the discussion.

"Well, then we have the answer to your question. If the zero is nothing, then it has been always there, because I think there was nothingness before the Big Bang." Franz had spoken directly to Paul.

I did not know that Franz could think and talk that way.

Victor no longer squinted.

The discussion made them forget their past. Victor had cracked opened a door to let them see something else. He had expanded the four walls of this classroom. They were spellbound. Nobody wanted this moment to pass. They had moved from the external, physical world into the expanse of their minds, considering concepts that had little to do with the harsh reality they lived with. Paul felt that somehow they together had taken another step into freedom, the freedom of their minds.

The bell rang. They did not notice. Victor knew for sure now that his students were not lost. His students would make it.

He had made them touch something beyond this planet.

Victor broke the spell by dismissing class. When he turned to leave, the men got up. One ran to the door and opened it. They all started clapping, cheering even after he had left.

"Andra moi ene pe musa polytropn hos malla pola planc ta"—the opening line of Homer's *Odyssey*. They kept reading and became bored. The teacher switched books and led them through the Greek mythology, although it was not part of the curriculum. That woke them up. He could see the magic attracting them.

Mr. Preuss, the Greek teacher, always had liquor on his breath, the same smell Paul's Latin teacher at home had carried around.

Do the classic languages do that to people?

The man also looked as sloppy as "Globe" had. He wore shirts that needed washing. The elbows of his jacket were shiny. His shoes had not seen a polish since he had bought them. Moreover, his tie wore dinner menus. The creases in his trousers had given way to worn bulges.

He knew his stuff, though. They talked about Zeus, the father of the many Greek gods. He led them into Hades at the center of the earth where the dead lived their dark lives. He was not out to teach them to speak the ancient Greek language, but rather to acquaint them with a mythology that is so very different from modern thinking, so different from the Bible, the Koran, or the teachings of Confucius. He wanted them to understand the evolution of a culture. The students listened to him in awe, and came to look forward to the "Preuss Hour," as they called it. He let them discover new perspectives and helped them to rethink their tomorrows. They felt that Preuss was giving something they could take with them.

Miss Pietrovski, a butterball of a woman, had come from Poland to Ansbach before the war. She had graduated with honors from the Sorbonne in Paris and was a senior member of the staff. Mr. Wagenraht felt fortunate that she had volunteered to work with the men.

"If you know Latin well, you'll have no problem picking up other languages like French, Spanish, Portuguese, and English," she gushed the first day. "They all come from Latin roots. And, of course, you will understand what the Pope is saying when he blesses you."

Paul thought she tried too hard to be funny, falling flat most of the time. Latin remained difficult and boring for him.

Butterball also was good at geography, often talking about the mountains, the gorges deep in the ocean, and the stream of warm seawater that crossed the Atlantic keeping France from slipping back into a new Ice Age. The ex-war men usually diddled around with their pencils as she droned on. And then, in her last class before the final tests, she let loose.

Her lecture started like all her other sessions, with her telling jokes about Caesar's affairs with the Egyptian queen, Cleopatra.

"By the way, did any of you ever read Caesar's *Mein Kampf?*"

Franz poked Paul, who was napping.

"Man, wake up, funny fairytales are on."

Paul took a deep breath.

"Asshole, I was dreaming of something nice. Did you have to wake me?"

"Mr. Berck are you with us again? Good! You see, those builders of the Third Reich did not have to reinvent all those horrible atrocities. Himmler copied some from earlier times when lions ate live people in front of kings, and their queens found it arousing."

The whole class came to. No joking, no extolling the virtues of Latin now; she was reading their mail.

She talked of Nero, the Roman, comparing him to Stalin and other dictators who murdered their mothers and let their wives rot in dungeons.

"We, the people, should be ashamed of our history. Cultures around the globe are not clean. Not only have they sprouted from red soils, they are nourished every hour of our days with blood of the innocent. We proudly keep on killing in the name of peace. You have been there. You understand what I am saying.

You want to change this, I know. That is why you are here. I hope we teachers have shown you that it is all right not to have perfect answers all the time. Horizons keep evading us, and what we do reach seems to evaporate into a time so much in need of forgiveness, compassion, and love. I also hope you are stronger now, more convinced of your own values, and know that you are winning.

"You must understand, too, that we teachers grew with you. We have accomplished this with your help. I wish I could say to you 'God bless you,' but I can't. For me He has looked the other way for too many times. But if you find Him out there, tell Him, please, I am looking for Him."

She stood there for a while and then left the classroom long before the bell rang.

Nobody moved. They hardly breathed, but sat as though chiseled in stone.

Paul returned to the scrap yard.

Wiesel hollered at him,"Where the hell have you been? Go light your torch, and get cutting that steel. How does fifty pennies an hour sound to you?"

The prices had been adjusted in the stores and other marketplaces. Fifty pennies would do.

Son of a gun, I got my job back. What do you know!

"Hey, Mr. Wiesel, good to see you. Yes, fifty is fine with me."

The Holzmanns had lowered Paul's rent to eight marks per month. He felt lucky to have a job and a good place to live.

Both school and work continued during the summer. Paul cut tons of bent, rusty iron. Sometimes he got sick from the smoke of burning paint. Wiesel told him to drink a lot of milk, which would help his lungs and stomach withstand the onslaught.

The "war" between the students and Father Krause culminated during a discussion of the miracles Christ performed, such as the few fishes and loaves He had used to nourish five thousand people, or the water He had turned into wine at the wedding in Cana.

"Men, this is the Evangelium, the Gospel. If you do not believe in what is written in there, you are no longer Christians."

This made Paul angry. "Father, would you please listen! Those are stories written by Jesus' disciples, translated by His followers, and interpreted by scholars for generations on end. I think they are nice stories, but what does God have to do with them?"

"You don't talk that way, young man. You obviously don't know anything about God!"

"Father Krause, I beg to differ. God was and is my mainstay in life. I have spent the last few years asking Him, praying to Him to help me endure the terrible things I lived through. Not you or anyone else can tell me that I am a godless man.

"Your problem is that you never have looked beyond the pages of your breviary you rattle off from every day. The way you see God does not have to be my way. I do not believe that Christus was conceived extraterrestrially. I cannot imagine that the Holy Mother of God went to heaven soul and body. Let me tell you, I prayed to her day after day as I marched the long way back and forth between our camp and the quarry. I kept praying to her when I was near death with typhoid fever. And ever since I met you, I am praying to her that you will find the light."

"Stop! Stop! You speak like the devil!"

This discourse had taken Father Krause beyond checking his watch, beyond raising his eyebrows. He screamed from the top of his lungs. Nobody ever had talked to him that way.

He turned around and looked at the cross that hung at the right side near the blackboard.

"Lord, please forgive him. He does not know what he is saying."

Now that *was blasphemy.*

Paul continued his cutting of steel. One day he was given sections that came from an old railroad bridge. The beams had been painted many times over during their life, since the railroad liberally used red lead paint on all treated surfaces. Paul remembered the coal car he had scaled during his escape had also worn such a coat of red lead.

He was about an hour into his shift when the stinging smoke became too much for his lungs. He felt dizzy and nauseated.

Just that afternoon, Mr. Wiesel had told him again, "Don't breathe that stuff. It'll make you sick.

How in hell can that be done, avoid breathing that smoke? I need a gas-mask, Mr. Wiesel!

Paul killed the torch, took off his gloves and goggles, and walked over to the office. He placed the gear and his leather leg protectors on the counter.

"Miss Hilde, I am coming to let you know that I don't want to work here any longer."

The payroll clerk got up from her desk and came over to Paul.

"Paul? What is the matter? You look sick, your face is so pale. Come, sit down. I'll get Wiesel. My God, you look awful!"

The foreman came on his bicycle, peddling hard. His lungs needed a minute to catch up. Squeezing his voice harder than usual, he said, "Damn it, Paul, I told you not to inhale this shit. Hilde, give him some milk. Paul, you sit down, take a few deep breaths."

"Mr. Wiesel, how can I not sniff that smoke and do my job? You know it can't be done. I must give up my job here. It's ruining my health. Please understand. I thank you for your concerns, your kindness, and your help, believe me I do."

"All right, enough said." he wiped a grimy hand across his forehead and gave Paul an appreciative nod. "Paul, you're an okay guy. You'll go places. Good luck. And Hilde, pay him for a full shift."

Wiesel stood by the open door and spit a couple of times hitting the front tire of his bike, then sped off on his rounds.

The fresh air and the milk helped the dizziness go away. When Paul got home, he felt better. He fixed himself a sandwich, counting his reserves while he ate lunch. He figured he could hold out for two months if he were frugal when shopping at Hornung's. He felt relieved. It gave him some time to look for another job, one without smoke. He'd miss Wiesel, though he did not quite understand why.

A couple days after the Krause confrontation, Mr. Schäufel stood in front of the class, his manner subdued. He halted at the podium, put down his books, and faced the students. Squinting, he said, "I need to talk to the people who attended Father Krause's session the day before yesterday. I would appreciate it if we could meet after class." The Catholics nodded. Another "Jesus!" look from Franz shot over to Paul. Now what?

"Mr. Berck, please, would you explain to us why the mathematical expression $n^{o} = 1$?"

"Mr. Schäufel, honestly, I have no clue, but I will guess. Maybe an equation approximating the temperature of nuclear explosions in the sun needed that expression to come out as a 1. I bet somebody made it up. Obviously, it is doing no harm. It was not in the way when they split uranium atoms over Japan."

Franz stepped on Paul's left foot, hard. Making a face, he whispered, "You idiot! He will suspend you for the rest of the course. If he does not, I will make him to do it. See, he is squinting, and I mean squinting!"

But the squinting Victor surprised Franz.

"Well, Mr. Berck, your answer is correct. Certain assumptions are necessary to keep mathematics alive. It is all very logical. Should you ever get in big with that science, you will discover that it is like a man-made lake. Some of us assume it is half empty of water while others will say it is half full." A "Jesus!" exploded from the last row. Edward Gerber had let it slip out.

"Mr. Schäufel, sir, you just tumbled my tower. I thought mathematics was an exact science. Is it not humankind's tool used to unearth our origin and to understand time in space? I seem to hear from you that the equation 1+1=2 is only true because we trust, assume that there is a 1 somewhere out there. Right?"

"Mr. Gerber, pick up the pieces of your tower and assume that by stacking brick onto brick you will be able to build a new, a better, and a stronger one." Victor admitted to himself that he had gotten in too deep, come too close to having no plausible answer for their challenging questions. These people here, sitting in front of him, were looking for solid, uncomplicated information. They wanted sturdy pegs to hang their hats on. He had thought about it a lot as he searched for a way to tell these young men that uncertainties will continue to be part of their life. How could he make them understand that there was not a thing out there for them to touch that was not tied to an assumption? How? "People, I let you go early today. You need time to think. We will talk about Mr. Krause some other time. Ite! Go in peace!"

When Victor left the school later that afternoon, he was in deep thought. He would tell Martha about the Gerber tower. His thoughts kept him from looking for traffic as he crossed Wagner Street, stepping out between two parked cars in front of a truck that could not stop.

Twenty-four men laid a flower on top of the coffin. Twenty-four men—for Number 3, August, had returned to pay his respects—took a hand full of earth from the pile next to the grave and scattered it with their tears three times into the hole. The hollow sound the falling soil made would stay with them forever.

The next morning they gathered in the classroom. They had lost their leader. One more time they were left behind, alone again. It was not fair.

"Paul, death was there all the time, every day, during those past years. You've been there. Friends, boys from my school, I kept on living while they went. I never cried about them. It did not phase me. Why is it, then, that now my heart feels ripped into pieces? Why now do I cry?" Franz wanted to know. "Mr. Schäufel, a stranger to me, is gone. I've known him only for a few months, yet all of a sudden, I feel I do not want to go on anymore. What is the matter with me?"

"I know, I feel the same. You see the shell we let grow around our souls, our hearts, is cracking. We have begun to breathe again. We had nothing to lose for so many years. We, only we were important. We had to survive, go on. That is changing. It is ironic that again death has to point this out to us.

"Franz, he left us not a stranger. He became our friend who reached out to give, not to take, or steal, or betray. What is the use to keep on living, you ask? He gave us a message. We still might not understand all of it, but still..."

"Paul, God must be awful short of good people up there."

Franz held his hand in front of his eyes. Paul leaned over and hugged him.

Mr. Wagenraht opened the door and slowly he walked over to the podium. Silence befell the classroom. He was alone this time.

He hesitated.

"Friends, I do not know what to say that could lessen the pain. Words will not do. You people have been there so many times, yet you find yourself in awe anew. You, and I, feel lost. So do his friends and family. We are grieving. Some of us might ask 'why him?' We feel that our dialog has been cut short. We still needed to talk about so many things. We wish we could undo what we said in anger, what we did uncaringly. We probably could have been more considerate at times, more gentle, supportive, nicer. Yes, we might feel that way, but we cannot change the past. We need to go on, pick up where he left.

"You have known him only for a short while. I am sure you learned to read his message, the message he lived. He taught all of us to accept, to help others in compassion, to be humble, to cherish good and genuine values, and to be true to ourselves—that message we must take, and we must run with it."

He paused for a moment and Eronimus stood up.

"Mr. Wagenraht, I believe I speak for all of us here. We loved that man. We looked up to him. We want to thank you for having shared him with us. Remembering Mr. Schäufel will always strengthen my confidence and my belief that there are good and decent people still walking this earth."

The men got up and applauded. Eronimus had spoken the right words, had taken a load off their souls. They all loved Victor Schäufel, yes. To go on without him would be hard to do, but they would do it.

"Thank you, Mr. Franke, I will pass on to Mrs. Schäufel how you people feel. Thank you. Thank you." After a short moment to compose himself, he continued. "We have about one month left to finish this course. I have decided to substitute for

Victor and be your teacher and mentor till October." They rose as one and gave him a standing ovation. He was deeply touched.

When Paul stopped at Hornung's to buy bread, he received condolences from the owner.

"I am sorry, Mr. Berck. You know, a few years back, Mr. Schäufel used to be my math teacher. I liked him, and he was good. He really knew how to make one understand that learning, life, and growing are all the same thing."

"Yes, he will be missed. My classmates and I are saddened beyond measure. We thought that death would leave us alone for a while. We thought his sickle had dulled, that death was resting. Seems we were wrong. We should have known better. Death will never stop, it is part of life. It is new for me to see it this way."

Kate, Kate, thank you! Without you, I would not have begun to understand this.

"During one of his last sessions with us, he tried to tell us about the uncertainties life brings. It took me a while to understand that by accepting uncertainties, we become able to dare, to overcome, and to live life being aware of its frailty.

"Mr. Hornung, may I ask, if you went to this Gymnasium here, why then did you choose to become a grocer?"

The "squirrel" glanced around to make sure nobody else was in his store. He was about to lay down one of his cards, tell a big secret.

The store was empty, yet he leaned over the counter whispering, "People, Mr. Berck, people will always need food. I am the one who fills that need. I am my own master. All I must do is count the eggs, weigh the cheese, cut the meat, and last but not least, see to it that there is plenty of money in my till. It is a simple business. There is no fame. If I fall, it is not far to the ground. I would not get hurt.

"Nobody ever has asked me a question like this. I do not know why I even answered you. If someone else would challenge me that way, I would render small talk. Often people do not know what to do with real answers.

"Please keep our discussion confidential. The loaf of bread is on me. Think, Mr. Berck, you are alive with wonderful days ahead of you. Leave things in the past, where they belong. Keep on walking from sunrise to sunrise. Yes, keep on walking!"

Did I ever misjudge him, and not only in one way! What a guy!

An elderly couple had entered the store. The new Hornung changed back into the former Hornung, a chameleon changing his colors. He wrung his hands like the hungry squirrel again, perking up his ears, listening to the needs of his customers, helping them decide which brand of pickles would go best with the potato salad they had planned for dinner.

Paul left the store not knowing what to think of Mr. Hornung.

Paul, don't wonder, don't judge. Keep your eyes on where you are going! Yes, Sir!

He had not been in his room for more than five minutes when Ludwig knocked.

"Hello, Mr. B. If I bring you some dinner, would you have time?"

"Ludwig, you are a rascal! Yes, I have time to talk to you."

"Three of my friends are here. Could you invite them also to come and listen to you?"

Paul looked at the boy, sensing his expectation. He needed to let go of his grief and begin to do what Mr. Hornung had suggested.

"You don't need to bribe me. I promised you we would talk some more. I am sorry you had to wait so long. Skip the dinner plate and bring up your friends."

I need to chase away those dark ghosts that came back with me from the funeral.

Four boys came storming upstairs. Ludwig introduced his friends to Paul as Heinz, Rasmus, and Peter. "I told them what I learned from you about clocks, and how you multiply figures in your head without using your fingers."

The tiny room got crowded in a hurry. Paul propped his pillow against the wall. Heinz and Peter settled at the foot of the bed, Indian fashion. Rasmus squatted on his feet on the floor and Ludwig brought over the chair from the table at the window. They looked at Paul anxiously waiting for the curtain to part.

"Well, guys, nice to meet you. Call me Paul. What do we want to talk about? Time?"

"Yes, time," answered one of the boys. "Ludwig told us you said when time dies it becomes infinity. I don't understand how time can die."

In memory of Victor, Paul squinted.

I hope this goes well. I don't want to snow these kids with thoughts they can't do anything with. A lot of what they want to talk about is far from being clear in my little head. I will try.

"Paul what do we need time for?"

"Right! The very first people on this earth, thousands of years ago, didn't have a watch, didn't boil their eggs for three minutes, didn't race against a clock to win trophies. What was time to them? When the sun rose, they knew the day had started. It ended when darkness fell. Did they know about time? Was time around some seventy million years ago when the dinosaurs roamed our planet? At this very moment, stars are born billions of light years away from us. Is time out there? Do those exploding gases need time to create new planets?" Paul could almost hear the spinning of their wheels. They sat there in awe wrestling for answers. Rasmus, unable to sit still, kneaded the bedspread like it was some sort of dough.

"Now, Paul, the dinosaurs could not count, I know that much. And there wasn't anybody else around who could."

"Yes, go on."

"So, if nobody was there to observe time, I guess time did not exist. Wow, did I say that?"

Heinz shook his head.

"What do you mean, time did not exist? We know from old fossils that there was life way before the dinosaurs. Beetles lived five hundred million years ago. Time measures that span. So time was there then."

Watch out, these young people will tie you into a loop.

"Paul, who is right? Heinz or Rasmus? They can't both be right, can they?"

"Peter, I believe time is a dimension. It has been there and it will always be there, whether someone is counting or not. Time has kept clicking away since our universe banged itself into existence. At that time, infinity gave way to a billion trillion years of universe. After that, time might as well go back to where it came from, to infinity."

The ice was getting thin, very thin.

The four looked at each other, then withdrew into their thoughts.

After much contemplation, Ludwig said, "Oh, Paul, you lost me. How about you guys?"

"Yeah, time out!" This pun sent them into peals of laughter.

"Where's the bathroom? Nature calls!"

"Wow, Ludwig wasn't kidding when he told us about you!"

Noisily they ran downstairs, leaving Paul to his thoughts.

Darkness had sneaked into the room. Paul turned on the tiffany lamp and it shed its cozy light.

Jesus, what an evening. Many a time I tried to reason and find answers to what time really consists of and where it came from. Sometimes, it looked like I was getting closer. Yes, I know, asymptotically closer only, because we will never be able to travel at the speed of light. If we could, we would beat time out of existence. That at least is what Mr. Einstein has said.

They came back laughing, gesticulating, loud and agitated. Paul himself felt elated.

What great kids! Thinking beyond the usual periphery of our realities always resets my perspective and puts my adrenaline on overtime.

"People, it is getting late. Time, yeah *time* will make sure that tomorrow morning gets here in a hurry. I will be here another month. If you like, we can discuss infinity some other evening, yes?"

Ludwig giggled. "Sir, you don't think we would let you leave here without telling us about infinity and the universe, the stars, and all that?"

"I promise to do that. But first I have to look for a new job so I can keep eating."

"Ah, Ludwig here can sneak food away from his mother. And I'll ask my father if he could use you in his carpenter shop."

"Rasmus, your father has a carpenter shop? Where?"

"Right down the street on the left side. It's in the back, which is why you don't see it. I'll ask tonight and let you know tomorrow."

Paul saw the sign in the morning on his way to school. "Cabinet Maker" it said in bold letters, and underneath, smaller, nicely centered, the added "Custom Carpentry." Unless one knew where to look, it was easy not to notice the black on white message.

When Paul returned from school that afternoon, there was a note from Rasmus pinned on Paul's door.

"My father would like to see you. Thanks for last night. Raz."

Ludwig came up the stairs. He carried a large plate covered with a red-and-white checkered napkin that matched the tablecloth.

"Hey, Mr. B., how was school? Mutti thought you might be hungry. All of us are holding our fingers crossed about your job."

"Ludwig, Ludwig, slow down. Why the plate? Fill me in, please."

"Well, last night after our talk about infinity and all that stuff we went downstairs. My parents wanted to know what we discussed."

"And?"

"Well, my father didn't say anything. He looked at me like he did not understand what my friends and I were reporting. My mother listened to us. She smiled here and there. She poured us some milk and said that the right question to ask about time would be to find out who made it. She also had the answer. 'God. God made it.' Do you think that's right?"

"We'll get to that in a few days. Meantime, think about it this way. God did not make anything. God is everything."

Ludwig looked at Paul.

"Mr. B., you better eat before it gets cold."

But, just as he shoveled in the first bite, someone banged on the door. Ludwig opened the door to find Rasmus.

"Did you read my note? When are you coming over? He's waiting for you."

"Good morning, gentlemen! During the coming week, this era will enter its final phase and culminate in our testing the status of the knowledge we have tried to convey, and you have absorbed. I know not how to put it in a gentler way: We will grade you. Sounds awful, I know, but that is what we will do. I have checked with your other teachers about your performance. I am proud to share that there is light at the end of the tunnel. We'll find out its lumens when you answer our quiz."

Mr. Wagenraht adjusted his butterfly bow tie with both hands and smiled pleasantly at the students. Then, ignoring Franz, who had raised his hand in the hopes of stalling the inevitable, he opened a ring binder and began.

"Victor had planned to complete his mathematics program with leading you to the edge. He had meant to guide you through the minefield of human assumptions into an area that expands farther than we can stretch our thoughts.

"He was going to ask you into what our universe keeps expanding. He wanted to know from you if you could fathom the concept of infinity. Could you reason that infinity is a real dimension without a beginning and, ignoring positive or negative, is never ending?

"I see a footnote down here at the bottom of this sheet. It says, 'If those people are in a receptive mood, I would like to ask them where and how eternity fits this very last equation.'"

Paul got up, so did Eronimus.

"Yes, Mr. Berck."

"Mr. Wagenraht, we do not know, do we? Eternity is a godly term. As so many other concepts, it came about because someone needed to answer questions that were asked either incorrectly or for which no answers existed."

Eronimus interjected, "Paul, I think eternity and infinity are not analogous. Mr. Wagenraht, excuse me, but I need to say this. I believe infinity is only possible within eternity. I really do."

Wagenraht thought how happy, how elated Victor would have been to hear their responses to his footnote. It is so sad that he cannot be part of this moment, he thought. Then again, he might be up there smiling at this congregation. Yes, of course, he has all the answers now. I'll ask Victor to let Father Krause know too.

"Mr. Franke, I suggest you take this up with your religion teacher tomorrow. It seems to me that Victor had mentioned something about a frustrating dispute between some of you men and the priest. Maybe—well, I leave this up to you."

Mr. Wagenraht came out from behind the lectern. He held a strip of blue paper between his index finger and thumb. The paper band was about eighteen inches long and about an inch wide.

"Let me demonstrate how one could imagine it, at least the 'no end' portion of this infinity concept. I am bringing the ends of the strip together. I twist one end by 180 degrees. Mr. Berck, be so kind, use this Tesa-Film here, and make the connection. Yes, thank you." He held his creation up for all to see: a twisted loop.

Wagenraht walked between the student desks."The mathematicians call this a 'Möbius Strip.' Please, Mr. Franz, take your pencil, make a mark right here on the face of the strip. Now let the pencil travel on that face. Yes, keep going."

Very carefully, Franz let the pencil go all around the paper strip. When he returned to his beginning mark, his pencil line had covered both sides of the structure in one continuous line.

"Hmm, so we have here a body with one face and one edge. If challenged, you probably would have said that there is no such thing. But you saw the pencil move continuously."

"Yes, sir, it does," Franz conceded, but challenged, "You are holding the band within the space of your hands. I don't believe you are telling us that you have a hold on infinity."

"No, of course not. 'Things' exist out there. Infinity might just be one of them. And then again it may be something we made up to fit our concepts."

Franz sat back down and looked over to Paul.

"Well? So he doesn't have the answers either."

"Franz, let's go and have a beer after school."

"Paul, I have no money. So, just tell me, what do you want?"

"Would you believe—nothing?"

"Shit, now I am worried."

They stopped by a small wine pub on Schneider Street. Wiesel, the scrap yard foreman, had taken Paul there a few times during the summer. It was after five in the afternoon. Men came here after work to punch out and to share their days with each other. The wine helped to ease their minds into a peaceful evening.

When Franz opened the door, they stepped into billowing blue smoke stacked in layers between ceiling and floor. Small and crowded, the place offered a maze of wooden tables that allowed very little room to walk in between. Coats and gear draped the back of the maplewood chairs, and red, cone-shaped metal shades covered the lightbulbs hanging above each table, their dimness enough to light up people's faces and their dirty hands. The men smoked cigarettes, some chewed on pipes that curved down from their lips like the letter S: Simbach pipes.

The tavern was alive with talk and laughter. Franz and Paul made their way to the bar.

"Hey guy, haven't seen you in a while. Don't you like me anymore? Is this your friend?"

Paul looked at the barmaid, thinking hard.

"Lisa?"

Nope, he'd picked the wrong name. He felt embarrassed that he didn't remember her name though he had always flirted with her when he stopped by to have a glass of wine.

"You students! Shame on you. I'm in love with you, Paul baby, and you can't even think of my name. I guess I need to let you go."

Franz moved closer to her.

"Good evening, most beautiful," he oozed, then put his arm around her waist and whispered something into her ear.

Behind them in the back by the window a fellow shouted, "Heeeyyy, Belle, will you bring my beer? It is getting warm on your tray. Quit jabbering with those schoolboys!"

Belle, how could I forget?

"Gentlemen, may we sit here?"

The brawny man made a show of looking around, as though he didn't know whom Paul was addressing.

"Cut the crap and have a seat. What are you waiting for?"

Paul shook hands with the one who had spoken. The man nearly crushed his fingers and shook Paul's arm so hard that he felt pain right up his shoulder.

"Hi, the name is Teich, and this is my brother."

"I'm Paul. This here is Franz, my friend."

The place buzzed with the merry noise of chatting voices, laughter, clanging glasses, chairs scraping across the pocked wooden floor. Paul ordered two glasses of young wine harvested from vineyards up the Neckar River near Heilbronn. Belle brought a pitcher of the milky brew.

"Hey, Belle baby, I'll take care of that. These two blokes look to me like students."

The brother got a couple crumpled D-Marks from his shirt pocket and handed it to her.

"Keep the change, girl. When are you getting off tonight?" He tried to catch her hand, but she was faster.

"Ha! Naw, I wouldn't want to tell you that. You go home to your wife, you hear!"

Paul lifted his glass.

"Here is to you, Mr. Teich's brother, and thank you. Yup, we are students."

"You're pretty old for still going to school. Did you get hung up a few times on the way?"

"Yes. Hung up we got, over there in those miserable French prison camps."

Teich looked at his brother. He shook his head and put a big, heavy paw on Paul's shoulder.

"Man, I'm sorry. I have a big mouth!"

Franz held his wineglass by the stem and kept turning it round and around. The cardboard coaster went with it. He lifted his head a little and, addressing no one in particular, he said, "How could you have known? Besides you're right, we are a little old for still going to school."

Teich bought a round of ham sandwiches, with hard-boiled eggs and pickles on the side.

"What are you going to do after you are done with school?" Franz, wolfing down the hearty bread, told them that he did not know yet. He needed time to find his way back into life.

Teich's brother folded his hands and cracked his knuckles. Paul saw the large fingers, the skin apparently made of leather, with oily dirt painted into its wrinkles. His fingernails were black with grime. The reddish flannel shirt, frayed around the collar, had one torn sleeve. A smell of old sweat and diesel oil drifted over from these roundhouse men. It mixed in with the bouquet of this pub, the wine, the beer, smoke, sausage, eggs, and pickles.

Teich scratched the unshaven face with his chafed hand.

"Yup, I know what you mean. My brother and I were lucky. We never became prisoners. The Americans kept us working. They needed us railroad engineers to run trains all over the country. Right after the war, they had a soldier ride with us in the engine cab. But that lasted only a short while. Too bad, because we smoked Lucky Strikes, ate white bread, and drank whiskey when he was around. Now, both of us are working the dayshift at the roundhouse behind the station."

Belle brought another pitcher of wine. The "schoolboys" and the railroaders talked until late into the night. Eventually, Paul got up.

"Franz, we better go. We have homework to do. We're still in school, you know, and close to finals."

Teich and his brother, his name remaining a closely guarded secret, stood up. Both swayed a little as they came to hug Franz and Paul goodbye.

Father Krause's test consisted of declaring with them the *Confiteor Deo Omnipotenti*.

"I hope I did not fail you. If I did, God will forgive me. And I ask you to forgive as well."

He got his stole from under his vest and turned its purple-colored side out as he hung it over his shoulders. He came down from the podium and raised his right hand.

"Ego te absolvo."

Taking the stole off and holding it up by the white-and-gold rimmed face of it, he made the sign of the cross.

"In nomine patris, ite, and take hold of your lives. He will be with you. Amen."

As always before, Paul had made it with a C average, and that was fine with him.

Mr. Hornung furnished a few bottles of wine for the farewell party. Paul invited Inge. She came using the reusable ticket. Others had family and girlfriends with them. They danced. They were happy, yet their uncertain tomorrows already reached into their evening.

They will leave this town and never meet again. They will fend for themselves, without Wagenraht, Victor, Krause, Preuss, the Holzmanns, and the gaslights in the alleys of Ansbach.

Order Form

Qty.	Title	Price	Can. Price	Total
	A Long Walk **- Claus Hackenberger**	**$19.95**	**$25.95 CN**	
			Shipping and Handling Add $3.50 for orders in the US/Add $7.50 for Global Priority	
			Sales tax (WA state residents only, add 8.6%)	
			Total enclosed	

Telephone Orders:
Call 1-800-461-1931
Have your VISA or
MasterCard ready.

Fax Orders:
425-398-1380
Fill out this order form and fax.

Postal Orders:
Hara Publishing
P.O. Box 19732
Seattle, WA 98109

E-mail Orders:
harapub@foxinternet.net

Method of Payment:

☐ Check or Money Order

☐ VISA

☐ MasterCard

Expiration Date: ____________

Card #: ____________

Signature: ____________

Name ____________
Address ____________
City ____________ **State** ____ **ZIP** ____________
Phone (**)** ____________ **Fax (** **)** ____________

Quantity discounts are available.
Call 425-398-3679 for more information.
Thank you for your order!